Jacob's Room

Jacob's Room

VIRGINIA WOOLF

Annotated and with an introduction
by Vara Neverow

Mark Hussey, General Editor

A Harvest Book • Harcourt, Inc.
Orlando Austin New York San Diego London

www.HarcourtBooks.com

Illustration credits appear on page 325, which constitutes
a continuation of the copyright page.

Library of Congress Cataloging-in-Publication Data
Woolf, Virginia, 1882–1941.
Jacob's room/Virginia Woolf; annotated and with an introduction
by Vara Neverow; Mark Hussey, general editor.—Annotated ed., 1st ed.
p. cm.—(A Harvest book)
Includes bibliographical references.
1. World War, 1914–1918—England—Fiction. 2. Young men—Fiction.
3. England—Fiction. 4. Psychological fiction. 5. Experimental fiction.
I. Neverow, Vara. II. Hussey, Mark, 1956– III. Title.
PR6045.O72J3 2008
823'.912—dc22 2008002967
ISBN 978-0-15-603479-1

Text set in Garamond MT
Designed by Cathy Riggs

Printed in the United States of America

First annotated edition
A C E G I K J H F D B

Contents

ILLUSTRATIONS

Jacob's Room

VIRGINIA WOOLF

VIRGINIA WOOLF was born into what she once described as "a very communicative, literate, letter writing, visiting, articulate, late nineteenth century world." Her parents, Leslie and Julia Stephen, both previously widowed, began their marriage in 1878 with four young children: Laura (1870–1945), the daughter of Leslie Stephen and his first wife, Harriet Thackeray (1840–1875); and George (1868–1934), Gerald (1870–1937), and Stella Duckworth (1869–1897), the children of Julia Prinsep (1846–1895) and Herbert Duckworth (1833–1870). In the first five years of their marriage, the Stephens had four more children. Their third child, Virginia, was born in 1882, the year her father began work on the monumental *Dictionary of National Biography* that would earn him a knighthood in 1902. Virginia, her sister, Vanessa (1879–1961), and brothers, Thoby (1880–1906) and Adrian (1883–1948), all were born in the tall house at 22 Hyde Park Gate in London, where the eight children lived with numerous servants, their eminent and irascible father, and their beautiful mother, who, in Woolf's words, was "in the very centre of that great Cathedral space that was childhood."

Woolf's parents knew many of the intellectual luminaries of the late Victorian era well, counting among their close friends novelists such as George Meredith, Thomas Hardy, and Henry James. Woolf's great-aunt Julia Margaret Cameron was a pioneering photographer who made portraits of the poets Alfred

Tennyson and Robert Browning, of the naturalist Charles Darwin, and of the philosopher and historian Thomas Carlyle, among many others. Beginning in the year Woolf was born, the entire Stephen family moved to Talland House in St. Ives, Cornwall, for the summer. There the younger children would spend their days playing cricket in the garden, frolicking on the beach, or taking walks along the coast, from where they could look out across the bay to the Godrevy lighthouse.

The early years of Woolf's life were marred by traumatic events. When she was thirteen, her mother, exhausted by a punishing schedule of charitable visits among the sick and poor, died from a bout of influenza. Woolf's half sister Stella took over the household responsibilities and bore the brunt of their self-pitying father's sorrow until she escaped into marriage in 1897 with Jack Hills, a young man who had been a favorite of Julia's. Within three months, Stella (who was pregnant) was dead, most likely from peritonitis. In this year, which she called "the first really *lived* year of my life," Woolf began a diary. Over the next twelve years, she would record in its pages her voracious reading, her impressions of people and places, feelings about her siblings, and events in the daily life of the large household.[1]

In addition to the premature deaths of her mother and half sister, there were other miseries in Woolf's childhood. In autobiographical writings and letters, Woolf referred to the sexual abuse she suffered at the hands of her two older half brothers, George and Gerald Duckworth. George, in one instance, explained his behavior to a family doctor as his effort to comfort his half sister for the fatal illness of their father. Sir Leslie died

---

[1]Woolf's early diary is published as *A Passionate Apprentice: The Early Journals, 1897–1909,* edited by Mitchell A. Leaska. A 1909 notebook discovered in 2002 has been published as *Carlyle's House and Other Sketches,* edited by David Bradshaw (London: Hesperus, 2003).

from cancer in 1904, and shortly thereafter the four Stephen children—Vanessa, Virginia, Thoby, and Adrian—moved together to the then-unfashionable London neighborhood of Bloomsbury. When Thoby Stephen began to bring his Cambridge University friends to the house on Thursday evenings, what would later become famous as the "Bloomsbury Group" began to form.

In an article marking the centenary of her father's birth, Woolf recalled his "allowing a girl of fifteen the free run of a large and quite unexpurgated library"—an unusual opportunity for a Victorian young woman, and evidence of the high regard Sir Leslie had for his daughter's intellectual talents. In her diary, she recorded the many different kinds of books her father recommended to her—biographies and memoirs, philosophy, history, and poetry. Although he believed that women should be "as well educated as men," Woolf's mother held that "to serve is the fulfilment of women's highest nature." The young Stephen children were first taught at home by their mother and father, with little success. Woolf herself received no formal education beyond some classes in Greek and Latin in the Ladies' Department of King's College in London, beginning in the fall of 1897. In 1899 she began lessons in Greek with Clara Pater, sister of the renowned Victorian critic Walter Pater, and in 1902 she was tutored in the classics by Janet Case (who also later involved her in work for women's suffrage). Such homeschooling was a source of some bitterness later in her life, as she recognized the advantages that derived from the expensive educations her brothers and half brothers received at private schools and university. Yet she also realized that her father's encouragement of her obviously keen intellect had given her an eclectic foundation. In the early years of Bloomsbury, she reveled in the opportunity to discuss ideas with her brother Thoby and his friends, among whom were Lytton Strachey, Clive Bell, and

E. M. Forster. From them, she heard, too, about an intense young man named Leonard Woolf, whom she had met briefly when visiting Thoby at Cambridge, and also in 1904 when he came to dinner at Gordon Square just before leaving for Ceylon (now called Sri Lanka), where he was to administer a far-flung outpost of the British Empire.

Virginia Woolf's first publications were unsigned reviews and essays in an Anglo-Catholic newspaper called the *Guardian,* beginning in December 1904. In the fall of 1906, she and Vanessa went with a family friend, Violet Dickinson, to meet their brothers in Greece. The trip was spoiled by Vanessa's falling ill, and when she returned to London, Virginia found both her brother Thoby—who had returned earlier—and her sister seriously ill. After a misdiagnosis by his doctors, Thoby died from typhoid fever on November 20, leaving Virginia to maintain a cheerful front while her sister and Violet Dickinson recovered from their own illnesses. Two days after Thoby's death, Vanessa agreed to marry his close friend Clive Bell.

While living in Bloomsbury, Woolf had begun to write a novel that would go through many drafts before it was published in 1915 as *The Voyage Out*. In these early years of independence, her social circle widened. She became close to the art critic Roger Fry, organizer of the First Post-Impressionist Exhibition in London in 1910, and also entered the orbit of the famed literary hostess Lady Ottoline Morrell (cruelly caricatured as Hermione Roddice in D. H. Lawrence's 1920 novel *Women in Love*). Her political consciousness also began to emerge. In 1910 she volunteered for the movement for women's suffrage. She also participated that February in a daring hoax that embarrassed the British Navy and led to questions being asked in the House of Commons: She and her brother Adrian, together with some other Cambridge friends, gained access to a secret warship by dressing up and posing as the Emperor of Abyssinia and his retinue. The "Dreadnought Hoax" was front-page news, complete with photographs of the phony Ethiopians with flowing robes, blackened faces, and false beards.

To the British establishment, one of the most embarrassing aspects of the Dreadnought affair was that a woman had taken part in the hoax. Vanessa Bell was concerned at what might have happened to her sister had she been discovered on the ship. She was also increasingly worried about Virginia's erratic health, and by the early summer 1910 had discussed with Dr. George Savage, one of the family's doctors, the debilitating headaches her sister suffered; Dr. Savage prescribed several weeks in a nursing home. Another element in Vanessa's concern was that Virginia was twenty-eight and still unmarried. Clive Bell and Virginia had, in fact, engaged in a hurtful flirtation soon after the birth of Vanessa's first child in 1908. Although she had been proposed to twice in 1909 and once in 1911, Virginia had not taken these offers very seriously.

Dropping by Vanessa's house on a July evening in 1911, Virginia met Leonard Woolf, recently back on leave from Ceylon. Soon after this, Leonard became a lodger at the house Virginia shared with Adrian, the economist John Maynard Keynes, and the painter Duncan Grant. Leonard decided to resign from the Colonial Service, hoping that Virginia would agree to marry him. After some considerable hesitation, she did, and they married in August 1912.

By the end of that year, Woolf was again suffering from the tremendous headaches that afflicted her throughout her life, and in 1913 she was again sent to a nursing home for what was then called a "rest cure." In September of that year, she took an overdose of a sleeping drug and was under care until the following spring. In early 1915 she suffered a severe breakdown and was ill throughout most of the year in which her first novel was published.

Despite this difficult beginning, Virginia and Leonard Woolf's marriage eventually settled into a pattern of immense productivity and mutual support. Leonard worked for a time for the Women's Cooperative Guild, and became increasingly involved with advising the Labour Party and writing on international politics, as well as editing several periodicals. Virginia began to establish herself as an important novelist and influential critic. In 1917 the Woolfs set up their own publishing house, the Hogarth Press, in their home in Richmond. Their first publication was *Two Stories*—Leonard's "Three Jews" and Virginia's experimental "The Mark on the Wall." They had decided to make their livings by writing, and in 1919, a few months before Woolf's second novel, *Night and Day,* was published, they bought a cottage in the village of Rodmell in Sussex. After moving back into London from Richmond in 1923, Woolf would spend summers at Monk's House, returning to the social whirl of the city in the fall.

"The Mark on the Wall" was one of a number of what Woolf called "sketches" that she began to write around the time she and Leonard bought their printing press. *Night and Day* was the last of her books to be published in England by another press. In 1919 Hogarth published her short story *Kew Gardens,* with two woodcuts by Vanessa Bell, and two years later came *Monday or Tuesday,* the only collection of her short fiction published in Woolf's lifetime. Her next novel was *Jacob's Room* (1922), a slim elegy to the generation of 1914, and to her beloved brother Thoby, whose life of great promise had also been cut short so suddenly. Woolf had written to her friend Margaret Llewelyn Davies in 1916 that the Great War, as it was then called, was a "preposterous masculine fiction" that made her "steadily more feminist," and in her fiction and nonfiction she began to articulate and illuminate the connections between the patriarchal status quo, the relatively subordinate position of

women, and war making. Thinking about a novel she was calling "The Hours," Woolf wrote in her diary in 1923 that she
wanted to criticize "the social system." Her inclusion in the
novel of a shell-shocked war veteran named Septimus Warren
Smith would confuse many of the early reviewers of her fourth
novel, *Mrs. Dalloway* (1925), but others recognized that Woolf
was breaking new ground in the way she rendered consciousness and her understanding of human subjectivity.

By the time she wrote *Mrs. Dalloway,* Woolf was also a sought-
after essayist and reviewer who, like many of her celebrated
contemporaries, was staking out her own particular piece of
modernist territory. The Hogarth Press published radical young
writers like Katherine Mansfield, T. S. Eliot, and Gertrude Stein.
Approached by Harriet Shaw Weaver with part of the manuscript of James Joyce's *Ulysses* in 1918, the Woolfs turned it down.
Their own small press could not cope with the long and complex manuscript, nor could Leonard Woolf find a commercial
printer willing to risk prosecution for obscenity by producing it.
In 1924 the Hogarth Press became the official English publisher
of the works of Sigmund Freud, translated by Lytton Strachey's
brother James. Woolf's own literary criticism was collected in a
volume published in 1925, *The Common Reader*—a title signaling
her distrust of academics and love of broad, eclectic reading.

The staggering range of Woolf's reading is reflected in the
more than five hundred essays and reviews she published during her lifetime. Her critical writing is concerned not only with
the canonical works of English literature from Chaucer to her
contemporaries, but also ranges widely through lives of the obscure, memoirs, diaries, letters, and biographies. Models of the
form, her essays comprise a body of work that has only recently
begun to attract the kind of recognition her fiction has received.

In 1922 Woolf met "the lovely and gifted aristocrat" Vita
Sackville-West, already a well-known poet and novelist. Their

close friendship slowly turned into a love affair, glowing most intensely from about 1925 to 1928, before modulating into friendship once more in the 1930s. The period of their intimacy was extremely creative for both writers, Woolf publishing essays such as "Mr. Bennett and Mrs. Brown" and "Letter to a Young Poet," as well as three very different novels: *To the Lighthouse* (1927), which evoked her own childhood and had at its center the figure of a modernist woman artist, Lily Briscoe; *Orlando* (1928), a fantastic biography inspired by Vita's own remarkable family history; and *The Waves* (1931), a mystical and profoundly meditative work that pushed Woolf's concept of novel form to its limit. Woolf also published a second *Common Reader* in 1932, and the "biography" of *Flush,* Elizabeth Barrett Browning's dog (1933). She went with Sackville-West to Cambridge in the fall of 1928 to deliver the second of the two lectures on which her great feminist essay *A Room of One's Own* (1929) is based.

As the political situation in Europe in the 1930s moved inexorably to its crisis in 1939, Woolf began to collect newspaper clippings about the relations between the sexes in England, France, Germany, and Italy. The scrapbooks she made became the matrix from which developed the perspectives of her penultimate novel, *The Years* (1937), and the arguments of her pacifist-feminist polemic *Three Guineas* (1938). In 1937 Vanessa's eldest son, Julian Bell, was killed serving as an ambulance driver in the Spanish Civil War. Woolf later wrote to Vanessa that she had written *Three Guineas* partly as an argument with Julian. Her work on *The Years* was grindingly slow and difficult. Ironically, given Woolf's reputation as a highbrow, it became a bestseller in the United States, even being published in an Armed Services edition. While she labored over the novel in 1934, the news came of the death of Roger Fry, one of her oldest and closest friends and the former lover of her sister, Vanessa. Reluctantly, given her distaste for the conventions of biography, Woolf agreed to write his life, which was published in 1940.

In 1939, to relieve the strain of writing Fry's biography, Woolf began to write a memoir, "A Sketch of the Past," which remained unpublished until 1976, when the manuscripts were edited by Jeanne Schulkind for a collection of Woolf's autobiographical writings, *Moments of Being*. Withdrawing with Leonard to Monk's House in Sussex, where they could see the German airplanes flying low overhead on their way to bomb London, Woolf continued to write for peace and correspond with anti-war activists in Europe and the United States. She began to write her last novel, *Between the Acts,* in the spring of 1938, but by early 1941 was dissatisfied with it. Before completing her final revisions, Woolf ended her own life, walking into the River Ouse on the morning of March 28, 1941. To her sister, Vanessa, she wrote, "I can hardly think clearly any more. If I could I would tell you what you and the children have meant to me. I think you know." In her last note to Leonard, she told him he had given her "complete happiness," and asked him to destroy all her papers.

BY THE END of the twentieth century, Virginia Woolf had become an iconic figure, a touchstone for the feminism that revived in the 1960s as well as for the conservative backlash of the 1980s. Hailed by many as a radical writer of genius, she has also been dismissed as a narrowly focused snob. Her image adorns T-shirts, postcards, and even a beer advertisement, while phrases from her writings occur in all kinds of contexts, from peace-march slogans to highbrow book reviews. That Woolf is one of those figures on whom the myriad competing narratives of twentieth- and twenty-first-century Western culture inscribe themselves is testified to by the enormous number of biographical works about her published in the decades since her nephew Quentin Bell broke the ground in 1972 with his two-volume biography of his aunt.

Argument continues about the work and life of Virginia Woolf: about her experience of incest, her madness, her class attitudes, her sexuality, the difficulty of her prose, her politics, her feminism, and her legacy. Perhaps, though, these words from her essay "How Should One Read a Book?" are our best guide: "The only advice, indeed, that one person can give another about reading is to take no advice, to follow your own instincts, to use your own reason, to come to your own conclusions."

—MARK HUSSEY, GENERAL EDITOR

CHRONOLOGY

Information is arranged in this order: 1. Virginia Woolf's family and her works; 2. Cultural and political events; 3. Significant publications and works of art.

1878   Marriage of Woolf's parents, Leslie Stephen (1832–1904) and Julia Prinsep Duckworth (née Jackson) (1846–1895). Leslie Stephen publishes *Samuel Johnson,* first volume in the English Men of Letters series.
England at war in Afghanistan.

1879   Vanessa Stephen (Bell) born (d. 1961). Edward Burne-Jones paints Julia Stephen as the Virgin Mary in *The Annunciation.* Leslie Stephen, *Hours in a Library,* 3rd series.
Somerville and Lady Margaret Hall Colleges for women founded at Oxford University.
Anglo-Zulu war in South Africa.

1880   Thoby Stephen born (d. 1906).
William Gladstone becomes prime minister for second time. First Boer War begins (1880–81). Deaths of Gustave Flaubert (b. 1821) and George Eliot (b. 1819). Lytton Strachey born (d. 1932).
Fyodor Dostoyevsky, *The Brothers Karamazov.*

1881　　Leslie Stephen buys lease of Talland House, St. Ives, Cornwall.

Cambridge University Tripos exams opened to women. Henrik Ibsen, *Ghosts;* Henry James, *The Portrait of a Lady, Washington Square;* Christina Rossetti, *A Pageant and Other Poems;* D. G. Rossetti, *Ballads and Sonnets;* Oscar Wilde, *Poems.*

1882　　Adeline Virginia Stephen (Virginia Woolf) born January 25. Leslie Stephen begins work as editor of the *Dictionary of National Biography* (*DNB*); publishes *The Science of Ethics.* The Stephen family spends its first summer at Talland House.

Married Women's Property Act enables women to buy, sell, and own property and keep their own earnings. Triple Alliance between Germany, Italy, and Austria. Phoenix Park murders of British officials in Dublin, Ireland. James Joyce born (d. 1941). Death of Charles Darwin (b. 1809).

1883　　Adrian Leslie Stephen born (d. 1948). Julia Stephen's *Notes from Sick Rooms* published.

Olive Schreiner, *The Story of an African Farm;* Robert Louis Stevenson, *Treasure Island.*

1884　　Leslie Stephen delivers the Clark Lectures at Cambridge University.

Third Reform Act extends the franchise in England. Friedrich Engels, *The Origin of the Family, Private Property and the State;* John Ruskin, *The Storm-Cloud of the Nineteenth Century;* Mark Twain, *The Adventures of Huckleberry Finn.*

1885   First volume of Leslie Stephen's *Dictionary of National Biography* published.

Redistribution Act further extends the franchise in England. Ezra Pound born (d. 1972); D. H. Lawrence born (d. 1930).

George Meredith, *Diana of the Crossways;* Émile Zola, *Germinal.*

1887   Queen Victoria's Golden Jubilee.

Arthur Conan Doyle, *A Study in Scarlet;* H. Rider Haggard, *She;* Thomas Hardy, *The Woodlanders.*

1891   Leslie Stephen gives up the *DNB* editorship. Laura Stephen (1870–1945) is placed in an asylum.

William Gladstone elected prime minister of England a fourth time.

Thomas Hardy, *Tess of the D'Urbervilles;* Oscar Wilde, *The Picture of Dorian Gray.*

1895   Death of Julia Stephen.

Armenian Massacres in Turkey. Discovery of X-rays by William Röntgen; Guglielmo Marconi discovers radio; invention of the cinematograph. Trials of Oscar Wilde.

Thomas Hardy, *Jude the Obscure;* H. G. Wells, *The Time Machine;* Oscar Wilde, *The Importance of Being Earnest.*

1896   Vanessa Stephen begins drawing classes three afternoons a week.

Death of William Morris (b. 1834); F. Scott Fitzgerald born (d. 1940).

Anton Chekhov, *The Seagull.*

1897 Woolf attends Greek and history classes at King's College, London, and begins to keep a regular diary. Vanessa, Virginia, and Thoby watch Queen Victoria's Diamond Jubilee procession. Stella Duckworth (b. 1869) marries Jack Hills in April, but dies in July. Gerald Duckworth (1870–1937) establishes a publishing house.
Paul Gauguin, *Where Do We Come From? What Are We? Where Are We Going?;* Bram Stoker, *Dracula.*

1898 Spanish-American War (1898–99). Marie Curie discovers radium. Death of Stéphane Mallarmé (b. 1842).
H. G. Wells, *The War of the Worlds;* Oscar Wilde, *The Ballad of Reading Gaol.*

1899 Woolf begins Latin and Greek lessons with Clara Pater. Thoby Stephen goes up to Trinity College, Cambridge University, entering with Lytton Strachey, Leonard Woolf (1880–1969), and Clive Bell (1881–1964).
The Second Boer War begins (1899–1902) in South Africa. Ernest Hemingway born (d. 1961).

1900 Woolf and Vanessa attend the Trinity College Ball at Cambridge University.
Deaths of Friedrich Nietzsche (b. 1844), John Ruskin (b. 1819), and Oscar Wilde (b. 1854).
Sigmund Freud, *The Interpretation of Dreams.*

1901 Vanessa enters Royal Academy Schools.
Queen Victoria dies January 22. Edward VII becomes king. Marconi sends messages by wireless telegraphy from Cornwall to Newfoundland.

1902 Woolf begins classics lessons with Janet Case. Adrian Stephen enters Trinity College, Cambridge University. Leslie Stephen is knighted.

Joseph Conrad, *Heart of Darkness;* Henry James, *The Wings of the Dove;* William James, *The Varieties of Religious Experience.*

1903 The Wright Brothers fly a biplane 852 feet. Women's Social and Political Union founded in England by Emmeline Pankhurst.

1904 Sir Leslie Stephen dies. George Duckworth (1868–1934) marries Lady Margaret Herbert. The Stephen children—Vanessa, Virginia, Thoby, and Adrian—move to 46 Gordon Square, in the Bloomsbury district of London. Woolf contributes to F. W. Maitland's biography of her father. Leonard Woolf comes to dine before sailing for Ceylon. Woolf travels in Italy and France. Her first publication is an unsigned review in the *Guardian,* a church weekly.

"Empire Day" inaugurated in London and in Britain's colonies.

Anton Chekhov, *The Cherry Orchard;* Henry James, *The Golden Bowl.*

1905 Woolf begins teaching weekly adult education classes at Morley College. Thoby invites Cambridge friends to their home for "Thursday Evenings"—the beginnings of the Bloomsbury Group. Woolf travels with Adrian to Portugal and Spain. The Stephens visit Cornwall for the first time since their mother's death.

Revolution in Russia.

Albert Einstein, *Special Theory of Relativity;* E. M. Forster, *Where Angels Fear to Tread;* Sigmund Freud, *Essays in the Theory of Sexuality;* Edith Wharton, *The House of Mirth;* Oscar Wilde, *De Profundis.*

1906   The Stephens travel to Greece. Vanessa and Thoby fall ill. Thoby dies November 20; on November 22, Vanessa agrees to marry Clive Bell.

Deaths of Paul Cézanne (b. 1839) and Henrik Ibsen (b. 1828). Samuel Beckett born (d. 1989).

1907   Woolf moves with her brother Adrian to Fitzroy Square. Vanessa marries Clive Bell.

First Cubist exhibition in Paris. W. H. Auden born (d. 1973).

Joseph Conrad, *The Secret Agent;* E. M. Forster, *The Longest Journey;* Edmund Gosse, *Father and Son;* Pablo Picasso, *Demoiselles d'Avignon.*

1908   Birth of Vanessa Bell's first child, Julian. Woolf travels to Italy with Vanessa and Clive Bell.

Herbert Asquith becomes prime minister.

E. M. Forster, *A Room with a View;* Gertrude Stein, *Three Lives.*

1909   Woolf receives a legacy of £2,500 on the death of her Quaker aunt, Caroline Emelia Stephen. Lytton Strachey proposes marriage to Woolf, but they both quickly realize this would be a mistake. Woolf meets Lady Ottoline Morrell for the first time. She travels to the Wagner festival in Bayreuth.

Chancellor of the Exchequer David Lloyd George (1863–1945) introduces a "People's Budget," taxing wealth to pay for social reforms. A constitutional crisis ensues when the House of Lords rejects it. Death of George Meredith (b. 1828).

Filippo Marinetti, "The Founding and Manifesto of Futurism"; Henri Matisse, *Dance.*

1910   Woolf participates in the Dreadnought Hoax. She volunteers for the cause of women's suffrage. Birth of Vanessa Bell's second child, Quentin (d. 1996).

First Post-Impressionist Exhibition ("Manet and the Post-Impressionists") organized by Roger Fry (1866–1934) at the Grafton Galleries in London. Edward VII dies May 6. George V becomes king. Death of Leo Tolstoy (b. 1828).

E. M. Forster, *Howards End;* Igor Stravinsky, *The Firebird.*

1911   Woolf rents Little Talland House in Sussex. Leonard Woolf returns from Ceylon; in November, he, Adrian Stephen, John Maynard Keynes (1883–1946), Woolf, and Duncan Grant (1885–1978) share a house together at Brunswick Square in London.

Ernest Rutherford makes first model of atomic structure. Rupert Brooke, *Poems;* Joseph Conrad, *Under Western Eyes;* D. H. Lawrence, *The White Peacock;* Katherine Mansfield, *In a German Pension;* Ezra Pound, *Canzoni;* Edith Wharton, *Ethan Frome.*

1912   Woolf leases Asheham House in Sussex. Marries Leonard on August 10; they move to Clifford's Inn, London.

Captain Robert Scott's expedition reaches the South Pole, but he and his companions die on the return

journey. The *Titanic* sinks. Second Post-Impression-
ist Exhibition, for which Leonard Woolf serves as
secretary.
Marcel Duchamp, *Nude Descending a Staircase;* Wassily
Kandinsky, *Concerning the Spiritual in Art;* Thomas
Mann, *Death in Venice;* George Bernard Shaw, *Pygmalion.*

1913 *The Voyage Out* manuscript delivered to Gerald Duckworth. Woolf enters a nursing home in July; in September, she attempts suicide.
Roger Fry founds the Omega Workshops.
Sigmund Freud, *Totem and Taboo;* D. H. Lawrence, *Sons
and Lovers;* Marcel Proust, *Du côté de chez Swann;* Igor
Stravinsky, *Le Sacre du printemps.*

1914 Leonard Woolf, *The Wise Virgins;* he reviews Freud's
The Psychopathology of Everyday Life.
World War I ("The Great War") begins in August.
Home Rule Bill for Ireland passed.
Clive Bell, *Art;* James Joyce, *Dubliners;* Wyndham Lewis
et al., "Vorticist Manifesto" (in *BLAST*); Gertrude
Stein, *Tender Buttons.*

1915 *The Voyage Out,* Woolf's first novel, published by Duck-
worth. In April the Woolfs move to Hogarth House in
Richmond. Woolf begins again to keep a regular diary.
First Zeppelin attack on London. Death of Rupert
Brooke (b. 1887).
Joseph Conrad, *Victory;* Ford Madox Ford, *The Good Sol-
dier;* D. H. Lawrence, *The Rainbow;* Dorothy Richardson,
Pointed Roofs.

1916 Woolf discovers Charleston, where her sister, Vanessa (no longer living with her husband, Clive), moves in October with her sons, Julian and Quentin, and Duncan Grant (with whom she is in love) and David Garnett (with whom Duncan is in love).
Easter Rising in Dublin. Death of Henry James (b. 1843).
Albert Einstein, *General Theory of Relativity;* James Joyce, *A Portrait of the Artist as a Young Man;* Dorothy Richardson, *Backwater.*

1917 The Hogarth Press established by Leonard and Virginia Woolf in Richmond. Their first publication is their own *Two Stories,* with woodcuts by Dora Carrington (1893–1932).
Russian Bolshevik Revolution destroys the rule of the czar. The United States enters the European war.
T. S. Eliot, *Prufrock and Other Observations;* Sigmund Freud, *Introduction to Psychoanalysis;* Carl Jung, *The Unconscious;* Dorothy Richardson, *Honeycomb;* W. B. Yeats, *The Wild Swans at Coole.*

1918 Woolf meets T. S. Eliot (1888–1965). Harriet Shaw Weaver comes to tea with the manuscript of James Joyce's *Ulysses.* Vanessa Bell and Duncan Grant's daughter, Angelica Garnett, born; her paternity is kept secret from all but a very few intimates.
Armistice signed November 11; Parliamentary Reform Act gives votes in Britain to women of thirty and older and to all men.
G. M. Hopkins, *Poems;* James Joyce, *Exiles;* Katherine Mansfield, *Prelude* (Hogarth Press); Marcel Proust, *À*

l'ombre des jeunes filles en fleurs; Lytton Strachey, *Eminent Victorians;* Rebecca West, *The Return of the Soldier.*

1919 The Woolfs buy Monk's House in Sussex. Woolf's second novel, *Night and Day,* is published by Duckworth. Her essay "Modern Novels" (republished in 1925 as "Modern Fiction") appears in the *Times Literary Supplement; Kew Gardens* published by Hogarth Press.

Bauhaus founded by Walter Gropius in Weimar. Sex Disqualification (Removal) Act opens many professions and public offices to women. Election of first woman member of Parliament, Nancy Astor. Treaty of Versailles imposes harsh conditions on postwar Germany, opposed by John Maynard Keynes, who writes *The Economic Consequences of the Peace.* League of Nations created. T. S. Eliot, "Tradition and the Individual Talent," *Poems;* Dorothy Richardson, *The Tunnel, Interim;* Robert Wiene, *The Cabinet of Dr. Caligari* (film).

1920 The Memoir Club, comprising thirteen original members of the Bloomsbury Group, meets for the first time. *The Voyage Out* and *Night and Day* are published in the United States by George H. Doran.

Mohandas Gandhi initiates mass passive resistance against British rule in India.

T. S. Eliot, *The Sacred Wood;* Sigmund Freud, *Beyond the Pleasure Principle;* Roger Fry, *Vision and Design;* D. H. Lawrence, *Women in Love;* Katherine Mansfield, *Bliss and Other Stories;* Ezra Pound, *Hugh Selwyn Mauberley;* Marcel Proust, *Le Côté de Guermantes I;* Edith Wharton, *The Age of Innocence.*

1921 Woolf's short story collection *Monday or Tuesday* published by Hogarth Press, which will from this time publish all her books in England. The book is also published in the United States by Harcourt Brace, which from now on is her American publisher.

Aldous Huxley, *Crome Yellow;* Pablo Picasso, *Three Musicians;* Luigi Pirandello, *Six Characters in Search of an Author;* Marcel Proust, *Le Côté de Guermantes II, Sodome et Gomorrhe I;* Dorothy Richardson, *Deadlock;* Lytton Strachey, *Queen Victoria.*

1922   *Jacob's Room* published. Woolf meets Vita Sackville-West (1892–1962) for the first time.

Bonar Law elected prime minister. Mussolini comes to power in Italy. Irish Free State established. British Broadcasting Company (BBC) formed. Discovery of Tutankhamen's tomb in Egypt. Death of Marcel Proust (b. 1871).

T. S. Eliot, *The Waste Land;* James Joyce, *Ulysses;* Katherine Mansfield, *The Garden Party;* Marcel Proust, *Sodome et Gomorrhe II;* Ludwig Wittgenstein, *Tractatus Logico-Philosophicus.*

1923   The Woolfs travel to Spain, stopping in Paris on the way home. Hogarth Press publishes *The Waste Land.*

Stanley Baldwin succeeds Bonar Law as prime minister. Death of Katherine Mansfield (b. 1888).

Mina Loy, *Lunar Baedeker;* Marcel Proust, *La Prisonnière;* Dorothy Richardson, *Revolving Lights;* Rainer Maria Rilke, *Duino Elegies.*

1924   The Woolfs move to Tavistock Square. Woolf lectures on "Character in Fiction" to the Heretics Society at Cambridge University.

The Labour Party takes office for the first time under

the leadership of Ramsay MacDonald but is voted out within the year. Death of Joseph Conrad (b. 1857). E. M. Forster, *A Passage to India;* Thomas Mann, *The Magic Mountain.*

1925   *Mrs. Dalloway* and *The Common Reader* published. Woolf stays with Vita Sackville-West at her house, Long Barn, for the first time.

Nancy Cunard, *Parallax;* F. Scott Fitzgerald, *The Great Gatsby;* Ernest Hemingway, *In Our Time;* Adolf Hitler, *Mein Kampf;* Franz Kafka, *The Trial;* Alain Locke, ed., *The New Negro;* Marcel Proust, *Albertine disparue;* Dorothy Richardson, *The Trap;* Gertrude Stein, *The Making of Americans.*

1926   Woolf lectures on "How Should One Read a Book?" at Hayes Court School. "Cinema" published in *Arts* (New York), "Impassioned Prose" in *Times Literary Supplement,* and "On Being Ill" in *New Criterion.* Meets Gertrude Stein (1874–1946).

The General Strike in support of mine workers in England lasts nearly two weeks.

Ernest Hemingway, *The Sun Also Rises;* Langston Hughes, *The Weary Blues;* Franz Kafka, *The Castle;* A. A. Milne, *Winnie-the-Pooh.*

1927   *To the Lighthouse,* "The Art of Fiction," "Poetry, Fiction and the Future," and "Street Haunting" published. The Woolfs travel with Vita Sackville-West and her husband, Harold Nicolson, to Yorkshire to see the total eclipse of the sun. They buy their first car.

Charles Lindbergh flies the Atlantic solo.

E. M. Forster, *Aspects of the Novel;* Ernest Hemingway, *Men without Women;* Franz Kafka, *Amerika;* Marcel

Proust, *Le Temps retrouvé;* Gertrude Stein, *Four Saints in Three Acts.*

1928   *Orlando: A Biography* published. In October, Woolf delivers two lectures at Cambridge on which she will base *A Room of One's Own.* Femina-Vie Heureuse prize awarded to *To the Lighthouse.*
The Equal Franchise Act gives the vote to all women over twenty-one. Sound films introduced. Death of Thomas Hardy (b. 1840).
Djuna Barnes, *Ladies Almanack;* Radclyffe Hall, *The Well of Loneliness;* D. H. Lawrence, *Lady Chatterley's Lover;* Evelyn Waugh, *Decline and Fall;* W. B. Yeats, *The Tower.*

1929   *A Room of One's Own* published. "Women and Fiction" in *The Forum* (New York).
Labour Party returned to power under Prime Minister MacDonald. Discovery of penicillin. Museum of Modern Art opens in New York. Wall Street crash.
William Faulkner, *The Sound and the Fury;* Ernest Hemingway, *A Farewell to Arms;* Nella Larsen, *Passing.*

1930   Woolf meets the pioneering composer, writer, and suffragette Ethel Smyth (1858–1944), with whom she forms a close friendship.
Death of D. H. Lawrence (b. 1885).
W. H. Auden, *Poems;* T. S. Eliot, *Ash Wednesday;* William Faulkner, *As I Lay Dying;* Sigmund Freud, *Civilisation and Its Discontents.*

1931   *The Waves* is published. First of six articles by Woolf about London published in *Good Housekeeping;* "Introductory Letter" to *Life As We Have Known It.* Lectures to London branch of National Society for Women's Service on "Professions for Women." Meets John Lehmann (1907–1987), who will become a partner in the Hogarth Press.

Growing financial crisis throughout Europe and beginning of the Great Depression.

1932   *The Common Reader, Second Series* and "Letter to a Young Poet" published. Woolf invited to give the 1933 Clark Lectures at Cambridge, which she declines.

Death of Lytton Strachey (b. 1880).

Aldous Huxley, *Brave New World.*

1933   *Flush: A Biography,* published. The Woolfs travel by car to Italy.

Adolf Hitler becomes chancellor of Germany, establishing the totalitarian dictatorship of his National Socialist (Nazi) Party.

T. S. Eliot, *The Use of Poetry and the Use of Criticism;* George Orwell, *Down and Out in Paris and London;* Gertrude Stein, *The Autobiography of Alice B. Toklas;* Nathanael West, *Miss Lonelyhearts;* W. B. Yeats, *The Collected Poems.*

1934   Woolf meets W. B. Yeats at Ottoline Morrell's house. Writes "Walter Sickert: A Conversation."

George Duckworth dies. Roger Fry dies.

Samuel Beckett, *More Pricks Than Kicks;* Nancy Cunard, ed., *Negro: An Anthology;* F. Scott Fitzgerald, *Tender Is the Night;* Wyndham Lewis, *Men Without Art;* Henry Miller, *Tropic of Cancer;* Ezra Pound, *ABC of Reading;* Evelyn Waugh, *A Handful of Dust.*

1935   The Woolfs travel to Germany, where they accidentally get caught up in a parade for Göring. They return to England via Italy and France.

1936   Woolf reads "Am I a Snob?" to the Memoir Club, and publishes "Why Art Today Follows Politics" in the *Daily Worker.*
Death of George V, who is succeeded by Edward VIII, who then abdicates to marry Wallis Simpson. George VI becomes king. Spanish Civil War (1936–38) begins when General Franco, assisted by Germany and Italy, attacks the Republican government. BBC television begins.
Djuna Barnes, *Nightwood;* Charlie Chaplin, *Modern Times* (film); Aldous Huxley, *Eyeless in Gaza;* J. M. Keynes, *The General Theory of Employment, Interest and Money;* Rose Macaulay, *Personal Pleasures;* Margaret Mitchell, *Gone with the Wind.*

1937   *The Years* published. Woolf's nephew Julian Bell killed in the Spanish Civil War.
Neville Chamberlain becomes prime minister.
Zora Neale Hurston, *Their Eyes Were Watching God;* David Jones, *In Parenthesis;* Pablo Picasso, *Guernica;* John Steinbeck, *Of Mice and Men;* J. R. R. Tolkien, *The Hobbit.*

1938   *Three Guineas* published.
Germany annexes Austria. Chamberlain negotiates the Munich Agreement ("Peace in our time"), ceding Czech territory to Hitler.
Samuel Beckett, *Murphy;* Elizabeth Bowen, *The Death of the Heart;* Jean-Paul Sartre, *La Nausée.*

1939   The Woolfs visit Sigmund Freud, living in exile in
London having fled the Nazis. They move to Mecklenburgh Square.

Germany occupies Czechoslovakia; Italy occupies Alba-
nia; Russia makes a nonaggression pact with Germany.
Germany invades Poland and war is declared by Britain
and France on Germany, September 3. Deaths of W. B.
Yeats (b. 1865), Sigmund Freud (b. 1856), and Ford
Madox Ford (b. 1873).

James Joyce, *Finnegans Wake;* John Steinbeck, *The Grapes
of Wrath;* Nathanael West, *The Day of the Locust.*

1940   *Roger Fry: A Biography* published. "Thoughts on Peace
in an Air Raid" in the *New Republic.* Woolf lectures on
"The Leaning Tower" to the Workers Educational Association in Brighton.

The Battle of Britain leads to German night bombings
of English cities. The Woolfs' house at Mecklenburgh
Square is severely damaged, as is their former house
at Tavistock Square. Hogarth Press is moved out of
London.

Ernest Hemingway, *For Whom the Bell Tolls;* Christina
Stead, *The Man Who Loved Children.*

1941   Woolf drowns herself, March 28, in the River Ouse in
Sussex. *Between the Acts* published in July.

Death of James Joyce (b. 1882).

Rebecca West, *Black Lamb and Grey Falcon.*

INTRODUCTION
by Vara Neverow

"Something in my own voice"

JACOB'S ROOM, Virginia Woolf's third novel, is not a conventional work. Rather, it is a classic example of high modernism and is usually considered Woolf's first truly experimental long work. Woolf's experiment in *Jacob's Room* was not an isolated event and was undoubtedly influenced by the work of other writers, some of them published by Leonard and Virginia Woolf's own Hogarth Press. Katherine Mansfield's experimental short story *Prelude* was published by the press in 1918 and may have influenced Woolf's vision for *Jacob's Room* as an elegiac work. Mansfield's story was based on her childhood experiences growing up in New Zealand, the memories triggered by time spent with her brother, Leslie Beauchamp, while he was training in England to serve as an officer in the Great War (he was killed in 1915). Hope Mirrlees's *Paris: A Poem,* which Virginia Woolf hand-set for publication in 1920, may have been a stylistic influence on *Jacob's Room* (see Briggs, "Modernism's" 91–92). The Woolfs also considered publishing James Joyce's *Ulysses* in 1918 but foresaw legal risks related to England's obscenity laws (the novel was published in 1922 in France, where the constraints on expression were less rigorous—see Marshik 157–66). Although Woolf found Joyce's work to be somewhat too forthright about bodily functions and sexuality, she was intrigued and even somewhat intimidated by his experimental style. The

Hogarth Press also published T. S. Eliot's *Poems* in 1919 and *The Waste Land* in 1922.[1]

As Woolf writes in a diary entry, having completed the manuscript of *Jacob's Room:* "There's no doubt in my mind that I have found out how to begin (at 40) to say something in my own voice" (*Diary* 2: 186). In terms of what might be considered character development and a plotline in *Jacob's Room,* Woolf has intentionally abandoned the conventions. In the same diary entry, she notes that Leonard Woolf, her husband, declared the work to be a literary triumph, saying with regard to the characters that "the people are ghosts . . . puppets, moved hither & thither by fate" (*Diary* 2: 186). In the holograph draft, Woolf writes on the first page, "Reflections upon beginning a work of fiction to be called, perhaps, Jacob's Room. . . . Let us suppose that the Room will hold it together" (Bishop, *Holograph* 1), suggesting that spaces, occupied and otherwise, will construct and contain the narrative.

"A new form for a new novel"

FROM THE FIRST, Woolf envisioned *Jacob's Room* as something radically different from the contemporary literary template, "a new form for a new novel" (*Diary* 2: 13), writing in her diary on the day after her thirty-eighth birthday:

> I figure that the approach will be entirely different this time: no scaffolding; scarcely a brick to be seen; all crepuscular, but the heart, the passion, humour, everything as bright as fire in the mist. Then I'll find room for so much—a gaiety—an inconsequence—a light spirited stepping at my sweet will. (*Diary* 2: 13–14)

Her experiment in *Jacob's Room* evolves from earlier forays into new narrative approaches. In the same diary entry, she muses: "Suppose one thing should open out of another—As in An Unwritten Novel—only not for 10 pages but 200 or so" (*Jacob's Room* was 259 pages in the first Hogarth Press edition). She speculates that if she is "sufficiently mistress of things," she will be able to intertwine elements of experimental techniques from earlier short works and "conceive mark on the wall, K[ew]. G[ardens]. & unwritten novel taking hands & dancing in unity" (*Diary* 2: 14).

"The Mark on the Wall" was paired with Leonard Woolf's "Three Jews" in a volume titled *Two Stories* (1917), the Hogarth Press's first published book. The story line of "The Mark on the Wall" is slight, indeed insignificant. The narrator ruminates about various themes including the Great War (which had, by 1917, reached the stage of stalemate between the combatants). At intervals, the narrator is distracted by a strange spot on the wall and wonders if it is a nail. As it turns out, the spot is a snail,[2] and the story ends without any significant denouement. *Kew Gardens* was published by the Hogarth Press in 1919. The impressionistic use of color in the story (see Hussey, *Singing* 70) predicts the painterly elements of *Jacob's Room*. The narrative traces four couples walking through Kew Gardens, offering glimpses of their thoughts, but also focusing intently on the activities of a snail and several insects.

This swerve away from the human experience recurs in *Jacob's Room*. Thus, in addition to the minor characters in the novel, there are other living things (like the snail's view of the world in *Kew Gardens*[3]) such as butterflies, birds, dogs, and even plants that have no interest in human existence at all and are concentrating on their own existences. From a human perspective, Jacob, trying to classify a dead moth he has captured for his collection, illustrates an intellectual challenge, a mental activity (21). Other beings in the world go about their own business. Thus, a sparrow "fl[ies] past the window trailing a straw ... from a stack stood by a barn in a farmyard," as Fanny Elmer realizes in despair that Jacob "would forget her" (130). Similarly indifferent to human emotions, "A fox pads stealthily. A leaf turns on its edge," as Betty Flanders and Mrs. Jarvis stand on the moors at midnight together (140).

Woolf's "An Unwritten Novel" was first published in the *London Mercury* in 1920. The random events of the story line evolve from a chance encounter of several travelers in the compartment of a train. The narrator, reading a newspaper story on the Versailles Treaty that formally ended the Great War in 1919, eventually begins to chat with the remaining passenger and imagine what sort of person she is. Woolf uses the modernist strategy of stream of consciousness to depict the narrator's associative and sometimes disjointed thought process.

Woolf's experimental objectives seem to have been fully realized in *Jacob's Room,* for there truly is "scarcely a brick to be seen." By drastically redefining the form of the novel, Woolf was consciously rebelling against the traditions of the Victorians and their successors, the Edwardians.[4] These writers, including H. G. Wells, Arnold Bennett, and John Galsworthy, were the establishment competitors against whom Woolf was vying for a market niche—if not market share—in the literary forum of the day. To capture the attention of a select readership, her product had to be distinctive. Woolf, claiming her territory in "Modern Fiction" (1925, first published in a different version in the *Times Literary Supplement* in 1919 under the title "Modern Novels"), attacks these writers rather savagely, sounding remarkably like Jacob himself ranting against his predecessors and asserting that "the flesh and blood of the future depends entirely upon six young men" (112):

The writer seems constrained . . . by some powerful and unscrupulous tyrant who has him in thrall, to provide a plot, to provide comedy, tragedy, love interest, and an air of probability embalming the whole so impeccable that if all his figures were to come to life they would find themselves dressed down to the last button of their coats. (149)

Woolf's vision for the novel of the future in "Modern Fiction" focuses on the minutiae of daily life, as does *Jacob's Room,* emphasizing the random realities of lived experience:

Examine for a moment an ordinary mind on an ordinary day. The mind receives a myriad impressions — trivial, fantastic, evanescent, or engraved with the sharpness of steel. From all sides they come, an incessant shower of innumerable atoms; . . . the accent falls differently from of old. . . . Life is not a series of gig lamps symmetrically arranged; life is a luminous halo, a semi-transparent envelope surrounding us from the beginning of consciousness to the end. Is it not the task of the novelist to convey this varying, this unknown and uncircumscribed spirit[?] ("Modern Fiction" 150)

What the Reviewers Said

THE "LUMINOUS HALO" mentioned in "Modern Fiction" is very similar indeed to Woolf's vision of *Jacob's Room* as "a fire in the mist" with nary "a brick to be seen." Yet, as one would expect, the reception of a novel written according to these precepts was mixed. Arnold Bennett's response to *Jacob's Room* was provocative. He comments: "I have seldom read a cleverer book . . . [I]t is exquisitely written. But the characters do not

vitally survive in the mind because the author has been obsessed
by details of originality and cleverness" (Majumdar and McLaurin 113).[5] Other reviewers had a more nuanced take on the
novel. In an unsigned review for the *Times Literary Supplement,*
A. S. McDowell recognizes the nature of Woolf's experiment,
noting that the novel "is not Jacob's history simply, nor anyone
else's, but the queer simultaneity of life, with all those incongruous threads which now run parallel, now intersect, and then part
as unaccountably" (Majumdar and McLaurin 96)—and yet,
there is something missing: "We should have to say that [the
novel] does not create personas and characters as we secretly desire to know them" (Majumdar and McLaurin 97). Lewis Bettany, writing for the *Daily News,* snidely refers to "an irritating
feature of Mrs Woolf's new story, which is so full of parenthe-
ses and suppressions, so tedious in its rediscoveries of the obvious, and so marred by its occasional lapses into indecency, that
I found great difficulty in discovering what it was all about"
(Majumdar and McLaurin 98). W. L. Courtney, the reviewer for
the *Daily Telegraph,* growls, "The old craving for a plot still remains in our unregenerate breasts," but concludes his critique,
"But if you want to know what a modern novel is like, you have
only to read *Jacob's Room* . . . In its tense, syncopated movements,
its staccato impulsiveness, do you not discern the influence of
Jazz?" (Majumdar and McLaurin 103, 105). And Rebecca West,
reviewing for the *New Statesman,* quips: "Very strongly has Mrs
Woolf preferred Jacob's room to his company. Jacob lives, but
that is hearsay. Jacob dies; there could be nothing more negative
than the death of one who never (that we could learn for certain) lived. But his room we know." As a consequence of these
and other peculiarities in the work, West classifies *Jacob's Room*
as "a portfolio" rather than a novel, declaring that "Mrs Woolf
has . . . provided us with a demonstration that she is at once a

negligible novelist and a supremely important writer" (Majumdar and McLaurin 100–1).

"Ja—cob! Ja—cob!"

JACOB'S ROOM ostensibly focuses on the evasive protagonist, Jacob Flanders, but Jacob himself is often eclipsed by the narrator who traces Jacob's life from his late Victorian boyhood through the brief flowering of his manhood in the early twentieth century. The novel concludes shortly after Jacob's untimely death, which occurs at some unspecified point during World War I, in Woolf's time known as the Great War, a catastrophic and futile global conflict that dragged on from August 1914 to November 1918, leaving millions dead in its wake.

Jacob is relatively privileged. He is intelligent and physically beautiful, reasonably well-read and perhaps a bit too pleased with himself. The narrator describes Jacob at Cambridge University, in the prime of his youth, enjoying his privileges and certain of his future:

> He looked satisfied; indeed masterly; which expression changed slightly as he stood there, the sound of the clock conveying to him (it may be) a sense of old buildings and time; and himself the inheritor; and then to-morrow; and friends; at the thought of whom, in sheer confidence and pleasure, it seemed, he yawned and stretched himself. (44)

But the clock chiming is ominous. Throughout the novel repeated references to clocks, watches, and the passing of time in general forewarn the reader of the inevitable—the moment that the Great War will begin and put an end to all tomorrows for young men like Jacob. In the thirteenth chapter, time converges as the disparate activities of multiple characters are glimpsed at precisely five P.M. on a summer day in London. The emphasis on a specific and exact time suggests that Woolf was recalling that Great Britain declared war on Germany on August 4, 1914, at seven P.M. It was not until eleven A.M. on the morning of November 11, 1918, that the hostilities came to an end with the signing of a truce — but the war did not officially conclude until the signing of the Treaty of Versailles in 1919.

The reader first sees Jacob as a child, perhaps six years old, straying away from his mother and brothers and getting lost while wandering on the beach at St. Ives, Cornwall. Betty Flanders, his mother, tells Jacob's older brother, Archer, to find him. Calling "Ja—cob! Ja—cob!" repeatedly and to no avail, Archer unenthusiastically seeks Jacob (it is Betty who actually finds Jacob just as the tide is coming in on the rocky beach). This call, with its "extraordinary sadness. Pure from all body, pure from all passion" (5), is repeated at the end of the novel by two of the characters who loved Jacob most. Clara Durrant, a young woman who had dared to hope Jacob would propose to her, and who never voices her emotions, aches helplessly for him and twice in a few moments thinks silently: "Jacob! Jacob!" (176). Richard Bonamy, Jacob's Cambridge friend and would-be lover, stands in Jacob's room, knowing that Jacob is dead and will never return, and cries aloud: "Jacob! Jacob!" (187).

During Jacob's adventure at the beach, he captures a defenseless crab and finds a sheep's skull, keeping the jawbone despite his mother's protests. The crab, struggling to escape from Jacob's toy bucket (6, 11), is often seen as a symbol of Jacob's own entrapment within the confines of society. Jacob's character as an adolescent is sketched out in a bit more depth and breadth than his early childhood, which is limited to a single afternoon and evening. For example, the reader knows that

Thoby Stephen, early 1880s (aged four or five, seated on a balustrade with a shrimping net), photograph by Lock & Whitfield; original albumen print (36i in Leslie Stephen Photograph Album).

Jacob, perhaps twelve years old, has chosen the works of Lord Byron as a gift when his Latin tutor moves on to a new position (19), and that he enjoys, like the Stephen siblings (Woolf, *A Passionate Apprentice* 144–45), classifying the butterflies and moths he enthusiastically collects (20–21). Also like the Stephen siblings, Jacob plays cricket (27). The narrator provides no specific information regarding Jacob's educational experience, although he attends Rugby School, a prestigious educational institution (19). Perhaps Woolf expects her reader to be familiar with Thomas Hughes's popular Victorian-era novel, *Tom Brown's Schooldays* (1857) and therefore in need of no further information. How Mrs. Flanders, Jacob's mother, can afford to send her son to an expensive public school given her "poverty" (12) remains unclear. Perhaps Jacob has won a scholarship; perhaps Captain Barfoot, Betty Flanders's married admirer (12), has paid the bills. Throughout the novel, Jacob's relationship with his mother seems awkward, although she does wish the best for him—and there are few indications that Jacob keeps in touch with his brothers, Archer and John.

As a university student at Cambridge, and later as a graduate, Jacob's views and tendencies become more apparent. For example, Jacob despises social climbers (33), rejects the traditions and aesthetics of the previous generation (34–35, 111–12), thrives on informal but intense debates with his university friends (for example, 44–45, 49, 77, 106), regards women with some disdain (31, 159), and possibly has a sexual relationship with at least one male friend (45) while at university and, perhaps, a continuing intimate relationship with Richard Bonamy (106, 174).

Jacob's day-to-day existence is filled with pleasant trivialities. He plays chess against himself (120) and reads for pleasure. He peruses newspapers and periodicals (93, 101–2, 145); he studies Plato's dialogues (114–15) and researches Christopher Marlowe's plays (111); he annotates John Donne's poems, giving his own copy to one of his lovers (169); he abominates the minor scholar who has expurgated lewd passages from William Wycherley's plays (70) and crafts his essay on the "Ethics of Indecency" in response (79)—a work that he knows will be rejected by the prestigious periodicals to which he submits, possibly because it is too indecent to publish (70; see Marshik 1–13; Briggs, "In Search" 98–101). Jacob, despite his advocacy of free expression, has a queasy moment when he comes face-to-face with inde-

cency "in the raw," and is fleetingly revolted by the realization
that "beauty goes hand in hand with stupidity" (83), but he is
clearly torn between the austere life of the mind and the rollick-
ing but sometimes nasty life of the flesh. In this instance, after
feigning a headache, he succumbs to carnality (84).

Thus, like many of his favorite writers, Jacob enjoys the var-
ied indulgences of the flesh. Even though his clothing is shabby
(28, 153) and his rooms are sparsely furnished (37, 71), he relishes
eating the dinners paid for by friends and acquaintances (105,
136, 146, 165), getting drunk (76, 116, 132), and smoking good ci-
gars (105, 152). He goes on sailing adventures possibly financed
by his friend Timmy Durrant (36, 46–48), and meets a suitable
young woman, Clara Durrant, Timmy's sister, to whom, as noted
above, he never proposes. Trapped in the conventions of her social class, Clara is just the type of woman who would encumber
Jacob's lifestyle. As he realizes, his marriage to her would force
him to participate in the formal high-society events, which he
finds excruciatingly boring (90, 145–46). In need of an income
after attending university, he holds a position at a law firm (93),
though his earnings never seem to meet his expenditures.

Instead of marrying, Jacob has various illicit relationships.
His first female lover, Florinda, perhaps takes advantage of him,
claiming she has no surname and continually touting her virginity. She initially enchants Jacob, who thinks of her as being "wild
and frail and beautiful, . . . thus the women of the Greeks were"
(79–80). Possibly, as Sue Roe suggests in her introduction to the
novel, Florinda is a student at the Slade School of Art (xxvi).
Florinda's lodgings are "half studio," and her bohemian decor
of silver stars and rosaries suggests an artistic inclination (78).
Jacob is sufficiently obtuse to believe that "little prostitutes" like
Florinda have "an inviolable fidelity" (98). Both Jacob and the
narrator seem to view Florinda as a dim-witted semiprofes-
sional prostitute, though she may just be promiscuous (79–80).

Roe suggests that Florinda is actually an intelligent woman who recognizes Jacob's contempt for her (xxvi) and strikes back by finding another lover (xxviii–xxix). Regardless, it is deeply ironic that immediately after Jacob's arrogant assertion he sees Florinda going "up Greek Street" with another man (98). Momentarily stunned and angry, Jacob returns to his rooms dejected, but rapidly recovers from the shock as he redirects his feelings and becomes engaged in reading the prime minister's speech on Irish Home Rule in the newspaper (102). Although short of cash, Jacob manages to pay for his fox-hunting expenses (105, 186) and for casual sex with prostitutes out of his own pocket (109), as well as paying for his rental chair in Hyde Park, extravagantly overpaying the "ticket-collector" (179).

Later, Jacob becomes involved with Fanny Elmer, an artist's model and probably an art student at the Slade School. Like Florinda, Fanny initiates the relationship (Roe suggests that she makes a prostitute's offer to him by deliberately dropping her glove [179 n4]). Unlike Florinda, who moves on and becomes involved with Nick Bramham,[6] the painter whom Fanny abandons for Jacob, Fanny is completely besotted with Jacob and lovelorn to the point of contemplating "drown[ing herself] in the Thames" (147). Jacob abruptly leaves Fanny when he inherits a modest legacy from a distant female relative (131), although he does continue to correspond with her (180). At the end of the novel, Fanny continues to yearn for him desperately (as do both Clara and Richard) and solaces herself by writing poems (180).

Rather than investing or saving the inheritance, Jacob replicates in miniature the Grand Tour of the Continent that was the tradition for well-to-do young men in the Victorian and Edwardian periods. Of course, as it turns out, squandering the inheritance is a kind of carpe diem, allowing Jacob to enjoy the fleeting pleasures of life before his premature demise. In Paris he becomes involved with some rather peculiar people: the painter Teddy Cruttendon and his companion Jinny Carslake, with whom he, perhaps, samples a brief ménage à trois during their visit to Versailles (135–37).[7] While traveling by rail through Italy, Jacob fantasizes about becoming a vagabond living on bread and wine once he exhausts his funds (143), but nothing comes of this daydream.

Exhilarated in anticipation of arriving in Greece, Jacob is initially disappointed by contemporary Greece in all its modern coarseness (144). He slips into depression because he is lonely and bored, so miserable in fact that "he bec[omes] like a man about to be executed" (145)—but when he ventures to the ancient archaeological sites, he regains his sense of philhellenic excitement about being in Greece (148–49, 152, 155–57). When, by chance, he meets Sandra Wentworth Williams, an older and sexually experienced married woman whose husband tolerates—or even facilitates—her affairs, Jacob eventually succumbs to her seductive maneuvers and to the tale she tells of her unhappy childhood. Ensnared by her worldly ways (154, 166–69), Jacob suffers from the "hook" of desire (155). He returns from Greece during the height of the London Season[8] still obsessed with Sandra and has a difficult encounter with his friend Bonamy, who is devastated to find out that, just as he had dreaded, Jacob has fallen in love with a woman (174). In a state of emotional discomfort, Jacob spends hours sitting in his rented chair in Hyde Park doing nothing in particular (173, 179), although his mother is under the impression that he is "hard at work after his delightful journey" (183). Purely by chance, the Reverend Andrew Floyd sees a young man passing through Piccadilly Circus and realizes that it is Jacob, but doesn't feel comfortable approaching him (183)[9]—and then, after that accidental sighting, the reader never glimpses Jacob again.

In terms of his personal decisions and character traits, Jacob is somewhat inclined to squander his resources; he is also easily bored (31, 145), endearingly naive (79, 154), shockingly insensitive (130), and obtuse and lazy (163). Jacob is almost reflexively misogynistic (31, 159), although there are brief moments when he views women as his equals. For example, he fleetingly wants "to figure out a comradeship all spirited on [Florinda's] side, protective on his, yet equal on both, for women, . . . are just the same as men" (80); but generally he regards members of the opposite sex as inferior and irrelevant—or as playthings provided for his physical pleasure. If one were to sum up Jacob's attributes and tendencies, one would have to conclude that he is not exceptional. Rather, he is ordinary and typical, a representative composite of university- and public-school-educated men of the 1900s. And, tragically, he, like so many other young men of his generation and class, is also ultimately a sacrificial victim in a pointless conflict, a helpless cog in the machinery of war (164), a futile casualty.

The Ultimate Sacrifice

JACOB'S VICTIMIZATION is marked in several passages as he politely consents without resistance to the demands of others. One such episode occurs while he is visiting the Durrants in Cornwall, where he is recruited for a role in a private theatrical: " 'Poor Jacob,' said Mrs. Durrant, quietly, as if she had known him all his life. 'They're going to make you act in their play' " (62). The battlefronts in the Great War were, of course, referred to as "theaters of war." As Paul Fussell notes in *The Great War and Modern Memory,* Sir Henry Newbolt, a close friend of General Douglas Haig, who was responsible for the western theater of the war, envisioned the battlefield as analogous to a game of cricket. He wrote the energetic lines "The river of death has brimmed his banks, / And England's far, and Honor a name; / But the voice of a schoolboy rallies the ranks: / 'Play up! Play up! And play the game!'" to inspire the men at the front to fight to the death (26). Like cricket, a game that Jacob played at Rugby, so, too, does fox hunting "mimic war" (96), as Fussell notes, citing Siegfried Sassoon's *Memoirs of a Fox-Hunting Man* (1928) as another instance of manliness and valor tainted by the carnage of the war.

David Roessel argues that on Guy Fawkes Night "Jacob has been marked as a sacrificial victim; he becomes, in effect, a replacement for the image burned on November 5" (53) as he is festooned with paper flowers and glass grapes by the revelers (see note to page 76). Jacob's status in this context is also linked through the grape motif to the mythic Dionysus, one of the dying-and-rising gods of the ancient Mediterranean mystery religions (see Neverow, "Return" 213–14). In a third instance of self-sacrifice, Jacob meekly allows himself to be blindfolded for a game at the raucous party where his devoted friend Dick Graves, "being a little drunk, very faithful, and very simpleminded, told [Helen Askew] that he thought Jacob the greatest man he had ever known," and Helen envisions the two of them as "heroes" (116).

As scholars have noted over the years, the reader's encounters with Jacob himself are transitory, and his absences foreshadow his inevitable death. Even the title itself refers not to Jacob, the protagonist, but to his *room*. In the final chapter, Jacob's mother and his close friend Richard Bonamy sort through his belongings to bring closure to his life, but neither the reader nor the narrator knows the location of Jacob's last resting place—his final room. However, in lieu of closure, the narrator repeats her description of his rooms in the final chapter, moving backward chronologically as if Jacob's life were unraveling along with the narrative. First, the description of

Jacob's room on Lamb's Conduit Street from the fifth chapter
is repeated almost verbatim in the final chapter:

> The eighteenth century has its distinction. These houses
> were built, say, a hundred and fifty years ago. The rooms
> are shapely, the ceilings high; over the doorways a rose or
> a ram's skull is carved in the wood. Even the panels,
> painted in raspberry-coloured paint, have their distinction.
> (71; and see 186)

The passage "Listless is the air in an empty room, just
swelling the curtain; ... One fibre in the wicker arm-chair
creaks, though no one sits there" (38), describing Jacob's room
at Cambridge, is reiterated in the final chapter (186). Bishop describes this particular repetition as "a meditation on mortality
itself. ... After reading the last line we raise our eyes from the
page and hear the creak of our own chair, conscious of the
room we too must ultimately leave" (introduction xxxiii).

About the Narrator

WHILE JACOB is hard to find in *Jacob's Room,* the nameless narrator is a ubiquitous and sometimes annoying presence. She
identifies herself as female and ten years older than Jacob
halfway through the novel (98) and seems to be of the same
class as Jacob, but the reader knows very little else about her.
While all narrators control the reader's access to the characters,
in this instance the narrator seems to be randomly secretive and
even taunts the reader about what she knows and the reader
does not (e.g., 74). But at another, more somber level, one might
view her as a composite of the mythic Greek Fates. As Clotho,

the narrator spins the thread of Jacob's life; as Lachesis, she measures its length; as Atropos, it is she who "slits the thin-spun life" (Milton, "Lycidas" 70–76).

It is the narrator's decision to render the protagonist as a cipher, a conundrum, an absence, and a shadow (72), and to depict anyone who attempts to comprehend him as a moth fluttering at the entrance of a cavern (74). Sometimes the narrator is omniscient—but sometimes she is not. Sometimes she provides credible information—but sometimes she is just a fallible observer (73), a distant acquaintance (69), a predatory gossip (162), or an eavesdropper (106). Sometimes she is even an outsider, as, for example, when she observes Jacob's life in his environment at Cambridge University from a distance (43). Alex Zwerdling notes that "she is pictured . . . so far away from the action that she literally can't hear the words of the characters" (902). Possibly she is a secret admirer of Jacob (see Knowles 106). The narrator is so inconsistent that James Hafley contends that there are not one but two narrators: "While one of them is saying that Jacob is essentially unknowable, the other is doing a very good job of disproving that by making the rest of the characters as knowable as they can possibly be" (52). Certainly and somewhat disturbingly the narrator is both a stalker (like the lovelorn Fanny Elmer, who lurks in the neighborhood of the Foundling Hospital in the hope of seeing Jacob walk by [127] or imagines proximity to him even when he is gone [147]) and a trespasser, skulking outside Jacob's rooms, following Jacob home (101), or even entering Jacob's rooms when he is away (37–38). The narrator's erratic style is evident even in a brief passage such as the account of Jacob's first visit to the Acropolis (158), as her tone shifts rapidly, from mocking to affectionate, from playful to satirical, from caustic to melancholic (regarding the narrator, see also Morgenstern).

Are There Characters in *Jacob's Room*?

THE NARRATOR is also easily distracted by minor characters entirely irrelevant to Jacob's existence. Bishop accounts for 172
named and 25 unnamed characters (introduction xxvii; see also
Neverow, "Return" 207). These minor characters are sometimes
no more than their names, but sometimes they possess their
own sketchy lives. Mrs. Pascoe, a working-class woman living in
an isolated cottage on the Cornwall coast, appears several times
in the manuscript and in the novel, depicted as earthy and res-
olute, an artifact from another century (52–54, 185). However,
characters like the frail and fidgety Mrs. Withers, who anxiously
confides to a man named Oliver Skelton at a party that her
husband is cold toward her (115), and Mrs. Grandage, living in
the London suburb of Surbiton, who believes that "the kettle
never boils so well on a sunny morning" (171), never reappear.
According to Bishop, their presence "honour[s] the non-
combatants" in a book that "memorializes not only Jacob, but
those who are left behind" by the impending war (introduction
xxviii). By introducing these random characters, the narrator
positions Jacob's story as one among hundreds of millions, deliberately diminishing his importance and thus challenging literary traditions in which the protagonist must overshadow the
other characters. Although he is frequently described as "distinguished" (29, 61, 71, 153, 163), Jacob is ultimately indistinguish-
able. In the last days, months, or years of his short life, he will
be clad in the officer's uniform intended to obliterate individuality. After that, he will be unrecognizable, perhaps lost at sea,
perhaps a corpse decaying in the mud, perhaps blown to bits,
perhaps nothing but putrefaction. As the narrator notes in
passing, Jacob's "walking-stick was like all the others" in the
pigeonholes of the checkroom of the British Museum, indistin-

guishable from similar items except by a number on one of innumerable "white discs" (113).

Certainly if Jacob were a conventional protagonist in a plot-driven novel, the cast of characters would be far smaller. But even typically important characters—Jacob's family members, friends, lovers, and acquaintances—are indistinct. Jacob's younger brother, John, is mentioned only twelve times in the novel; Archer, his older brother, is mentioned twenty-seven times. But Jacob himself mentions his own siblings by name only once (108; he also refers to "my brother" once [168]). Only Jacob's mother, Betty, is equally developed as a character in the novel. Her intriguing relationship with Captain Barfoot, her marriage offer from Reverend Floyd, her friendship with Mrs. Jarvis, her letter writing, her passion for her chickens all combine to make Betty a substantial presence. However, if one were to use E. M. Forster's differentiation between "flat," or one-dimensional, and "round," or three-dimensional, characters to analyze the novel, neither Jacob himself nor his mother would be considered sufficiently fully developed to qualify as "round" (67–78).

The Shock of the Modern

READERS WILL realize from the very first page that *Jacob's Room* is not the kind of novel one can skim through or skip to the end to find out what happened. The novel begins in medias res (in the middle of things) and focuses on Betty Flanders, Jacob's mother, rather than Jacob himself. The first words are from a letter Betty is writing: "there was nothing for it but to leave" (3). The narrator's reference to this unspecified incident is never explained or mentioned again, although critics have speculated about its implications.[10] Throughout the novel, the narrator routinely offers the reader scraps of information without explanation, though, occasionally, she sorts things out a few sentences later. While in more conventional works the narrator actively assists the reader, clarifying the sequence of events and explaining what has occurred, in *Jacob's Room* the reader must actually decipher the work independently.

Thus Woolf's innovative narrative strategies in *Jacob's Room* may still startle readers in the twenty-first century. As she does in subsequent works as well, Woolf experiments in *Jacob's Room* with such modernist techniques as stream of consciousness (the sustained access to the character's random, associative inner perceptions and thoughts) and free indirect monologue (a character's thoughts modulated through the medium of the narrator) rather than relying on extensive narrative explication and detailed dialogue. Furthermore, the modernist techniques used in the visual arts are evident in the work. Clive Bell, Woolf's brother-in-law, noted in his review of *Jacob's Room* for the *Dial* Woolf's "almost painterlike vision" in the style of "the French impressionists" (Majumdar and McLaurin 144), and the narrative strategies also incorporate what is known as ekphrasis (see Wall), the depiction of visual artworks in words (e.g., 4). Woolf also experiments with photographic imagery (Gillespie 143–44; Neverow, "Thinking" 77–85) and cinematic techniques (Holtby) such as the freeze-frame (Bishop, "Shaping" 17). The author of a contemporary unsigned review for the *Yorkshire Post* observes that "The method . . . is snapshot photography [and] the result is a crowded album of little pictures— of Jacob as a boy; of Jacob's mother and home at Scarborough; of Jacob at Cambridge; . . . of Jacob's room, empty . . . after Jacob (we gather) has been killed in the war" (Majumdar and McLaurin 107).

The Holograph Draft: Revising the Text

THE EXISTING holograph draft (see Bishop, *Holograph,* "Shaping"; see also Flint) shows that Woolf made significant changes as she crafted the framework of the novel, crossing out passages, changing characters' names, developing sections that were later eliminated. In the manuscript, the novel begins with Jacob on the beach ("Beyond the rock lay a pool shine green something shiny on the sand. A few small fish, left by the tide, beat with up & down with their tails" [Bishop, *Holograph* 2]), rather than with the emphasis on Jacob's mother in tears: "'So, of course,' wrote Betty Flanders, pressing her heels rather deeper in the sand, 'there was nothing for it but to leave'... [H]er eyes fixed, and tears slowly filled them" (3). In both the draft and the final version, at the very end of the novel Betty Flanders, knowing that her son is dead, stands bemused in Jacob's rooms, holding his shoes and asking his friend Bonamy what she should do with them. In the published version, this is the last line of the novel. In the draft, Woolf wrote (and then struck out): "They both laughed: The room waved behind her tears" (Bishop, *Holograph* 275). Thus in the published version, Betty's tears begin, rather than end the novel.

In the draft, the names of characters metamorphose rapidly. Betty Flanders's admirer and faithful Wednesday visitor makes his first appearance as Captain Bingham (Bishop, *Holograph* 7), rather than as Captain Barfoot (Bishop, *Holograph* 21). Jacob refers to his uncle, the mysterious "Mohammedan," as "Uncle Eliot" (Bishop, *Holograph* 36) who eventually becomes Uncle Morty. A character named Borwick (Bishop, *Holograph* 81) evolves into Richard Bonamy (Bishop, *Holograph* 106), but is also briefly named Arthur Raisley (Bishop, *Holograph* 106); Angela Edwards (Bishop, *Holograph* 50), a student at the Cambridge women's college, Newnham, is renamed Angela Williams

(Bishop, *Holograph* 52). In the final version, this entire segment disappears from the novel, reappearing, heavily edited, as "A Woman's College from the Outside" in *Atalanta's Garland: Being the Book of the Edinburgh University Women's Union* (November 1926) (Flint 365; Roe xxix–xxxii; see also Woolf, "A Society").

Some of the minor characters in the draft have more substantial attributes that were later edited out. Mrs. Pascoe's life is delineated far more graphically—"~~in this four-roomed cottage an~~ there would be no escaping the body. Its functions are detestable. An earth closet out in the rain[11]—sickness—a woman's period—~~copul~~—copulation upstairs in the double bed, ~~or here before the fire perhaps~~" (Bishop, *Holograph* 57–58). In the draft, Mrs. Pascoe reads about the wedding of Lady Cynthia Mosley; however, Lady Cynthia's marriage to Oswald Mosley, the founder of the British Union of Fascists, took place in 1920, years after Jacob's death in the war. Woolf omits any reference to a surname in the published version, leaving it to the reader to determine that it is the Lady Cynthia Charteris who married Herbert Asquith, the second son of Prime Minister Asquith, in Westminster Abbey in 1910. Nick Bramham's emotional turmoil after Fanny Elmer has left him is omitted entirely from the published version but is detailed in the draft (Bishop, *Holograph* 175). When Jacob and Sandra clamber up to the Acropolis, one draft version includes Jacob imagining that "[h]e had already climbed them [the gates of the Acropolis] lifted her over them, broken them down" (Bishop, *Holograph* 265), and another ends with the strike-out "~~She kissed him~~" (Bishop, *Holograph* 268), while in the published version, the narrator has completely lost track of the couple: "They had vanished" (169).

Woolf even incorporates a variation of her own earliest remembered sensory experiences into the holograph. In "A Sketch of the Past," a memoir she began in 1939, Woolf recalls lying half asleep, half awake, in bed in the nursery at St Ives ... hearing the waves breaking, one, two, one, two, and sending a splash of water over the beach; and then breaking, one, two, one, two, behind a yellow blind ... hearing the blind draw its little acorn across the floor as the wind blew the blind out ... of lying and hearing this splash and seeing this light, and feeling, it is almost impossible that I should be here; of feeling the purest ecstasy I can conceive. (64–65)

Woolf transfers variants of these memories to Jacob himself in the draft. For example, she writes: "The blind was thin yellow; ~~like a curving~~ cut, for the nursery window was open ... The little trailing noise ~~of the~~ knob on blind cord ~~again~~ made him open his eyes"[12] (Bishop, *Holograph* 4; Lee 23–24). However, these details do not appear in the final version.

Publishing *Jacob's Room*

IT WAS A tremendous triumph for Woolf when the Hogarth Press, the venture she and her husband Leonard Woolf had launched in 1917, published *Jacob's Room,* the first full-length work released by the press. Unlike the hand-set and hand-printed publications with small print runs such as *Two Stories* (1917), Katherine Mansfield's *Prelude* (1918), Virginia Woolf's *Kew Gardens* (1919), T. S. Eliot's *Poems* (1919), and Hope Mirrlees's *Paris: A Poem* (1919), *Jacob's Room,* both because of its length and the number of copies required, had to be outsourced to R. & R. Clark of Edinburgh (Bishop, introduction xxxiii), a commercial printer. As Bishop observes:

> The publishing of *Jacob's Room* marks a pivotal point in the career of Virginia Woolf as both writer and publisher: she takes over her own means of production, inaugurates the

commercial phase of the Press, and simultaneously begins the consolidation of the Hogarth Press as a name brand, an imprint whose wolf's-head logo conferred the stamp of quality. (Introduction xxiv)

The dust jacket of *Jacob's Room* was as experimental and controversial as the contents and was the first dust jacket designed for the Hogarth Press by Woolf's sister, the painter Vanessa Bell.[13] The cover was a paean to Roger Fry's vision for the arts. Fry had promoted his passionate advocacy for the Postimpressionist style of painting through the avant-garde exhibits he organized at the Grafton Galleries in London in 1910 and 1912. His Omega Workshops (1913–1921) venture was a modernist rebellion against the style of the arts and crafts movement of the late nineteenth century that, nonetheless, continued the tradition by producing beautifully crafted, useful objects such as home decor items and jewelry. Printed in cinnamon and black (Willis 60), Bell's dust jacket sketches a curtain draped at the top and pulled back on either side of the suggestive edge of a table holding a vase with three free-form flowers. The title and the author's name are inscribed in a calligraphic style. *Jacob's Room* was first published in Britain on October 22, 1922, by the Hogarth Press, and in America by Harcourt Brace and Company on February 8, 1923.

"Mind the Gap"

BISHOP NOTES that "in the Hogarth edition there are four different sizes of breaks, ranging from one to four-line spaces, where in the Harcourt Brace edition they are all regularized as one-line spaces." He asks, quite appropriately, "Why should we care?" since Woolf did not seem to be disturbed by the American formatting ("Mind" 34). However, as Bishop argues in his article "Mind the Gap: The Spaces in *Jacob's Room*," these differing spaces delineate significant shifts in the narrative.[14] He offers a detailed explanation of the spacing variants and contends that "the absence of a space break, or even a variation in the size of the space break, can affect our response to the text" ("Mind" 35). One example will suffice. In the British edition, Jacob's sighting of Florinda "turning up Greek Street upon another man's arm" is separated by a two-line space from the sentence "The light from the arc lamp drenched him from head to toe" (98). The larger gap between the lines, according to Bishop, shows the reader exactly "where Jacob's horror sinks in. Or when time stops" ("Mind" 39). Francesca Kazan sees the spacing of paragraphs and chapters as a pictorial device. Thus we can think of *Jacob's Room* as a series of frames:

> The work is graphically arranged in discrete bordered blocks: it is divided into fourteen chapters of varying length, and these fourteen units are further divided into a number of fragments, each set off from the other by a white border of blankness. The last, single-page chapter is complete in itself, and finally reveals what has previously been veiled—Jacob's death. . . . There is also another level of framing at work in *Jacob's Room:* within the discrete fragment certain passages operate in special contrast to the rest of the narrative—a moment of stillness or quiet interrupts the incessant murmur of voices, and thus appears as if framed or set apart. (703)

Self-Censorship and the Obscenity Laws

THE PUBLICATION of *Jacob's Room* marked Woolf's exhilarating declaration of independence from intrusive and interfering editors. Her earlier novels, *The Voyage Out* (1915) and *Night and Day* (1919), were both published by Duckworth and Company, a publishing house founded by her half brother Gerald Duckworth. Quite simply, Woolf did not respect Gerald's capabilities as an editor. In a diary entry regarding her second novel, *Night and Day,* she notes, with revulsion, how she "thought of [her] novel destined to be pawed & snored over by him" (*Diary* 1: 129). She also had other issues with him. Her memoirs describe her unpleasant recollections of being sexually molested as a child by Gerald ("A Sketch of the Past" 67–68) and later, as an adolescent and young woman, by her other half brother George Duckworth ("22 Hyde Park Gate" 169, 177).

Having her work scrutinized and evaluated by her half brother was not the only impediment Woolf faced. Raised in the late Victorian period, Woolf felt that her creative expression was blocked early on by a ghostly feminine presence she satirically calls "the Angel in the House" in her 1931 essay "Professions for Women." As she states: "Had I not killed her, she would have killed me. She would have plucked the heart out of my writing" (59). Even when "the Angel was dead" (60), Woolf still did not feel that she (or, for that matter, any woman of her era) would ever be able to voice her ideas freely. Women were held to a different standard than men. Thus it was "unfitting for her as a woman to say" anything "about the passions" because "[m]en, her reason told her, would be shocked" (61).

Last, but definitely not least, there was the daunting legal machinery of censorship, which restricted expression not on the basis of gender but on the basis of social purity. Writers and publishers of the era were liable under strict obscenity laws in Britain and could be severely fined. As Celia Marshik notes, the 1868 *Regina v. Hicklin* trial, "conducted under the auspices of Lord Campbell's Act of 1857," justified harsh scrutiny of literary expression. This act, although purportedly not intended to affect "serious literature," nonetheless "authorized the seizure and destruction of all copies of an 'obscene' publication,'" regardless of the intentions of author or publisher. Without a doubt, "the vagueness of the Act's language all but ensured that literature would eventually fall under its purview," sending a chilling message to the literary community (see Marshik 22–23).

The Patriarchal Machine

DESPITE SIGNIFICANT obstacles, Woolf speaks far more candidly in *Jacob's Room* of sexuality and other taboo topics than in her earlier work (as some of her reviewers took note[15]). Woolf was keenly conscious that men of her own social class not only had much greater sexual freedom (see Froula), they also had far greater access to education and were financially much more independent than women. Woolf sees these elements of oppression and exclusion as interrelated. Thus *Jacob's Room* reveals the machinery that drives multiple levels of the social system. While women's lives are "irresistibly driven" by the "force" of rigid gender rules (160), the same "unseizable force" propels both male sexuality (164) and the buildup to the impending war (164). Woolf positions Jacob's libertine lifestyle in direct contrast with the living conditions of the young women who pass through his life[16] (see Ohmann; Karen Lawrence; Ingram). While Jacob retains his social standing regardless of his sexual adventures, a woman like Clara Durrant must maintain her virtue at all costs. Because of her class, Clara does not have the freedoms of the "little prostitute" Florinda or the bohemian painter's model Fanny Elmer, but their independence is not linked to any sort of fiscal security. Florinda lives in seedy lodgings and is so financially strapped that she tries to wiggle out of paying for her tea by claiming that the waitress put broken glass in the sugar bowl

(79). Fanny shares a room with a schoolteacher (128) and almost swoons over Jacob's pocket change when she first meets him (124), equating his physical beauty with his innate male access to money. Ironically, although Jacob can afford his own rooms and pay for many of his pleasures, from the perspective of high-society gossips, Jacob himself "ha[s]n't a penny" (163). Such subtle distinctions of gender-based social stratification are evident throughout the novel.

Constructing *Jacob's Room*

VIRGINIA WOOLF chose to use personal experiences as raw materials for her fiction. Thus *Jacob's Room* draws extensively on her own life, memories, and observations. Although *Jacob's Room* is certainly not a memoir or an (auto)biography, it does have some of the attributes of an occasionally playful and sometimes rueful roman à clef (a novel with a key), a literary form using a fictional facade to depict aspects of the author's life and of real people the author knew.[17] And despite its experimental nature, *Jacob's Room* has deep allegiances to traditional novelistic approaches. The novel has a great deal in common with the picaresque tradition exemplified by Henry Fielding's *Tom Jones*—although the protagonist of that novel ends up happily married despite his brush with death. The comedic elements in *Jacob's Room* are noted by a number of scholars, though they do not necessarily agree on what is meant to be funny in the novel. Sebastian D. G. Knowles argues that "the narrator hovers over the inhabitants of the novel with a smug superiority, cracking jokes at the expense of everyone but Jacob himself" (98), while Catherine Nelson-McDermott asserts that "*Jacob's Room* is an extremely pessimistic and caustic text; its humor is angry, even eviscerating. The book's central character is unflatteringly presented by the narrator because he is in training to be a patriarch" (84).

Jacob's Room also draws on the attributes of the popular bildungsroman, a coming-of-age novel. Judy Little sees the novel as a parody of the genre and points out that "[t]he musing and amused narrator mocks the structure of her story; she mocks the conventions of the hero's progress; and, by implication, she mocks the values behind those conventions" (105). As she notes, "It seems almost as though Virginia Woolf deliberately chose the traditions of the *Bildungsroman* in order to play havoc with them" (109). Instead of the protagonist's steady process of maturation, Jacob's activities lead nowhere significant and result in nothing noteworthy—his life is delightfully trivial until it is suddenly snuffed out.

For Zwerdling, the novel is not just a strongly satirical commentary on society, it is also an elegy. Humor and satire in *Jacob's Room* are intermingled with grieving for the dead—but definitely not in a sentimental fashion. Thus Zwerdling asks rhetorically: "Is this any way to treat a young man whose life is about to be snuffed out? Why does Woolf challenge the ancient wisdom that dictates '*De mortuis nil nisi bonum*' [Speak no evil of the dead]. Is there some meanness of spirit evident in the games she plays with her characters?" But, as he observes, Woolf "was no more interested in a cult of war heroes than she had been in a religion of eminent Victorians. . . . Woolf's elegy for the young men who died in the war is revisionist: there is nothing grand about Jacob; the sacrifice of his life seems perfectly pointless, not even a cautionary tale" (902–3).

Of course Zwerdling is not the only scholar to recognize the elegiac elements in the novel. Tammy Clewell argues that Woolf is "promoting a new consciousness of death [in] *Jacob's Room*" and thereby "does more than criticize the tenacious persistence of consolatory mourning rituals. The novel also responds to . . . the reduction of death to insignificance [because of] the modern emergence of the secular individual whose values derive solely from earthly satisfactions" (201). Roger Moss notes that "writing and weeping, ink and tears, come together again in a piece of writing that enacts mourning" (42); and Karen Smythe contends that Woolf "uses the novel form in the exploration and alteration of elegiac conventions (such as incantation) that originated in poetic technique," creating what Smythe terms "fiction-elegy" (65).

Crafting Jacob

Thoby Stephen

In 1906 Virginia and Vanessa traveled (along with Virginia's friend Violet Dickinson) to Greece to meet their brothers, Thoby and Adrian. During the tour of Greece, Vanessa became ill, and later both Thoby and Violet contracted typhoid fever. When Thoby returned to England, he was misdiagnosed with malaria and was not properly treated for typhoid. While Violet recovered, Thoby died at the age of twenty-six on November 20 of that year. At the end of the manuscript of *Jacob's Room,* Woolf wrote:

Atque in perpetuum, frater, ave atque vale
Julian Thoby Stephen
(1880–1906)
Atque in perpetuum, frater, ave atque vale (Lee 227)[18]

Unquestionably, there is a very strong resemblance between Thoby Stephen and Jacob Flanders. At prep school, Thoby was an unexceptional student in most respects. Yet if Thoby was indifferent to schoolwork during his adolescence, he was passionate about entomology, a fascination he shared with his sisters.

Thoby Stephen, by George Charles Beresford, sepia-toned platinotype print, 1902–1906.

Jacob, too, is fascinated by "bug-hunting" (Lee 31–32; see also Woolf, *A Passionate Apprentice* 144–45, and "A Sketch of the Past" 104). Shakespeare and Greek literature also sparked Thoby's interest as he matured. He engaged during term breaks in excited literary disputes with Virginia, who, although denied the formal education of her brothers, was inspired to study Greek, first with Clara Pater (the sister of Walter Pater) and later with Janet Case. This educational divide between the sexes recurs in subtle ways throughout the novel; for example, the female narrator is not able to participate in the debate in Simeon's rooms at Cambridge; instead, she seems to be eavesdropping from outside (43; see also Zwerdling; Karen Lawrence; Ingram). The fascination

with things Greek is a recurrent motif that builds steadily toward Jacob's visit to Greece itself.[19] Jacob's Greek dictionary
and photographs "from the Greeks" are among the items the
narrator notes when she sneaks into his room while he is in the
dining hall (37) at Cambridge. At the end of the Guy Fawkes
Night's revelry in chapter 6, Jacob, wandering the London
streets with Timmy Durrant, declares recklessly, "Probably . . .
we are the only people in the world who know what the Greeks
meant" (77). But for Woolf, this arrogant philhellenic obsession
(see Fowler) is also related to her own sense of gender exclusion,
as she subtly indicates in "On Not Knowing Greek," an essay
she began to write in August 1922 (Hussey, *Virginia Woolf A to Z*
196) just a few months prior to the publication of *Jacob's Room*.

Thoby went up to Cambridge in 1899 and became (as had
his father, Leslie Stephen) a member of the Cambridge Conversazione Society, the elite secret organization known informally
as the Apostles. Other members of the society included Thoby's
closest friends Clive Bell, Lytton Strachey, and Leonard Woolf.
They called Thoby the Goth because of his distinctive personality traits, traits evidenced in Jacob's character as well.
Hermione Lee, in her biography of Virginia Woolf, lists the
many adjectives Woolf used in *Jacob's Room* to describe Jacob's
"Thoby-esque" attributes, including "awkward, distinguished-
looking, unworldly, excitable," as well as "authoritative, healthy,
severe, tolerant, regal, childlike, judicious, solid, shy, slow, barbaric, monolithic"—descriptors that Woolf also uses to describe Thoby himself in her memoir "A Sketch of the Past" (Lee
113–14). Woolf wryly incorporated a dose of Thoby's own irresistible magnetism into Jacob's character, for women and men
alike fall in love with the inarticulate and somewhat lethargic,
but statuesquely beautiful young man. In fact, Jacob is so
statuesque that three different women—Florinda (81), Fanny

Elmer (180), and Sandra Wentworth Williams (153)—specifically see his resemblance to sculpture, and Clara Durrant associates Jacob with the towering nineteenth-century statue of the mythic warrior Achilles (176). Richard Bonamy also, perhaps, compares Jacob to a statue—maybe that of Lord Nelson in Trafalgar Square—since he twice thinks of Jacob's resemblance to a "British Admiral" (153, 174).

The Cambridge Apostles devoted themselves to passionate argumentation and debate. Guided by G. E. Moore's philosophical perspective, they were committed to the values of friendship that he advocated. Julie Anne Taddeo indicates that the members of the "Brotherhood" of the Cambridge Apostles, especially during the Edwardian period when Thoby's friends Lytton Strachey, John Maynard Keynes, and Leonard Woolf were active members, had a deep investment in what they variously termed a "new style of love," "Brotherly Love" or "Higher Sodomy," a mode of intimacy based on the ancient Greek model of Platonic love. " 'Passing the love of women,' . . . romantic friendships also contributed to the formation of 'manliness' " among the Apostles (Taddeo 199). In a very oblique passage in *Jacob's Room,* the narrator describes Professor Sopwith's advocacy for the same sort of "manliness" and sums up the nature of his discourse as "thin silver disks which dissolve in young men's minds like silver . . . the impress always the same—a Greek boy's head" (39–40). "Overall," Taddeo argues, "the Brothers described their relations with the opposite sex as 'always degraded' " (207), an observation that may illuminate Jacob's intermittent attacks of misogyny (31, 159), his shudder of revulsion at Florinda when he realizes that "beauty goes hand in hand with stupidity," and his yearning for "male society" and the "cloistered" life of Cambridge (83). Richard Bonamy's abrupt spasm of hatred toward women (174) when he realizes that Jacob has fallen in love is triggered by his realization that Jacob has chosen intimacy with the opposite sex over "Higher Sodomy."

The Stephen siblings' move to Bloomsbury was a daring act of liberation from the stuffy and constrained life they had led in Kensington. Thoby quickly reinvented the culture of the Apostles with his "Thursday Evenings" at 46 Gordon Square, where the Stephen siblings had taken up residence after the death of their father in 1904. The Thursday Evenings were the embryonic origin of the Bloomsbury Group, and even after Thoby's death the gatherings continued (as Woolf describes in "A Sketch of the Past," and "Old Bloomsbury"). The radical difference was that Thoby's sisters, Vanessa and Virginia, were present during these debates. Although the Apostles are never explicitly mentioned in *Jacob's Room,* nor is there any direct reference to a social community similar to the Bloomsbury Group, the synergy of heated deliberation, extended reflection on ideas, and intimate camaraderie typical of the interactions among Thoby's friends are described in the novel. Jacob in Bloomsbury and his sparsely furnished sitting room, his sexual adventures, and his intimacy with bohemians all seem to be based on aspects of the Bloomsbury experiment.

As Woolf notes, her own exposure to these young men's sexual inclinations was quite an eye-opener:

> I knew there were buggers in Plato's Greece; I suspected—it was not a question you could just ask Thoby—that there were buggers in . . . Trinity [College], Cambridge; but it never occurred to me that there were buggers even now in the Stephens' sitting room at Gordon Square. I did not realise that love, far from being a thing they never mentioned, was in fact a thing which they seldom ceased to discuss. ("Old Bloomsbury" 194)

It was Lytton Strachey who breached the protective membrane of sexual prudery for Virginia Stephen and her now-married sister by pointing to a stain on Vanessa's white dress and saying, "Semen?" (195). The moment of emancipation was intoxicating—and the word *bugger* was immediately integrated into the vocabulary of the formerly sheltered maidens (194). Jacob's own early and extreme innocence seems to parallel Virginia's own naïveté.

Rupert Brooke

Woolf combined several young male prototypes to craft Jacob. In addition to Thoby's characteristics, she incorporated elements of her friend Rupert Brooke into Jacob's composite identity (see Briggs, "In Search" 87). Born in 1887, Brooke was a longtime friend of the Stephen siblings, a brother in the Cambridge Apostles, and an intimate of some members of the Bloomsbury Group for a time. Like Jacob—and like Thoby—Brooke was an exceptionally beautiful young man, adored by both women and men. When he was six years old, Brooke spent a holiday at St. Ives at the same time the Stephen siblings were at Talland House. At the end of chapter 2, Jacob goes up to Cambridge in 1906, the same year that Brooke did. Jacob's fascination with Elizabethan literature parallels Brooke's own interests. The narrator's description of the afternoon Jacob spends in the British Museum Reading Room collating editions of Christopher Marlowe's works is probably an allusion to Brooke's interest in Marlowe and his role in founding the Marlowe Dramatic Society.[20] Brooke's sexual adventures, although they do not precisely mirror Jacob's, are quite similar. Like Brooke, Jacob has some homosexual leanings but also recoils from such relationships. Instances in the novel include the homoerotic scene with Simeon at Cambridge: "Intimacy—the room was full of it, still, deep, like a pool. Without need of

Rupert Brooke, by Gwendolen ("Gwen") Raverat (née Darwin),
pencil, 1910.

movement or speech it rose softly and washed over everything,
mollifying, kindling, and coating the mind with the lustre of
pearl" (45). There is also the playful tussle that follows an argument with Richard Bonamy (who is deeply in love with Jacob
throughout the work) (107), a motif that is reiterated later, describing how Bonamy would "play round [Jacob] like an affectionate spaniel" and how "(as likely as not) they would end by
rolling on the floor" (174).[21] Even Jacob's bouts of depression
may be echoes of Brooke's emotional crisis in 1913.

Brooke's "personal beauty," as Woolf notes in her review
of his posthumously published *Collected Poems,* was "so conven-
tionally handsome and English as to make it inexpressive or

expressive only of something that one might be inclined half-humourously to disparage. He was the type of English young manhood at its healthiest and most vigorous" ("Rupert Brooke" 279). In an elegiac tone, Woolf concludes the review: "One turns from the thought of him not with a sense of completeness and finality, but rather to wonder and to question still: what would he have been, what would he have done?" ("Rupert Brooke" 282). So, too, throughout *Jacob's Room,* the reader is reminded of what Jacob never will be. Woolf resented, indeed loathed what Rupert Brooke became without his consent after his death—the pretty poster boy the recruiters and warmongers used to drum up support for the war effort. She detested "the peculiar irony of [Brooke's] canonisation" and offered grateful praise to "any one who helps us remember that volatile, irreverent, and extremely vivacious spirit before the romantic public took possession of his fame" ("Rupert Brooke" 203; see also *Diary* 1: 171; Levenback, "Virginia Woolf and Rupert Brooke" 5–6).

Poetry in the War

RUPERT BROOKE'S "The Soldier," the final poem in a sonnet sequence reflecting on the war entitled "1914," was shamelessly exploited as propaganda much to Woolf's disgust. "The Soldier" begins: "If I should die, think only this of me: / That there's some corner of a foreign field / That is for ever England" (1–3). As it happened, Brooke died of blood poisoning en route to the front at Gallipoli, having seen only brief action in the war. He never experienced the bitter disillusionment that others of his generation endured, though many speculate that he would have joined the war poets in outrage against the slaughter. Poets like Wilfred Owen (who was killed two weeks before the Armistice) and Siegfried Sassoon (who survived the war) reveal the true catastrophe that combatants faced at the front, a horror that neither the upper echelons of the military nor the civilians on the home front ever saw or understood. Owen famously challenges the ancient traditions depicting war as glory. In his caustic and sardonic poem "Dulce et Decorum Est,"[22] Owen exposes the brutal lie crafted by the classical Roman poet Horace and perpetrated for centuries by the warmongers who avow that it is sweet and fitting to die for one's fatherland. Owen's poem vividly images the actual charnel house of the battlefield and excoriates the enthusiasts who market this horror to "children ardent / for some desperate glory" as a gallant sacrifice of life and limb (26).

The narrator's chilling observation in *Jacob's Room* about the abbreviated lives of young men at Cambridge University is a memento mori (see Wall). The narrator has already seen the future—in fact, to her, it is the tragic and irrevocable past. But the young men reading peacefully, their legs flung over the arms of chairs, or sprawling over tables, cannot. These "simple young men" are blissfully unaware that "there is no need to think of them grown old."[23] The narrator's bleak observation contrasts starkly with Laurence Binyon's highly patriotic poem extolling the war dead, "For the Fallen," first published in the *Times* in September 1914.[24] The poem begins: "They went with songs to the battle, they were young . . . / They shall not grow old, as we that are left grow old" (9, 13), suggesting that their so-called ultimate sacrifice was noble and gallant. Woolf might also be alluding to W. B. Yeats's "In Memory of Major Robert Gregory," a poem written late in the war, in which the speaker bitterly reflects: "What made us dream that he could comb grey hair?" (88).[25] As J. M. Winter argues, the number of deaths of privileged young men were proportionately higher than those in other ranks. "Officers were drawn from the well-educated and well-to-do middle and upper classes" and "these groups suffered disproportionately heavy losses during the First World War" (460).[26]

Sassoon's "The Hero" was published in *The Old Huntsman and Other Poems,* a volume Woolf reviewed in the *Times Literary Supplement* in 1918. The poem begins in the heroic mode: "'Jack fell as he'd have wished,' the Mother said"; but the poem quickly shifts to harsh reality and the contemptuous recollections of "the Brother Officer" who had brought the news and "thought how 'Jack,' cold-footed, useless swine, ... tried / To get sent home, and how, at last, he died, / Blown to small bits" (13, 15–17). Owen's "S.I.W." (an acronym for "self-inflicted wound") shows a variant of unheroic death at the front, describing the suicide of a terrified recruit who puts a rifle in his mouth and pulls the trigger: "With him they buried the muzzle his teeth had kissed / And truthfully wrote the Mother 'Tim died smiling'" (32–33). Both of these poems expose the way that death at the front during the Great War was tarted up by the military to fit the valiant tradition of war stories. And as readers, we just do not know what Betty Flanders was told regarding Jacob's death. Whether it was true or otherwise, she was almost certainly informed that he had died heroically.

Glimpsing Virginia Stephen and Lytton Strachey in *Jacob's Room*

THE CHARACTER of Clara Durrant draws on the experiences of the young Virginia Stephen and her sister, Vanessa. In her memoirs, Virginia Woolf recalls with bitterness a life strikingly like

Clara's in terms of social demands placed on unmarried young women. In "A Sketch of the Past," Woolf refers to her adolescence and young adulthood at 22 Hyde Park Gate as life in a "cage" (116), an experience of being "tortured and fretted and made numb with non-being" (136). Like Clara, Woolf endured tea-table rituals (e.g., "Sketch" 118, 148; "22 Hyde" 164–65), dinner parties and dances (e.g., "Sketch" 155–57), the boring young men (e.g., "Sketch" 149–50) and the equally boring old men (e.g., "Sketch" 158; "22 Hyde" 164–65), and the stings of the gossips ("Sketch" 157; "22 Hyde" 164–66, 173, 176; "Old Bloomsbury" 200–1). Jacob's closest friend, Richard Bonamy, is undoubtedly modeled affectionately on Lytton Strachey, one of Thoby Stephen's closest friends from Cambridge. A joyfully flagrant homosexual, Strachey was a member of the Cambridge Apostles. Bonamy, who is just as painfully and pointlessly obsessed with Jacob as Clara Durrant is, has in common with Strachey not only his homosexual orientation, but "a Wellington nose" (70, 87, 163). When Strachey wrote to Virginia Woolf on October 9, 1922, having just read *Jacob's Room,* he praised the novel and observed with amusement: "I am such a Bonamy" (Woolf and Strachey 144). Aside from Strachey's sexuality, his published work also is echoed in the novel. Bonamy's knowledge of French literature is a reference to Strachey's *Landmarks in French Literature,* published in 1912. The gossips (Woolf calls them "character-mongers") avoid direct mention of "Dick" Bonamy's sexual orientation as they note that "it is precisely a woman like Clara that men of that temperament need" (163). Not coincidentally, Strachey was one of Virginia Woolf's suitors. He proposed to Virginia Woolf in February 1909, and she accepted, but they both realized that the arrangement would be a disaster and quickly extricated themselves (Strachey went on to encourage Leonard Woolf to propose to Virginia).

The Marriage Market on the Eve of War

ALTHOUGH JACOB is vaguely interested in Clara Durrant, a suitable young woman of the upper class whom he could marry, thereby stabilizing his shaky finances and enhancing his career options, Jacob never makes an offer to Clara. As a bachelor, Jacob does not lose market value, but Clara gradually devolves from maiden to dusty virgin, "chained to a rock," a captive of society (129). One of the most satirical aspects of the novel is its bitterly caustic and yet elegiac inversion of the traditional marriage plot, a favorite subgenre of writers such as Jane Austen. Such novels are fraught with the anxiety that the young woman protagonist will not win a marriage proposal from the man of her dreams, but in the end almost everyone lives happily ever after. But *Jacob's Room* is a nightmarish travesty of the happy ending—instead, it is the ending of happiness. The Belle Epoque, the "Beautiful Era," lasted from the late nineteenth century until the onset of the war. A cosmopolitan paradise for the privileged, the period was marked by great strides in technology, and, temporarily, the resolution of political conflicts through diplomacy rather than military hostilities. Refined society life was at the peak of elegance and cultured behavior at the very same time that Europe was teetering on the edge of war. In the novel, Rose Shaw, a society matchmaker, declares histrionically that "Life is wicked—life is detestable" (90) when one of her marriage traps fails to snare the prey; a few paragraphs later, the narrator repeats a variant of Rose's phrase, "Oh, life is damnable, life is wicked," having just observed that "Jimmy feeds crows in Flanders and Helen visits hospitals" (100). Encapsulated in this single phrase is the essence of the moment— the war, expected to be a brief encounter and a quick triumph, became a war without end (Fussell 71–74). Civilization collapsed into chaos. The eligible young men who should have

married died in agony, while many of the young women they
would have married remained single.[27]

The Endless War in *Jacob's Room*

JACOB'S ROOM is set in the lull before the storm. The horror is
what follows. It is an obscene thing, and thus occurs mostly off-
stage, like violence in a classical Greek play, or, for that matter,
like Jacob and Florinda having sex in the bedroom (95), or Jacob
and Sandra Wentworth Williams disappearing into the darkness
at the Acropolis (169). The novel is haunted both by illicit sexuality (see Harris) and by motifs of death and war, a collective
elegy in which Woolf expresses not just her grief for her beloved
brother but also for her friend Rupert Brooke, and for Leonard
Woolf's brother Cecil, who was killed in the Great War. Implicitly, she also grieves for all the millions of young men who died
or were wounded in the carnage of World War I. And the novel
itself does not just foreshadow the war that had taken place before it was published, it is also the necropolis of other recent and
ancient wars—in fact, of war itself. Mark Hussey, in *Virginia
Woolf and War,* provides a powerful overview of war in Woolf's
novels in "Living in a War Zone," and notes that a particular war
was under way when the volume was published (that war is now
known as the First Persian Gulf War[28]). Other relevant contribu-
tions to Hussey's volume include William Handley's "War and
the Politics of Narration in *Jacob's Room,*" and Josephine O'Brien
Schaefer's "The Great War and 'This late age of world's experience' in Cather and Woolf." Karen Levenback's *Virginia Woolf
and the Great War* provides a valuable historical context for the
war in *Jacob's Room.*

There are numerous explicit references in *Jacob's Room* to
particular wars, beginning with the Trojan War (the ancient con-

flict between the Greeks and the Trojans over the abduction of Helen, the wife of Menelaus, by Paris, the son of Priam, king of Troy). For example, what might seem to be just a passing reference to changing weather is actually an invocation both of an impending and an ancient war: "Violent was the wind now rushing down the Sea of Marmara between Greece and the plains of Troy" (169) reports the narrator as Jacob and Sandra Wentworth Williams clamber up the Acropolis at night. The reference to the Sea of Marmara, an inland body of water that divides the Turkish city of Istanbul and connects the Black Sea to the Aegean Sea, is a reminder to historically knowledgeable readers of the Battle of Gallipoli, fought on the landmass where the Sea of Marmara meets the strait of the Dardanelles (formerly known as the Hellespont) during World War I. The Australian and New Zealand Army Corps (ANZAC), the main forces that fought for the British Empire at Gallipoli, were confronted with a travesty of horrendous living conditions, insufficient medical provisions, and bungled strategic planning. Similarly, "the plains of Troy" is not just a passing allusion to a mythical site but a deliberate reference to Homer's description of "windy Ilium" in *The Iliad* as well as to the nineteenth-century German archaeologist Heinrich Schliemann's claim that he had discovered the remains of Troy in Turkey, near the Dardanelles, where a naval attack in World War I went awry and three of sixteen British battleships were sunk by the enemy's mines. Similarly, the statue in Hyde Park of the mythic Greek warrior Achilles, who was slain in the Trojan War while avenging the death of Patroclus, his lover, is another obvious reference to the ancient war. And, though the reference is slight, one must note that Clara Durrant's Aberdeen terrier is named Troy.[29]

The statue of Achilles in Hyde Park is the centerpiece of a monument erected "by the women of England" (as it says on the base of the memorial) in honor of the Duke of Wellington, who

Bronze statue of Achilles—the Wellington Monument in Hyde Park, London.

defeated Napoleon at Waterloo in 1815. The fusion of these two great war heroes in this monument, one ancient and mythical and the other legendary and revered, was meant to elevate Wellington to the level of the greatest warrior of all. But, at least for the narrator, the combination reveals not that heroes should be honored, but that war is a continuum of conflict, a relentless and irresistible killing machine, an "unseizable force" (164). Referring to the current war, the narrator describes the deaths of young men in just such a cold, mechanical fashion (164).

Memento Mori

A DESCRIPTION of death in war is an obvious memento mori (reminder of death), and, as many critics have noted, *Jacob's Room* is riddled with such reminders referring not only to the protagonist's death, but to the deaths of millions of others past, present, and future. Jacob merges with these dead. His surname, Flanders, is a direct reference to the Ypres Salient, the area surrounding the ancient city (*Ieper* in Dutch) of the same name in western Belgium, one of the bloodiest battlefields in World War I. The blunt statement "now Jimmy feeds crows in Flanders" makes the point even clearer. Other characters' names used as reminders of death include Mrs. Wargrave, Oliver Skelton, Mrs. Withers, Dick Graves, and Mme. Lucien Gravé.

A particularly obvious memento mori is the motif of the skull: the sheep's skull Jacob finds on the beach at St. Ives (6); the death's-head hawk moth marked with the pattern of a skull on its back that Rebecca, the Flanders's family servant, finds in the kitchen, a wonderful addition to Jacob's butterfly and moth collection (21); the "ram's skull" motif that the narrator says was often carved above doorways in eighteenth-century houses such as the one where Jacob has his rooms in Bloomsbury (71) (the ram being the sign of Mars, the Roman god of war, known as Ares in Greek).

Among the other reminders of death are the burial places of the dead and their remains. There are coffins, graves and graveyards, tombstones and tombs, effigies, skeletons, bones, and carrion. For example, there is Seabrook Flanders's expensive coffin buried six feet deep in a crowded churchyard strewn with slanted tombstones and green crosses. There are the ornate tombs of the Duke of Wellington and Lord Nelson in St. Paul's Cathedral. There are the "turbaned" burial sites of Muslims (169), the engraved epitaphs on tombstones in the back of

Death's-head hawk moth (*Acherontia atropos*).

a van crossing Waterloo Bridge (117), and a coffinlike black box
with Jacob's name on it in white lettering in his Bloomsbury
sitting room (71). There are Roman skeletons buried on the
moors above Scarborough (141), Phoenician traders beneath
the earth in Cornwall (184), and mummies in the British Museum (114). And in the natural world, there are the delicate but
disgustingly carnivorous butterflies on the Yorkshire moors,
"settl[ing] on little bones lying on the turf" and "feast[ing] upon
bloody entrails dropped by a hawk" (22), while in the New Forest, Purple Emperor butterflies feed on "putrid carrion at the
base of an oak tree" (130). And there is also what is missing—

Victorian-era photograph of King's College Chapel.

a monument to those who are not there. The narrator does not ever mention but knows, since she foresees the future at other points in the novel (e.g., 100, 137), that after the armistice in 1918 and the punitive Treaty of Versailles in 1919, the Cenotaph would be erected on Whitehall in London to honor the missing war dead, *cenotaph* literally meaning "empty grave."

Allyson Booth identifies even more cumulative references to the war, and Susan Bennett Smith points out that the references to boots, shoes, and horses are all allusions to the impending war and death. These instances include the heavy combat boots under the white gowns worn by the militaristic choir marching into King's College Chapel (30) as they "pass into service" (a double entendre blending religion with military duty); and the riderless horse, traditionally used in funeral processions to honor

the fallen warrior,[30] that so terrifies Clara as she walks her dog
with Mr. Bowley in Hyde Park (177). There is even Seabrook
Flanders's absurd death from failing to change his boots (13).
Smith notes that these and other similar references "connote
militarism and manly stubbornness, both of which prove fatal,"
and she drives home the ironic juxtaposition of Jacob and the
Duke, noting: "The Duke died an old man and a war hero; Jacob,
a meaningless casualty, dies young with his promise unfulfilled"
(2; see also Bradshaw 26–28).

Among the reminders of death, there are the poppy petals
"pressed to silk" between the pages of Jacob's Greek dictionary (38), which might seem to be a decorative detail but actually constitute a particularly vivid reference to war and death.
The poppy has been permanently linked to the Great War by
the famous 1915 poem "In Flanders Fields,"[31] written by John
McCrae, a Canadian army physician serving at the front in
Ypres:

> In Flanders fields the poppies blow
> Between the crosses, row on row,
> That mark our place;
> . . . .
> We are the Dead. Short days ago,
> We lived, felt dawn, saw sunset glow,
> Loved, and were loved, and now we lie
> In Flanders fields. (1–3, 6–9)

The terrible sadness of McCrae's poem is offset by its belliger-
ent final stanza, a jingoistic plea urging the living to "take up our
quarrel with the foe" and avenge the dead.

As Woolf (who studied both Greek and Roman literature)
would almost certainly have known, the poppy has much deeper

roots in the poetry of war than McCrae's "In Flanders Fields." In Homer's *Iliad,* the epic Greek account of the Trojan War that celebrates the heroic traditions of war, a young man, slain in battle by the Greeks, "bow[s] his head to one side like a poppy that in a garden is laden with its fruit and the rains of spring" (II.viii, 306). In Virgil's *Aeneid,* an epic of the founding of Rome after the fall of Troy, a youth's death is similarly described:

> Down fell the beauteous youth: the yawning wound
> Gush'd out a purple stream, and stain'd the ground.
> His snowy neck reclines upon his breast,
> Like a fair flow'r by the keen share oppress'd,
> Like a white poppy sinking on the plain,
> Whose heavy head is overcharg'd with rain. (IX: 578–83)

The exquisite simile of the drooping flower transmutes the mutilated bodies of young men dying from ghastly slaughter and agony into ornamental loveliness.

Deciphering *Jacob's Room*

READERS WHO wish to begin to interpret the coding of *Jacob's Room* not only need to construct their own mental montage of the characters, but to piece together the fragmented events, interpret the narrator's hints and patterns of repetition, and tease out the intricate meanings and allusions of the novel. Exploring the nuanced implications of Woolf's fleeting references to literary works, historical events, famous people, and cultural details reveals the remarkable complexity of the work. The annotations to this edition provide a map for such a journey. And, of course, investigating the scholarship on *Jacob's Room* is an

essential component of this endeavor. Thus this volume provides extensive recommendations for further reading.

Jacob's Room is a many-faceted work. In terms of literary expression, the novel is an intriguing experiment in technique, but
it is also a euphoric and liberating achievement for the author
herself, who having at last said "something in [her] own voice"
also had been able to launch her novel from her own press. The
literary significance of *Jacob's Room* is, of course, linked to its fas-
cinating use of modernist strategies. But the novel is more than
the sum of its form. The work is an elegy for a generation and
for an era; a heartfelt protest against wars past, present, and future; a stinging critique of patriarchy and gender hierarchy; an
exploration of the maze of sexualities, desires, and transgres-
sion; and a lens through which the reader can glimpse the
writer's own lived experience. All of these attributes seem — indeed are — tremendously serious. But they are not presented in
a solemn or dour fashion. Just as the author wished, *Jacob's Room*
is glowing with "the heart, the passion, humour, everything as
bright as fire in the mist," and indeed she did "find room for so
much — a gaiety — an inconsequence — a light spirited stepping
at [her] own sweet will" (*Diary* 2: 13–14) in a work that also
bravely confronts the bitter fact of death.

NOTES

[1]See Michael North, *Reading 1922: Return to the Scene of the Modern* (New York:
Oxford University Press, 1999); Michael Levenson, ed., *The Cambridge Com-
panion to Modernism* (Cambridge: Cambridge University Press, 1999); Peter
Stansky, *On or About December 1910: Early Bloomsbury and Its Intimate World*
(Cambridge: Harvard University Press, 1996).

[2]Karen Smythe analyzes the recurrent snail motif in Woolf's work in "Virginia Woolf's Elegaic Enterprise."

[3]"[A]ll these objects lay across the snail's progress between one stalk and another to his goal. Before he had decided whether to circumvent the arched tent of a dead leaf or to breast it there came past the bed the feet of other human beings" ("Kew Gardens" 92).

[4]The Edwardian period (1901–1910) was the time of King Edward VII's monarchy. Woolf called her own cohort of writers "Georgians," referring to the period when George V became king, in 1910.

[5]And Woolf's response in her first version of "Mr. Bennett and Mrs. Brown" (1923) was stinging, referring to his comments as "a symptom of the respectful hostility which is the only healthy relation between old and young" (Majumdar and McLaurin 115).

[6]Nick Bramham may—or may not—be the father of Florinda's unborn child, but seems to be prepared to do the gentlemanly thing and confer legitimacy on the child by marrying Florinda (178).

[7]The multiple, heavily revised drafts of this chapter include a suggestive passage that hints at something rather kinky: "The queer thing about this argument was that it was all stuck about, ~~forever,~~ in ~~all~~ their minds with pink hyacinths; a lozenge shaped bed; a yew hedge; & the figure of Priapus, ~~which stands~~ or some other tapering White God . . . made Jacob feel a new kind of person" (Bishop, *Holograph* 196). Priapus was a minor Greek fertility deity and god of the male genitalia.

[8]It is unclear from the chronology whether Jacob has returned during the summer of 1913 or 1914, the year the Great War began.

[9]Reverend Floyd's glimpse of Jacob is mentioned earlier in the novel as well (20); Fanny, Florinda, and Clara (127, 178, 184) each momentarily think they see Jacob, their hopes raised and then dashed.

[10]David Bradshaw argues that the situation relates to Betty giving birth to her third son too long after her husband's death (6–9).

[11]At Monk's House, Leonard and Virginia did not have an indoor water closet (a flush toilet) until 1926.

[12]None of Woolf's insertions written above the crossed-out text has been included.

[13]It can be viewed online at: http://library.vicu.utoronto.ca/exhibitions/bloomsbury/covers/vbell/jacobs.htm

[14]Recent editions of *Jacob's Room* reinstate the Hogarth Press spacing. See the

2007 W. W. Norton edition edited by Suzanne Raitt, and the 2004 Shakespeare Head Press edition edited by Edward L. Bishop.

[15]Gerald Gould, writing for the *Saturday Review,* refers to Jacob's "rather sordid sexual experiences of the transitory kind" (Majumdar and McLaurin 106), and Lewis Bettany, as noted above, thinks the novel is "marred by its occasional lapses into indecency" (Majumdar and McLaurin 98).

[16]Those women in the novel who are financially independent are either spinsters or widows—including "Old Miss Birkbeck" who leaves a hundred pounds to Jacob (131).

[17]Other examples of the roman à clef from the period include D. H. Lawrence's *Women in Love* (1920), in which the protagonist, Rupert Birkin, is modeled on the author himself, and the character Hermione Roddice is a surrogate for Lady Ottoline Morrell. The character of Gudrun seems to be Katherine Mansfield.

[18]Translated as, "And forever, Brother, hail and farewell," the phrase is from the last lines of the elegiac poem (number 101) written by the Roman poet Catullus for his dead brother.

[19]Much of chapter 12 is based on Virginia Stephen's diary from the trip to Greece in 1906 (see *A Passionate Apprentice*).

[20]Jacob's plan to "read incredibly dull essays upon Marlowe to [his] friends" may be an insider joke about the Memoir Club, founded in 1920 and consisting initially of thirteen Bloomsbury Group members who met regularly to read their work to one another (see Hussey, *Virginia Woolf A to Z* 158).

[21]The intimate scene with Simeon at Cambridge prefigures several instances of similar language describing same-sex desire in *Mrs. Dalloway* (32, 75). The scene where Jacob and Bonamy are wrestling is also replicated in *Mrs. Dalloway* when Septimus Smith remembers Evans, the man he had loved who was killed in action in World War I (84)—and in D. H. Lawrence's *Women in Love* in the intensely homoerotic naked wrestling match between Birkin and Gerald in the chapter suggestively entitled "Gladiator." (See Dunn, Goldman regarding homosexuality and the dog motif in Woolf's work.)

[22]Owen's poem ends with the full Latin phrase from Horace's *Odes* (III.ii.13): "dulce et decorum est pro patria mori," which means "sweet and proper it is to die for your country" (160, 161).

[23]There are other ironic observations about the future for Jacob and his peers. For example, as Jacob recoils angrily after Mme. Lucien Gravé has taken an

illicit photograph of him at the Acropolis, the narrator notes: "This violent disillusionment is generally to be expected in young men in the prime of life, sound of wind and limb, who will soon become fathers of families and directors of banks" (159). Soon they will become cannon fodder and worms' meat instead.

24Edward Elgar set three poems by Binyon to music. "For the Fallen" was first performed in Leeds on May 3, 1916.

25Gregory, the son of Yeats's dear friend Lady Gregory, died when his British Royal Air Force plane was downed by Italian Allied forces by what we now call "friendly fire."

26The idea of the lost generation has been challenged by Robert Wohl in *The Generation of 1914,* arguing that the term refers to "the severe losses suffered within a small and clearly defined ruling class" and that, over all, Britain's casualties were not as severe as those of the other European nations (120).

27The phrase is a miniature synopsis of *Testament of Youth* (1933), Vera Brittain's memoir of her experience during the war in which she lost not only her fiancé but also her brother and many dear male friends. In fact, the war changed everything for women of the upper classes. Even women's clothing was affected by the war, as women's new and active roles emphasized mobility over modesty, making the restrictive clothing that covered even their ankles an obstacle to performing their tasks (see R. L. Shep, *The Great War: Styles & Patterns of the 1910s* [Fort Bragg, CA: R. L. Shep Publications, 1998]; see also Gilbert and Gubar; Ouditt). Young women like Clara Durrant in *Jacob's Room,* who had once been sheltered, chaperoned, and protected from any hint of indecency or glimpse of male nudity, suddenly found themselves, like Brittain, serving in the Voluntary Aid Detachment (VAD) and assisting professional nurses with the war effort by emptying the bedpans and changing the dressings on the wounds of dying young men.

28Ironically enough, the so-called Second Persian Gulf War is under way at this writing, and the president of the United States has warned that World War III may be launched before he leaves office.

29Leslie Stephen, Woolf's father, had a dog named Troy.

30David Bradshaw notes that in ancient times the horse traditionally was buried with the warrior (27).

31The poem was originally published in *Punch* on December 8, 1915.

For their invaluable help in many profound ways, I give my heartfelt thanks to June Dunn, Mark Hussey, Jane Lilienfeld, and David Turk. In sadness, I honor and remember a friend beloved of many Woolfians:

Atque in perpetuum, amica, ave atque vale
Julia Briggs OBE
(1943–2007)
Atque in perpetuum.

WORKS CITED

Binyon, Laurence. "For the Fallen." In *Selected Poems of Laurence Binyon*, 77–78. New York: Macmillan, 1922.

Bishop, Edward L. Introduction. *Jacob's Room*, by Virginia Woolf. Edited and with an introduction and notes by Edward L. Bishop, xi–xxxvii. Oxford: Shakespeare Head Press, 2004.

———. "Mind the Gap: The Spaces in *Jacob's Room*." *Woolf Studies Annual* 10 (2004): 31–49.

———. "The Shaping of *Jacob's Room*: Woolf's Manuscript Revisions." *Twentieth Century Literature* 32.1 (Spring 1986): 115–23.

———. *Virginia Woolf's* Jacob's Room: *The Holograph Draft*. Transcribed and edited by Edward L. Bishop. New York: Pace University Press, 1998.

Booth, Allyson. "The Architecture of Loss: Teaching *Jacob's Room* as a War Novel." In *Re: Reading, Re: Writing, Re: Teaching Virginia Woolf: Selected Papers from the Fourth Annual Conference on Virginia Woolf*, 65–79. New York: Pace University Press, 1995.

Bradshaw, David. *Winking, Buzzing, Carpet-Beating: Reading* Jacob's Room. Southport: Virginia Woolf Society of Great Britain, 2003.

Briggs, Julia. "In Search of Jacob: *Jacob's Room* (1922)." In *Virginia Woolf: An Inner Life*, 84–108. Orlando: Harcourt, 2005.

———. "Modernism's Lost Hope: Virginia Woolf, Hope Mirrlees and the Printing of *Paris*." In *Reading Virginia Woolf*, 80–95. Edinburgh: Edinburgh University Press, 2006.

Brittain, Vera. *Testament of Youth*. New York: Macmillan, 1933.

Brooke, Rupert. "1914." In *The Collected Poems of Rupert Brooke*, 105–12. 1915. Reprint, Charleston, SC: BiblioBazaar, 2006.

———. "The Soldier." Ibid.: 111.

Clewell, Tammy. "Consolation Refused: Virginia Woolf, the Great War, and Modernist Mourning." *Modern Fiction Studies* 50.1 (Spring 2004): 198–223.

Dunn, June Elizabeth. "'Beauty Shines on Two Dogs Doing What Two Women Must Not Do': Puppy Love, Same-Sex Desire and Homosexual Coding in *Mrs. Dalloway.*" In *Virginia Woolf: Turning the Centuries: Selected Papers from the Ninth Annual Conference on Virginia Woolf.* Edited by Ann Ardis and Bonnie Kime Scott, 176–82. New York: Pace University Press, 2000.

Flint, Kate. "Revising *Jacob's Room*: Virginia Woolf, Women, and Language." *The Review of English Studies.* New Series. 42.167. (August 1991): 361–79.

Forster, E. M. *Aspects of the Novel.* New York: Harcourt Brace Jovanovich, 1954.

Fowler, Rowena. "Moments and Metamorphoses: Virginia Woolf's Greece." *Comparative Literature* 51.3 (Summer 1999): 218–41.

Froula, Christine. "On French and British Freedoms: Early Bloomsbury and the Brothels of Modernism." *Modernism/modernity* 12.4 (November 2005): 553–80.

Fussell, Paul. *The Great War and Modern Memory.* New York: Oxford University Press, 1975.

Gilbert, Sandra M., and Susan Gubar. "Soldier's Heart: Literary Men, Literary Women, and the Great War." In *No Man's Land: The Place of the Woman Writer in the Twentieth Century: Vol. 2, Sexchanges,* 258–323. New Haven, CT: Yale University Press, 1989.

Gillespie, Diane F. "'Her Kodak Pointed at His Head': Virginia Woolf and Photography." In *The Multiple Muses of Virginia Woolf.* Edited by Diane F. Gillespie, 113–47. Columbia: University of Missouri Press, 1993.

Goldman, Jane. "'Ce chien est à moi': Virginia Woolf and the Signifying Dog." *Woolf Studies Annual* 13 (2007): 49–86.

Hafley, James. *The Glass Roof: Virginia Woolf as Novelist.* New York: Russell and Russell, 1963.

Handley, William. "War and the Politics of Narration in *Jacob's Room.*" In Mark Hussey, editor, *Virginia Woolf and War:* 110–33.

Harris, Susan C. "The Ethics of Indecency: Censorship, Sexuality, and the Voice of the Academy in the Narration of *Jacob's Room.*" *Twentieth Century Literature* 43.4 (Winter 1997): 420–38.

Holtby, Winifred. "Cinematograph." In *Virginia Woolf: A Critical Memoir.* Chicago: Cassandra Editions, 1978.

Homer. *The Iliad.* Translated by Augustus Taber Murray. Cambridge: Harvard University Press, 1925.

Horace. *The Odes of Horace: Bilingual Edition.* Edited by David Ferry. New York: Farrar, Straus and Giroux, 1997.

Hussey, Mark. "Living in a War Zone: An Introduction to Virginia Woolf as a War Novelist." In Hussey, *Virginia Woolf and War:* 1–13.

————. *The Singing of the Real World: The Philosophy of Virginia Woolf's Fiction.* Columbus: Ohio State University Press, 1986.

————, ed. *Virginia Woolf and War: Fiction, Reality, and Myth.* Reprint, Syracuse, NY: Syracuse University Press, 1992.

————. *Virginia Woolf A to Z: The Essential Reference to Her Life and Writings.* New York: Oxford University Press, 1995.

Ingram, Angela. "'The Sacred Edifices': Virginia Woolf and Some of the Sons of Culture." In *Virginia Woolf and Bloomsbury.* Edited by Jane Marcus, 125–45. Bloomington: Indiana University Press, 1987.

Kazan, Francesca. "Description and the Pictorial in *Jacob's Room.*" *ELH* 55.3 (Autumn 1988): 701–19.

Knowles, Sebastian D. G. "Narrative Death and Desire: The Three Senses of Humor in *Jacob's Room.*" *Woolf Studies Annual* 5 (1999): 97–114.

Lawrence, D. H. *Women in Love.* 1920. Reprint, New York: Penguin, 1995.

Lawrence, Karen. "Gender and Narrative Voice in *Jacob's Room* and *A Portrait of the Artist as a Young Man.*" In *James Joyce: The Centennial Symposium.* Edited by Morris Beja, Phillip Herring, Maurice Harmon, and David Norris, 31–38. Urbana: University of Illinois Press, 1986.

Lee, Hermione. *Virginia Woolf.* New York: Knopf, 1997.

Levenback, Karen. "Virginia Woolf and Rupert Brooke: Poised Between Olympus and the 'Real World.'" *Virginia Woolf Miscellany* 33 (Fall 1989): 5–6.

————. *Virginia Woolf and the Great War.* Syracuse, NY: Syracuse University Press, 1999.

Little, Judy. "*Jacob's Room* as Comedy: Woolf's Parodic *Bildungsroman.*" In *New Feminist Essays.* Edited by Jane Marcus, 105–24. Lincoln: University of Nebraska Press, 1981.

Majumdar, Robin, and Allen McLaurin, eds. *Virginia Woolf: The Critical Heritage.* Boston: Routledge and Kegan Paul, 1975.

Marshik, Celia. *British Modernism and Censorship.* Cambridge: Cambridge University Press, 2006.

McCrae, John. *In Flanders Fields and Other Poems, 3.* New York: G. P. Putnam's Sons, 1919.

Milton, John. "Lycidas." In *The Major Works.* Edited by Stephen Orgel and Jonathan Goldberg, 39–44. 1991. Reprint, New York: Oxford University Press, 2003.

Morgenstern, Barry. "The Self-Conscious Narrator in *Jacob's Room.*" *Modern Fiction Studies* 18 (1972): 351–61.

Moss, Roger. "*Jacob's Room* and the Eighteenth Century: From Elegy to Essay." *Critical Quarterly* 23.3 (1981): 39–54.

Nelson-McDermott, Catherine. "Disorderly Conduct: Parody and Coded Humor in *Jacob's Room* and *The Years*." *Woolf Studies Annual* 5 (1999): 79–95.

Neverow, Vara. "The Return of the Great Goddess: Immortal Virginity, Sexual Autonomy, and Lesbian Possibility in *Jacob's Room*." *Woolf Studies Annual* 10 (2004): 203–31.

———. "Thinking Back Through Our Mothers, Thinking in Common: Virginia Woolf's Photographic Imagination and the Community of Narrators in *Jacob's Room, A Room of One's Own,* and *Three Guineas*." In *Virginia Woolf and Communities: Selected Papers from the Eighth Annual Conference on Virginia Woolf*. Edited by Jeanette McVicker and Laura Davis, 65–90. New York: Pace University Press, 1999.

Ohmann, Carol. "Culture and Anarchy in *Jacob's Room*." *Contemporary Literature* 18.2 (Spring 1977): 160–72.

Ouditt, Sharon. *Fighting Forces, Writing Women: Identity and Ideology in the First World War*. New York: Routledge, 1994.

Owen, Wilfred. "Dulce et Decorum Est." In *The War Poets: An Anthology of the War Poetry of the 20th Century*. Edited with an introduction by Oscar Williams, 37. New York: John Day Company, 1945.

———. "S.I.W." In *The Works of Wilfred Owen*. Introduction and notes by Owen Knowles, 84–85. 1994. Reprint, Ware, Hertfordshire: Wordsworth, 2002.

Roe, Sue. *Jacob's Room,* by Virginia Woolf. Edited with an introduction and notes by Sue Roe, xi–xlii. Harmondsworth: Penguin, 1992.

Roessel, David. "Guy Fawkes Day and the Versailles Peace in 'The Hollow Men.'" *English Language Notes* 28.1 (September 1990): 52–58.

Sassoon, Siegfried. "The Hero." In *The Old Huntsman and Other Poems,* 48. 1918. Reprint, Whitefish, MT: Kessinger Publishing, 2004.

Schaefer, Josephine O'Brien. "The Great War and 'This late age of world's experience' in Cather and Woolf." In Hussey, *Virginia Woolf and War:* 134–50.

Smith, Susan Bennett. "What the Duke of Wellington is Doing in *Jacob's Room*." *Virginia Woolf Miscellany* 36 (Spring 1991): 2.

Smythe, Karen. "Virginia Woolf's Elegiac Enterprise." *NOVEL: A Forum on Fiction* 26.1 (Autumn 1992): 64–79.

Taddeo, Julie Anne. "Plato's Apostles: Edwardian Cambridge and the 'New Style of Love.'" *Journal of the History of Sexuality* 8.2 (October 1997): 196–228.

Virgil. *The Aeneid*. Translated by John Dryden, edited by Frederick M. Keener. New York: Penguin, 1997.

Wall, Kathleen. "Significant Form in *Jacob's Room*: Ekphrasis and the Elegy." *Texas Studies in Literature and Language* 44.3 (Fall 2002): 301–23.

Willis, Jr., J. H. *Leonard and Virginia Woolf as Publishers: The Hogarth Press 1917–1941.* Charlottesville: University of Virginia Press, 1992.

Winter, J. M. "Britain's 'Lost Generation' of the First World War." *Population Studies* 31.3 (November 1977): 449–66.

Wohl, Robert. *The Generation of 1914.* London: Weidenfeld and Nicolson, 1980.

Woolf, Virginia . "Kew Gardens." In *Virginia Woolf: The Complete Shorter Fiction.* Edited by Susan Dick, 90–95. New York: Harcourt Brace Jovanovich, 1989.

———. "The Mark on the Wall." In *Virginia Woolf: The Complete Shorter Fiction,* 83–89.

———. "Modern Fiction." In *The Common Reader: First Series.* Edited and with an introduction by Andrew McNeillie, 146–54. San Diego: Harcourt, 1984.

———. *Mrs. Dalloway.* Annotated and with an introduction by Bonnie Kime Scott. Orlando: Harcourt, 2005.

———. "Old Bloomsbury." In *Moments of Being.* Edited by Jeanne Schulkind, 179–201. San Diego: Harcourt, 1985.

———. "On Not Knowing Greek." In *Collected Essays* I, 1–13. New York: Harcourt Brace Jovanovich, 1966.

———. *A Passionate Apprentice: The Early Journals, 1897–1909.* Edited by Mitchell A. Leaska. San Diego: Harcourt, 1990.

———. "Professions for Women." In *Women and Writing.* Edited and with an introduction by Michèle Barrett, 57–63. New York: Harcourt Brace Jovanovich, 1980.

———. "Rupert Brooke." In *Essays,* vol. 2. Edited by Andrew McNeillie, 277–84. San Diego: Harcourt Brace Jovanovich, 1987.

———. "A Sketch of the Past." In *Moments of Being,* 61–159.

———. "A Society." In *Virginia Woolf: The Complete Shorter Fiction,* 124–36.

———. "22 Hyde Park Gate." In *Moments of Being,* 162–77.

———. "An Unwritten Novel." In *Virginia Woolf: The Complete Shorter Fiction,* 112–21.

———. "A Woman's College from the Outside." In *Virginia Woolf: The Complete Shorter Fiction,* 145–48.

——— and Lytton Strachey. *Virginia Woolf and Lytton Strachey Letters.* Selected and edited by Leonard Woolf and James Strachey. New York: Harcourt Brace Jovanovich, 1956.

Yeats, W. B. "In Memory of Major Robert Gregory." In *Selected Poems and Two Plays of William Butler Yeats.* Edited and with an introduction by M. L. Rosenthal, 52–55. 1966. Reprint, New York: Macmillan, 1977.

Zwerdling, Alex. "*Jacob's Room:* Woolf's Satiric Elegy." *ELH* 48.4 (Winter 1981): 894–913.

Jacob's Room

ONE

"SO OF COURSE," wrote Betty Flanders, pressing her heels
rather deeper in the sand, "there was nothing for it but to leave."

Slowly welling from the point of her gold nib, pale blue ink
dissolved the full stop; for there her pen stuck; her eyes fixed,
and tears slowly filled them. The entire bay quivered; the lighthouse wobbled; and she had the illusion that the mast of Mr.
Connor's little yacht was bending like a wax candle in the sun.
She winked quickly. Accidents were awful things. She winked
again. The mast was straight; the waves were regular; the lighthouse was upright; but the blot had spread.

". . . nothing for it but to leave," she read.

"Well, if Jacob doesn't want to play" (the shadow of Archer,
her eldest son, fell across the notepaper and looked blue on the
sand, and she felt chilly—it was the third of September already),
"if Jacob doesn't want to play"—what a horrid blot! It must be
getting late.

"Where *is* that tiresome little boy?" she said. "I don't see
him. Run and find him. Tell him to come at once." ". . . but mer-
cifully," she scribbled, ignoring the full stop, "everything seems
satisfactorily arranged, packed though we are like herrings in a
barrel, and forced to stand the perambulator which the landlady
quite naturally won't allow. . . ."

Such were Betty Flanders's letters to Captain Barfoot—
many-paged, tear-stained. Scarborough is seven hundred miles
from Cornwall: Captain Barfoot is in Scarborough: Seabrook is
dead. Tears made all the dahlias in her garden undulate in red
waves and flashed the glass house in her eyes, and spangled the
kitchen with bright knives, and made Mrs. Jarvis, the rector's
wife, think at church, while the hymn-tune played and Mrs.
Flanders bent low over her little boys' heads, that marriage is a
fortress and widows stray solitary in the open fields, picking up
stones, gleaning a few golden straws, lonely, unprotected, poor
creatures. Mrs. Flanders had been a widow for these two years.

"JA—COB! JA—COB!" Archer shouted.

"SCARBOROUGH," MRS. FLANDERS wrote on the envelope,
and dashed a bold line beneath; it was her native town; the hub
of the universe. But a stamp? She ferreted in her bag; then held
it up mouth downwards; then fumbled in her lap, all so vigorously that Charles Steele in the Panama hat suspended his paint-
brush.

Like the antennae of some irritable insect it positively
trembled. Here was that woman moving—actually going to get
up—confound her! He struck the canvas a hasty violet-black
dab. For the landscape needed it. It was too pale—greys flowing into lavenders, and one star or a white gull suspended just
so—too pale as usual. The critics would say it was too pale, for
he was an unknown man exhibiting obscurely, a favourite with
his landladies' children, wearing a cross on his watch chain, and
much gratified if his landladies liked his pictures—which they
often did.

"JA—COB! JA—COB!" Archer shouted.

———————

EXASPERATED BY the noise, yet loving children, Steele picked nervously at the dark little coils on his palette.

"I saw your brother—I saw your brother," he said, nodding his head, as Archer lagged past him, trailing his spade, and scowling at the old gentleman in spectacles.

"Over there—by the rock," Steele muttered, with his brush between his teeth, squeezing out raw sienna, and keeping his eyes fixed on Betty Flanders's back.

"Ja—cob! Ja—cob!" shouted Archer, lagging on after a second.

The voice had an extraordinary sadness. Pure from all body, pure from all passion, going out into the world, solitary, unanswered, breaking against rocks—so it sounded.

STEELE FROWNED; but was pleased by the effect of the black—it was just *that* note which brought the rest together. "Ah, one may learn to paint at fifty! There's Titian . . ." and so, having found the right tint, up he looked and saw to his horror a cloud over the bay.

Mrs. Flanders rose, slapped her coat this side and that to get the sand off, and picked up her black parasol.

THE ROCK was one of those tremendously solid brown, or rather black, rocks which emerge from the sand like something primitive. Rough with crinkled limpet shells and sparsely strewn with locks of dry seaweed, a small boy has to stretch his legs far apart, and indeed to feel rather heroic, before he gets to the top.

But there, on the very top, is a hollow full of water, with a sandy bottom; with a blob of jelly stuck to the side, and some mussels. A fish darts across. The fringe of yellow-brown seaweed flutters, and out pushes an opal-shelled crab——

"Oh, a huge crab," Jacob murmured——and begins his journey on weakly legs on the sandy bottom. Now! Jacob plunged his hand. The crab was cool and very light. But the water was thick with sand, and so, scrambling down, Jacob was about to jump, holding his bucket in front of him, when he saw, stretched entirely rigid, side by side, their faces very red, an enormous man and woman.

An enormous man and woman (it was early-closing day) were stretched motionless, with their heads on pocket-handkerchiefs, side by side, within a few feet of the sea, while two or three gulls gracefully skirted the incoming waves, and settled near their boots.

The large red faces lying on the bandanna handkerchiefs stared up at Jacob. Jacob stared down at them. Holding his bucket very carefully, Jacob then jumped deliberately and trotted away very nonchalantly at first, but faster and faster as the waves came creaming up to him and he had to swerve to avoid them, and the gulls rose in front of him and floated out and settled again a little farther on. A large black woman was sitting on the sand. He ran towards her.

"Nanny! Nanny!" he cried, sobbing the words out on the crest of each gasping breath.

The waves came round her. She was a rock. She was covered with the seaweed which pops when it is pressed. He was lost.

There he stood. His face composed itself. He was about to roar when, lying among the black sticks and straw under the cliff, he saw a whole skull—perhaps a cow's skull, a skull, perhaps, with the teeth in it. Sobbing, but absent-mindedly, he ran farther and farther away until he held the skull in his arms.

"THERE HE IS!" cried Mrs. Flanders, coming round the rock and covering the whole space of the beach in a few seconds. "What has he got hold of? Put it down, Jacob! Drop it this moment! Something horrid, I know. Why didn't you stay with us?

Naughty little boy! Now put it down. Now come along both of you," and she swept round, holding Archer by one hand and fumbling for Jacob's arm with the other. But he ducked down and picked up the sheep's jaw, which was loose.

Swinging her bag, clutching her parasol, holding Archer's hand, and telling the story of the gunpowder explosion in which poor Mr. Curnow had lost his eye, Mrs. Flanders hurried up the steep lane, aware all the time in the depths of her mind of some buried discomfort.

There on the sand not far from the lovers lay the old sheep's skull without its jaw. Clean, white, wind-swept, sand-rubbed, a more unpolluted piece of bone existed nowhere on the coast of Cornwall. The sea holly would grow through the eye-sockets; it would turn to powder, or some golfer, hitting his ball one fine day, would disperse a little dust.—No, but not in lodgings, thought Mrs. Flanders. It's a great experiment coming so far with young children. There's no man to help with the perambulator. And Jacob is such a handful; so obstinate already.

"Throw it away, dear, do," she said, as they got into the road; but Jacob squirmed away from her; and the wind rising, she took out her bonnet-pin, looked at the sea, and stuck it in afresh. The wind was rising. The waves showed that uneasiness, like something alive, restive, expecting the whip, of waves before a storm. The fishing-boats were leaning to the water's brim. A pale yellow light shot across the purple sea; and shut. The lighthouse was lit. "Come along," said Betty Flanders. The sun blazed in their faces and gilded the great blackberries trembling out from the hedge which Archer tried to strip as they passed.

"Don't lag, boys. You've got nothing to change into," said Betty, pulling them along, and looking with uneasy emotion at the earth displayed so luridly, with sudden sparks of light from greenhouses in gardens, with a sort of yellow and black mutability, against this blazing sunset, this astonishing agitation and vitality of colour, which stirred Betty Flanders and made her think of responsibility and danger. She gripped Archer's hand. On she plodded up the hill.

"What did I ask you to remember?" she said.

"I don't know," said Archer.

"Well, I don't know either," said Betty, humorously and simply, and who shall deny that this blankness of mind, when combined with profusion, mother wit, old wives' tales, haphazard ways, moments of astonishing daring, humour, and sentimentality—who shall deny that in these respects every woman is nicer than any man?

Well, Betty Flanders, to begin with.

She had her hand upon the garden gate.

"The meat!" she exclaimed, striking the latch down.

She had forgotten the meat.

There was Rebecca at the window.

THE BARENESS of Mrs. Pearce's front room was fully displayed at ten o'clock at night when a powerful oil lamp stood on the middle of the table. The harsh light fell on the garden; cut straight across the lawn; lit up a child's bucket and a purple aster and reached the hedge. Mrs. Flanders had left her sewing on the table. There were her large reels of white cotton and her steel spectacles; her needle-case; her brown wool wound round an old postcard. There were the bulrushes and the *Strand* magazines; and the linoleum sandy from the boys' boots. A daddy-long-legs shot from corner to corner and hit the lamp globe. The wind blew straight dashes of rain across the window, which flashed silver as they passed through the light. A single leaf tapped hurriedly, persistently, upon the glass. There was a hurricane out at sea.

ARCHER COULD not sleep.

Mrs. Flanders stooped over him. "Think of the fairies," said Betty Flanders. "Think of the lovely, lovely birds settling down on their nests. Now shut your eyes and see the old mother bird with a worm in her beak. Now turn and shut your eyes," she murmured, "and shut your eyes."

The lodging-house seemed full of gurgling and rushing; the cistern overflowing; water bubbling and squeaking and running along the pipes and streaming down the windows.

"What's all that water rushing in?" murmured Archer.

"It's only the bath water running away," said Mrs. Flanders.

Something snapped out of doors.

"I say, won't that steamer sink?" said Archer, opening his eyes.

"Of course it won't," said Mrs. Flanders. "The Captain's in bed long ago. Shut your eyes, and think of the fairies, fast asleep, under the flowers."

"I THOUGHT he'd never get off—such a hurricane," she whispered to Rebecca, who was bending over a spirit-lamp in the small room next door. The wind rushed outside, but the small flame of the spirit-lamp burnt quietly, shaded from the cot by a book stood on edge.

"Did he take his bottle well?" Mrs. Flanders whispered, and Rebecca nodded and went to the cot and turned down the quilt, and Mrs. Flanders bent over and looked anxiously at the baby, asleep, but frowning. The window shook, and Rebecca stole like a cat and wedged it. The two women murmured over the spirit-lamp, plotting the eternal conspiracy of hush and clean bottles while the wind raged and gave a sudden wrench at the cheap fastenings.

Both looked round at the cot. Their lips were pursed. Mrs. Flanders crossed over to the cot.

"Asleep?" whispered Rebecca, looking at the cot.

Mrs. Flanders nodded.

"Good-night, Rebecca," Mrs. Flanders murmured, and Rebecca called her ma'm, though they were conspirators plotting the eternal conspiracy of hush and clean bottles.

Mrs. Flanders had left the lamp burning in the front room. There were her spectacles, her sewing; and a letter with the Scarborough postmark. She had not drawn the curtains either.

The light blazed out across the patch of grass; fell on the child's green bucket with the gold line round it, and upon the aster which trembled violently beside it. For the wind was tearing across the coast, hurling itself at the hills, and leaping, in sudden gusts, on top of its own back. How it spread over the town in the hollow! How the lights seemed to wink and quiver in its fury, lights in the harbour, lights in bedroom windows high up! And rolling dark waves before it, it raced over the Atlantic, jerking the stars above the ships this way and that.

There was a click in the front sitting-room. Mr. Pearce had extinguished the lamp. The garden went out. It was but a dark patch. Every inch was rained upon. Every blade of grass was bent by rain. Eyelids would have been fastened down by the rain. Lying on one's back one would have seen nothing but muddle and confusion—clouds turning and turning, and something yellow-tinted and sulphurous in the darkness.

The little boys in the front bedroom had thrown off their blankets and lay under the sheets. It was hot; rather sticky and steamy. Archer lay spread out, with one arm striking across the pillow. He was flushed; and when the heavy curtain blew out a little he turned and half-opened his eyes. The wind actually stirred the cloth on the chest of drawers, and let in a little light, so that the sharp edge of the chest of drawers was visible, running straight up, until a white shape bulged out; and a silver streak showed in the looking-glass.

In the other bed by the door Jacob lay asleep, fast asleep, profoundly unconscious. The sheep's jaw with the big yellow teeth in it lay at his feet. He had kicked it against the iron bed-rail.

Outside the rain poured down more directly and powerfully as the wind fell in the early hours of the morning. The aster was beaten to the earth. The child's bucket was half-full of rain-water; and the opal-shelled crab slowly circled round the bottom, trying with its weakly legs to climb the steep side; trying again and falling back, and trying again and again.

Two

"MRS. FLANDERS"—"Poor Betty Flanders"—"Dear Betty"—
"She's very attractive still"—"Odd she don't marry again!"
"There's Captain Barfoot to be sure — calls every Wednesday as
regular as clockwork, and never brings his wife."

"But that's Ellen Barfoot's fault," the ladies of Scarborough
said. "She don't put herself out for no one."

"A man likes to have a son—that we know."

"Some tumours have to be cut; but the sort my mother had
you bear with for years and years, and never even have a cup of
tea brought up to you in bed."

(Mrs. Barfoot was an invalid.)

ELIZABETH FLANDERS, of whom this and much more than this
had been said and would be said, was, of course, a widow in her
prime. She was half-way between forty and fifty. Years and sorrow between them; the death of Seabrook, her husband; three
boys; poverty; a house on the outskirts of Scarborough; her
brother, poor Morty's, downfall and possible demise — for where
was he? what was he? Shading her eyes, she looked along the road
for Captain Barfoot—yes, there he was, punctual as ever; the at-
tentions of the Captain—all ripened Betty Flanders, enlarged her
figure, tinged her face with jollity, and flooded her eyes for no reason that any one could see perhaps three times a day.

True, there's no harm in crying for one's husband, and the tombstone, though plain, was a solid piece of work, and on summer's days when the widow brought her boys to stand there one felt kindly towards her. Hats were raised higher than usual; wives tugged their husbands' arms. Seabrook lay six foot beneath, dead these many years; enclosed in three shells; the crevices sealed with lead, so that, had earth and wood been glass, doubtless his very face lay visible beneath, the face of a young man whiskered, shapely, who had gone out duck-shooting and refused to change his boots.

"Merchant of this city," the tombstone said; though why Betty Flanders had chosen so to call him when, as many still remembered, he had only sat behind an office window for three months, and before that had broken horses, ridden to hounds, farmed a few fields, and run a little wild—well, she had to call him something. An example for the boys.

Had he, then, been nothing? An unanswerable question, since even if it weren't the habit of the undertaker to close the eyes, the light so soon goes out of them. At first, part of herself; now one of a company, he had merged in the grass, the sloping hillside, the thousand white stones, some slanting, others upright, the decayed wreaths, the crosses of green tin, the narrow yellow paths, and the lilacs that drooped in April, with a scent like that of an invalid's bedroom, over the churchyard wall. Seabrook was now all that; and when, with her skirt hitched up, feeding the chickens, she heard the bell for service or funeral, that was Seabrook's voice—the voice of the dead.

The rooster had been known to fly on her shoulder and peck her neck, so that now she carried a stick or took one of the children with her when she went to feed the fowls.

"Wouldn't you like my knife, mother?" said Archer.

Sounding at the same moment as the bell, her son's voice mixed life and death inextricably, exhilaratingly.

"What a big knife for a small boy!" she said. She took it to please him. Then the rooster flew out of the hen-house, and, shouting to Archer to shut the door into the kitchen garden, Mrs. Flanders set her meal down, clucked for the hens, went bustling about the orchard, and was seen from over the way by Mrs. Cranch, who, beating her mat against the wall, held it for a moment suspended while she observed to Mrs. Page next door that Mrs. Flanders was in the orchard with the chickens.

Mrs. Page, Mrs. Cranch, and Mrs. Garfit could see Mrs. Flanders in the orchard because the orchard was a piece of Dods Hill enclosed; and Dods Hill dominated the village. No words can exaggerate the importance of Dods Hill. It was the earth; the world against the sky; the horizon of how many glances can best be computed by those who have lived all their lives in the same village, only leaving it once to fight in the Crimea, like old George Garfit, leaning over his garden gate smoking his pipe. The progress of the sun was measured by it; the tint of the day laid against it to be judged.

"Now she's going up the hill with little John," said Mrs. Cranch to Mrs. Garfit, shaking her mat for the last time, and bustling indoors.

Opening the orchard gate, Mrs. Flanders walked to the top of Dods Hill, holding John by the hand. Archer and Jacob ran in front or lagged behind; but they were in the Roman fortress when she came there, and shouting out what ships were to be seen in the bay. For there was a magnificent view—moors behind, sea in front, and the whole of Scarborough from one end to the other laid out flat like a puzzle. Mrs. Flanders, who was growing stout, sat down in the fortress and looked about her.

The entire gamut of the view's changes should have been known to her; its winter aspect, spring, summer and autumn; how storms came up from the sea; how the moors shuddered

and brightened as the clouds went over; she should have noted
the red spot where the villas were building; and the criss-cross
of lines where the allotments were cut; and the diamond flash
of little glass houses in the sun. Or, if details like these escaped
her, she might have let her fancy play upon the gold tint of the
sea at sunset, and thought how it lapped in coins of gold upon
the shingle. Little pleasure boats shoved out into it; the black
arm of the pier hoarded it up. The whole city was pink and gold;
domed; mist-wreathed; resonant; strident. Banjoes strummed;
the parade smelt of tar which stuck to the heels; goats suddenly
cantered their carriages through crowds. It was observed how
well the Corporation had laid out the flower-beds. Sometimes a
straw hat was blown away. Tulips burnt in the sun. Numbers of
sponge-bag trousers were stretched in rows. Purple bonnets
fringed soft, pink, querulous faces on pillows in bath chairs. Triangular hoardings were wheeled along by men in white coats.
Captain George Boase had caught a monster shark. One side of
the triangular hoarding said so in red, blue, and yellow letters;
and each line ended with three differently coloured notes of
exclamation.

So that was a reason for going down into the Aquarium,
where the sallow blinds, the stale smell of spirits of salt, the
bamboo chairs, the tables with ash-trays, the revolving fish, the
attendant knitting behind six or seven chocolate boxes (often
she was quite alone with the fish for hours at a time) remained
in the mind as part of the monster shark, he himself being only
a flabby yellow receptacle, like an empty Gladstone bag in a
tank. No one had ever been cheered by the Aquarium; but the
faces of those emerging quickly lost their dim, chilled expression when they perceived that it was only by standing in a queue
that one could be admitted to the pier. Once through the turn-
stiles, every one walked for a yard or two very briskly; some

flagged at this stall; others at that. But it was the band that drew them all to it finally; even the fishermen on the lower pier taking up their pitch within its range.

The band played in the Moorish kiosk. Number nine went up on the board. It was a waltz tune. The pale girls, the old widow lady, the three Jews lodging in the same boarding-house, the dandy, the major, the horse-dealer, and the gentleman of independent means, all wore the same blurred, drugged expression, and through the chinks in the planks at their feet they could see the green summer waves, peacefully, amiably, swaying round the iron pillars of the pier.

But there was a time when none of this had any existence (thought the young man leaning against the railings). Fix your eyes upon the lady's skirt; the grey one will do — above the pink silk stockings. It changes; drapes her ankles — the nineties; then it amplifies — the seventies; now it's burnished red and stretched above a crinoline — the sixties; a tiny black foot wearing a white cotton stocking peeps out. Still sitting there? Yes — she's still on the pier. The silk now is sprigged with roses, but somehow one no longer sees so clearly. There's no pier beneath us. The heavy chariot may swing along the turnpike road, but there's no pier for it to stop at, and how grey and turbulent the sea is in the seventeenth century! Let's to the museum. Cannon-balls; arrowheads; Roman glass and a forceps green with verdigris. The Rev. Jaspar Floyd dug them up at his own expense early in the forties in the Roman camp on Dods Hill — see the little ticket with the faded writing on it.

And now, what's the next thing to see in Scarborough?

MRS. FLANDERS sat on the raised circle of the Roman camp, patching Jacob's breeches; only looking up as she sucked the end of her cotton, or when some insect dashed at her, boomed in her ear, and was gone.

John kept trotting up and slapping down in her lap grass or dead leaves which he called "tea," and she arranged them methodically but absent-mindedly, laying the flowery heads of the grasses together, thinking how Archer had been awake again last night; the church clock was ten or thirteen minutes fast; she wished she could buy Garfit's acre.

"THAT'S AN orchid leaf, Johnny. Look at the little brown spots. Come, my dear. We must go home. Ar—cher! Ja—cob!"

"Ar—cher—Ja—cob!" Johnny piped after her, pivoting round on his heel, and strewing the grass and leaves in his hands as if he were sowing seed. Archer and Jacob jumped up from behind the mound where they had been crouching with the intention of springing upon their mother unexpectedly, and they all began to walk slowly home.

"Who is that?" said Mrs. Flanders, shading her eyes.

"That old man in the road?" said Archer, looking below.

"He's not an old man," said Mrs. Flanders. "He's—no, he's not—I thought it was the Captain, but it's Mr. Floyd. Come along, boys."

"Oh, bother Mr. Floyd!" said Jacob, switching off a thistle's head, for he knew already that Mr. Floyd was going to teach them Latin, as indeed he did for three years in his spare time, out of kindness, for there was no other gentleman in the neighbourhood whom Mrs. Flanders could have asked to do such a thing, and the elder boys were getting beyond her, and must be got ready for school, and it was more than most clergymen would have done, coming round after tea, or having them in his own room—as he could fit it in—for the parish was a very large one, and Mr. Floyd, like his father before him, visited cottages miles away on the moors, and, like old Mr. Floyd, was a great scholar, which made it so unlikely—she had never dreamt of such a thing. Ought she to have guessed? But let alone being a scholar he was eight years younger than she was. She knew his mother—old Mrs. Floyd. She had tea there. And it was that very evening when she came back from having tea with old Mrs. Floyd that she found the note in the hall and took it into the kitchen with her when she went to give Rebecca the fish, thinking it must be something about the boys.

"Mr. Floyd brought it himself, did he?—I think the cheese must be in the parcel in the hall—oh, in the hall——" for she was reading. No, it was not about the boys.

"Yes, enough for fish-cakes to-morrow certainly— Perhaps Captain Barfoot——" she had come to the word "love." She went into the garden and read, leaning against the walnut tree to steady herself. Up and down went her breast. Seabrook came so vividly before her. She shook her head and was looking through her tears at the little shifting leaves against the yellow sky when three geese, half-running, half-flying, scuttled across the lawn with Johnny behind them, brandishing a stick.

Mrs. Flanders flushed with anger.

"How many times have I told you?" she cried, and seized him and snatched his stick away from him.

"But they'd escaped!" he cried, struggling to get free.

"You're a very naughty boy. If I've told you once, I've told you a thousand times. I won't *have* you chasing the geese!" she said, and crumpling Mr. Floyd's letter in her hand, she held Johnny fast and herded the geese back into the orchard.

"How could I think of marriage!" she said to herself bitterly, as she fastened the gate with a piece of wire. She had always disliked red hair in men, she thought, thinking of Mr. Floyd's appearance, that night when the boys had gone to bed. And pushing her work-box away, she drew the blotting-paper towards her, and read Mr. Floyd's letter again, and her breast went up and down when she came to the word "love," but not so fast this time, for she saw Johnny chasing the geese, and knew that it was impossible for her to marry any one—let alone Mr. Floyd, who was so much younger than she was, but what a nice man—and such a scholar too.

"Dear Mr. Floyd," she wrote.—"Did I forget about the cheese?" she wondered, laying down her pen. No, she had told Rebecca that the cheese was in the hall. "I am much surprised . . ." she wrote.

But the letter which Mr. Floyd found on the table when he got up early next morning did not begin "I am much surprised," and it was such a motherly, respectful, inconsequent, regretful letter that he kept it for many years; long after his marriage with Miss Wimbush, of Andover; long after he had left the village. For he asked for a parish in Sheffield, which was given him; and, sending for Archer, Jacob, and John to say good-bye, he told them to choose whatever they liked in his study to remember him by. Archer chose a paper-knife, because he did not like to choose anything too good; Jacob chose the works of Byron in one volume; John, who was still too young to make a proper choice, chose Mr. Floyd's kitten, which his brothers thought an absurd choice, but Mr. Floyd upheld him when he said: "It has fur like you." Then Mr. Floyd spoke about the King's Navy (to which Archer was going); and about Rugby (to which Jacob was going); and next day he received a silver salver and went—first to Sheffield, where he met Miss Wimbush, who was on a visit to her uncle, then to Hackney—then to Maresfield House, of which he became the principal, and finally, becoming editor of a well-known series of Ecclesiastical Biographies, he retired to Hampstead with his wife and daughter, and is often to be seen feeding the ducks on Leg of Mutton Pond. As for Mrs. Flanders's letter—when he looked for it the other day he could not find it, and did not like to ask his wife whether she had put it away. Meeting Jacob in Piccadilly lately, he recognized him after three seconds. But Jacob had grown such a fine young man that Mr. Floyd did not like to stop him in the street.

"DEAR ME," said Mrs. Flanders, when she read in the *Scarborough and Harrogate Courier* that the Rev. Andrew Floyd, etc., etc., had been made Principal of Maresfield House, "that must be our Mr. Floyd."

A slight gloom fell upon the table. Jacob was helping himself to jam; the postman was talking to Rebecca in the kitchen; there was a bee humming at the yellow flower which nodded at the open window. They were all alive, that is to say, while poor Mr. Floyd was becoming Principal of Maresfield House.

Mrs. Flanders got up and went over to the fender and stroked Topaz on the neck behind the ears.

"Poor Topaz," she said (for Mr. Floyd's kitten was now a very old cat, a little mangy behind the ears, and one of these days would have to be killed).

"Poor old Topaz," said Mrs. Flanders, as he stretched himself out in the sun, and she smiled, thinking how she had had him gelded, and how she did not like red hair in men. Smiling, she went into the kitchen.

Jacob drew rather a dirty pocket-handkerchief across his face. He went upstairs to his room.

THE STAG-BEETLE dies slowly (it was John who collected the beetles). Even on the second day its legs were supple. But the butterflies were dead. A whiff of rotten eggs had vanquished the pale clouded yellows which came pelting across the orchard and up Dods Hill and away on to the moor, now lost behind a furze bush, then off again helter-skelter in a broiling sun. A fritillary basked on a white stone in the Roman camp. From the valley came the sound of church bells. They were all eating roast beef in Scarborough; for it was Sunday when Jacob caught the pale clouded yellows in the clover field, eight miles from home.

Rebecca had caught the death's-head moth in the kitchen.

A strong smell of camphor came from the butterfly boxes.

Mixed with the smell of camphor was the unmistakable smell of seaweed. Tawny ribbons hung on the door. The sun beat straight upon them.

The upper wings of the moth which Jacob held were undoubtedly marked with kidney-shaped spots of a fulvous hue. But there was no crescent upon the underwing. The tree had fallen the night he caught it. There had been a volley of pistol-shots suddenly in the depths of the wood. And his mother had taken him for a burglar when he came home late. The only one of her sons who never obeyed her, she said.

Morris called it "an extremely local insect found in damp or marshy places." But Morris is sometimes wrong. Sometimes Jacob, choosing a very fine pen, made a correction in the margin.

The tree had fallen, though it was a windless night, and the lantern, stood upon the ground, had lit up the still green leaves and the dead beech leaves. It was a dry place. A toad was there. And the red underwing had circled round the light and flashed and gone. The red underwing had never come back, though Jacob had waited. It was after twelve when he crossed the lawn and saw his mother in the bright room, playing patience, sitting up.

"How you frightened me!" she had cried. She thought something dreadful had happened. And he woke Rebecca, who had to be up so early.

There he stood pale, come out of the depths of darkness, in the hot room, blinking at the light.

No, it could not be a straw-bordered underwing.

The mowing-machine always wanted oiling. Barnet turned it under Jacob's window, and it creaked—creaked, and rattled across the lawn and creaked again.

Now it was clouding over.

Back came the sun, dazzlingly.

It fell like an eye upon the stirrups, and then suddenly and yet very gently rested upon the bed, upon the alarum clock, and upon the butterfly box stood open. The pale clouded yellows had pelted over the moor; they had zigzagged across the purple clover. The fritillaries flaunted along the hedgerows. The blues settled on little bones lying on the turf with the sun beating on them, and the painted ladies and the peacocks feasted upon bloody entrails dropped by a hawk. Miles away from home, in a hollow among teasles beneath a ruin, he had found the commas. He had seen a white admiral circling higher and higher round an oak tree, but he had never caught it. An old cottage woman living alone, high up, had told him of a purple butterfly which came every summer to her garden. The fox cubs played in the gorse in the early morning, she told him. And if you looked out at dawn you could always see two badgers. Sometimes they knocked each other over like two boys fighting, she said.

"YOU WON'T go far this afternoon, Jacob," said his mother, popping her head in at the door, "for the Captain's coming to say good-bye." It was the last day of the Easter holidays.

Wednesday was Captain Barfoot's day. He dressed himself very neatly in blue serge, took his rubber-shod stick—for he was lame and wanted two fingers on the left hand, having served his country—and set out from the house with the flagstaff precisely at four o'clock in the afternoon.

At three Mr. Dickens, the bath-chair man, had called for Mrs. Barfoot.

"Move me," she would say to Mr. Dickens, after sitting on the esplanade for fifteen minutes. And again, "That'll do, thank you, Mr. Dickens." At the first command he would seek the sun; at the second he would stay the chair there in the bright strip.

An old inhabitant himself, he had much in common with Mrs. Barfoot—James Coppard's daughter. The drinking-fountain, where West Street joins Broad Street, is the gift of James Coppard, who was mayor at the time of Queen Victoria's jubilee, and Coppard is painted upon municipal watering-carts and over shop windows, and upon the zinc blinds of solicitors' consulting-room windows. But Ellen Barfoot never visited the Aquarium (though she had known Captain Boase, who had caught the shark, quite well), and when the men came by with the posters she eyed them superciliously, for she knew that she would never see the Pierrots, or the brothers Zeno, or Daisy Budd and her troupe of performing seals. For Ellen Barfoot in her bath-chair on the esplanade was a prisoner—civilization's prisoner—all the bars of her cage falling across the esplanade on sunny days when the town hall, the drapery stores, the swimming-bath, and the memorial hall striped the ground with shadow.

An old inhabitant himself, Mr. Dickens would stand a little behind her, smoking his pipe. She would ask him questions— who people were—who now kept Mr. Jones's shop—then about the season—and had Mrs. Dickens tried, whatever it might be—the words issuing from her lips like crumbs of dry biscuit.

She closed her eyes. Mr. Dickens took a turn. The feelings of a man had not altogether deserted him, though as you saw him coming towards you, you noticed how one knobbed black boot swung tremulously in front of the other; how there was a shadow between his waistcoat and his trousers; how he leant forward unsteadily, like an old horse who finds himself suddenly out of the shafts drawing no cart. But as Mr. Dickens sucked in the smoke and puffed it out again, the feelings of a man were perceptible in his eyes. He was thinking how Captain Barfoot was now on his way to Mount Pleasant; Captain Barfoot, his master. For at home in the little sitting-room above the mews, with the canary in the window, and the girls at the sewing-machine, and Mrs. Dickens huddled up with the rheumatics—at home where he was made little of, the thought of being in the employ of Captain Barfoot supported him. He liked to think that while he chatted with Mrs. Barfoot on the front, he helped the Captain on his way to Mrs. Flanders. He, a man, was in charge of Mrs. Barfoot, a woman.

Turning, he saw that she was chatting with Mrs. Rogers. Turning again, he saw that Mrs. Rogers had moved on. So he came back to the bath-chair, and Mrs. Barfoot asked him the time, and he took out his great silver watch and told her the time very obligingly, as if he knew a great deal more about the time and everything than she did. But Mrs. Barfoot knew that Captain Barfoot was on his way to Mrs. Flanders.

INDEED HE was well on his way there, having left the tram, and seeing Dods Hill to the south-east, green against a blue sky that was suffused with dust colour on the horizon. He was marching up the hill. In spite of his lameness there was something military in his approach. Mrs. Jarvis, as she came out of the Rectory gate, saw him coming, and her Newfoundland dog, Nero, slowly swept his tail from side to side.

"Oh, Captain Barfoot!" Mrs. Jarvis exclaimed.

"Good-day, Mrs. Jarvis," said the Captain.

They walked on together, and when they reached Mrs. Flanders's gate Captain Barfoot took off his tweed cap, and said, bowing very courteously:

"Good-day to you, Mrs. Jarvis."

And Mrs. Jarvis walked on alone.

She was going to walk on the moor. Had she again been pacing her lawn late at night? Had she again tapped on the study window and cried: "Look at the moon, look at the moon, Herbert!"

And Herbert looked at the moon.

Mrs. Jarvis walked on the moor when she was unhappy, going as far as a certain saucer-shaped hollow, though she always meant to go to a more distant ridge; and there she sat down, and took out the little book hidden beneath her cloak and read a few lines of poetry, and looked about her. She was not very unhappy, and, seeing that she was forty-five, never perhaps would be very unhappy, desperately unhappy that is, and leave her husband, and ruin a good man's career, as she sometimes threatened.

Still there is no need to say what risks a clergyman's wife runs when she walks on the moor. Short, dark, with kindling eyes, a pheasant's feather in her hat, Mrs. Jarvis was just the sort of woman to lose her faith upon the moors—to confound her God with the universal that is—but she did not lose her faith, did not leave her husband, never read her poem through, and went on walking the moors, looking at the moon behind the elm trees, and feeling as she sat on the grass high above Scarborough . . . Yes, yes, when the lark soars; when the sheep, moving a step or two onwards, crop the turf, and at the same time set their bells tinkling; when the breeze first blows, then dies down, leaving the cheek kissed; when the ships on the sea below seem to cross each other and pass on as if drawn by an invisible hand; when there are distant concussions in the air and phantom horsemen galloping, ceasing; when the horizon swims blue, green, emotional—then Mrs. Jarvis, heaving a sigh, thinks to herself, "If only some one could give me . . . if I could give some one. . . ." But she does not know what she wants to give, nor who could give it her.

"MRS. FLANDERS stepped out only five minutes ago, Captain," said Rebecca. Captain Barfoot sat him down in the arm-chair to wait. Resting his elbows on the arms, putting one hand over the other, sticking his lame leg straight out, and placing the stick with the rubber ferrule beside it, he sat perfectly still. There was something rigid about him. Did he think? Probably the same thoughts again and again. But were they "nice" thoughts, interesting thoughts? He was a man with a temper; tenacious; faithful. Women would have felt, "Here is law. Here is order. Therefore we must cherish this man. He is on the Bridge at night," and, handing him his cup, or whatever it might be, would run on to visions of shipwreck and disaster, in which all the passengers come tumbling from their cabins, and there is the captain, buttoned in his pea-jacket, matched with the storm, vanquished by it but by none other. "Yet I have a soul," Mrs. Jarvis would bethink her, as Captain Barfoot suddenly blew his nose in a great red bandanna handkerchief, "and it's the man's stupidity that's the cause of this, and the storm's my storm as well as his" . . . so Mrs. Jarvis would bethink her when the Captain dropped in to see them and found Herbert out, and spent two or three hours, almost silent, sitting in the arm-chair. But Betty Flanders thought nothing of the kind.

"Oh, Captain," said Mrs. Flanders, bursting into the drawing-room, "I had to run after Barker's man . . . I hope Rebecca . . . I hope Jacob . . ."

She was very much out of breath, yet not at all upset, and as she put down the hearth-brush which she had bought of the oil-man, she said it was hot, flung the window further open, straightened a cover, picked up a book, as if she were very confident, very fond of the Captain, and a great many years younger than he was. Indeed, in her blue apron she did not look more than thirty-five. He was well over fifty.

She moved her hands about the table; the Captain moved his head from side to side, and made little sounds, as Betty went on chattering, completely at his ease — after twenty years.

"Well," he said at length, "I've heard from Mr. Polegate."

He had heard from Mr. Polegate that he could advise nothing better than to send a boy to one of the universities.

"Mr. Floyd was at Cambridge ... no, at Oxford ... well, at one or the other," said Mrs. Flanders.

She looked out of the window. Little windows, and the lilac and green of the garden were reflected in her eyes.

"Archer is doing very well," she said. "I have a very nice report from Captain Maxwell."

"I will leave you the letter to show Jacob," said the Captain, putting it clumsily back in its envelope.

"Jacob is after his butterflies as usual," said Mrs. Flanders irritably, but was surprised by a sudden afterthought, "Cricket begins this week, of course."

"Edward Jenkinson has handed in his resignation," said Captain Barfoot.

"Then you will stand for the Council?" Mrs. Flanders exclaimed, looking the Captain full in the face.

"Well, about that," Captain Barfoot began, settling himself rather deeper in his chair.

JACOB FLANDERS, therefore, went up to Cambridge in October, 1906.

THREE

"THIS IS NOT a smoking-carriage," Mrs. Norman protested, nervously but very feebly, as the door swung open and a powerfully built young man jumped in. He seemed not to hear her. The train did not stop before it reached Cambridge, and here she was shut up alone, in a railway carriage, with a young man.

She touched the spring of her dressing-case, and ascertained that the scent-bottle and a novel from Mudie's were both handy (the young man was standing up with his back to her, putting his bag in the rack). She would throw the scent-bottle with her right hand, she decided, and tug the communication cord with her left. She was fifty years of age, and had a son at college. Nevertheless, it is a fact that men are dangerous. She read half a column of her newspaper; then stealthily looked over the edge to decide the question of safety by the infallible test of appearance. . . . She would like to offer him her paper. But do young men read the *Morning Post?* She looked to see what he was reading—the *Daily Telegraph*.

Taking note of socks (loose), of tie (shabby), she once more reached his face. She dwelt upon his mouth. The lips were shut. The eyes bent down, since he was reading. All was firm, yet youthful, indifferent, unconscious—as for knocking one down! No, no, no! She looked out of the window, smiling slightly now, and then came back again, for he didn't notice her.

Grave, unconscious ... now he looked up, past her ... he seemed so out of place, somehow, alone with an elderly lady ... then he fixed his eyes—which were blue—on the landscape. He had not realized her presence, she thought. Yet it was none of *her* fault that this was not a smoking-carriage—if that was what he meant.

Nobody sees any one as he is, let alone an elderly lady sitting opposite a strange young man in a railway carriage. They see a whole—they see all sorts of things—they see themselves. ... Mrs. Norman now read three pages of one of Mr. Norris's novels. Should she say to the young man (and after all he was just the same age as her own boy): "If you want to smoke, don't mind me"? No: he seemed absolutely indifferent to her presence ... she did not wish to interrupt.

But since, even at her age, she noted his indifference, presumably he was in some way or other—to her at least—nice, handsome, interesting, distinguished, well built, like her own boy? One must do the best one can with her report. Anyhow, this was Jacob Flanders, aged nineteen. It is no use trying to sum people up. One must follow hints, not exactly what is said, nor yet entirely what is done—for instance, when the train drew into the station, Mr. Flanders burst open the door, and put the lady's dressing-case out for her, saying, or rather mumbling: "Let me" very shyly; indeed he was rather clumsy about it.

"Who ..." said the lady, meeting her son; but as there was a great crowd on the platform and Jacob had already gone, she did not finish her sentence. As this was Cambridge, as she was staying there for the week-end, as she saw nothing but young men all day long, in streets and round tables, this sight of her fellow-traveller was completely lost in her mind, as the crooked pin dropped by a child into the wishing-well twirls in the water and disappears for ever.

———

THEY SAY the sky is the same everywhere. Travellers, the ship-wrecked, exiles, and the dying draw comfort from the thought, and no doubt if you are of a mystical tendency, consolation, and even explanation, shower down from the unbroken surface. But above Cambridge—anyhow above the roof of King's College Chapel—there is a difference. Out at sea a great city will cast a brightness into the night. Is it fanciful to suppose the sky, washed into the crevices of King's College Chapel, lighter, thinner, more sparkling than the sky elsewhere? Does Cambridge burn not only into the night, but into the day?

Look, as they pass into service, how airily the gowns blow out, as though nothing dense and corporeal were within. What sculptured faces, what certainty, authority controlled by piety, although great boots march under the gowns. In what orderly procession they advance. Thick wax candles stand upright; young men rise in white gowns; while the subservient eagle bears up for inspection the great white book.

An inclined plane of light comes accurately through each window, purple and yellow even in its most diffused dust, while, where it breaks upon stone, that stone is softly chalked red, yellow, and purple. Neither snow nor greenery, winter nor summer, has power over the old stained glass. As the sides of a lantern protect the flame so that it burns steady even in the wildest night—burns steady and gravely illumines the tree-trunks—so inside the Chapel all was orderly. Gravely sounded the voices; wisely the organ replied, as if buttressing human faith with the assent of the elements. The white-robed figures crossed from side to side; now mounted steps, now descended, all very orderly.

... If you stand a lantern under a tree every insect in the forest creeps up to it—a curious assembly, since though they scramble and swing and knock their heads against the glass, they seem to have no purpose—something senseless inspires them.

One gets tired of watching them, as they amble round the lantern and blindly tap as if for admittance, one large toad being the most besotted of any and shouldering his way through the rest. Ah, but what's that? A terrifying volley of pistol-shots rings out—cracks sharply; ripples spread—silence laps smooth over sound. A tree—a tree has fallen, a sort of death in the forest. After that, the wind in the trees sounds melancholy.

But this service in King's College Chapel—why allow women to take part in it? Surely, if the mind wanders (and Jacob looked extraordinarily vacant, his head thrown back, his hymn-book open at the wrong place), if the mind wanders it is because several hat shops and cupboards upon cupboards of coloured dresses are displayed upon rush-bottomed chairs. Though heads and bodies may be devout enough, one has a sense of individuals—some like blue, others brown; some feathers, others pansies and forget-me-nots. No one would think of bringing a dog into church. For though a dog is all very well on a gravel path, and shows no disrespect to flowers, the way he wanders down an aisle, looking, lifting a paw, and approaching a pillar with a purpose that makes the blood run cold with horror (should you be one of a congregation—alone, shyness is out of the question), a dog destroys the service completely. So do these women—though separately devout, distinguished, and vouched for by the theology, mathematics, Latin, and Greek of their husbands. Heaven knows why it is. For one thing, thought Jacob, they're as ugly as sin.

Now there was a scraping and murmuring. He caught Timmy Durrant's eye; looked very sternly at him; and then, very solemnly, winked.

"WAVERLEY," THE VILLA on the road to Girton was called, not that Mr. Plumer admired Scott or would have chosen any name at all, but names are useful when you have to entertain undergraduates, and as they sat waiting for the fourth undergraduate, on Sunday at lunch-time, there was talk of names upon gates.

"How tiresome," Mrs. Plumer interrupted impulsively. "Does anybody know Mr. Flanders?"

Mr. Durrant knew him; and therefore blushed slightly, and said, awkwardly, something about being sure — looking at Mr. Plumer and hitching the right leg of his trouser as he spoke. Mr. Plumer got up and stood in front of the fireplace. Mrs. Plumer laughed like a straightforward friendly fellow. In short, anything more horrible than the scene, the setting, the prospect, even the May garden being afflicted with chill sterility and a cloud choosing that moment to cross the sun, cannot be imagined. There was the garden, of course. Every one at the same moment looked at it. Owing to the cloud, the leaves ruffled grey, and the sparrows — there were two sparrows.

"I think," said Mrs. Plumer, taking advantage of the momentary respite, while the young men stared at the garden, to look at her husband, and he, not accepting full responsibility for the act, nevertheless touched the bell.

There can be no excuse for this outrage upon one hour of human life, save the reflection which occurred to Mr. Plumer as he carved the mutton, that if no don ever gave a luncheon party, if Sunday after Sunday passed, if men went down, became lawyers, doctors, members of Parliament, business men — if no don ever gave a luncheon party———

"Now, does lamb make the mint sauce, or mint sauce make the lamb?" he asked the young man next him, to break a silence which had already lasted five minutes and a half.

"I don't know, sir," said the young man, blushing very vividly.

At this moment in came Mr. Flanders. He had mistaken the time.

Now, though they had finished their meat, Mrs. Plumer took a second helping of cabbage. Jacob determined, of course, that he would eat his meat in the time it took her to finish her cabbage, looking once or twice to measure his speed—only he was infernally hungry. Seeing this, Mrs. Plumer said that she was sure Mr. Flanders would not mind—and the tart was brought in. Nodding in a peculiar way, she directed the maid to give Mr. Flanders a second helping of mutton. She glanced at the mutton. Not much of the leg would be left for luncheon.

It was none of her fault—since how could she control her father begetting her forty years ago in the suburbs of Manchester? and once begotten, how could she do other than grow up cheese-paring, ambitious, with an instinctively accurate notion of the rungs of the ladder and an ant-like assiduity in pushing George Plumer ahead of her to the top of the ladder? What was at the top of the ladder? A sense that all the rungs were beneath one apparently; since by the time that George Plumer became Professor of Physics, or whatever it might be, Mrs. Plumer could only be in a condition to cling tight to her eminence, peer down at the ground, and goad her two plain daughters to climb the rungs of the ladder.

"I was down at the races yesterday," she said, "with my two little girls."

It was none of *their* fault either. In they came to the drawing-room, in white frocks and blue sashes. They handed the cigarettes. Rhoda had inherited her father's cold grey eyes. Cold grey eyes George Plumer had, but in them was an abstract light. He could talk about Persia and the Trade winds, the Reform Bill and the cycle of the harvests. Books were on his shelves by Wells and Shaw; on the table serious sixpenny weeklies written by pale men in muddy boots—the weekly creak and screech of brains rinsed in cold water and wrung dry—melancholy papers.

"I don't feel that I know the truth about anything till I've read them both!" said Mrs. Plumer brightly, tapping the table of contents with her bare red hand, upon which the ring looked so incongruous.

"Oh God, oh God, oh God!" exclaimed Jacob, as the four undergraduates left the house. "Oh, my God!"

"BLOODY BEASTLY!" he said, scanning the street for lilac or bicycle — anything to restore his sense of freedom.

"Bloody beastly," he said to Timmy Durrant, summing up his discomfort at the world shown him at lunch-time, a world capable of existing — there was no doubt about that — but so unnecessary, such a thing to believe in — Shaw and Wells and the serious sixpenny weeklies! What were they after, scrubbing and demolishing, these elderly people? Had they never read Homer, Shakespeare, the Elizabethans? He saw it clearly outlined against the feelings he drew from youth and natural inclination. The poor devils had rigged up this meagre object. Yet something of pity was in him. Those wretched little girls——

The extent to which he was disturbed proves that he was already agog. Insolent he was and inexperienced, but sure enough the cities which the elderly of the race have built upon the skyline showed like brick suburbs, barracks, and places of discipline against a red and yellow flame. He was impressionable; but the word is contradicted by the composure with which he hollowed his hand to screen a match. He was a young man of substance.

Anyhow, whether undergraduate or shop boy, man or woman, it must come as a shock about the age of twenty — the world of the elderly — thrown up in such black outline upon what we are; upon the reality; the moors and Byron; the sea and the lighthouse; the sheep's jaw with the yellow teeth in it; upon the obstinate irrepressible conviction which makes youth so intolerably disagreeable — "I am what I am, and intend to be it,"

for which there will be no form in the world unless Jacob makes
one for himself. The Plumers will try to prevent him from making it. Wells and Shaw and the serious sixpenny weeklies will sit
on its head. Every time he lunches out on Sunday—at dinner
parties and tea parties—there will be this same shock—horror—discomfort—then pleasure, for he draws into him at
every step as he walks by the river such steady certainty, such re-
assurance from all sides, the trees bowing, the grey spires soft
in the blue, voices blowing and seeming suspended in the air,
the springy air of May, the elastic air with its particles—chestnut bloom, pollen, whatever it is that gives the May air its po-
tency, blurring the trees, gumming the buds, daubing the green.
And the river too runs past, not at flood, nor swiftly, but cloy-
ing the oar that dips in it and drops white drops from the blade,
swimming green and deep over the bowed rushes, as if lavishly
caressing them.

Where they moored their boat the trees showered down, so
that their topmost leaves trailed in the ripples and the green
wedge that lay in the water being made of leaves shifted in leaf-
breadths as the real leaves shifted. Now there was a shiver of
wind—instantly an edge of sky; and as Durrant ate cherries he
dropped the stunted yellow cherries through the green wedge
of leaves, their stalks twinkling as they wriggled in and out, and
sometimes one half-bitten cherry would go down red into the
green. The meadow was on a level with Jacob's eyes as he lay
back; gilt with buttercups, but the grass did not run like the thin
green water of the graveyard grass about to overflow the tombstones, but stood juicy and thick. Looking up, backwards, he
saw the legs of children deep in the grass, and the legs of cows.
Munch, munch, he heard; then a short step through the grass;
then again munch, munch, munch, as they tore the grass short
at the roots. In front of him two white butterflies circled higher
and higher round the elm tree.

"Jacob's off," thought Durrant looking up from his novel. He kept reading a few pages and then looking up in a curiously methodical manner, and each time he looked up he took a few cherries out of the bag and ate them abstractedly. Other boats passed them, crossing the backwater from side to side to avoid each other, for many were now moored, and there were now white dresses and a flaw in the column of air between two trees, round which curled a thread of blue—Lady Miller's picnic party. Still more boats kept coming, and Durrant, without getting up, shoved their boat closer to the bank.

"Oh-h-h-h," groaned Jacob, as the boat rocked, and the trees rocked, and the white dresses and the white flannel trousers drew out long and wavering up the bank.

"Oh-h-h-h!" He sat up, and felt as if a piece of elastic had snapped in his face.

"THEY'RE FRIENDS of my mother's," said Durrant. "So old Bow took no end of trouble about the boat."

And this boat had gone from Falmouth to St. Ives Bay, all round the coast. A larger boat, a ten-ton yacht, about the twentieth of June, properly fitted out, Durrant said . . .

"There's the cash difficulty," said Jacob.

"My people'll see to that," said Durrant (the son of a banker, deceased).

"I intend to preserve my economic independence," said Jacob stiffly. (He was getting excited.)

"My mother said something about going to Harrogate," he said with a little annoyance, feeling the pocket where he kept his letters.

"Was that true about your uncle becoming a Mohammedan?" asked Timmy Durrant.

Jacob had told the story of his Uncle Morty in Durrant's room the night before.

"I expect he's feeding the sharks, if the truth were known," said Jacob. "I say, Durrant, there's none left!" he exclaimed, crumpling the bag which had held the cherries, and throwing it into the river. He saw Lady Miller's picnic party on the island as he threw the bag into the river.

A sort of awkwardness, grumpiness, gloom came into his eyes.

"Shall we move on . . . this beastly crowd . . ." he said.

So up they went, past the island.

THE FEATHERY white moon never let the sky grow dark; all night the chestnut blossoms were white in the green; dim was the cow-parsley in the meadows.

The waiters at Trinity must have been shuffling china plates like cards, from the clatter that could be heard in the Great Court. Jacob's rooms, however, were in Neville's Court; at the top; so that reaching his door one went in a little out of breath; but he wasn't there. Dining in Hall, presumably. It will be quite dark in Neville's Court long before midnight, only the pillars opposite will always be white, and the fountains. A curious effect the gate has, like lace upon pale green. Even in the window you hear the plates; a hum of talk, too, from the diners; the Hall lit up, and the swing-doors opening and shutting with a soft thud. Some are late.

Jacob's room had a round table and two low chairs. There were yellow flags in a jar on the mantelpiece; a photograph of his mother; cards from societies with little raised crescents, coats of arms, and initials; notes and pipes; on the table lay paper ruled with a red margin—an essay, no doubt—"Does History consist of the Biographies of Great Men?" There were books enough; very few French books; but then any one who's worth anything reads just what he likes, as the mood takes him, with extravagant enthusiasm. Lives of the Duke of Wellington,

for example; Spinoza; the works of Dickens; the *Faery Queen;* a
Greek dictionary with the petals of poppies pressed to silk between the pages; all the Elizabethans. His slippers were incredibly shabby, like boats burnt to the water's rim. Then there were
photographs from the Greeks, and a mezzotint from Sir
Joshua—all very English. The works of Jane Austen, too, in
deference, perhaps, to some one else's standard. Carlyle was a
prize. There were books upon the Italian painters of the Renaissance, a *Manual of the Diseases of the Horse,* and all the usual text-
books. Listless is the air in an empty room, just swelling the
curtain; the flowers in the jar shift. One fibre in the wicker arm-
chair creaks, though no one sits there.

COMING DOWN the steps a little sideways (Jacob sat on the
window-seat talking to Durrant; he smoked, and Durrant
looked at the map), the old man, with his hands locked behind
him, his gown floating black, lurched, unsteadily, near the wall;
then, upstairs he went into his room. Then another, who raised
his hand and praised the columns, the gate, the sky; another,
tripping and smug. Each went up a staircase; three lights were
lit in the dark windows.

If any light burns above Cambridge, it must be from three
such rooms; Greek burns here; science there; philosophy on the
ground floor. Poor old Huxtable can't walk straight;—Sopwith,
too, has praised the sky any night these twenty years; and Cowan
still chuckles at the same stories. It is not simple, or pure, or
wholly splendid, the lamp of learning, since if you see them
there under its light (whether Rossetti's on the wall, or Van
Goch reproduced, whether there are lilacs in the bowl or rusty
pipes), how priestly they look! How like a suburb where you go
to see a view and eat a special cake! "We are the sole purveyors
of this cake." Back you go to London; for the treat is over.

Old Professor Huxtable, performing with the method of a clock his change of dress, let himself down into his chair; filled his pipe; chose his paper; crossed his feet; and extracted his glasses. The whole flesh of his face then fell into folds as if props were removed. Yet strip a whole seat of an underground railway carriage of its heads and old Huxtable's head will hold them all. Now, as his eye goes down the print, what a procession tramps through the corridors of his brain, orderly, quick-stepping, and reinforced, as the march goes on, by fresh runnels, till the whole hall, dome, whatever one calls it, is populous with ideas. Such a muster takes place in no other brain. Yet sometimes there he'll sit for hours together, gripping the arm of the chair, like a man holding fast because stranded, and then, just because his corn twinges, or it may be the gout, what execrations, and, dear me, to hear him talk of money, taking out his leather purse and grudging even the smallest silver coin, secretive and suspicious as an old peasant woman with all her lies. Strange paralysis and constriction—marvellous illumination. Serene over it all rides the great full brow, and sometimes asleep or in the quiet spaces of the night you might fancy that on a pillow of stone he lay triumphant.

SOPWITH, MEANWHILE, advancing with a curious trip from the fireplace, cut the chocolate cake into segments. Until midnight or later there would be undergraduates in his room, sometimes as many as twelve, sometimes three or four; but nobody got up when they went or when they came; Sopwith went on talking. Talking, talking, talking—as if everything could be talked—the soul itself slipped through the lips in thin silver disks which dissolve in young men's minds like silver, like moonlight. Oh, far away they'd remember it, and deep in dulness gaze back on it, and come to refresh themselves again.

"Well, I never. That's old Chucky. My dear boy, how's the world treating you?" And in came poor little Chucky, the unsuccessful provincial, Stenhouse his real name, but of course Sopwith brought back by using the other everything, everything, "all I could never be"—yes, though next day, buying his newspaper and catching the early train, it all seemed to him childish, absurd; the chocolate cake, the young men; Sopwith summing things up; no, not all; he would send his son there. He would save every penny to send his son there. Sopwith went on talking; twining stiff fibres of awkward speech—things young men blurted out—plaiting them round his own smooth garland, making the bright side show, the vivid greens, the sharp thorns, manliness. He loved it. Indeed to Sopwith a man could say anything, until perhaps he'd grown old, or gone under, gone deep, when the silver disks would tinkle hollow, and the inscription read a little too simple, and the old stamp look too pure, and the impress always the same—a Greek boy's head. But he would respect still. A woman, divining the priest, would, involuntarily, despise.

COWAN, ERASMUS COWAN, sipped his port alone, or with one rosy little man, whose memory held precisely the same span of time; sipped his port, and told his stories, and without book before him intoned Latin, Virgil and Catullus, as if language were wine upon his lips. Only—sometimes it will come over one— what if the poet strode in? "*This* my image?" he might ask, pointing to the chubby man, whose brain is, after all, Virgil's representative among us, though the body gluttonize, and as for arms, bees, or even the plough, Cowan takes his trips abroad with a French novel in his pocket, a rug about his knees, and is thankful to be home again in his place, in his line, holding up in his snug little mirror the image of Virgil, all rayed round with good stories of the dons of Trinity and red beams of port. But language is wine upon his lips. Nowhere else would Virgil hear the like. And though, as she goes sauntering along the Backs, old Miss Umphelby sings him melodiously enough, accurately too, she is always brought up by this question as she reaches Clare Bridge: "But if I met him, what should I wear?"—and then, taking her way up the avenue towards Newnham, she lets her fancy play upon other details of men's meeting with women which have never got into print. Her lectures, therefore, are not half so well attended as those of Cowan, and the thing she might have said in elucidation of the text for ever left out. In short, face a teacher with the image of the taught and the mirror breaks. But Cowan sipped his port, his exaltation over, no longer the representative of Virgil. No, the builder, assessor, surveyor, rather; ruling lines between names, hanging lists above doors. Such is the fabric through which the light must shine, if shine it can—the light of all these languages, Chinese and Russian, Persian and Arabic, of symbols and figures, of history, of things that are known and things that are about to be known. So that if at night, far out at sea over the tumbling waves, one saw a haze on the waters, a city illuminated, a whiteness even in the sky, such as that now over the Hall of Trinity where they're still dining, or washing up plates, that would be the light burning there—the light of Cambridge.

"LET'S GO ROUND to Simeon's room," said Jacob, and they rolled up the map, having got the whole thing settled.

ALL THE LIGHTS were coming out round the court, and falling on the cobbles, picking out dark patches of grass and single daisies. The young men were now back in their rooms. Heaven knows what they were doing. What was it that could *drop* like that? And leaning down over a foaming window-box, one stopped another hurrying past, and upstairs they went and down they went, until a sort of fulness settled on the court, the hive full of bees, the bees home thick with gold, drowsy, humming, suddenly vocal; the Moonlight Sonata answered by a waltz.

THE MOONLIGHT SONATA tinkled away; the waltz crashed. Although young men still went in and out, they walked as if keeping engagements. Now and then there was a thud, as if some heavy piece of furniture had fallen, unexpectedly, of its own accord, not in the general stir of life after dinner. One supposed that young men raised their eyes from their books as the furniture fell. Were they reading? Certainly there was a sense of concentration in the air. Behind the grey walls sat so many young men, some undoubtedly reading, magazines, shilling shockers, no doubt; legs, perhaps, over the arms of chairs; smoking; sprawling over tables, and writing while their heads went round in a circle as the pen moved—simple young men, these, who would—but there is no need to think of them grown old; others eating sweets; here they boxed; and, well, Mr. Hawkins must have been mad suddenly to throw up his window and bawl: "Jo—seph! Jo—seph!" and then he ran as hard as ever he could across the court, while an elderly man, in a green apron, carrying an immense pile of tin covers, hesitated, balanced, and then went on. But this was a diversion. There were young men who read, lying in shallow arm-chairs, holding their books as if they had hold in their hands of something that would see them through; they being all in a torment, coming from midland towns, clergymen's sons. Others read Keats. And those long histories in many volumes—surely some one was now beginning at the beginning in order to understand the Holy Roman Empire, as one must. That was part of the concentration, though it would be dangerous on a hot spring night—dangerous, perhaps, to concentrate too much upon single books, actual chapters, when at any moment the door opened and Jacob appeared;

or Richard Bonamy, reading Keats no longer, began making long pink spills from an old newspaper, bending forward, and looking eager and contented no more, but almost fierce. Why? Only perhaps that Keats died young—one wants to write poetry too and to love—oh, the brutes! It's damnably difficult. But, after all, not so difficult if on the next staircase, in the large room, there are two, three, five young men all convinced of this—of brutality, that is, and the clear division between right and wrong. There was a sofa, chairs, a square table, and the window being open, one could see how they sat—legs issuing here, one there crumpled in a corner of the sofa; and, presumably, for you could not see him, somebody stood by the fender, talking. Anyhow, Jacob, who sat astride a chair and ate dates from a long box, burst out laughing. The answer came from the sofa corner; for his pipe was held in the air, then replaced. Jacob wheeled round. He had something to say to *that,* though the sturdy red-haired boy at the table seemed to deny it, wagging his head slowly from side to side; and then, taking out his penknife, he dug the point of it again and again into a knot in the table, as if affirming that the voice from the fender spoke the truth—which Jacob could not deny. Possibly, when he had done arranging the date-stones, he might find something to say to it—indeed his lips opened—only then there broke out a roar of laughter.

The laughter died in the air. The sound of it could scarcely have reached any one standing by the Chapel, which stretched along the opposite side of the court. The laughter died out, and only gestures of arms, movements of bodies, could be seen shaping something in the room. Was it an argument? A bet on the boat races? Was it nothing of the sort? What was shaped by the arms and bodies moving in the twilight room?

A step or two beyond the window there was nothing at all, except the enclosing buildings—chimneys upright, roofs horizontal; too much brick and building for a May night, perhaps.

And then before one's eyes would come the bare hills of
Turkey—sharp lines, dry earth, coloured flowers, and colour on
the shoulders of the women, standing naked-legged in the
stream to beat linen on the stones. The stream made loops of
water round their ankles. But none of that could show clearly
through the swaddlings and blanketings of the Cambridge
night. The stroke of the clock even was muffled; as if intoned
by somebody reverent from a pulpit; as if generations of learned
men heard the last hour go rolling through their ranks and issued it, already smooth and time-worn, with their blessing, for
the use of the living.

Was it to receive this gift from the past that the young man
came to the window and stood there, looking out across the
court? It was Jacob. He stood smoking his pipe while the last
stroke of the clock purred softly round him. Perhaps there had
been an argument. He looked satisfied; indeed masterly; which
expression changed slightly as he stood there, the sound of the
clock conveying to him (it may be) a sense of old buildings and
time; and himself the inheritor; and then to-morrow; and
friends; at the thought of whom, in sheer confidence and pleasure, it seemed, he yawned and stretched himself.

Meanwhile behind him the shape they had made, whether by
argument or not, the spiritual shape, hard yet ephemeral, as of
glass compared with the dark stone of the Chapel, was dashed
to splinters, young men rising from chairs and sofa corners,
buzzing and barging about the room, one driving another against
the bedroom door, which giving way, in they fell. Then Jacob
was left there, in the shallow arm-chair, alone with Masham? An-
derson? Simeon? Oh, it was Simeon. The others had all gone.

". . . JULIAN THE APOSTATE. . . ." Which of them said that
and the other words murmured round it? But about midnight
there sometimes rises, like a veiled figure suddenly woken, a

heavy wind; and this now flapping through Trinity lifted unseen leaves and blurred everything. "Julian the Apostate"—and then the wind. Up go the elm branches, out blow the sails, the old schooners rear and plunge, the grey waves in the hot Indian Ocean tumble sultrily, and then all falls flat again.

So, if the veiled lady stepped through the Courts of Trinity, she now drowsed once more, all her draperies about her, her head against a pillar.

"Somehow it seems to matter."

The low voice was Simeon's.

The voice was even lower that answered him. The sharp tap of a pipe on the mantelpiece cancelled the words. And perhaps Jacob only said "hum," or said nothing at all. True, the words were inaudible. It was the intimacy, a sort of spiritual suppleness, when mind prints upon mind indelibly.

"Well, you seem to have studied the subject," said Jacob, rising and standing over Simeon's chair. He balanced himself; he swayed a little. He appeared extraordinarily happy, as if his pleasure would brim and spill down the sides if Simeon spoke.

Simeon said nothing. Jacob remained standing. But intimacy—the room was full of it, still, deep, like a pool. Without need of movement or speech it rose softly and washed over everything, mollifying, kindling, and coating the mind with the lustre of pearl, so that if you talk of a light, of Cambridge burning, it's not languages only. It's Julian the Apostate.

But Jacob moved. He murmured good-night. He went out into the court. He buttoned his jacket across his chest. He went back to his rooms, and being the only man who walked at that moment back to his rooms, his footsteps rang out, his figure loomed large. Back from the Chapel, back from the Hall, back from the Library, came the sound of his footsteps, as if the old stone echoed with magisterial authority: "The young man—the young man—the young man—back to his rooms."

Four

WHAT'S THE USE of trying to read Shakespeare, especially in one of those little thin paper editions whose pages get ruffled, or stuck together with sea-water? Although the plays of Shakespeare had frequently been praised, even quoted, and placed higher than the Greek, never since they started had Jacob managed to read one through. Yet what an opportunity!

For the Scilly Isles had been sighted by Timmy Durrant lying like mountain-tops almost a-wash in precisely the right place. His calculations had worked perfectly, and really the sight of him sitting there, with his hand on the tiller, rosy gilled, with a sprout of beard, looking sternly at the stars, then at a compass, spelling out quite correctly his page of the eternal lesson-book, would have moved a woman. Jacob, of course, was not a woman. The sight of Timmy Durrant was no sight for him, nothing to set against the sky and worship; far from it. They had quarrelled. Why the right way to open a tin of beef, with Shakespeare on board, under conditions of such splendour, should have turned them to sulky schoolboys, none can tell. Tinned beef is cold eating, though; and salt water spoils biscuits; and the waves tumble and lollop much the same hour after hour—tumble and lollop all across the horizon. Now a spray of seaweed floats past—now a log of wood. Ships have been wrecked here. One or two go past, keeping their own side of the road. Timmy knew where they were bound, what their cargoes were, and, by looking through his glass, could tell the name of the line, and even guess what dividends it paid its shareholders. Yet that was no reason for Jacob to turn sulky.

The Scilly Isles had the look of mountain-tops almost a-wash. . . . Unfortunately, Jacob broke the pin of the Primus stove.

The Scilly Isles might well be obliterated by a roller sweeping straight across.

But one must give young men the credit of admitting that, though breakfast eaten under these circumstances is grim, it is sincere enough. No need to make conversation. They got out their pipes.

Timmy wrote up some scientific observations; and—what was the question that broke the silence—the exact time or the day of the month? anyhow, it was spoken without the least awkwardness; in the most matter-of-fact way in the world; and then Jacob began to unbutton his clothes and sat naked, save for his shirt, intending, apparently, to bathe.

The Scilly Isles were turning bluish; and suddenly blue, purple, and green flushed the sea; left it grey; struck a stripe which vanished; but when Jacob had got his shirt over his head the whole floor of the waves was blue and white, rippling and crisp, though now and again a broad purple mark appeared, like a bruise; or there floated an entire emerald tinged with yellow. He plunged. He gulped in water, spat it out, struck with his right arm, struck with his left, was towed by a rope, gasped, splashed, and was hauled on board.

The seat in the boat was positively hot, and the sun warmed his back as he sat naked with a towel in his hand, looking at the Scilly Isles which—confound it! the sail flapped. Shakespeare was knocked overboard. There you could see him floating merrily away, with all his pages ruffling innumerably; and then he went under.

Strangely enough, you could smell violets, or if violets were impossible in July, they must grow something very pungent on the mainland then. The mainland, not so very far off—you could see clefts in the cliffs, white cottages, smoke going up—wore an extraordinary look of calm, of sunny peace, as if wisdom and piety had descended upon the dwellers there. Now a cry sounded, as of a man calling pilchards in a main street. It wore an extraordinary look of piety and peace, as if old men smoked by the door, and girls stood, hands on hips, at the well, and horses stood; as if the end of the world had come, and cabbage fields and stone walls, and coast-guard stations, and, above all, the white sand bays with the waves breaking unseen by any one, rose to heaven in a kind of ecstasy.

But imperceptibly the cottage smoke droops, has the look of a mourning emblem, a flag floating its caress over a grave. The gulls, making their broad flight and then riding at peace, seem to mark the grave.

No doubt if this were Italy, Greece, or even the shores of Spain, sadness would be routed by strangeness and excitement and the nudge of a classical education. But the Cornish hills have stark chimneys standing on them; and, somehow or other, loveliness is infernally sad. Yes, the chimneys and the coast-guard stations and the little bays with the waves breaking unseen by any one make one remember the overpowering sorrow. And what can this sorrow be?

IT IS BREWED by the earth itself. It comes from the houses on the coast. We start transparent, and then the cloud thickens. All history backs our pane of glass. To escape is vain.

But whether this is the right interpretation of Jacob's gloom as he sat naked, in the sun, looking at the Land's End, it is impossible to say; for he never spoke a word. Timmy sometimes wondered (only for a second) whether his people bothered him. . . .

No matter. There are things that can't be said. Let's shake it off. Let's dry ourselves, and take up the first thing that comes handy. . . . Timmy Durrant's notebook of scientific observations.

"Now . . ." said Jacob.

It is a tremendous argument.

Some people can follow every step of the way, and even take a little one, six inches long, by themselves at the end; others remain observant of the external signs.

The eyes fix themselves upon the poker; the right hand takes the poker and lifts it; turns it slowly round, and then, very accurately, replaces it. The left hand, which lies on the knee, plays some stately but intermittent piece of march music. A deep breath is taken; but allowed to evaporate unused. The cat marches across the hearth-rug. No one observes her.

"That's about as near as I can get to it," Durrant wound up.

The next minute is quiet as the grave.

"It follows . . ." said Jacob.

Only half a sentence followed; but these half-sentences are like flags set on tops of buildings to the observer of external sights down below. What was the coast of Cornwall, with its violet scents, and mourning emblems, and tranquil piety, but a screen happening to hang straight behind as his mind marched up?

"It follows . . ." said Jacob.

"Yes," said Timmy, after reflection. "That is so."

Now Jacob began plunging about, half to stretch himself, half in a kind of jollity, no doubt, for the strangest sound issued from his lips as he furled the sail, rubbed the plates — gruff, tuneless — a sort of pæan, for having grasped the argument, for being master of the situation, sunburnt, unshaven, capable into the bargain of sailing round the world in a ten-ton yacht, which, very likely, he would do one of these days instead of settling down in a lawyer's office, and wearing spats.

"Our friend Masham," said Timmy Durrant, "would rather not be seen in our company as we are now." His buttons had come off.

"D'you know Masham's aunt?" said Jacob.

"Never knew he had one," said Timmy.

"Masham has millions of aunts," said Jacob.

"Masham is mentioned in Domesday Book," said Timmy.

"So are his aunts," said Jacob.

"His sister," said Timmy, "is a very pretty girl."

"That's what'll happen to you, Timmy," said Jacob.

"It'll happen to you first," said Timmy.

"But this woman I was telling you about—Masham's aunt——"

"Oh, do get on," said Timmy, for Jacob was laughing so much that he could not speak.

"Masham's aunt . . ."

Timmy laughed so much that he could not speak.

"Masham's aunt . . ."

"What is there about Masham that makes one laugh?" said Timmy.

"Hang it all—a man who swallows his tie-pin," said Jacob.

"Lord Chancellor before he's fifty," said Timmy.

"He's a gentleman," said Jacob.

"The Duke of Wellington was a gentleman," said Timmy.

"Keats wasn't."

"Lord Salisbury was."

"And what about God?" said Jacob.

The Scilly Isles now appeared as if directly pointed at by a golden finger issuing from a cloud; and everybody knows how portentous that sight is, and how these broad rays, whether they light upon the Scilly Isles or upon the tombs of crusaders in cathedrals, always shake the very foundations of scepticism and lead to jokes about God.

"Abide with me:
Fast falls the eventide;
The shadows deepen;
Lord, with me abide,"

sang Timmy Durrant.

"At my place we used to have a hymn which began

Great God, what do I see and hear?"

said Jacob.

Gulls rode gently swaying in little companies of two or
three quite near the boat; the cormorant, as if following his long
strained neck in eternal pursuit, skimmed an inch above the
water to the next rock; and the drone of the tide in the caves
came across the water, low, monotonous, like the voice of some
one talking to himself.

"Rock of Ages, cleft for me,
Let me hide myself in thee,"

sang Jacob.

Like the blunt tooth of some monster, a rock broke the surface; brown; overflown with perpetual waterfalls.

"Rock of Ages,"

Jacob sang, lying on his back, looking up into the sky at midday,
from which every shred of cloud had been withdrawn, so that
it was like something permanently displayed with the cover off.

BY SIX O'CLOCK a breeze blew in off an icefield; and by seven
the water was more purple than blue; and by half-past seven

there was a patch of rough gold-beater's skin round the Scilly Isles, and Durrant's face, as he sat steering, was of the colour of a red lacquer box polished for generations. By nine all the fire and confusion had gone out of the sky, leaving wedges of apple-green and plates of pale yellow; and by ten the lanterns on the boat were making twisted colours upon the waves, elongated or squat, as the waves stretched or humped themselves. The beam from the lighthouse strode rapidly across the water. Infinite millions of miles away powdered stars twinkled; but the waves slapped the boat, and crashed, with regular and appalling solemnity, against the rocks.

ALTHOUGH IT would be possible to knock at the cottage door and ask for a glass of milk, it is only thirst that would compel the intrusion. Yet perhaps Mrs. Pascoe would welcome it. The summer's day may be wearing heavy. Washing in her little scullery, she may hear the cheap clock on the mantelpiece tick, tick, tick . . . tick, tick, tick. She is alone in the house. Her husband is out helping Farmer Hosken; her daughter married and gone to America. Her elder son is married too, but she does not agree with his wife. The Wesleyan minister came along and took the younger boy. She is alone in the house. A steamer, probably bound for Cardiff, now crosses the horizon, while near at hand one bell of a foxglove swings to and fro with a bumble-bee for clapper.

These white Cornish cottages are built on the edge of the cliff; the garden grows gorse more readily than cabbages; and for hedge, some primeval man has piled granite boulders. In one of these, to hold, an historian conjectures, the victim's blood, a basin has been hollowed, but in our time it serves more tamely to seat those tourists who wish for an uninterrupted view of the Gurnard's Head. Not that any one objects to a blue print dress and a white apron in a cottage garden.

"Look—she has to draw her water from a well in the garden."

"Very lonely it must be in winter, with the wind sweeping over those hills, and the waves dashing on the rocks."

Even on a summer's day you hear them murmuring.

Having drawn her water, Mrs. Pascoe went in. The tourists regretted that they had brought no glasses, so that they might have read the name of the tramp steamer. Indeed, it was such a fine day that there was no saying what a pair of field-glasses might not have fetched into view. Two fishing luggers, presumably from St. Ives Bay, were now sailing in an opposite direction from the steamer, and the floor of the sea became alternately clear and opaque. As for the bee, having sucked its fill of honey, it visited the teasle and thence made a straight line to Mrs. Pascoe's patch, once more directing the tourists' gaze to the old woman's print dress and white apron, for she had come to the door of the cottage and was standing there.

There she stood, shading her eyes and looking out to sea.

For the millionth time, perhaps, she looked at the sea. A peacock butterfly now spread himself upon the teasle, fresh and newly emerged, as the blue and chocolate down on his wings testified. Mrs. Pascoe went indoors, fetched a cream pan, came out, and stood scouring it. Her face was assuredly not soft, sensual, or lecherous, but hard, wise, wholesome rather, signifying in a room full of sophisticated people the flesh and blood of life. She would tell a lie, though, as soon as the truth. Behind her on the wall hung a large dried skate. Shut up in the parlour she prized mats, china mugs, and photographs, though the mouldy little room was saved from the salt breeze only by the depth of a brick, and between lace curtains you saw the gannet drop like a stone, and on stormy days the gulls came shuddering through the air, and the steamers' lights were now high, now deep. Melancholy were the sounds on a winter's night.

The picture papers were delivered punctually on Sunday, and she pored long over Lady Cynthia's wedding at the Abbey. She, too, would have liked to ride in a carriage with springs. The soft, swift syllables of educated speech often shamed her few rude ones. And then all night to hear the grinding of the Atlantic upon the rocks instead of hansom cabs and footmen whistling for motor cars. . . . So she may have dreamed, scouring her cream pan. But the talkative, nimble-witted people have taken themselves to towns. Like a miser, she has hoarded her feelings within her own breast. Not a penny piece has she changed all these years, and, watching her enviously, it seems as if all within must be pure gold.

The wise old woman, having fixed her eyes upon the sea, once more withdrew. The tourists decided that it was time to move on to the Gurnard's Head.

THREE SECONDS later Mrs. Durrant rapped upon the door.

"Mrs. Pascoe?" she said.

Rather haughtily, she watched the tourists cross the field path. She came of a Highland race, famous for its chieftains.

Mrs. Pascoe appeared.

"I envy you that bush, Mrs. Pascoe," said Mrs. Durrant, pointing the parasol with which she had rapped on the door at the fine clump of St. John's wort that grew beside it. Mrs. Pascoe looked at the bush deprecatingly.

"I expect my son in a day or two," said Mrs. Durrant. "Sailing from Falmouth with a friend in a little boat. . . . Any news of Lizzie yet, Mrs. Pascoe?"

Her long-tailed ponies stood twitching their ears on the road twenty yards away. The boy, Curnow, flicked flies off them occasionally. He saw his mistress go into the cottage; come out again; and pass, talking energetically to judge by the movements of her hands, round the vegetable plot in front of the cottage.

Mrs. Pascoe was his aunt. Both women surveyed a bush. Mrs. Durrant stooped and picked a sprig from it. Next she pointed (her movements were peremptory; she held herself very upright) at the potatoes. They had the blight. All potatoes that year had the blight. Mrs. Durrant showed Mrs. Pascoe how bad the blight was on her potatoes. Mrs. Durrant talked energetically; Mrs. Pascoe listened submissively. The boy Curnow knew that Mrs. Durrant was saying that it is perfectly simple; you mix the powder in a gallon of water; "I have done it with my own hands in my own garden," Mrs. Durrant was saying.

"You won't have a potato left—you won't have a potato left," Mrs. Durrant was saying in her emphatic voice as they reached the gate. The boy Curnow became as immobile as stone.

Mrs. Durrant took the reins in her hands and settled herself on the driver's seat.

"Take care of that leg, or I shall send the doctor to you," she called back over her shoulder; touched the ponies; and the carriage started forward. The boy Curnow had only just time to swing himself up by the toe of his boot. The boy Curnow, sitting in the middle of the back seat, looked at his aunt.

Mrs. Pascoe stood at the gate looking after them; stood at the gate till the trap was round the corner; stood at the gate, looking now to the right, now to the left; then went back to her cottage.

Soon the ponies attacked the swelling moor road with striving forelegs. Mrs. Durrant let the reins fall slackly, and leant backwards. Her vivacity had left her. Her hawk nose was thin as a bleached bone through which you almost see the light. Her hands, lying on the reins in her lap, were firm even in repose. The upper lip was cut so short that it raised itself almost in a sneer from the front teeth. Her mind skimmed leagues where Mrs. Pascoe's mind adhered to its solitary patch. Her mind skimmed leagues as the ponies climbed the hill road. Forwards and backwards she cast her mind, as if the roofless cottages, mounds of slag, and cottage gardens overgrown with foxglove and bramble cast shade upon her mind. Arrived at the summit, she stopped the carriage. The pale hills were round her, each scattered with ancient stones; beneath was the sea, variable as a southern sea; she herself sat there looking from hill to sea, upright, aquiline, equally poised between gloom and laughter. Suddenly she flicked the ponies so that the boy Curnow had to swing himself up by the toe of his boot.

THE ROOKS SETTLED; the rooks rose. The trees which they touched so capriciously seemed insufficient to lodge their numbers. The tree-tops sang with the breeze in them; the branches creaked audibly and dropped now and then, though the season was midsummer, husks or twigs. Up went the rooks and down again, rising in lesser numbers each time as the sager birds made ready to settle, for the evening was already spent enough to make the air inside the wood almost dark. The moss was soft; the tree-trunks spectral. Beyond them lay a silvery meadow. The pampas grass raised its feathery spears from mounds of green at the end of the meadow. A breadth of water gleamed. Already the convolvulus moth was spinning over the flowers. Orange and purple, nasturtium and cherry pie, were washed into the twilight, but the tobacco plant and the passion flower, over which the great moth spun, were white as china. The rooks creaked their wings together on the tree-tops, and were settling down for sleep when, far off, a familiar sound shook and trembled—increased—fairly dinned in their ears—scared sleepy wings into the air again—the dinner bell at the house.

AFTER SIX DAYS of salt wind, rain, and sun, Jacob Flanders had put on a dinner jacket. The discreet black object had made its

appearance now and then in the boat among tins, pickles, pre-
served meats, and as the voyage went on had become more and
more irrelevant, hardly to be believed in. And now, the world
being stable, lit by candle-light, the dinner jacket alone pre-
served him. He could not be sufficiently thankful. Even so his
neck, wrists, and face were exposed without cover, and his
whole person, whether exposed or not, tingled and glowed so
as to make even black cloth an imperfect screen. He drew back
the great red hand that lay on the table-cloth. Surreptitiously it
closed upon slim glasses and curved silver forks. The bones of
the cutlets were decorated with pink frills—and yesterday he
had gnawn ham from the bone! Opposite him were hazy, semi-
transparent shapes of yellow and blue. Behind them, again, was
the grey-green garden, and among the pear-shaped leaves of the
escallonia fishing-boats seemed caught and suspended. A sailing
ship slowly drew past the women's backs. Two or three figures
crossed the terrace hastily in the dusk. The door opened and
shut. Nothing settled or stayed unbroken. Like oars rowing now
this side, now that, were the sentences that came now here, now
there, from either side of the table.

"Oh, Clara, Clara!" exclaimed Mrs. Durrant, and Timothy
Durrant adding, "Clara, Clara," Jacob named the shape in
yellow gauze Timothy's sister, Clara. The girl sat smiling and
flushed. With her brother's dark eyes, she was vaguer and
softer than he was. When the laugh died down she said: "But,
mother, it was true. He said so, didn't he? Miss Eliot agreed
with us. . . ."

But Miss Eliot, tall, grey-headed, was making room beside
her for the old man who had come in from the terrace. The dinner would never end, Jacob thought, and he did not wish it to
end, though the ship had sailed from one corner of the window-
frame to the other, and a light marked the end of the pier. He
saw Mrs. Durrant gaze at the light. She turned to him.

"Did you take command, or Timothy?" she said. "Forgive me if I call you Jacob. I've heard so much of you." Then her eyes went back to the sea. Her eyes glazed as she looked at the view.

"A little village once," she said, "and now grown. . . ." She rose, taking her napkin with her, and stood by the window.

"Did you quarrel with Timothy?" Clara asked shyly. "I should have."

Mrs. Durrant came back from the window.

"It gets later and later," she said, sitting upright, and looking down the table. "You ought to be ashamed—all of you. Mr. Clutterbuck, you ought to be ashamed." She raised her voice, for Mr. Clutterbuck was deaf.

"We *are* ashamed," said a girl. But the old man with the beard went on eating plum tart. Mrs. Durrant laughed and leant back in her chair, as if indulging him.

"We put it to you, Mrs. Durrant," said a young man with thick spectacles and a fiery moustache. "I say the conditions were fulfilled. She owes me a sovereign."

"Not *before* the fish—*with* it, Mrs. Durrant," said Charlotte Wilding.

"That was the bet; with the fish," said Clara seriously. "Begonias, mother. To eat them with his fish."

"Oh dear," said Mrs. Durrant.

"Charlotte won't pay you," said Timothy.

"How dare you . . ." said Charlotte.

"That privilege will be mine," said the courtly Mr. Wortley, producing a silver case primed with sovereigns and slipping one coin on to the table. Then Mrs. Durrant got up and passed down the room, holding herself very straight, and the girls in yellow and blue and silver gauze followed her, and elderly Miss Eliot in her velvet; and a little rosy woman, hesitating at the door, clean, scrupulous, probably a governess. All passed out at the open door.

"WHEN YOU ARE as old as I am, Charlotte," said Mrs. Durrant, drawing the girl's arm within hers as they paced up and down the terrace.

"Why are you so sad?" Charlotte asked impulsively.

"Do I seem to you sad? I hope not," said Mrs. Durrant.

"Well, just now. You're *not* old."

"Old enough to be Timothy's mother." They stopped.

Miss Eliot was looking through Mr. Clutterbuck's telescope at the edge of the terrace. The deaf old man stood beside her, fondling his beard, and reciting the names of the constellations: "Andromeda, Bootes, Sidonia, Cassiopeia. . . ."

"Andromeda," murmured Miss Eliot, shifting the telescope slightly.

Mrs. Durrant and Charlotte looked along the barrel of the instrument pointed at the skies.

"There are *millions* of stars," said Charlotte with conviction. Miss Eliot turned away from the telescope. The young men laughed suddenly in the dining-room.

"Let *me* look," said Charlotte eagerly.

"The stars bore me," said Mrs. Durrant, walking down the terrace with Julia Eliot. "I read a book once about the stars. . . . What are they saying?" She stopped in front of the dining-room window. "Timothy," she noted.

"The silent young man," said Miss Eliot.

"Yes, Jacob Flanders," said Mrs. Durrant.

"Oh, mother! I didn't recognize you!" exclaimed Clara Durrant, coming from the opposite direction with Elsbeth. "How delicious," she breathed, crushing a verbena leaf.

Mrs. Durrant turned and walked away by herself.

"Clara!" she called. Clara went to her.

"How unlike they are!" said Miss Eliot.

Mr. Wortley passed them, smoking a cigar.

"Every day I live I find myself agreeing . . ." he said as he passed them.

"It's so interesting to guess . . ." murmured Julia Eliot.

"When first we came out we could see the flowers in that bed," said Elsbeth.

"We see very little now," said Miss Eliot.

"She must have been so beautiful, and everybody loved her, of course," said Charlotte. "I suppose Mr. Wortley . . ." she paused.

"Edward's death was a tragedy," said Miss Eliot decidedly.

Here Mr. Erskine joined them.

"There's no such thing as silence," he said positively. "I can hear twenty different sounds on a night like this without counting your voices."

"Make a bet of it?" said Charlotte.

"Done," said Mr. Erskine. "One, the sea; two, the wind; three, a dog; four . . ."

The others passed on.

"Poor Timothy," said Elsbeth.

"A very fine night," shouted Miss Eliot into Mr. Clutterbuck's ear.

"Like to look at the stars?" said the old man, turning the telescope towards Elsbeth.

"Doesn't it make you melancholy—looking at the stars?" shouted Miss Eliot.

"Dear me no, dear me no," Mr. Clutterbuck chuckled when he understood her. "Why should it make me melancholy? Not for a moment—dear me no."

"Thank you, Timothy, but I'm coming in," said Miss Eliot. "Elsbeth, here's a shawl."

"I'm coming in," Elsbeth murmured with her eye to the telescope. "Cassiopeia," she murmured. "Where are you all?" she asked, taking her eye away from the telescope. "How dark it is!"

MRS. DURRANT sat in the drawing-room by a lamp winding a ball of wool. Mr. Clutterbuck read the *Times*. In the distance stood a second lamp, and round it sat the young ladies, flashing scissors over silver-spangled stuff for private theatricals. Mr. Wortley read a book.

"Yes; he is perfectly right," said Mrs. Durrant, drawing herself up and ceasing to wind her wool. And while Mr. Clutterbuck read the rest of Lord Lansdowne's speech she sat upright, without touching her ball.

"Ah, Mr. Flanders," she said, speaking proudly, as if to Lord Lansdowne himself. Then she sighed and began to wind her wool again.

"Sit *there*," she said.

Jacob came out from the dark place by the window where he had hovered. The light poured over him, illuminating every cranny of his skin; but not a muscle of his face moved as he sat looking out into the garden.

"I want to hear about your voyage," said Mrs. Durrant.

"Yes," he said.

"Twenty years ago we did the same thing."

"Yes," he said. She looked at him sharply.

"He is extraordinarily awkward," she thought, noticing how he fingered his socks. "Yet so distinguished-looking."

"In those days . . ." she resumed, and told him how they had sailed . . . "my husband, who knew a good deal about sailing, for he kept a yacht before we married" . . . and then how rashly they had defied the fishermen, "almost paid for it with our lives, but so proud of ourselves!" She flung the hand out that held the ball of wool.

"Shall I hold your wool?" Jacob asked stiffly.

"You do that for your mother," said Mrs. Durrant, looking at him again keenly, as she transferred the skein. "Yes, it goes much better."

He smiled; but said nothing.

Elsbeth Siddons hovered behind them with something silver on her arm.

"We want," she said. . . . "I've come . . ." she paused.

"Poor Jacob," said Mrs. Durrant, quietly, as if she had known him all his life. "They're going to make you act in their play."

"How I love you!" said Elsbeth, kneeling beside Mrs. Durrant's chair.

"Give me the wool," said Mrs. Durrant.

"He's come—he's come!" cried Charlotte Wilding. "I've won my bet!"

"There's another bunch higher up," murmured Clara Durrant, mounting another step of the ladder. Jacob held the ladder as she stretched out to reach the grapes high up on the vine.

"There!" she said, cutting through the stalk. She looked semi-transparent, pale, wonderfully beautiful up there among the vine leaves and the yellow and purple bunches, the lights swimming over her in coloured islands. Geraniums and begonias stood in pots along planks; tomatoes climbed the walls.

"The leaves really want thinning," she considered, and one green one, spread like the palm of a hand, circled down past Jacob's head.

"I have more than I can eat already," he said, looking up.

"It does seem absurd . . ." Clara began, "going back to London. . . ."

"Ridiculous," said Jacob, firmly.

"Then . . ." said Clara, "you must come next year, properly," she said, snipping another vine leaf, rather at random.

"If . . . if . . ."

A child ran past the greenhouse shouting. Clara slowly descended the ladder with her basket of grapes.

"One bunch of white, and two of purple," she said, and she placed two great leaves over them where they lay curled warm in the basket.

"I have enjoyed myself," said Jacob, looking down the greenhouse.

"Yes, it's been delightful," she said vaguely.

"Oh, Miss Durrant," he said, taking the basket of grapes; but she walked past him towards the door of the greenhouse.

"You're too good—too good," she thought, thinking of Jacob, thinking that he must not say that he loved her. No, no, no.

The children were whirling past the door, throwing things high into the air.

"Little demons!" she cried. "What have they got?" she asked Jacob.

"Onions, I think," said Jacob. He looked at them without moving.

"NEXT AUGUST, remember, Jacob," said Mrs. Durrant, shaking hands with him on the terrace where the fuchsia hung, like a scarlet ear-ring, behind her head. Mr. Wortley came out of the window in yellow slippers, trailing the *Times* and holding out his hand very cordially.

"Good-bye," said Jacob. "Good-bye," he repeated. "Good-bye," he said once more. Charlotte Wilding flung up her bedroom window and cried out: "Good-bye, Mr. Jacob!"

"Mr. Flanders!" cried Mr. Clutterbuck, trying to extricate himself from his beehive chair. "Jacob Flanders!"

"Too late, Joseph," said Mrs. Durrant.

"Not to sit for me," said Miss Eliot, planting her tripod upon the lawn.

FIVE

"I RATHER THINK," said Jacob, taking his pipe from his mouth, "it's in Virgil," and pushing back his chair, he went to the window.

The rashest drivers in the world are, certainly, the drivers of post-office vans. Swinging down Lamb's Conduit Street, the scarlet van rounded the corner by the pillar box in such a way as to graze the kerb and make the little girl who was standing on tiptoe to post a letter look up, half frightened, half curious. She paused with her hand in the mouth of the box; then dropped her letter and ran away. It is seldom only that we see a child on tiptoe with pity—more often a dim discomfort, a grain of sand in the shoe which it's scarcely worth while to remove—that's our feeling, and so—Jacob turned to the bookcase.

Long ago great people lived here, and coming back from Court past midnight stood, huddling their satin skirts, under the carved door-posts while the footman roused himself from his mattress on the floor, hurriedly fastened the lower buttons of his waistcoat, and let them in. The bitter eighteenth-century rain rushed down the kennel. Southampton Row, however, is chiefly remarkable nowadays for the fact that you will always find a man there trying to sell a tortoise to a tailor. "Showing off the tweed, sir; what the gentry wants is something singular to catch the eye, sir—and clean in their habits, sir!" So they display their tortoises.

At Mudie's corner in Oxford Street all the red and blue beads had run together on the string. The motor omnibuses were locked. Mr. Spalding going to the city looked at Mr. Charles Budgeon bound for Shepherd's Bush. The proximity of the omnibuses gave the outside passengers an opportunity to stare into each other's faces. Yet few took advantage of it. Each had his own business to think of. Each had his past shut in him like the leaves of a book known to him by heart; and his friends could only read the title, James Spalding, or Charles Budgeon, and the passengers going the opposite way could read nothing at all—save "a man with a red moustache," "a young man in grey smoking a pipe." The October sunlight rested upon all these men and women sitting immobile; and little Johnnie Sturgeon took the chance to swing down the staircase, carrying his large mysterious parcel, and so dodging a zigzag course between the wheels he reached the pavement, started to whistle a tune and was soon out of sight—for ever. The omnibuses jerked on, and every single person felt relief at being a little nearer to his journey's end, though some cajoled themselves past the immediate engagement by promise of indulgence beyond—steak and kidney pudding, drink, or a game of dominoes in the smoky corner of a city restaurant. Oh yes, human life is very tolerable on the top of an omnibus in Holborn, when the policeman holds up his arm and the sun beats on your back, and if there is such a thing as a shell secreted by man to fit man himself here we find it, on the banks of the Thames, where the great streets join and St. Paul's Cathedral, like the volute on the top of the snail shell, finishes it off. Jacob, getting off his omnibus, loitered up the steps, consulted his watch, and finally made up his mind to go in. . . . Does it need an effort? Yes. These changes of mood wear us out.

Dim it is, haunted by ghosts of white marble, to whom the organ for ever chaunts. If a boot creaks, it's awful; then the order; the discipline. The verger with his rod has life ironed out beneath him. Sweet and holy are the angelic choristers. And for ever round the marble shoulders, in and out of the folded fingers, go the thin high sounds of voice and organ. For ever requiem—repose. Tired with scrubbing the steps of the Prudential Society's office, which she did year in year out, Mrs. Lidgett took her seat beneath the great Duke's tomb, folded her hands, and half closed her eyes. A magnificent place for an old woman to rest in, by the very side of the great Duke's bones, whose victories mean nothing to her, whose name she knows not, though she never fails to greet the little angels opposite, as she passes out, wishing the like on her own tomb, for the leathern curtain of the heart has flapped wide, and out steal on tiptoe thoughts of rest, sweet melodies. . . . Old Spicer, jute merchant, thought nothing of the kind though. Strangely enough he'd never been in St. Paul's these fifty years, though his office windows looked on the churchyard. "So that's all? Well, a gloomy old place. . . . Where's Nelson's tomb? No time now— come again—a coin to leave in the box. . . . Rain or fine is it? Well, if it would only make up its mind!" Idly the children stray in—the verger dissuades them—and another and another . . . man, woman, man, woman, boy . . . casting their eyes up, pursing their lips, the same shadow brushing the same faces; the leathern curtain of the heart flaps wide.

Nothing could appear more certain from the steps of St. Paul's than that each person is miraculously provided with coat, skirt, and boots; an income; an object. Only Jacob, carrying in his hand Finlay's *Byzantine Empire,* which he had bought in Ludgate Hill, looked a little different; for in his hand he carried a book, which book he would at nine-thirty precisely, by his own fireside, open and study, as no one else of all these multitudes would do.

They have no houses. The streets belong to them; the shops; the churches; theirs the innumerable desks; the stretched office lights; the vans are theirs, and the railway slung high above the street. If you look closer you will see that three elderly men at a little distance from each other run spiders along the pavement as if the street were their parlour, and here, against the wall, a woman stares at nothing, boot-laces extended, which she does not ask you to buy. The posters are theirs too; and the news on them. A town destroyed; a race won. A homeless people, circling beneath the sky whose blue or white is held off by a ceiling cloth of steel filings and horse dung shredded to dust.

There, under the green shade, with his head bent over white paper, Mr. Sibley transferred figures to folios, and upon each desk you observe, like provender, a bunch of papers, the day's nutriment, slowly consumed by the industrious pen. Innumerable overcoats of the quality prescribed hung empty all day in the corridors, but as the clock struck six each was exactly filled, and the little figures, split apart into trousers or moulded into a single thickness, jerked rapidly with angular forward motion along the pavement; then dropped into darkness. Beneath the pavement, sunk in the earth, hollow drains lined with yellow light for ever conveyed them this way and that, and large letters upon enamel plates represented in the underworld the parks, squares, and circuses of the upper. "Marble Arch—Shepherd's Bush"—to the majority the Arch and the Bush are eternally white letters upon a blue ground. Only at one point—it may be Acton, Holloway, Kensal Rise, Caledonian Road—does the name mean shops where you buy things, and houses, in one of which, down to the right, where the pollard trees grow out of the paving stones, there is a square curtained window, and a bedroom.

Long past sunset an old blind woman sat on a camp-stool with her back to the stone wall of the Union of London and Smith's Bank, clasping a brown mongrel tight in her arms and singing out loud, not for coppers, no, from the depths of her gay wild heart—her sinful, tanned heart—for the child who fetches her is the fruit of sin, and should have been in bed, curtained, asleep, instead of hearing in the lamplight her mother's wild song, where she sits against the Bank, singing not for coppers, with her dog against her breast.

Home they went. The grey church spires received them; the hoary city, old, sinful, and majestic. One behind another, round or pointed, piercing the sky or massing themselves, like sailing ships, like granite cliffs, spires and offices, wharves and factories crowd the bank; eternally the pilgrims trudge; barges rest in mid stream heavy laden; as some believe, the city loves her prostitutes.

But few, it seems, are admitted to that degree. Of all the carriages that leave the arch of the Opera House, not one turns eastward, and when the little thief is caught in the empty marketplace no one in black-and-white or rose-coloured evening dress blocks the way by pausing with a hand upon the carriage door to help or condemn—though Lady Charles, to do her justice, sighs sadly as she ascends her staircase, takes down Thomas à Kempis, and does not sleep till her mind has lost itself tunnelling into the complexity of things. "Why? Why? Why?" she sighs. On the whole it's best to walk back from the Opera House. Fatigue is the safest sleeping draught.

The autumn season was in full swing. Tristan was twitching his rug up under his armpits twice a week; Isolde waved her scarf in miraculous sympathy with the conductor's baton. In all parts of the house were to be found pink faces and glittering breasts. When a Royal hand attached to an invisible body slipped out and withdrew the red and white bouquet reposing on the scarlet ledge, the Queen of England seemed a name worth dying for. Beauty, in its hothouse variety (which is none of the worst), flowered in box after box; and though nothing was said of profound importance, and though it is generally agreed that wit deserted beautiful lips about the time that Walpole died—at any rate when Victoria in her nightgown descended to meet her ministers, the lips (through an opera glass) remained red, adorable. Bald distinguished men with gold-headed canes strolled down the crimson avenues between the stalls, and only broke from intercourse with the boxes when the lights went down, and the conductor, first bowing to the Queen, next to the bald-headed men, swept round on his feet and raised his wand.

Then two thousand hearts in the semi-darkness remembered, anticipated, travelled dark labyrinths; and Clara Durrant said farewell to Jacob Flanders, and tasted the sweetness of death in effigy; and Mrs. Durrant, sitting behind her in the dark of the box, sighed her sharp sigh; and Mr. Wortley, shifting his position behind the Italian Ambassador's wife, thought that Brangaena was a trifle hoarse; and suspended in the gallery many feet above their heads, Edward Whittaker surreptitiously held a torch to his miniature score; and ... and ...

In short, the observer is choked with observations. Only to prevent us from being submerged by chaos, nature and society between them have arranged a system of classification which is simplicity itself; stalls, boxes, amphitheatre, gallery. The moulds are filled nightly. There is no need to distinguish details. But the difficulty remains—one has to choose. For though I have no wish to be Queen of England—or only for a moment—I would willingly sit beside her; I would hear the Prime Minister's gossip; the countess whisper, and share her memories of halls and gardens; the massive fronts of the respectable conceal after all their secret code; or why so impermeable? And then, doffing one's own headpiece, how strange to assume for a moment some one's—any one's—to be a man of valour who has ruled the Empire; to refer while Brangaena sings to the fragments of

Sophocles, or see in a flash, as the shepherd pipes his tune, bridges and aqueducts. But no—we must choose. Never was there a harsher necessity! or one which entails greater pain, more certain disaster; for wherever I seat myself, I die in exile: Whittaker in his lodging-house; Lady Charles at the Manor.

A YOUNG MAN with a Wellington nose, who had occupied a seven-and-sixpenny seat, made his way down the stone stairs when the opera ended, as if he were still set a little apart from his fellows by the influence of the music.

At midnight Jacob Flanders heard a rap on his door.

"By Jove!" he exclaimed. "You're the very man I want!" and without more ado they discovered the lines which he had been seeking all day; only they come not in Virgil, but in Lucretius.

"YES; THAT SHOULD make him sit up," said Bonamy, as Jacob stopped reading. Jacob was excited. It was the first time he had read his essay aloud.

"Damned swine!" he said, rather too extravagantly; but the praise had gone to his head. Professor Bulteel, of Leeds, had issued an edition of Wycherley without stating that he had left out, disembowelled, or indicated only by asterisks, several indecent words and some indecent phrases. An outrage, Jacob said; a breach of faith; sheer prudery; token of a lewd mind and a disgusting nature. Aristophanes and Shakespeare were cited. Modern life was repudiated. Great play was made with the professional title, and Leeds as a seat of learning was laughed to scorn. And the extraordinary thing was that these young men were perfectly right—extraordinary, because, even as Jacob copied his pages, he knew that no one would ever print them; and sure enough back they came from the *Fortnightly*, the *Contemporary*, the *Nineteenth Century*—when Jacob threw them into the black wooden box where he kept his mother's letters, his old flannel trousers, and a note or two with the Cornish postmark. The lid shut upon the truth.

This black wooden box, upon which his name was still legible in white paint, stood between the long windows of the sitting-room. The street ran beneath. No doubt the bedroom was behind. The furniture — three wicker chairs and a gate-legged table — came from Cambridge. These houses (Mrs. Garfit's daughter, Mrs. Whitehorn, was the landlady of this one) were built, say, a hundred and fifty years ago. The rooms are shapely, the ceilings high; over the doorway a rose, or a ram's skull, is carved in the wood. The eighteenth century has its distinction. Even the panels, painted in raspberry-coloured paint, have their distinction. . . .

"Distinction"—Mrs. Durrant said that Jacob Flanders was "distinguished-looking." "Extremely awkward," she said, "but so distinguished-looking." Seeing him for the first time that no doubt is the word for him. Lying back in his chair, taking his pipe from his lips, and saying to Bonamy: "About this opera now" (for they had done with indecency). "This fellow Wagner" . . . distinction was one of the words to use naturally, though, from looking at him, one would have found it difficult to say which seat in the opera house was his, stalls, gallery, or dress circle. A writer? He lacked self-consciousness. A painter? There was something in the shape of his hands (he was descended on his mother's side from a family of the greatest antiquity and deepest obscurity) which indicated taste. Then his mouth—but surely, of all futile occupations this of cataloguing features is the worst. One word is sufficient. But if one cannot find it?

"I LIKE JACOB Flanders," wrote Clara Durrant in her diary. "He is so unworldly. He gives himself no airs and one can say what one likes to him, though he's frightening because . . ." But

Mr. Letts allows little space in his shilling diaries. Clara was not the one to encroach upon Wednesday. Humblest, most candid of women! "No, no, no," she sighed, standing at the greenhouse door, "don't break—don't spoil"—what? Something infinitely wonderful.

But then, this is only a young woman's language, one, too, who loves, or refrains from loving. She wished the moment to continue for ever precisely as it was that July morning. And moments don't. Now, for instance, Jacob was telling a story about some walking tour he'd taken, and the inn was called "The Foaming Pot," which, considering the landlady's name . . . They shouted with laughter. The joke was indecent.

Then Julia Eliot said "the silent young man," and as she dined with Prime Ministers, no doubt she meant: "If he is going to get on in the world, he will have to find his tongue."

Timothy Durrant never made any comment at all.

The housemaid found herself very liberally rewarded.

Mr. Sopwith's opinion was as sentimental as Clara's, though far more skilfully expressed.

Betty Flanders was romantic about Archer and tender about John; she was unreasonably irritated by Jacob's clumsiness in the house.

Captain Barfoot liked him best of the boys; but as for saying why . . .

It seems then that men and women are equally at fault. It seems that a profound, impartial, and absolutely just opinion of our fellow-creatures is utterly unknown. Either we are men, or we are women. Either we are cold, or we are sentimental. Either we are young, or growing old. In any case life is but a procession of shadows, and God knows why it is that we embrace them so eagerly, and see them depart with such anguish, being shadows. And why, if this and much more than this is true, why are we yet surprised in the window corner by a sudden vision that the young man in the chair is of all things in the world the most real, the most solid, the best known to us—why indeed? For the moment after we know nothing about him.

Such is the manner of our seeing. Such the conditions of our love.

("I'M TWENTY-TWO. It's nearly the end of October. Life is thoroughly pleasant, although unfortunately there are a great number of fools about. One must apply oneself to something or other—God knows what. Everything is really very jolly—except getting up in the morning and wearing a tail coat.")

"I say, Bonamy, what about Beethoven?"

("Bonamy is an amazing fellow. He knows practically every-thing—not more about English literature than I do—but then he's read all those Frenchmen.")

"I rather suspect you're talking rot, Bonamy. In spite of what you say, poor old Tennyson. . . ."

("The truth is one ought to have been taught French. Now, I suppose, old Barfoot is talking to my mother. That's an odd affair to be sure. But I can't see Bonamy down there. Damn London!") for the market carts were lumbering down the street.

"What about a walk on Saturday?"

("What's happening on Saturday?")

Then, taking out his pocket-book, he assured himself that the night of the Durrants' party came next week.

But though all this may very well be true—so Jacob thought and spoke—so he crossed his legs—filled his pipe—sipped his whisky, and once looked at his pocket-book, rum-pling his hair as he did so, there remains over something which can never be conveyed to a second person save by Jacob him-self. Moreover, part of this is not Jacob but Richard Bonamy—the room; the market carts; the hour; the very moment of his-tory. Then consider the effect of sex—how between man and woman it hangs wavy, tremulous, so that here's a valley, there's a peak, when in truth, perhaps, all's as flat as my hand. Even the exact words get the wrong accent on them. But something is always impelling one to hum vibrating, like the hawk moth, at the mouth of the cavern of mystery, endowing Jacob Flanders with all sorts of qualities he had not at all—for though, certainly, he sat talking to Bonamy, half of what he said was too dull to repeat; much unintelligible (about unknown people and Parliament); what remains is mostly a matter of guess work. Yet over him we hang vibrating.

"Yes," said Captain Barfoot, knocking out his pipe on Betty Flanders's hob, and buttoning his coat. "It doubles the work, but I don't mind that."

He was now town councillor. They looked at the night, which was the same as the London night, only a good deal more transparent. Church bells down in the town were striking eleven o'clock. The wind was off the sea. And all the bedroom windows were dark—the Pages were asleep; the Garfits were asleep; the Cranches were asleep—whereas in London at this hour they were burning Guy Fawkes on Parliament Hill.

SIX

THE FLAMES had fairly caught.

"There's St. Paul's!" some one cried.

As the wood caught the city of London was lit up for a second; on other sides of the fire there were trees. Of the faces which came out fresh and vivid as though painted in yellow and red, the most prominent was a girl's face. By a trick of the firelight she seemed to have no body. The oval of the face and hair hung beside the fire with a dark vacuum for background. As if dazed by the glare, her green-blue eyes stared at the flames. Every muscle of her face was taut. There was something tragic in her thus staring—her age between twenty and twenty-five.

A hand descending from the chequered darkness thrust on her head the conical white hat of a pierrot. Shaking her head, she still stared. A whiskered face appeared above her. They dropped two legs of a table upon the fire and a scattering of twigs and leaves. All this blazed up and showed faces far back, round, pale, smooth, bearded, some with billycock hats on; all intent; showed too St. Paul's floating on the uneven white mist, and two or three narrow, paper-white, extinguisher-shaped spires.

The flames were struggling through the wood and roaring up when, goodness knows where from, pails flung water in beautiful hollow shapes, as of polished tortoiseshell; flung again and again; until the hiss was like a swarm of bees; and all the faces went out.

"Oh Jacob," said the girl, as they pounded up the hill in the dark, "I'm so frightfully unhappy!"

Shouts of laughter came from the others—high, low; some before, others after.

The hotel dining-room was brightly lit. A stag's head in plaster was at one end of the table; at the other some Roman bust blackened and reddened to represent Guy Fawkes, whose night it was. The diners were linked together by lengths of paper roses, so that when it came to singing "Auld Lang Syne" with their hands crossed a pink and yellow line rose and fell the entire length of the table. There was an enormous tapping of green wine-glasses. A young man stood up, and Florinda, taking one of the purplish globes that lay on the table, flung it straight at his head. It crushed to powder.

"I'm so frightfully unhappy!" she said, turning to Jacob, who sat beside her.

The table ran, as if on invisible legs, to the side of the room, and a barrel organ decorated with a red cloth and two pots of paper flowers reeled out waltz music.

Jacob could not dance. He stood against the wall smoking a pipe.

"We think," said two of the dancers, breaking off from the rest, and bowing profoundly before him, "that you are the most beautiful man we have ever seen."

So they wreathed his head with paper flowers. Then somebody brought out a white and gilt chair and made him sit on it. As they passed, people hung glass grapes on his shoulders, until he looked like the figure-head of a wrecked ship. Then Florinda got upon his knee and hid her face in his waistcoat. With one hand he held her; with the other, his pipe.

———

"Now LET US talk," said Jacob, as he walked down Haverstock Hill between four and five o'clock in the morning of November the sixth arm-in-arm with Timmy Durrant, "about something sensible."

THE GREEKS—yes, that was what they talked about—how when all's said and done, when one's rinsed one's mouth with every literature in the world, including Chinese and Russian (but these Slavs aren't civilized), it's the flavour of Greek that remains. Durrant quoted Aeschylus—Jacob Sophocles. It is true that no Greek could have understood or professor refrained from pointing out— Never mind; what is Greek for if not to be shouted on Haverstock Hill in the dawn? Moreover, Durrant never listened to Sophocles, nor Jacob to Aeschylus. They were boastful, triumphant; it seemed to both that they had read every book in the world; known every sin, passion, and joy. Civilizations stood round them like flowers ready for picking. Ages lapped at their feet like waves fit for sailing. And surveying all this, looming through the fog, the lamplight, the shades of London, the two young men decided in favour of Greece.

"Probably," said Jacob, "we are the only people in the world who know what the Greeks meant."

They drank coffee at a stall where the urns were burnished and little lamps burnt along the counter.

Taking Jacob for a military gentleman, the stall-keeper told him about his boy at Gibraltar, and Jacob cursed the British army and praised the Duke of Wellington. So on again they went down the hill talking about the Greeks.

A STRANGE THING—when you come to think of it—this love of Greek, flourishing in such obscurity, distorted, discouraged, yet leaping out, all of a sudden, especially on leaving crowded rooms, or after a surfeit of print, or when the moon floats among the waves of the hills, or in hollow, sallow, fruitless London days, like a specific; a clean blade; always a miracle. Jacob knew no more Greek than served him to stumble through a play. Of ancient history he knew nothing. However, as he tramped into London it seemed to him that they were making the flagstones ring on the road to the Acropolis, and that if Socrates saw them coming he would bestir himself and say "my fine fellows," for the whole sentiment of Athens was entirely after his heart; free, venturesome, high-spirited. . . . She had called him Jacob without asking his leave. She had sat upon his knee. Thus did all good women in the days of the Greeks.

At this moment there shook out into the air a wavering, quavering, doleful lamentation which seemed to lack strength to unfold itself, and yet flagged on; at the sound of which doors in back streets burst sullenly open; workmen stumped forth.

FLORINDA WAS sick.

MRS. DURRANT, sleepless as usual, scored a mark by the side of certain lines in the *Inferno.*

CLARA SLEPT buried in her pillows; on her dressing-table dishevelled roses and a pair of long white gloves.

STILL WEARING the conical white hat of a pierrot, Florinda was sick.

The bedroom seemed fit for these catastrophes—cheap, mustard-coloured, half attic, half studio, curiously ornamented with silver paper stars, Welshwomen's hats, and rosaries pendent from the gas brackets. As for Florinda's story, her name had been bestowed upon her by a painter who had wished it to signify that the flower of her maidenhood was still unplucked. Be that as it may, she was without a surname, and for parents had only the photograph of a tombstone beneath which, she said, her father lay buried. Sometimes she would dwell upon the size of it, and rumour had it that Florinda's father had died from the growth of his bones which nothing could stop; just as her mother enjoyed the confidence of a Royal master, and now and again Florinda herself was a Princess, but chiefly when drunk. Thus deserted, pretty into the bargain, with tragic eyes and the lips of a child, she talked more about virginity than women mostly do; and had lost it only the night before, or cherished it beyond the heart in her breast, according to the man she talked to. But did she always talk to men? No, she had her confidante: Mother Stuart. Stuart, as the lady would point out, is the name of a Royal house; but what that signified, and what her business was, no one knew; only that Mrs. Stuart got postal orders every Monday morning, kept a parrot, believed in the transmigration of souls, and could read the future in tea leaves. Dirty lodging-house wallpaper she was behind the chastity of Florinda.

Now Florinda wept, and spent the day wandering the streets; stood at Chelsea watching the river swim past; trailed along the shopping streets; opened her bag and powdered her cheeks in omnibuses; read love letters, propping them against the milk pot in the A.B.C. shop; detected glass in the sugar bowl; accused the waitress of wishing to poison her; declared that young men stared at her; and found herself towards evening slowly saunter-ing down Jacob's street, when it struck her that she liked that man Jacob better than dirty Jews, and sitting at his table (he was copying his essay upon the Ethics of Indecency), drew off her gloves and told him how Mother Stuart had banged her on the head with the tea-cosy.

Jacob took her word for it that she was chaste. She prattled, sitting by the fireside, of famous painters. The tomb of her fa-ther was mentioned. Wild and frail and beautiful she looked, and thus the women of the Greeks were, Jacob thought; and this was life; and himself a man and Florinda chaste.

She left with one of Shelley's poems beneath her arm. Mrs. Stuart, she said, often talked of him.

Marvellous are the innocent. To believe that the girl herself transcends all lies (for Jacob was not such a fool as to believe implicitly), to wonder enviously at the unanchored life — his own seeming petted and even cloistered in comparison — to have at hand as sovereign specifics for all disorders of the soul Adonais and the plays of Shakespeare; to figure out a comradeship all spirited on her side, protective on his, yet equal on both, for women, thought Jacob, are just the same as men — innocence such as this is marvellous enough, and perhaps not so foolish after all.

For when Florinda got home that night she first washed her head; then ate chocolate creams; then opened Shelley. True, she was horribly bored. What on earth was it *about?* She had to wager with herself that she would turn the page before she ate another. In fact she slept. But then her day had been a long one, Mother Stuart had thrown the tea-cosy;—there are formidable sights in the streets, and though Florinda was ignorant as an owl, and would never learn to read even her love letters correctly, still she had her feelings, liked some men better than others, and was entirely at the beck and call of life. Whether or not she was a virgin seems a matter of no importance whatever. Unless, indeed, it is the only thing of any importance at all.

Jacob was restless when she left him.

All night men and women seethed up and down the well-known beats. Late home-comers could see shadows against the blinds even in the most respectable suburbs. Not a square in snow or fog lacked its amorous couple. All plays turned on the same subject. Bullets went through heads in hotel bedrooms almost nightly on that account. When the body escaped mutilation, seldom did the heart go to the grave unscarred. Little else was talked of in theatres and popular novels. Yet we say it is a matter of no importance at all.

What with Shakespeare and Adonais, Mozart and Bishop Berkeley—choose whom you like—the fact is concealed and the evenings for most of us pass reputably, or with only the sort of tremor that a snake makes sliding through the grass. But then concealment by itself distracts the mind from the print and the sound. If Florinda had had a mind, she might have read with clearer eyes than we can. She and her sort have solved the question by turning it to a trifle of washing the hands nightly before going to bed, the only difficulty being whether you prefer your water hot or cold, which being settled, the mind can go about its business unassailed.

But it did occur to Jacob, half-way through dinner, to wonder whether she had a mind.

THEY SAT AT a little table in the restaurant.

Florinda leant the points of her elbows on the table and held her chin in the cup of her hands. Her cloak had slipped behind her. Gold and white with bright beads on her she emerged, her face flowering from her body, innocent, scarcely tinted, the eyes gazing frankly about her, or slowly settling on Jacob and resting there. She talked:

"You know that big black box the Australian left in my room ever so long ago? . . . I do think furs make a woman look old. . . . That's Bechstein come in now. . . . I was wondering what you looked like when you were a little boy, Jacob." She nibbled her roll and looked at him.

"Jacob. You're like one of those statues. . . . I think there are lovely things in the British Museum, don't you? Lots of lovely things . . ." she spoke dreamily. The room was filling; the heat increasing. Talk in a restaurant is dazed sleep-walkers' talk, so many things to look at—so much noise—other people talking. Can one overhear? Oh, but they mustn't overhear *us*.

"That's like Ellen Nagle—that girl . . ." and so on.

"I'm awfully happy since I've known you, Jacob. You're such a *good* man."

The room got fuller and fuller; talk louder; knives more clattering.

"Well, you see what makes her say things like that is . . ."

She stopped. So did every one.

"To-morrow . . . Sunday . . . a beastly . . . you tell me . . . go then!" Crash! And out she swept.

It was at the table next them that the voice spun higher and higher. Suddenly the woman dashed the plates to the floor. The man was left there. Everybody stared. Then—"Well, poor chap, we mustn't sit staring. What a go! Did you hear what she said? By God, he looks a fool! Didn't come up to the scratch, I suppose. All the mustard on the table-cloth. The waiters laughing."

Jacob observed Florinda. In her face there seemed to him something horribly brainless—as she sat staring.

OUT SHE SWEPT, the black woman with the dancing feather in her hat.

Yet she had to go somewhere. The night is not a tumultuous black ocean in which you sink or sail as a star. As a matter of fact it was a wet November night. The lamps of Soho made large greasy spots of light upon the pavement. The by-streets were dark enough to shelter man or woman leaning against the doorways. One detached herself as Jacob and Florinda approached.

"She's dropped her glove," said Florinda.

Jacob, pressing forward, gave it her.

Effusively she thanked him; retraced her steps; dropped her glove again. But why? For whom?

Meanwhile, where had the other woman got to? And the man?

The street lamps do not carry far enough to tell us. The voices, angry, lustful, despairing, passionate, were scarcely more than the voices of caged beasts at night. Only they are not caged, nor beasts. Stop a man; ask him the way; he'll tell it you; but one's afraid to ask him the way. What does one fear?—the human eye. At once the pavement narrows, the chasm deepens. There! They've melted into it—both man and woman. Further on, blatantly advertising its meritorious solidity, a boarding-house exhibits behind uncurtained windows its testimony to the soundness of London. There they sit, plainly illuminated, dressed like ladies and gentlemen, in bamboo chairs. The widows of business men prove laboriously that they are related to judges. The wives of coal merchants instantly retort that their fathers kept coachmen. A servant brings coffee, and the crochet basket has to be moved. And so on again into the dark, passing a girl here for sale, or there an old woman with only matches to offer, passing the crowd from the Tube station, the women with veiled hair, passing at length no one but shut doors, carved door-posts, and a solitary policeman, Jacob, with Florinda on his arm, reached his room and, lighting the lamp, said nothing at all.

"I don't like you when you look like that," said Florinda.

THE PROBLEM is insoluble. The body is harnessed to a brain. Beauty goes hand in hand with stupidity. There she sat staring at the fire as she had stared at the broken mustard-pot. In spite of defending indecency, Jacob doubted whether he liked it in the raw. He had a violent reversion towards male society, cloistered rooms, and the works of the classics; and was ready to turn with wrath upon whoever it was who had fashioned life thus.

Then Florinda laid her hand upon his knee.

After all, it was none of her fault. But the thought saddened him. It's not catastrophes, murders, deaths, diseases, that age and kill us; it's the way people look and laugh, and run up the steps of omnibuses.

Any excuse, though, serves a stupid woman. He told her his head ached.

But when she looked at him, dumbly, half-guessing, half-understanding, apologizing perhaps, anyhow saying as he had said, "It's none of my fault," straight and beautiful in body, her face like a shell within its cap, then he knew that cloisters and classics are no use whatever. The problem is insoluble.

SEVEN

ABOUT THIS TIME a firm of merchants having dealings with the East put on the market little paper flowers which opened on touching water. As it was the custom also to use finger-bowls at the end of dinner, the new discovery was found of excellent service. In these sheltered lakes the little coloured flowers swam and slid; surmounted smooth slippery waves, and sometimes foundered and lay like pebbles on the glass floor. Their fortunes were watched by eyes intent and lovely. It is surely a great discovery that leads to the union of hearts and foundation of homes. The paper flowers did no less.

It must not be thought, though, that they ousted the flowers of nature. Roses, lilies, carnations in particular, looked over the rims of vases and surveyed the bright lives and swift dooms of their artificial relations. Mr. Stuart Ormond made this very observation; and charming it was thought; and Kitty Craster married him on the strength of it six months later. But real flowers can never be dispensed with. If they could, human life would be a different affair altogether. For flowers fade; chrysanthemums are the worst; perfect over night; yellow and jaded next morning—not fit to be seen. On the whole, though the price is sinful, carnations pay best;—it's a question, however, whether it's wise to have them wired. Some shops advise it. Certainly it's the only way to keep them at a dance; but whether it is necessary at dinner parties, unless the rooms are very hot, remains in dispute. Old Mrs. Temple used to recommend an ivy leaf—just one—dropped into the bowl. She said it kept the water pure for days and days. But there is some reason to think that old Mrs. Temple was mistaken.

THE LITTLE CARDS, however, with names engraved on them, are a more serious problem than the flowers. More horses' legs have been worn out, more coachmen's lives consumed, more hours of sound afternoon time vainly lavished than served to win us the battle of Waterloo, and pay for it into the bargain. The little demons are the source of as many reprieves, calamities, and anxieties as the battle itself. Sometimes Mrs. Bonham has just gone out; at others she is at home. But, even if the cards should be superseded, which seems unlikely, there are unruly powers blowing life into storms, disordering sedulous mornings, and uprooting the stability of the afternoon—dressmakers, that is to say, and confectioners' shops. Six yards of silk will cover one body; but if you have to devise six hundred shapes for it, and twice as many colours?—in the middle of which there is the urgent question of the pudding with tufts of green cream and battlements of almond paste. It has not arrived.

The flamingo hours fluttered softly through the sky. But regularly they dipped their wings in pitch black; Notting Hill, for instance, or the purlieus of Clerkenwell. No wonder that Italian remained a hidden art, and the piano always played the same sonata. In order to buy one pair of elastic stockings for Mrs. Page, widow, aged sixty-three, in receipt of five shillings outdoor relief, and help from her only son employed in Messrs. Mackie's dye-works, suffering in winter with his chest, letters must be written, columns filled up in the same round, simple hand that wrote in Mr. Letts's diary how the weather was fine, the children demons, and Jacob Flanders unworldly. Clara Durrant procured the stockings, played the sonata, filled the vases, fetched the pudding, left the cards, and when the great invention of paper flowers to swim in finger-bowls was discovered, was one of those who most marvelled at their brief lives.

Nor were there wanting poets to celebrate the theme. Edwin Mallett, for example, wrote his verses ending:

And read their doom in Chloe's eyes,

which caused Clara to blush at the first reading, and to laugh at the second, saying that it was just like him to call her Chloe when her name was Clara. Ridiculous young man! But when, between ten and eleven on a rainy morning, Edwin Mallett laid his life at her feet she ran out of the room and hid herself in her bedroom, and Timothy below could not get on with his work all that morning on account of her sobs.

"Which is the result of enjoying yourself," said Mrs. Durrant severely, surveying the dance programme all scored with the same initials, or rather they were different ones this time — R.B. instead of E.M.; Richard Bonamy it was now, the young man with the Wellington nose.

"But I could never marry a man with a nose like that," said Clara.

"Nonsense," said Mrs. Durrant.

"But I am too severe," she thought to herself. For Clara, losing all vivacity, tore up her dance programme and threw it in the fender.

Such were the very serious consequences of the invention of paper flowers to swim in bowls.

"PLEASE," SAID Julia Eliot, taking up her position by the curtain almost opposite the door, "don't introduce me. I like to look on. The amusing thing," she went on, addressing Mr.

Salvin, who, owing to his lameness, was accommodated with a chair, "the amusing thing about a party is to watch the people — coming and going, coming and going."

"Last time we met," said Mr. Salvin, "was at the Farquhars. Poor lady! She has much to put up with."

"Doesn't she look charming?" exclaimed Miss Eliot, as Clara Durrant passed them.

"And which of them . . . ?" asked Mr. Salvin, dropping his voice and speaking in quizzical tones.

"There are so many . . ." Miss Eliot replied. Three young men stood at the doorway looking about for their hostess.

"You don't remember Elizabeth as I do," said Mr. Salvin, "dancing Highland reels at Banchorie. Clara lacks her mother's spirit. Clara is a little pale."

"What different people one sees here!" said Miss Eliot.

"Happily we are not governed by the evening papers," said Mr. Salvin.

"I never read them," said Miss Eliot. "I know nothing about politics," she added.

"The piano is in tune," said Clara, passing them, "but we may have to ask some one to move it for us."

"Are they going to dance?" asked Mr. Salvin.

"Nobody shall disturb you," said Mrs. Durrant peremptorily as she passed.

"Julia Eliot. It *is* Julia Eliot!" said old Lady Hibbert, holding out both her hands. "And Mr. Salvin. What is going to happen to us, Mr. Salvin? With all my experience of English politics — My dear, I was thinking of your father last night — one of my oldest friends, Mr. Salvin. Never tell me that girls of ten are incapable of love! I had all Shakespeare by heart before I was in my teens, Mr. Salvin!"

"You don't say so," said Mr. Salvin.

"But I do," said Lady Hibbert.

"OH, MR. SALVIN, I'm so sorry. . . ."

"I will remove myself if you'll kindly lend me a hand," said Mr. Salvin.

"You shall sit by my mother," said Clara. "Everybody seems to come in here. . . . Mr. Calthorp, let me introduce you to Miss Edwards."

"ARE YOU GOING away for Christmas?" said Mr. Calthorp.

"If my brother gets his leave," said Miss Edwards.

"What regiment is he in?" said Mr. Calthorp.

"The Twentieth Hussars," said Miss Edwards.

"Perhaps he knows my brother?" said Mr. Calthorp.

"I am afraid I did not catch your name," said Miss Edwards.

"Calthorp," said Mr. Calthorp.

"BUT WHAT proof was there that the marriage service was actually performed?" said Mr. Crosby.

"There is no reason to doubt that Charles James Fox . . ." Mr. Burley began; but here Mrs. Stretton told him that she knew his sister well; had stayed with her not six weeks ago; and thought the house charming, but bleak in winter.

"GOING ABOUT as girls do nowadays——" said Mrs. Forster.

Mr. Bowley looked round him, and catching sight of Rose Shaw moved towards her, threw out his hands, and exclaimed: "Well!"

"Nothing!" she replied. "Nothing at all—though I left them alone the entire afternoon on purpose."

"Dear me, dear me," said Mr. Bowley. "I will ask Jimmy to breakfast."

"But who could resist her?" cried Rose Shaw. "Dearest Clara—I know we mustn't try to stop you . . ."

"You and Mr. Bowley are talking dreadful gossip, I know," said Clara.

"Life is wicked—life is detestable!" cried Rose Shaw.

"THERE'S NOT much to be said for this sort of thing, is there?" said Timothy Durrant to Jacob.

"Women like it."

"Like what?" said Charlotte Wilding, coming up to them.

"Where have you come from?" said Timothy. "Dining somewhere, I suppose."

"I don't see why not," said Charlotte.

"People must go downstairs," said Clara, passing. "Take Charlotte, Timothy. How d'you do, Mr. Flanders."

"How d'you do, Mr. Flanders," said Julia Eliot, holding out her hand. "What's been happening to you?"

> "Who is Silvia? what is she?
> That all our swains commend her?"

sang Elsbeth Siddons.

Every one stood where they were, or sat down if a chair was empty.

"Ah," sighed Clara, who stood beside Jacob, half-way through.

> "Then to Silvia let us sing,
>   That Silvia is excelling;
> She excels each mortal thing
>   Upon the dull earth dwelling.
> To her let us garlands bring,"

sang Elsbeth Siddons.

"Ah!" Clara exclaimed out loud, and clapped her gloved

hands; and Jacob clapped his bare ones; and then she moved forward and directed people to come in from the doorway.

"You are living in London?" asked Miss Julia Eliot.

"Yes," said Jacob.

"In rooms?"

"Yes."

"There is Mr. Clutterbuck. You always see Mr. Clutterbuck here. He is not very happy at home, I am afraid. They say that Mrs. Clutterbuck . . ." she dropped her voice. "That's why he stays with the Durrants. Were you there when they acted Mr. Wortley's play? Oh, no, of course not—at the last moment, did you hear—you had to go to join your mother, I remember, at Harrogate—At the last moment, as I was saying, just as everything was ready, the clothes finished and everything—Now Elsbeth is going to sing again. Clara is playing her accompaniment or turning over for Mr. Carter, I think. No, Mr. Carter is playing by himself—This is *Bach*," she whispered, as Mr. Carter played the first bars.

"ARE YOU fond of music?" said Mrs. Durrant.

"Yes. I like hearing it," said Jacob. "I know nothing about it."

"Very few people do that," said Mrs. Durrant. "I daresay you were never taught. Why is that, Sir Jasper?—Sir Jasper Bigham—Mr. Flanders. Why is nobody taught anything that they ought to know, Sir Jasper?" She left them standing against the wall.

Neither of the gentlemen said anything for three minutes, though Jacob shifted perhaps five inches to the left, and then as many to the right. Then Jacob grunted, and suddenly crossed the room.

"Will you come and have something to eat?" he said to Clara Durrant.

"Yes, an ice. Quickly. Now," she said.

Downstairs they went.

But half-way down they met Mr. and Mrs. Gresham, Herbert Turner, Sylvia Rashleigh, and a friend, whom they had dared to bring, from America, "knowing that Mrs. Durrant—wishing to show Mr. Pilcher.—Mr. Pilcher from New York—This is Miss Durrant."

"Whom I have heard so much of," said Mr. Pilcher, bowing low.

SO CLARA left him.

Eight

ABOUT HALF-PAST nine Jacob left the house, his door slamming, other doors slamming, buying his paper, mounting his omnibus, or, weather permitting, walking his road as other people do. Head bent down, a desk, a telephone, books bound in green leather, electric light.... "Fresh coals, sir?" ... "Your tea, sir." ... Talk about football, the Hotspurs, the Harlequins; six-thirty *Star* brought in by the office boy; the rooks of Gray's Inn passing overhead; branches in the fog thin and brittle; and through the roar of traffic now and again a voice shouting: "Verdict—verdict—winner—winner," while letters accumulate in a basket, Jacob signs them, and each evening finds him, as he takes his coat down, with some muscle of the brain new stretched.

Then, sometimes a game of chess; or pictures in Bond Street, or a long way home to take the air with Bonamy on his arm, meditatively marching, head thrown back, the world a spectacle, the early moon above the steeples coming in for praise, the sea-gulls flying high, Nelson on his column surveying the horizon, and the world our ship.

Meanwhile, poor Betty Flanders's letter, having caught the second post, lay on the hall table—poor Betty Flanders writing her son's name, Jacob Alan Flanders, Esq., as mothers do, and the ink pale, profuse, suggesting how mothers down at Scarborough scribble over the fire with their feet on the fender, when tea's cleared away, and can never, never say, whatever it may be—probably this—Don't go with bad women, do be a good boy; wear your thick shirts; and come back, come back, come back to me.

But she said nothing of the kind. "Do you remember old Miss Wargrave, who used to be so kind when you had the whooping-cough?" she wrote; "she's dead at last, poor thing. They would like it if you wrote. Ellen came over and we spent a nice day shopping. Old Mouse gets very stiff, and we have to walk him up the smallest hill. Rebecca, at last, after I don't know how long, went into Mr. Adamson's. Three teeth, he says, must come out. Such mild weather for the time of year, the little buds actually on the pear trees. And Mrs. Jarvis tells me——" Mrs. Flanders liked Mrs. Jarvis, always said of her that she was too good for such a quiet place, and, though she never listened to her discontent and told her at the end of it (looking up, sucking her thread, or taking off her spectacles) that a little peat wrapped round the iris roots keeps them from the frost, and Parrot's great white sale is Tuesday next, "do remember,"—Mrs. Flanders knew precisely how Mrs. Jarvis felt; and how interesting her letters were, about Mrs. Jarvis, could one read them year in, year out—the unpublished works of women, written by the fireside in pale profusion, dried by the flame, for the blotting-paper's worn to holes and the nib cleft and clotted. Then Captain Barfoot. Him she called "the Captain," spoke of frankly, yet never without reserve. The Captain was enquiring for her about Garfit's acre; advised chickens; could promise profit; or had the sciatica; or Mrs. Barfoot had been indoors for weeks; or the Captain says things look bad, politics that is, for as Jacob knew, the Captain would sometimes talk, as the evening waned, about Ireland or India; and then Mrs. Flanders would fall musing about Morty, her brother, lost all these years—had the natives got him, was his ship sunk—would the Admiralty tell her?—the Captain knocking his pipe out, as Jacob knew, rising to go, stiffly stretching to pick up Mrs. Flanders's wool which had rolled beneath the chair. Talk of the chicken farm came back and back, the woman, even at fifty, impulsive at heart, sketching on the cloudy future flocks of Leghorns, Cochin Chinas, Orpingtons; like Jacob in the blur of her outline; but powerful as he was; fresh and vigorous, running about the house, scolding Rebecca.

The letter lay upon the hall table; Florinda coming in that night took it up with her, put it on the table as she kissed Jacob, and Jacob seeing the hand, left it there under the lamp, between the biscuit-tin and the tobacco-box. They shut the bedroom door behind them.

The sitting-room neither knew nor cared. The door was shut; and to suppose that wood, when it creaks, transmits anything save that rats are busy and wood dry is childish. These old houses are only brick and wood, soaked in human sweat, grained with human dirt. But if the pale blue envelope lying by the biscuit-box had the feelings of a mother, the heart was torn by the little creak, the sudden stir. Behind the door was the obscene thing, the alarming presence, and terror would come over her as at death, or the birth of a child. Better, perhaps, burst in and face it than sit in the antechamber listening to the little creak, the sudden stir, for her heart was swollen, and pain threaded it. My son, my son—such would be her cry, uttered to hide her vision of him stretched with Florinda, inexcusable, irrational, in a woman with three children living at Scarborough. And the fault lay with Florinda. Indeed, when the door opened and the couple came out, Mrs. Flanders would have flounced upon her—only it was Jacob who came first, in his dressing-gown, amiable, authoritative, beautifully healthy, like a baby after an airing, with an eye clear as running water. Florinda

followed, lazily stretching; yawning a little; arranging her hair at
the looking-glass—while Jacob read his mother's letter.

LET US CONSIDER letters—how they come at breakfast, and
at night, with their yellow stamps and their green stamps, im-
mortalized by the postmark—for to see one's own envelope on
another's table is to realize how soon deeds sever and become
alien. Then at last the power of the mind to quit the body is
manifest, and perhaps we fear or hate or wish annihilated this
phantom of ourselves, lying on the table. Still, there are letters
that merely say how dinner's at seven; others ordering coal;
making appointments. The hand in them is scarcely perceptible,
let alone the voice or the scowl. Ah, but when the post knocks
and the letter comes always the miracle seems repeated—
speech attempted. Venerable are letters, infinitely brave, forlorn,
and lost.

Life would split asunder without them. "Come to tea, come
to dinner, what's the truth of the story? have you heard the
news? life in the capital is gay; the Russian dancers. . . ." These
are our stays and props. These lace our days together and make
of life a perfect globe. And yet, and yet . . . when we go to dinner, when pressing finger-tips we hope to meet somewhere
soon, a doubt insinuates itself; is this the way to spend our days?
the rare, the limited, so soon dealt out to us—drinking tea? dining out? And the notes accumulate. And the telephones ring.
And everywhere we go wires and tubes surround us to carry the
voices that try to penetrate before the last card is dealt and the
days are over. "Try to penetrate," for as we lift the cup, shake
the hand, express the hope, something whispers, Is this all? Can
I never know, share, be certain? Am I doomed all my days to
write letters, send voices, which fall upon the tea-table, fade
upon the passage, making appointments, while life dwindles, to
come and dine? Yet letters are venerable; and the telephone

valiant, for the journey is a lonely one, and if bound together by notes and telephones we went in company, perhaps—who knows?—we might talk by the way.

Well, people have tried. Byron wrote letters. So did Cowper. For centuries the writing-desk has contained sheets fit precisely for the communications of friends. Masters of language, poets of long ages, have turned from the sheet that endures to the sheet that perishes, pushing aside the tea-tray, drawing close to the fire (for letters are written when the dark presses round a bright red cave), and addressed themselves to the task of reaching, touching, penetrating the individual heart. Were it possible! But words have been used too often; touched and turned, and left exposed to the dust of the street. The words we seek hang close to the tree. We come at dawn and find them sweet beneath the leaf.

Mrs. Flanders wrote letters; Mrs. Jarvis wrote them; Mrs. Durrant too; Mother Stuart actually scented her pages, thereby adding a flavour which the English language fails to provide; Jacob had written in his day long letters about art, morality, and politics to young men at college. Clara Durrant's letters were those of a child. Florinda—the impediment between Florinda and her pen was something impassable. Fancy a butterfly, gnat, or other winged insect, attached to a twig which, clogged with mud, it rolls across a page. Her spelling was abominable. Her sentiments infantile. And for some reason when she wrote she declared her belief in God. Then there were crosses—tear stains; and the hand itself rambling and redeemed only by the fact—which always did redeem Florinda—by the fact that she cared. Yes, whether it was for chocolate creams, hot baths, the shape of her face in the looking-glass, Florinda could no more pretend a feeling than swallow whisky. Incontinent was her rejection. Great men are truthful, and these little prostitutes, staring in the fire, taking out a powder-puff, decorating lips at an

inch of looking-glass, have (so Jacob thought) an inviolable
fidelity.

Then he saw her turning up Greek Street upon another
man's arm.

THE LIGHT from the arc lamp drenched him from head to toe.
He stood for a minute motionless beneath it. Shadows chequered the street. Other figures, single and together, poured out,
wavered across, and obliterated Florinda and the man.

The light drenched Jacob from head to toe. You could see
the pattern on his trousers; the old thorns on his stick; his shoe
laces; bare hands; and face.

It was as if a stone were ground to dust; as if white sparks
flew from a livid whetstone, which was his spine; as if the
switchback railway, having swooped to the depths, fell, fell, fell.
This was in his face.

Whether we know what was in his mind is another question. Granted ten years' seniority and a difference of sex, fear of
him comes first; this is swallowed up by a desire to help — over-
whelming sense, reason, and the time of night; anger would follow close on that—with Florinda, with destiny; and then up
would bubble an irresponsible optimism. "Surely there's enough
light in the street at this moment to drown all our cares in gold!"
Ah, what's the use of saying it? Even while you speak and look
over your shoulder towards Shaftesbury Avenue, destiny is chip-
ping a dent in him. He has turned to go. As for following him
back to his rooms, no — that we won't do.

Yet that, of course, is precisely what one does. He let himself in and shut the door, though it was only striking ten on one
of the city clocks. No one can go to bed at ten. Nobody was
thinking of going to bed. It was January and dismal, but Mrs.
Wagg stood on her doorstep, as if expecting something to happen. A barrel-organ played like an obscene nightingale beneath

wet leaves. Children ran across the road. Here and there one could see brown panelling inside the hall door. . . . The march that the mind keeps beneath the windows of others is queer enough. Now distracted by brown panelling; now by a fern in a pot; here improvising a few phrases to dance with the barrel-organ; again snatching a detached gaiety from a drunken man; then altogether absorbed by words the poor shout across the street at each other (so outright, so lusty)—yet all the while having for centre, for magnet, a young man alone in his room.

"LIFE IS WICKED—life is detestable," cried Rose Shaw.

The strange thing about life is that though the nature of it must have been apparent to every one for hundreds of years, no one has left any adequate account of it. The streets of London have their map; but our passions are uncharted. What are you going to meet if you turn this corner?

"Holborn straight ahead of you," says the policeman. Ah, but where are you going if instead of brushing past the old man with the white beard, the silver medal, and the cheap violin, you let him go on with his story, which ends in an invitation to step somewhere, to his room, presumably, off Queen's Square, and there he shows you a collection of birds' eggs and a letter from the Prince of Wales's secretary, and this (skipping the interme-diate stages) brings you one winter's day to the Essex coast, where the little boat makes off to the ship, and the ship sails and you behold on the skyline the Azores; and the flamingoes rise; and there you sit on the verge of the marsh drinking rum-punch, an outcast from civilization, for you have committed a crime, are infected with yellow fever as likely as not, and—fill in the sketch as you like.

As frequent as street corners in Holborn are these chasms in the continuity of our ways. Yet we keep straight on.

———

ROSE SHAW, talking in rather an emotional manner to Mr. Bowley at Mrs. Durrant's evening party a few nights back, said that life was wicked because a man called Jimmy refused to marry a woman called (if memory serves) Helen Aitken.

Both were beautiful. Both were inanimate. The oval tea-table invariably separated them, and the plate of biscuits was all he ever gave her. He bowed; she inclined her head. They danced. He danced divinely. They sat in the alcove; never a word was said. Her pillow was wet with tears. Kind Mr. Bowley and dear Rose Shaw marvelled and deplored. Bowley had rooms in the Albany. Rose was re-born every evening precisely as the clock struck eight. All four were civilization's triumphs, and if you persist that a command of the English language is part of our inheritance, one can only reply that beauty is almost always dumb. Male beauty in association with female beauty breeds in the onlooker a sense of fear. Often have I seen them—Helen and Jimmy—and likened them to ships adrift, and feared for my own little craft. Or again, have you ever watched fine collie dogs couchant at twenty yards' distance? As she passed him his cup there was that quiver in her flanks. Bowley saw what was up—asked Jimmy to breakfast. Helen must have confided in Rose. For my own part, I find it exceedingly difficult to interpret songs without words. And now Jimmy feeds crows in Flanders and Helen visits hospitals. Oh, life is damnable, life is wicked, as Rose Shaw said.

THE LAMPS of London uphold the dark as upon the points of burning bayonets. The yellow canopy sinks and swells over the great four-poster. Passengers in the mail-coaches running into London in the eighteenth century looked through leafless branches and saw it flaring beneath them. The light burns behind yellow blinds and pink blinds, and above fanlights, and down in basement windows. The street market in Soho is fierce with light. Raw meat, china mugs, and silk stockings blaze in it. Raw voices wrap themselves round the flaring gas-jets. Arms akimbo, they stand on the pavement bawling—Messrs. Kettle and Wilkinson; their wives sit in the shop, furs wrapped round their necks, arms folded, eyes contemptuous. Such faces as one sees. The little man fingering the meat must have squatted before the fire in innumerable lodging-houses, and heard and seen and known so much that it seems to utter itself even volubly from dark eyes, loose lips, as he fingers the meat silently, his face sad as a poet's, and never a song sung. Shawled women carry babies with purple eyelids; boys stand at street corners; girls look across the road—rude illustrations, pictures in a book whose pages we turn over and over as if we should at last find what we look for. Every face, every shop, bedroom window, public-house, and dark square is a picture feverishly turned—in search of what? It is the same with books. What do we seek through millions of pages? Still hopefully turning the pages—oh, here is Jacob's room.

HE SAT AT the table reading the *Globe*. The pinkish sheet was spread flat before him. He propped his face in his hand, so that the skin of his cheek was wrinkled in deep folds. Terribly severe he looked, set, and defiant. (What people go through in half an hour! But nothing could save him. These events are features of our landscape. A foreigner coming to London could scarcely miss seeing St. Paul's.) He judged life. These pinkish and greenish newspapers are thin sheets of gelatine pressed nightly over the brain and heart of the world. They take the impression of the whole. Jacob cast his eye over it. A strike, a murder, football, bodies found; vociferation from all parts of England simultaneously. How miserable it is that the *Globe* newspaper offers nothing better to Jacob Flanders! When a child begins to read history one marvels, sorrowfully, to hear him spell out in his new voice the ancient words.

The Prime Minister's speech was reported in something over five columns. Feeling in his pocket, Jacob took out a pipe and proceeded to fill it. Five minutes, ten minutes, fifteen minutes passed. Jacob took the paper over to the fire. The Prime Minister proposed a measure for giving Home Rule to Ireland. Jacob knocked out his pipe. He was certainly thinking about Home Rule in Ireland—a very difficult matter. A very cold night.

THE SNOW, which had been falling all night, lay at three o'clock in the afternoon over the fields and the hill. Clumps of withered grass stood out upon the hill-top; the furze bushes were black, and now and then a black shiver crossed the snow as the wind drove flurries of frozen particles before it. The sound was that of a broom sweeping—sweeping.

The stream crept along by the road unseen by any one. Sticks and leaves caught in the frozen grass. The sky was sullen grey and the trees of black iron. Uncompromising was the severity of the country. At four o'clock the snow was again falling. The day had gone out.

A window tinged yellow about two feet across alone combated the white fields and the black trees.... At six o'clock a man's figure carrying a lantern crossed the field.... A raft of twig stayed upon a stone, suddenly detached itself, and floated towards the culvert.... A load of snow slipped and fell from a fir branch.... Later there was a mournful cry.... A motor car came along the road shoving the dark before it.... The dark shut down behind it....

Spaces of complete immobility separated each of these movements. The land seemed to lie dead.... Then the old shepherd returned stiffly across the field. Stiffly and painfully the frozen earth was trodden under and gave beneath pressure like a treadmill. The worn voices of clocks repeated the fact of the hour all night long.

JACOB, TOO, heard them, and raked out the fire. He rose. He stretched himself. He went to bed.

NINE

THE COUNTESS of Rocksbier sat at the head of the table alone with Jacob. Fed upon champagne and spices for at least two centuries (four, if you count the female line), the Countess Lucy looked well fed. A discriminating nose she had for scents, prolonged, as if in quest of them; her underlip protruded a narrow red shelf; her eyes were small, with sandy tufts for eyebrows, and her jowl was heavy. Behind her (the window looked on Grosvenor Square) stood Moll Pratt on the pavement, offering violets for sale; and Mrs. Hilda Thomas, lifting her skirts, preparing to cross the road. One was from Walworth; the other from Putney. Both wore black stockings, but Mrs. Thomas was coiled in furs. The comparison was much in Lady Rocksbier's favour. Moll had more humour, but was violent; stupid too. Hilda Thomas was mealy-mouthed, all her silver frames aslant; egg-cups in the drawing-room; and the windows shrouded. Lady Rocksbier, whatever the deficiencies of her profile, had been a great rider to hounds. She used her knife with authority, tore her chicken bones, asking Jacob's pardon, with her own hands.

"Who is that driving by?" she asked Boxall, the butler.

"Lady Fittlemere's carriage, my lady," which reminded her to send a card to ask after his lordship's health. A rude old lady, Jacob thought. The wine was excellent. She called herself "an old woman"—"so kind to lunch with an old woman"—which flattered him. She talked of Joseph Chamberlain, whom she had known. She said that Jacob must come and meet—one of our celebrities. And the Lady Alice came in with three dogs on a leash, and Jackie, who ran to kiss his grandmother, while Boxall brought in a telegram, and Jacob was given a good cigar.

A FEW MOMENTS before a horse jumps it slows, sidles, gathers itself together, goes up like a monster wave, and pitches down on the further side. Hedges and sky swoop in a semicircle. Then as if your own body ran into the horse's body and it was your own forelegs grown with his that sprang, rushing through the air you go, the ground resilient, bodies a mass of muscles, yet you have command too, upright stillness, eyes accurately judging. Then the curves cease, changing to downright hammer strokes, which jar; and you draw up with a jolt; sitting back a little, sparkling, tingling, glazed with ice over pounding arteries, gasping: "Ah! ho! Hah!" the steam going up from the horses as they jostle together at the cross-roads, where the signpost is, and the woman in the apron stands and stares at the doorway. The man raises himself from the cabbages to stare too.

So Jacob galloped over the fields of Essex, flopped in the mud, lost the hunt, and rode by himself eating sandwiches, looking over the hedges, noticing the colours as if new scraped, cursing his luck.

He had tea at the Inn; and there they all were, slapping, stamping, saying, "After you," clipped, curt, jocose, red as the wattles of turkeys, using free speech until Mrs. Horsefield and her friend Miss Dudding appeared at the doorway with their skirts hitched up, and hair looping down. Then Tom Dudding rapped at the window with his whip. A motor car throbbed in the courtyard. Gentlemen, feeling for matches, moved out, and Jacob went into the bar with Brandy Jones to smoke with the rustics. There was old Jevons with one eye gone, and his clothes the colour of mud, his bag over his back, and his brains laid feet down in earth among the violet roots and the nettle roots; Mary Sanders with her box of wood; and Tom sent for beer, the half-witted son of the sexton—all this within thirty miles of London.

MRS. PAPWORTH, of Endell Street, Covent Garden, did for Mr. Bonamy in New Square, Lincoln's Inn, and as she washed up the dinner things in the scullery she heard the young gentlemen talking in the room next door. Mr. Sanders was there again; Flanders she meant; and where an inquisitive old woman gets a name wrong, what chance is there that she will faithfully report an argument? As she held the plates under water and then dealt them on the pile beneath the hissing gas, she listened: heard Sanders speaking in a loud rather overbearing tone of voice: "good," he said, and "absolute" and "justice" and "punish-ment," and "the will of the majority." Then her gentleman piped up; she backed him for argument against Sanders. Yet Sanders was a fine young fellow (here all the scraps went swirling round the sink, scoured after by her purple, almost nailless hands). "Women"—she thought, and wondered what Sanders and her gentleman did in *that* line, one eyelid sinking perceptibly as she mused, for she was the mother of nine—three still-born and one deaf and dumb from birth. Putting the plates in the rack she heard once more Sanders at it again ("He don't give Bonamy a chance," she thought). "Objective something," said Bonamy; and "common ground" and something else—all very long words, she noted. "Book learning does it," she thought to her-self, and, as she thrust her arms into her jacket, heard some-thing—might be the little table by the fire—fall; and then stamp, stamp, stamp—as if they were having at each other—round the room, making the plates dance.

"To-morrow's breakfast, sir," she said, opening the door; and there were Sanders and Bonamy like two bulls of Bashan driving each other up and down, making such a racket, and all them chairs in the way. They never noticed her. She felt motherly towards them. "Your breakfast, sir," she said, as they came near. And Bonamy, all his hair touzled and his tie flying, broke off, and pushed Sanders into the arm-chair, and said Mr. Sanders had smashed the coffee-pot and he was teaching Mr. Sanders——

Sure enough, the coffee-pot lay broken on the hearthrug.

"ANY DAY this week except Thursday," wrote Miss Perry, and this was not the first invitation by any means. Were all Miss Perry's weeks blank with the exception of Thursday, and was her only desire to see her old friend's son? Time is issued to spinster ladies of wealth in long white ribbons. These they wind round and round, round and round, assisted by five female servants, a butler, a fine Mexican parrot, regular meals, Mudie's library, and friends dropping in. A little hurt she was already that Jacob had not called.

"Your mother," she said, "is one of my oldest friends."

Miss Rosseter, who was sitting by the fire, holding the *Spectator* between her cheek and the blaze, refused to have a fire screen, but finally accepted one. The weather was then discussed, for in deference to Parkes, who was opening little tables, graver matters were postponed. Miss Rosseter drew Jacob's attention to the beauty of the cabinet.

"So wonderfully clever in picking things up," she said. Miss Perry had found it in Yorkshire. The North of England was discussed. When Jacob spoke they both listened. Miss Perry was bethinking her of something suitable and manly to say when the door opened and Mr. Benson was announced. Now there were

four people sitting in that room. Miss Perry aged 66; Miss Rosseter 42; Mr. Benson 38; and Jacob 25.

"My old friend looks as well as ever," said Mr. Benson, tapping the bars of the parrot's cage; Miss Rosseter simultaneously
praised the tea; Jacob handed the wrong plates; and Miss Perry
signified her desire to approach more closely. "Your brothers,"
she began vaguely.

"Archer and John," Jacob supplied her. Then to her pleasure
she recovered Rebecca's name; and how one day "when you
were all little boys, playing in the drawing-room——"

"But Miss Perry has the kettle-holder," said Miss Rosseter,
and indeed Miss Perry was clasping it to her breast. (Had she,
then, loved Jacob's father?)

"So clever"—"not so good as usual"—"I thought it most
unfair," said Mr. Benson and Miss Rosseter, discussing the Saturday *Westminster*. Did they not compete regularly for prizes?
Had not Mr. Benson three times won a guinea, and Miss Rosseter once ten and sixpence? Of course Everard Benson had a
weak heart, but still, to win prizes, remember parrots, toady
Miss Perry, despise Miss Rosseter, give tea-parties in his rooms
(which were in the style of Whistler, with pretty books on
tables), all this, so Jacob felt without knowing him, made him a
contemptible ass. As for Miss Rosseter, she had nursed cancer,
and now painted water-colours.

"Running away so soon?" said Miss Perry vaguely. "At
home every afternoon, if you've nothing better to do—except
Thursdays."

"I've never known you desert your old ladies once," Miss
Rosseter was saying, and Mr. Benson was stooping over the parrot's cage, and Miss Perry was moving towards the bell. . . .

THE FIRE BURNT clear between two pillars of greenish marble,
and on the mantelpiece there was a green clock guarded by Bri-

tannia leaning on her spear. As for pictures—a maiden in a
large hat offered roses over the garden gate to a gentleman in
eighteenth-century costume. A mastiff lay extended against a
battered door. The lower panes of the windows were of ground
glass, and the curtains, accurately looped, were of plush and
green too.

Laurette and Jacob sat with their toes in the fender side by
side, in two large chairs covered in green plush. Laurette's skirts
were short, her legs long, thin, and transparently covered. Her
fingers stroked her ankles.

"It's not exactly that I don't understand them," she was saying thoughtfully. "I must go and try again."

"What time will you be there?" said Jacob.

She shrugged her shoulders.

"To-morrow?"

No, not to-morrow.

"This weather makes me long for the country," she said,
looking over her shoulder at the back view of tall houses
through the window.

"I wish you'd been with me on Saturday," said Jacob.

"I used to ride," she said. She got up gracefully, calmly.
Jacob got up. She smiled at him. As she shut the door he put so
many shillings on the mantelpiece.

Altogether a most reasonable conversation; a most respectable room; an intelligent girl. Only Madame herself seeing Jacob
out had about her that leer, that lewdness, that quake of the surface (visible in the eyes chiefly), which threatens to spill the
whole bag of ordure, with difficulty held together, over the
pavement. In short, something was wrong.

NOT SO VERY long ago the workmen had gilt the final "y" in
Lord Macaulay's name, and the names stretched in unbroken
file round the dome of the British Museum. At a considerable

depth beneath, many hundreds of the living sat at the spokes of a cart-wheel copying from printed books into manuscript books; now and then rising to consult the catalogue; regaining their places stealthily, while from time to time a silent man replenished their compartments.

There was a little catastrophe. Miss Marchmont's pile overbalanced and fell into Jacob's compartment. Such things happened to Miss Marchmont. What was she seeking through millions of pages, in her old plush dress, and her wig of claret-coloured hair, with her gems and her chilblains? Sometimes one thing, sometimes another, to confirm her philosophy that colour is sound—or, perhaps, it has something to do with music. She could never quite say, though it was not for lack of trying. And she could not ask you back to her room, for it was "not very clean, I'm afraid," so she must catch you in the passage, or take a chair in Hyde Park to explain her philosophy. The rhythm of the soul depends on it—("how rude the little boys are!" she would say), and Mr. Asquith's Irish policy, and Shakespeare comes in, "and Queen Alexandra most graciously once acknowledged a copy of my pamphlet," she would say, waving the little boys magnificently away. But she needs funds to publish her book, for "publishers are capitalists—publishers are cowards." And so, digging her elbow into her pile of books it fell over.

Jacob remained quite unmoved.

But Fraser, the atheist, on the other side, detesting plush, more than once accosted with leaflets, shifted irritably. He abhorred vagueness—the Christian religion, for example, and old Dean Parker's pronouncements. Dean Parker wrote books and Fraser utterly destroyed them by force of logic and left his children unbaptized—his wife did it secretly in the washing basin— but Fraser ignored her, and went on supporting blasphemers, distributing leaflets, getting up his facts in the British Museum, always in the same check suit and fiery tie, but pale, spotted, irritable. Indeed, what a work—to destroy religion!

Jacob transcribed a whole passage from Marlowe.

Miss Julia Hedge, the feminist, waited for her books. They did not come. She wetted her pen. She looked about her. Her eye was caught by the final letters in Lord Macaulay's name. And she read them all round the dome—the names of great men which remind us—— "Oh damn," said Julia Hedge, "why didn't they leave room for an Eliot or a Brontë?"

Unfortunate Julia! wetting her pen in bitterness, and leaving her shoe laces untied. When her books came she applied herself to her gigantic labours, but perceived through one of the nerves of her exasperated sensibility how composedly, unconcernedly, and with every consideration the male readers applied themselves to theirs. That young man for example. What had he got to do except copy out poetry? And she must study statistics. There are more women than men. Yes; but if you let women work as men work, they'll die off much quicker. They'll become extinct. That was her argument. Death and gall and bitter dust were on her pen-tip; and as the afternoon wore on, red had worked into her cheek-bones and a light was in her eyes.

But what brought Jacob Flanders to read Marlowe in the British Museum?

YOUTH, YOUTH—something savage—something pedantic. For example, there is Mr. Masefield, there is Mr. Bennett. Stuff them into the flame of Marlowe and burn them to cinders. Let not a shred remain. Don't palter with the second rate. Detest your own age. Build a better one. And to set that on foot read incredibly dull essays upon Marlowe to your friends. For which purpose one must collate editions in the British Museum. One must do the thing oneself. Useless to trust to the Victorians, who disembowel, or to the living, who are mere publicists. The flesh and blood of the future depends entirely upon six young men. And as Jacob was one of them, no doubt he looked a little regal and pompous as he turned his page, and Julia Hedge disliked him naturally enough.

But then a pudding-faced man pushed a note towards Jacob, and Jacob, leaning back in his chair, began an uneasy murmured conversation, and they went off together (Julia Hedge watched them), and laughed aloud (she thought) directly they were in the hall.

Nobody laughed in the reading-room. There were shiftings, murmurings, apologetic sneezes, and sudden unashamed devastating coughs. The lesson hour was almost over. Ushers were collecting exercises. Lazy children wanted to stretch. Good ones scribbled assiduously—ah, another day over and so little done! And now and then was to be heard from the whole collection of human beings a heavy sigh, after which the humiliating old man would cough shamelessly, and Miss Marchmont hinnied like a horse.

Jacob came back only in time to return his books.

The books were now replaced. A few letters of the alphabet were sprinkled round the dome. Closely stood together in a ring round the dome were Plato, Aristotle, Sophocles, and Shakespeare; the literatures of Rome, Greece, China, India, Persia. One leaf of poetry was pressed flat against another leaf, one burnished letter laid smooth against another in a density of meaning, a conglomeration of loveliness.

"One does want one's tea," said Miss Marchmont, reclaiming her shabby umbrella.

Miss Marchmont wanted her tea, but could never resist a last look at the Elgin Marbles. She looked at them sideways, waving her hand and muttering a word or two of salutation which made Jacob and the other man turn round. She smiled at them amiably. It all came into her philosophy—that colour is sound, or perhaps it has something to do with music. And having done her service, she hobbled off to tea. It was closing time. The public collected in the hall to receive their umbrellas.

For the most part the students wait their turn very patiently. To stand and wait while some one examines white discs is soothing. The umbrella will certainly be found. But the fact leads you on all day through Macaulay, Hobbes, Gibbon; through octavos, quartos, folios; sinks deeper and deeper through ivory pages and morocco bindings into this density of thought, this conglomeration of knowledge.

Jacob's walking-stick was like all the others; they had muddled the pigeon-holes perhaps.

There is in the British Museum an enormous mind. Consider that Plato is there cheek by jowl with Aristotle; and Shakespeare with Marlowe. This great mind is hoarded beyond the power of any single mind to possess it. Nevertheless (as they take so long finding one's walking-stick) one can't help thinking how one might come with a notebook, sit at a desk, and read it all through. A learned man is the most venerable of all—a man like Huxtable of Trinity, who writes all his letters in Greek, they say, and could have kept his end up with Bentley. And then there is science, pictures, architecture,—an enormous mind.

They pushed the walking-stick across the counter. Jacob stood beneath the porch of the British Museum. It was raining. Great Russell Street was glazed and shining—here yellow, here, outside the chemist's, red and pale blue. People scuttled quickly close to the wall; carriages rattled rather helter-skelter down the streets. Well, but a little rain hurts nobody. Jacob walked off much as if he had been in the country; and late that night there he was sitting at his table with his pipe and his book.

The rain poured down. The British Museum stood in one solid immense mound, very pale, very sleek in the rain, not a quarter of a mile from him. The vast mind was sheeted with stone; and each compartment in the depths of it was safe and dry. The night-watchmen, flashing their lanterns over the backs of Plato and Shakespeare, saw that on the twenty-second of February neither flame, rat, nor burglar was going to violate these treasures—poor, highly respectable men, with wives and families at Kentish Town, do their best for twenty years to protect Plato and Shakespeare, and then are buried at Highgate.

Stone lies solid over the British Museum, as bone lies cool over the visions and heat of the brain. Only here the brain is Plato's brain and Shakespeare's; the brain has made pots and statues, great bulls and little jewels, and crossed the river of death this way and that incessantly, seeking some landing, now wrapping the body well for its long sleep; now laying a penny piece on the eyes; now turning the toes scrupulously to the East. Meanwhile, Plato continues his dialogue; in spite of the rain; in spite of the cab whistles; in spite of the woman in the mews behind Great Ormond Street who has come home drunk and cries all night long, "Let me in! Let me in!"

In the street below Jacob's room voices were raised.

But he read on. For after all Plato continues imperturbably. And Hamlet utters his soliloquy. And there the Elgin Marbles lie, all night long, old Jones's lantern sometimes recalling Ulysses, or a horse's head; or sometimes a flash of gold, or a mummy's sunk yellow cheek. Plato and Shakespeare continue; and Jacob, who was reading the *Phaedrus,* heard people vociferating round the lamp-post, and the woman battering at the door and crying, "Let me in!" as if a coal had dropped from the fire, or a fly, falling from the ceiling, had lain on its back, too weak to turn over.

The *Phaedrus* is very difficult. And so, when at length one reads straight ahead, falling into step, marching on, becoming (so it seems) momentarily part of this rolling, imperturbable en-

ergy, which has driven darkness before it since Plato walked the
Acropolis, it is impossible to see to the fire.

The dialogue draws to its close. Plato's argument is done.
Plato's argument is stowed away in Jacob's mind, and for five
minutes Jacob's mind continues alone, onwards, into the darkness. Then, getting up, he parted the curtains, and saw, with astonishing clearness, how the Springetts opposite had gone to
bed; how it rained; how the Jews and the foreign woman, at the
end of the street, stood by the pillar-box, arguing.

EVERY TIME the door opened and fresh people came in, those
already in the room shifted slightly; those who were standing
looked over their shoulders; those who were sitting stopped in
the middle of sentences. What with the light, the wine, the
strumming of a guitar, something exciting happened each time
the door opened. Who was coming in?

"That's Gibson."

"The painter?"

"But go on with what you were saying."

They were saying something that was far, far too intimate
to be said outright. But the noise of the voices served like a clapper in little Mrs. Withers's mind, scaring into the air flocks of
small birds, and then they'd settle, and then she'd feel afraid, put
one hand to her hair, bind both round her knees, and look up
at Oliver Skelton nervously, and say:

"Promise, *promise,* you'll tell no one." . . . so considerate he
was, so tender. It was her husband's character that she discussed. He was cold, she said.

Down upon them came the splendid Magdalen, brown,
warm, voluminous, scarcely brushing the grass with her san-
dalled feet. Her hair flew; pins seemed scarcely to attach the flying silks. An actress of course, a line of light perpetually beneath

her. It was only "My dear" that she said, but her voice went
jodelling between Alpine passes. And down she tumbled on the
floor, and sang, since there was nothing to be said, round ah's
and oh's. Mangin, the poet, coming up to her, stood looking
down at her, drawing at his pipe. The dancing began.

Grey-haired Mrs. Keymer asked Dick Graves to tell her
who Mangin was, and said that she had seen too much of this
sort of thing in Paris (Magdalen had got upon his knees; now
his pipe was in her mouth) to be shocked. "Who is that?" she
said, staying her glasses when they came to Jacob, for indeed he
looked quiet, not indifferent, but like some one on a beach,
watching.

"Oh, my dear, let me lean on you," gasped Helen Askew,
hopping on one foot, for the silver cord round her ankle had
worked loose. Mrs. Keymer turned and looked at the picture on
the wall.

"Look at Jacob," said Helen (they were binding his eyes for
some game).

And Dick Graves, being a little drunk, very faithful, and
very simple-minded, told her that he thought Jacob the greatest
man he had ever known. And down they sat cross-legged upon
cushions and talked about Jacob, and Helen's voice trembled,
for they both seemed heroes to her, and the friendship between
them so much more beautiful than women's friendships. Anthony Pollett now asked her to dance, and as she danced she
looked at them, over her shoulder, standing at the table, drinking together.

THE MAGNIFICENT world—the live, sane, vigorous world. . . .
These words refer to the stretch of wood pavement between
Hammersmith and Holborn in January between two and three
in the morning. That was the ground beneath Jacob's feet. It
was healthy and magnificent because one room, above a mews,

somewhere near the river, contained fifty excited, talkative, friendly people. And then to stride over the pavement (there was scarcely a cab or policeman in sight) is of itself exhilarating. The long loop of Piccadilly, diamond-stitched, shows to best advantage when it is empty. A young man has nothing to fear. On the contrary, though he may not have said anything brilliant, he feels pretty confident he can hold his own. He was pleased to have met Mangin; he admired the young woman on the floor; he liked them all; he liked that sort of thing. In short, all the drums and trumpets were sounding. The street scavengers were the only people about at the moment. It is scarcely necessary to say how well-disposed Jacob felt towards them; how it pleased him to let himself in with his latch-key at his own door; how he seemed to bring back with him into the empty room ten or eleven people whom he had not known when he set out; how he looked about for something to read, and found it, and never read it, and fell asleep.

INDEED, DRUMS and trumpets is no phrase. Indeed, Piccadilly and Holborn, and the empty sitting-room and the sitting-room with fifty people in it are liable at any moment to blow music into the air. Women perhaps are more excitable than men. It is seldom that any one says anything about it, and to see the hordes crossing Waterloo Bridge to catch the non-stop to Surbiton one might think that reason impelled them. No, no. It is the drums and trumpets. Only, should you turn aside into one of those little bays on Waterloo Bridge to think the matter over, it will probably seem to you all a muddle — all a mystery.

They cross the Bridge incessantly. Sometimes in the midst of carts and omnibuses a lorry will appear with great forest trees chained to it. Then, perhaps, a mason's van with newly lettered tombstones recording how some one loved some one who is buried at Putney. Then the motor car in front jerks forward, and

the tombstones pass too quick for you to read more. All the
time the stream of people never ceases passing from the Surrey
side to the Strand; from the Strand to the Surrey side. It seems
as if the poor had gone raiding the town, and now trapesed back
to their own quarters, like beetles scurrying to their holes, for
that old woman fairly hobbles towards Waterloo, grasping a
shiny bag, as if she had been out into the light and now made
off with some scraped chicken bones to her hovel underground.
On the other hand, though the wind is rough and blowing in
their faces, those girls there, striding hand in hand, shouting out
a song, seem to feel neither cold nor shame. They are hatless.
They triumph.

The wind has blown up the waves. The river races beneath
us, and the men standing on the barges have to lean all their
weight on the tiller. A black tarpaulin is tied down over a
swelling load of gold. Avalanches of coal glitter blackly. As
usual, painters are slung on planks across the great riverside hotels, and the hotel windows have already points of light in them.
On the other side the city is white as if with age; St. Paul's swells
white above the fretted, pointed, or oblong buildings beside it.
The cross alone shines rosy-gilt. But what century have we
reached? Has this procession from the Surrey side to the Strand
gone on for ever? That old man has been crossing the Bridge
these six hundred years, with the rabble of little boys at his heels,
for he is drunk, or blind with misery, and tied round with old
clouts of clothing such as pilgrims might have worn. He shuffles
on. No one stands still. It seems as if we marched to the sound
of music; perhaps the wind and the river; perhaps these same
drums and trumpets—the ecstasy and hubbub of the soul. Why,
even the unhappy laugh, and the policeman, far from judging
the drunk man, surveys him humorously, and the little boys
scamper back again, and the clerk from Somerset House has
nothing but tolerance for him, and the man who is reading half

a page of *Lothair* at the bookstall muses charitably, with his eyes off the print, and the girl hesitates at the crossing and turns on him the bright yet vague glance of the young.

Bright yet vague. She is perhaps twenty-two. She is shabby. She crosses the road and looks at the daffodils and the red tulips in the florist's window. She hesitates, and makes off in the direction of Temple Bar. She walks fast, and yet anything distracts her. Now she seems to see, and now to notice nothing.

TEN

THROUGH THE disused graveyard in the parish of St. Pancras, Fanny Elmer strayed between the white tombs which lean against the wall, crossing the grass to read a name, hurrying on when the grave-keeper approached, hurrying into the street, pausing now by a window with blue china, now quickly making up for lost time, abruptly entering a baker's shop, buying rolls, adding cakes, going on again so that any one wishing to follow must fairly trot. She was not drably shabby, though. She wore silk stockings, and silver-buckled shoes, only the red feather in her hat drooped, and the clasp of her bag was weak, for out fell a copy of Madame Tussaud's programme as she walked. She had the ankles of a stag. Her face was hidden. Of course, in this dusk, rapid movements, quick glances, and soaring hopes come naturally enough. She passed right beneath Jacob's window.

THE HOUSE was flat, dark, and silent. Jacob was at home engaged upon a chess problem, the board being on a stool between his knees. One hand was fingering the hair at the back of his head. He slowly brought it forward and raised the white queen from her square; then put her down again on the same spot. He filled his pipe; ruminated; moved two pawns; advanced the white knight; then ruminated with one finger upon the bishop. Now Fanny Elmer passed beneath the window.

She was on her way to sit to Nick Bramham the painter.

SHE SAT IN a flowered Spanish shawl, holding in her hand a yellow novel.

"A little lower, a little looser, so—better, that's right," Bramham mumbled, who was drawing her, and smoking at the same time, and was naturally speechless. His head might have been the work of a sculptor, who had squared the forehead, stretched the mouth, and left marks of his thumbs and streaks from his fingers in the clay. But the eyes had never been shut. They were rather prominent, and rather bloodshot, as if from staring and staring, and when he spoke they looked for a second disturbed, but went on staring. An unshaded electric light hung above her head.

As for the beauty of women, it is like the light on the sea, never constant to a single wave. They all have it; they all lose it. Now she is dull and thick as bacon; now transparent as a hanging glass. The fixed faces are the dull ones. Here comes Lady Venice displayed like a monument for admiration, but carved in alabaster, to be set on the mantelpiece and never dusted. A dapper brunette complete from head to foot serves only as an illustration to lie upon the drawing-room table. The women in the streets have the faces of playing cards; the outlines accurately filled in with pink or yellow, and the line drawn tightly round them. Then, at a top-floor window, leaning out, looking down, you see beauty itself; or in the corner of an omnibus; or squatted in a ditch—beauty glowing, suddenly expressive, withdrawn the moment after. No one can count on it or seize it or have it wrapped in paper. Nothing is to be won from the shops, and Heaven knows it would be better to sit at home than haunt the plate-glass windows in the hope of lifting the shining green, the glowing ruby, out of them alive. Sea glass in a saucer loses its lustre no sooner than silks do. Thus if you talk of a beautiful woman you mean only something flying fast which for a second uses the eyes, lips, or cheeks of Fanny Elmer, for example, to glow through.

She was not beautiful, as she sat stiffly; her underlip too prominent; her nose too large; her eyes too near together. She was a thin girl, with brilliant cheeks and dark hair, sulky just now, or stiff with sitting. When Bramham snapped his stick of charcoal she started. Bramham was out of temper. He squatted before the gas fire warming his hands. Meanwhile she looked at his drawing. He grunted. Fanny threw on a dressing-gown and boiled a kettle.

"By God, it's bad," said Bramham.

Fanny dropped on to the floor, clasped her hands round her knees, and looked at him, her beautiful eyes—yes, beauty, flying through the room, shone there for a second. Fanny's eyes seemed to question, to commiserate, to be, for a second, love itself. But she exaggerated. Bramham noticed nothing. And when the kettle boiled, up she scrambled, more like a colt or a puppy than a loving woman.

Now Jacob walked over to the window and stood with his hands in his pockets. Mr. Springett opposite came out, looked at his shop window, and went in again. The children drifted past, eyeing the pink sticks of sweetstuff. Pickford's van swung down the street. A small boy twirled from a rope. Jacob turned away. Two minutes later he opened the front door, and walked off in the direction of Holborn.

Fanny Elmer took down her cloak from the hook. Nick Bramham unpinned his drawing and rolled it under his arm.

They turned out the lights and set off down the street, holding on their way through all the people, motor cars, omnibuses, carts, until they reached Leicester Square, five minutes before Jacob reached it, for his way was slightly longer, and he had been stopped by a block in Holborn waiting to see the King drive by, so that Nick and Fanny were already leaning over the barrier in the promenade at the Empire when Jacob pushed through the swing doors and took his place beside them.

"Hullo, never noticed you," said Nick, five minutes later.

"Bloody rot," said Jacob.

"Miss Elmer," said Nick.

Jacob took his pipe out of his mouth very awkwardly.

Very awkward he was. And when they sat upon a plush sofa and let the smoke go up between them and the stage, and heard far off the high-pitched voices and the jolly orchestra breaking in opportunely he was still awkward, only Fanny thought: "What a beautiful voice!" She thought how little he said yet how firm it was. She thought how young men are dignified and aloof, and how unconscious they are, and how quietly one might sit beside Jacob and look at him. And how childlike he would be, come in tired of an evening, she thought, and how majestic; a little overbearing perhaps; "But I wouldn't give way," she thought. He got up and leant over the barrier. The smoke hung about him.

And for ever the beauty of young men seems to be set in smoke, however lustily they chase footballs, or drive cricket balls, dance, run, or stride along roads. Possibly they are soon to lose it. Possibly they look into the eyes of faraway heroes, and take their station among us half contemptuously, she thought (vibrating like a fiddle-string, to be played on and snapped). Anyhow, they love silence, and speak beautifully, each word falling like a disc new cut, not a hubble-bubble of small smooth coins such as girls use; and they move decidedly, as if they knew how long to stay and when to go—oh, but Mr. Flanders was only gone to get a programme.

"The dancers come right at the end," he said, coming back to them.

And isn't it pleasant, Fanny went on thinking, how young men bring out lots of silver coins from their trouser pockets, and look at them, instead of having just so many in a purse?

Then there she was herself, whirling across the stage in white flounces, and the music was the dance and fling of her own soul, and the whole machinery, rock and gear of the world was spun smoothly into those swift eddies and falls, she felt, as she stood rigid leaning over the barrier two feet from Jacob Flanders.

Her screwed-up black glove dropped to the floor. When Jacob gave it her, she started angrily. For never was there a more irrational passion. And Jacob was afraid of her for a moment— so violent, so dangerous is it when young women stand rigid; grasp the barrier; fall in love.

It was the middle of February. The roofs of Hampstead Garden Suburb lay in a tremulous haze. It was too hot to walk. A dog barked, barked, barked down in the hollow. The liquid shadows went over the plain.

The body after long illness is languid, passive, receptive of sweetness, but too weak to contain it. The tears well and fall as the dog barks in the hollow, the children skim after hoops, the country darkens and brightens. Beyond a veil it seems. Ah, but draw the veil thicker lest I faint with sweetness, Fanny Elmer sighed, as she sat on a bench in Judges Walk looking at Hampstead Garden Suburb. But the dog went on barking. The motor cars hooted on the road. She heard a far-away rush and humming. Agitation was at her heart. Up she got and walked. The grass was freshly green; the sun hot. All round the pond children were stooping to launch little boats; or were drawn back screaming by their nurses.

At mid-day young women walk out into the air. All the men are busy in the town. They stand by the edge of the blue pond. The fresh wind scatters the children's voices all about. *My* children, thought Fanny Elmer. The women stand round the pond, beating off great prancing shaggy dogs. Gently the baby is rocked in the perambulator. The eyes of all the nurses, mothers, and wandering women are a little glazed, absorbed. They gently nod instead of answering when the little boys tug at their skirts, begging them to move on.

And Fanny moved, hearing some cry—a workman's whistle perhaps—high in mid-air. Now, among the trees, it was the thrush trilling out into the warm air a flutter of jubilation, but fear seemed to spur him, Fanny thought; as if he too were anxious with such joy at his heart—as if he were watched as he sang, and pressed by tumult to sing. There! Restless, he flew to the next tree. She heard his song more faintly. Beyond it was the humming of the wheels and the wind rushing.

SHE SPENT tenpence on lunch.

"Dear, miss, she's left her umbrella," grumbled the mottled woman in the glass box near the door at the Express Dairy Company's shop.

"Perhaps I'll catch her," answered Milly Edwards, the waitress with the pale plaits of hair; and she dashed through the door.

"No good," she said, coming back a moment later with Fanny's cheap umbrella. She put her hand to her plaits.

"Oh, that door!" grumbled the cashier.

Her hands were cased in black mittens, and the finger-tips that drew in the paper slips were swollen as sausages.

"Pie and greens for one. Large coffee and crumpets. Eggs on toast. Two fruit cakes."

Thus the sharp voices of the waitresses snapped. The lunchers heard their orders repeated with approval; saw the next table served with anticipation. Their own eggs on toast were at last delivered. Their eyes strayed no more.

Damp cubes of pastry fell into mouths opened like triangular bags.

Nelly Jenkinson, the typist, crumbled her cake indifferently enough. Every time the door opened she looked up. What did she expect to see?

The coal merchant read the *Telegraph* without stopping, missed the saucer, and, feeling abstractedly, put the cup down on the table-cloth.

"Did you ever hear the like of that for impertinence?" Mrs. Parsons wound up, brushing the crumbs from her furs.

"Hot milk and scone for one. Pot of tea. Roll and butter," cried the waitresses.

The door opened and shut.

SUCH IS the life of the elderly.

It is curious, lying in a boat, to watch the waves. Here are three coming regularly one after another, all much of a size. Then, hurrying after them comes a fourth, very large and menacing; it lifts the boat; on it goes; somehow merges without accomplishing anything; flattens itself out with the rest.

What can be more violent than the fling of boughs in a gale, the tree yielding itself all up the trunk, to the very tip of the branch, streaming and shuddering the way the wind blows, yet never flying in dishevelment away?

The corn squirms and abases itself as if preparing to tug itself free from the roots, and yet is tied down.

Why, from the very windows, even in the dusk, you see a

swelling run through the street, an aspiration, as with arms out-stretched, eyes desiring, mouths agape. And then we peaceably subside. For if the exaltation lasted we should be blown like foam into the air. The stars would shine through us. We should go down the gale in salt drops — as sometimes happens. For the impetuous spirits will have none of this cradling. Never any swaying or aimlessly lolling for them. Never any making believe, or lying cosily, or genially supposing that one is much like an-other, fire warm, wine pleasant, extravagance a sin.

"People are so nice, once you know them."

"I couldn't think ill of her. One must remember——" But Nick perhaps, or Fanny Elmer, believing implicitly in the truth of the moment, fling off, sting the cheek, are gone like sharp hail.

"OH," SAID FANNY, bursting into the studio three-quarters of an hour late because she had been hanging about the neigh-bourhood of the Foundling Hospital merely for the chance of seeing Jacob walk down the street, take out his latch-key, and open the door, "I'm afraid I'm late"; upon which Nick said nothing and Fanny grew defiant.

"I'll never come again!" she cried at length.

"Don't, then," Nick replied, and off she ran without so much as good-night.

HOW EXQUISITE it was — that dress in Evelina's shop off Shaftesbury Avenue! It was four o'clock on a fine day early in April, and was Fanny the one to spend four o'clock on a fine day indoors? Other girls in that very street sat over ledgers, or drew long threads wearily between silk and gauze; or, festooned with ribbons in Swan and Edgars, rapidly added up pence and farthings on the back of the bill and twisted the yard and three-quarters in tissue paper and asked "Your pleasure?" of the next comer.

In Evelina's shop off Shaftesbury Avenue the parts of a woman were shown separate. In the left hand was her skirt. Twining round a pole in the middle was a feather boa. Ranged like the heads of malefactors on Temple Bar were hats—emerald and white, lightly wreathed or drooping beneath deep-dyed feathers. And on the carpet were her feet—pointed gold, or patent leather slashed with scarlet.

Feasted upon by the eyes of women, the clothes by four o'clock were flyblown like sugar cakes in a baker's window. Fanny eyed them too.

But coming along Gerrard Street was a tall man in a shabby coat. A shadow fell across Evelina's window—Jacob's shadow, though it was not Jacob. And Fanny turned and walked along Gerrard Street and wished that she had read books. Nick never read books, never talked of Ireland, or the House of Lords; and as for his finger-nails! She would learn Latin and read Virgil. She had been a great reader. She had read Scott; she had read Dumas. At the Slade no one read. But no one knew Fanny at the Slade, or guessed how empty it seemed to her; the passion for ear-rings, for dances, for Tonks and Steer—when it was only the French who could paint, Jacob said. For the moderns were futile; painting the least respectable of the arts; and why read anything but Marlowe and Shakespeare, Jacob said, and Fielding if you must read novels?

"Fielding," said Fanny, when the man in Charing Cross Road asked her what book she wanted.

She bought *Tom Jones*.

At ten o'clock in the morning, in a room which she shared with a school teacher, Fanny Elmer read *Tom Jones*—that mystic book. For this dull stuff (Fanny thought) about people with odd names is what Jacob likes. Good people like it. Dowdy women who don't mind how they cross their legs read *Tom Jones*—a mystic book; for there is something, Fanny thought, about books which if I had been educated I could have liked—much better than ear-rings and flowers, she sighed, thinking of the corridors at the Slade and the fancy-dress dance next week. She had nothing to wear.

They are real, thought Fanny Elmer, setting her feet on the mantelpiece. Some people are. Nick perhaps, only he was so stupid. And women never—except Miss Sargent, but she went off at lunch-time and gave herself airs. There they sat quietly of a night reading, she thought. Not going to music-halls; not looking in at shop windows; not wearing each other's clothes, like Robertson who had worn her shawl, and she had worn his waistcoat, which Jacob could only do very awkwardly; for he liked *Tom Jones*.

There it lay on her lap, in double columns, price three and sixpence; the mystic book in which Henry Fielding ever so many years ago rebuked Fanny Elmer for feasting on scarlet, in perfect prose, Jacob said. For he never read modern novels. He liked *Tom Jones*.

"I do like *Tom Jones*," said Fanny, at five-thirty that same day early in April when Jacob took out his pipe in the arm-chair opposite.

Alas, women lie! But not Clara Durrant. A flawless mind; a candid nature; a virgin chained to a rock (somewhere off Lowndes Square) eternally pouring out tea for old men in white waistcoats, blue-eyed, looking you straight in the face, playing Bach. Of all women, Jacob honoured her most. But to sit at a table with bread and butter, with dowagers in velvet, and never say more to Clara Durrant than Benson said to the parrot when old Miss Perry poured out tea, was an insufferable outrage upon the liberties and decencies of human nature—or words to that effect. For Jacob said nothing. Only he glared at the fire. Fanny laid down *Tom Jones*.

She stitched or knitted.

"What's that?" asked Jacob.

"For the dance at the Slade."

And she fetched her head-dress; her trousers; her shoes with red tassels. What should she wear?

"I shall be in Paris," said Jacob.

And what is the point of fancy-dress dances? thought Fanny. You meet the same people; you wear the same clothes; Mangin gets drunk; Florinda sits on his knee. She flirts outrageously—with Nick Bramham just now.

"In Paris?" said Fanny.

"On my way to Greece," he replied.

For, he said, there is nothing so detestable as London in May.

He would forget her.

A sparrow flew past the window trailing a straw—a straw from a stack stood by a barn in a farmyard. The old brown spaniel snuffs at the base for a rat. Already the upper branches of the elm trees are blotted with nests. The chestnuts have flirted their fans. And the butterflies are flaunting across the rides in the Forest. Perhaps the Purple Emperor is feasting, as Morris says, upon a mass of putrid carrion at the base of an oak tree.

Fanny thought it all came from *Tom Jones*. He could go alone with a book in his pocket and watch the badgers. He would take a train at eight-thirty and walk all night. He saw fire-flies, and brought back glow-worms in pill-boxes. He would hunt with the New Forest Staghounds. It all came from *Tom Jones;* and he would go to Greece with a book in his pocket and forget her.

She fetched her hand-glass. There was her face. And suppose one wreathed Jacob in a turban? There was his face. She lit the lamp. But as the daylight came through the window only half was lit up by the lamp. And though he looked terrible and magnificent and would chuck the Forest, he said, and come to the Slade, and be a Turkish knight or a Roman emperor (and he let her blacken his lips and clenched his teeth and scowled in the glass), still—there lay *Tom Jones*.

ELEVEN

"ARCHER," SAID Mrs. Flanders with that tenderness which mothers so often display towards their eldest sons, "will be at Gibraltar to-morrow."

The post for which she was waiting (strolling up Dods Hill while the random church bells swung a hymn tune about her head, the clock striking four straight through the circling notes; the glass purpling under a storm-cloud; and the two dozen houses of the village cowering, infinitely humble, in company under a leaf of shadow), the post, with all its variety of messages, envelopes addressed in bold hands, in slanting hands, stamped now with English stamps, again with Colonial stamps, or sometimes hastily dabbed with a yellow bar, the post was about to scatter a myriad messages over the world. Whether we gain or not by this habit of profuse communication it is not for us to say. But that letter-writing is practised mendaciously nowadays, particularly by young men travelling in foreign parts, seems likely enough.

For example, take this scene.

Here was Jacob Flanders gone abroad and staying to break his journey in Paris. (Old Miss Birkbeck, his mother's cousin, had died last June and left him a hundred pounds.)

"YOU NEEDN'T repeat the whole damned thing over again, Cruttendon," said Mallinson, the little bald painter who was sitting at a marble table, splashed with coffee and ringed with wine, talking very fast, and undoubtedly more than a little drunk.

"Well, Flanders, finished writing to your lady?" said Cruttendon, as Jacob came and took his seat beside them, holding in his hand an envelope addressed to Mrs. Flanders, near Scarborough, England.

"Do you uphold Velasquez?" said Cruttendon.

"By God, he does," said Mallinson.

"He always gets like this," said Cruttendon irritably.

Jacob looked at Mallinson with excessive composure.

"I'll tell you the three greatest things that were ever written in the whole of literature," Cruttendon burst out. " 'Hang there like fruit my soul,' " he began. . . .

"Don't listen to a man who don't like Velasquez," said Mallinson.

"Adolphe, don't give Mr. Mallinson any more wine," said Cruttendon.

"Fair play, fair play," said Jacob judicially. "Let a man get drunk if he likes. That's Shakespeare, Cruttendon. I'm with you there. Shakespeare had more guts than all these damned frogs put together. 'Hang there like fruit my soul,' " he began quoting, in a musical rhetorical voice, flourishing his wine-glass. "The devil damn you black, you cream-faced loon!" he exclaimed as the wine washed over the rim.

" 'Hang there like fruit my soul,' " Cruttendon and Jacob both began again at the same moment, and both burst out laughing.

"Curse these flies," said Mallinson, flicking at his bald head. "What do they take me for?"

"Something sweet-smelling," said Cruttendon.

"Shut up, Cruttendon," said Jacob. "The fellow has no manners," he explained to Mallinson very politely. "Wants to cut people off their drink. Look here. I want grilled bone. What's the French for grilled bone? Grilled bone, Adolphe. Now you juggins, don't you understand?"

"And I'll tell you, Flanders, the second most beautiful thing in the whole of literature," said Cruttendon, bringing his feet down on to the floor, and leaning right across the table, so that his face almost touched Jacob's face.

"'Hey diddle diddle, the cat and the fiddle,'" Mallinson interrupted, strumming his fingers on the table. "The most ex-qui-sitely beautiful thing in the whole of literature. . . . Cruttendon is a very good fellow," he remarked confidentially. "But he's a bit of a fool." And he jerked his head forward.

WELL, NOT A word of this was ever told to Mrs. Flanders; nor what happened when they paid the bill and left the restaurant, and walked along the Boulevard Raspaille.

Then here is another scrap of conversation; the time about eleven in the morning; the scene a studio; and the day Sunday.

"I tell you, Flanders," said Cruttendon, "I'd as soon have one of Mallinson's little pictures as a Chardin. And when I say that . . ." he squeezed the tail of an emaciated tube . . . "Chardin was a great swell. . . . He sells 'em to pay his dinner now. But wait till the dealers get hold of him. A great swell—oh, a very great swell."

"It's an awfully pleasant life," said Jacob, "messing away up here. Still, it's a stupid art, Cruttendon." He wandered off across the room. "There's this man, Pierre Louÿs now." He took up a book.

"Now my good sir, are you going to settle down?" said Cruttendon.

"That's a solid piece of work," said Jacob, standing a canvas on a chair.

"Oh, that I did ages ago," said Cruttendon, looking over his shoulder.

"You're a pretty competent painter in my opinion," said Jacob after a time.

"Now if you'd like to see what I'm after at the present moment," said Cruttendon, putting a canvas before Jacob. "There. That's it. That's more like it. That's . . ." he squirmed his thumb in a circle round a lamp globe painted white.

"A pretty solid piece of work," said Jacob, straddling his legs in front of it. "But what I wish you'd explain . . ."

MISS JINNY CARSLAKE, pale, freckled, morbid, came into the room.

"Oh Jinny, here's a friend. Flanders. An Englishman. Wealthy. Highly connected. Go on, Flanders. . . ."

Jacob said nothing.

"It's *that*—that's not right," said Jinny Carslake.

"No," said Cruttendon decidedly. "Can't be done."

He took the canvas off the chair and stood it on the floor with its back to them.

"Sit down, ladies and gentlemen. Miss Carslake comes from your part of the world, Flanders. From Devonshire. Oh, I thought you said Devonshire. Very well. She's a daughter of the church too. The black sheep of the family. Her mother writes her such letters. I say—have you one about you? It's generally Sundays they come. Sort of church-bell effect, you know."

"Have you met all the painter men?" said Jinny. "Was Mallinson drunk? If you go to his studio he'll give you one of his pictures. I say, Teddy . . ."

"Half a jiff," said Cruttendon. "What's the season of the year?" He looked out of the window.

"We take a day off on Sundays, Flanders."

"Will he . . ." said Jinny, looking at Jacob. "You . . ."

"Yes, he'll come with us," said Cruttendon.

———

AND THEN, here is Versailles.

Jinny stood on the stone rim and leant over the pond, clasped by Cruttendon's arms or she would have fallen in. "There! There!" she cried. "Right up to the top!" Some sluggish, sloping-shouldered fish had floated up from the depths to nip her crumbs. "You look," she said, jumping down. And then the dazzling white water, rough and throttled, shot up into the air. The fountain spread itself. Through it came the sound of military music far away. All the water was puckered with drops. A blue air-ball gently bumped the surface. How all the nurses and children and old men and young crowded to the edge, leant over and waved their sticks! The little girl ran stretching her arms towards her air-ball, but it sank beneath the fountain.

Edward Cruttendon, Jinny Carslake, and Jacob Flanders walked in a row along the yellow gravel path; got on to the grass; so passed under the trees; and came out at the summer-house where Marie Antoinette used to drink chocolate. In went Edward and Jinny, but Jacob waited outside, sitting on the handle of his walking-stick. Out they came again.

"Well?" said Cruttendon, smiling at Jacob.

Jinny waited; Edward waited; and both looked at Jacob.

"Well?" said Jacob, smiling and pressing both hands on his stick.

"Come along," he decided; and started off. The others followed him, smiling.

AND THEN they went to the little café in the by-street where people sit drinking coffee, watching the soldiers, meditatively knocking ashes into trays.

"But he's quite different," said Jinny, folding her hands over the top of her glass. "I don't suppose you know what Ted means when he says a thing like that," she said, looking at Jacob. "But I do. Sometimes I could kill myself. Sometimes he lies in bed all day long—just lies there. . . . I don't want you right on the table"; she waved her hands. Swollen iridescent pigeons were waddling round their feet.

"Look at that woman's hat," said Cruttendon. "How do they come to think of it? . . . No, Flanders, I don't think I could live like you. When one walks down that street opposite the British Museum—what's it called?—that's what I mean. It's all like that. Those fat women—and the man standing in the middle of the road as if he were going to have a fit . . ."

"Everybody feeds them," said Jinny, waving the pigeons away. "They're stupid old things."

"Well, I don't know," said Jacob, smoking his cigarette. "There's St. Paul's."

"I mean going to an office," said Cruttendon.

"Hang it all," Jacob expostulated.

"But you don't count," said Jinny, looking at Cruttendon. "You're mad. I mean, you just think of painting."

"Yes, I know. I can't help it. I say, will King George give way about the peers?"

"He'll jolly well have to," said Jacob.

"There!" said Jinny. "He really knows."

"You see, I would if I could," said Cruttendon, "but I simply can't."

"I *think* I could," said Jinny. "Only, it's all the people one dislikes who do it. At home, I mean. They talk of nothing else. Even people like my mother."

"Now if I came and lived here——" said Jacob. "What's my share, Cruttendon? Oh, very well. Have it your own way. Those silly birds, directly one wants them—they've flown away."

AND FINALLY under the arc lamps in the Gare des Invalides, with one of those queer movements which are so slight yet so definite, which may wound or pass unnoticed but generally in-

flict a good deal of discomfort, Jinny and Cruttendon drew together; Jacob stood apart. They had to separate. Something
must be said. Nothing was said. A man wheeled a trolley past
Jacob's legs so near that he almost grazed them. When Jacob recovered his balance the other two were turning away, though
Jinny looked over her shoulder, and Cruttendon, waving his
hand, disappeared like the very great genius that he was.

NO—MRS. FLANDERS was told none of this, though Jacob
felt, it is safe to say, that nothing in the world was of greater importance; and as for Cruttendon and Jinny, he thought them the
most remarkable people he had ever met—being of course unable to foresee how it fell out in the course of time that Cruttendon took to painting orchards; had therefore to live in Kent;
and must, one would think, see through apple blossom by this
time, since his wife, for whose sake he did it, eloped with a novelist; but no; Cruttendon still paints orchards, savagely, in solitude.
Then Jinny Carslake, after her affair with Lefanu the American
painter, frequented Indian philosophers, and now you find her
in pensions in Italy cherishing a little jeweller's box containing
ordinary pebbles picked off the road. But if you look at them
steadily, she says, multiplicity becomes unity, which is somehow
the secret of life, though it does not prevent her from following
the macaroni as it goes round the table, and sometimes, on
spring nights, she makes the strangest confidences to shy young
Englishmen.

Jacob had nothing to hide from his mother. It was only that
he could make no sense himself of his extraordinary excitement,
and as for writing it down——

"JACOB'S LETTERS are so like him," said Mrs. Jarvis, folding the
sheet.

"Indeed he seems to be having . . ." said Mrs. Flanders, and paused, for she was cutting out a dress and had to straighten the pattern, ". . . a very gay time."

Mrs. Jarvis thought of Paris. At her back the window was open, for it was a mild night; a calm night; when the moon seemed muffled and the apple trees stood perfectly still.

"I never pity the dead," said Mrs. Jarvis, shifting the cushion at her back, and clasping her hands behind her head. Betty Flanders did not hear, for her scissors made so much noise on the table.

"They are at rest," said Mrs. Jarvis. "And we spend our days doing foolish unnecessary things without knowing why."

Mrs. Jarvis was not liked in the village.

"You never walk at this time of night?" she asked Mrs. Flanders.

"It is certainly wonderfully mild," said Mrs. Flanders.

Yet it was years since she had opened the orchard gate and gone out on Dods Hill after dinner.

"It is perfectly dry," said Mrs. Jarvis, as they shut the orchard door and stepped on to the turf.

"I shan't go far," said Betty Flanders. "Yes, Jacob will leave Paris on Wednesday."

"Jacob was always my friend of the three," said Mrs. Jarvis.

"Now, my dear, I am going no further," said Mrs. Flanders. They had climbed the dark hill and reached the Roman camp.

The rampart rose at their feet—the smooth circle surrounding the camp or the grave. How many needles Betty Flanders had lost there! and her garnet brooch.

"It is much clearer than this sometimes," said Mrs. Jarvis, standing upon the ridge. There were no clouds, and yet there was a haze over the sea, and over the moors. The lights of Scarborough flashed, as if a woman wearing a diamond necklace turned her head this way and that.

"How quiet it is!" said Mrs. Jarvis.

Mrs. Flanders rubbed the turf with her toe, thinking of her garnet brooch.

Mrs. Jarvis found it difficult to think of herself to-night. It was so calm. There was no wind; nothing racing, flying, escaping. Black shadows stood still over the silver moors. The furze bushes stood perfectly still. Neither did Mrs. Jarvis think of God. There was a church behind them, of course. The church clock struck ten. Did the strokes reach the furze bush, or did the thorn tree hear them?

Mrs. Flanders was stooping down to pick up a pebble. Sometimes people do find things, Mrs. Jarvis thought, and yet in this hazy moonlight it was impossible to see anything, except bones, and little pieces of chalk.

"Jacob bought it with his own money, and then I brought Mr. Parker up to see the view, and it must have dropped——" Mrs. Flanders murmured.

Did the bones stir, or the rusty swords? Was Mrs. Flanders's twopenny-halfpenny brooch for ever part of the rich accumulation? and if all the ghosts flocked thick and rubbed shoulders with Mrs. Flanders in the circle, would she not have seemed perfectly in her place, a live English matron, growing stout?

The clock struck the quarter.

The frail waves of sound broke among the stiff gorse and the hawthorn twigs as the church clock divided time into quarters.

Motionless and broad-backed the moors received the statement "It is fifteen minutes past the hour," but made no answer, unless a bramble stirred.

Yet even in this light the legends on the tombstones could be read, brief voices saying, "I am Bertha Ruck," "I am Tom Gage." And they say which day of the year they died, and the New Testament says something for them, very proud, very emphatic, or consoling.

The moors accept all that too.

The moonlight falls like a pale page upon the church wall, and illumines the kneeling family in the niche, and the tablet set up in 1780 to the Squire of the parish who relieved the poor, and believed in God—so the measured voice goes on down the marble scroll, as though it could impose itself upon time and the open air.

Now a fox steals out from behind the gorse bushes.

Often, even at night, the church seems full of people. The pews are worn and greasy, and the cassocks in place, and the hymn-books on the ledges. It is a ship with all its crew aboard. The timbers strain to hold the dead and the living, the plough-men, the carpenters, the fox-hunting gentlemen and the farmers smelling of mud and brandy. Their tongues join together in syllabling the sharp-cut words, which for ever slice asunder time and the broad-backed moors. Plaint and belief and elegy, despair and triumph, but for the most part good sense and jolly indifference, go trampling out of the windows any time these five hundred years.

Still, as Mrs. Jarvis said, stepping out on to the moors, "How quiet it is!" Quiet at midday, except when the hunt scatters across it; quiet in the afternoon, save for the drifting sheep; at night the moor is perfectly quiet.

A garnet brooch has dropped into its grass. A fox pads stealthily. A leaf turns on its edge. Mrs. Jarvis, who is fifty years of age, reposes in the camp in the hazy moonlight.

"... and," said Mrs. Flanders, straightening her back, "I never cared for Mr. Parker."

"Neither did I," said Mrs. Jarvis. They began to walk home.

But their voices floated for a little above the camp. The moonlight destroyed nothing. The moor accepted everything. Tom Gage cries aloud so long as his tombstone endures. The

Roman skeletons are in safe keeping. Betty Flanders's darning needles are safe too and her garnet brooch. And sometimes at midday, in the sunshine, the moor seems to hoard these little treasures, like a nurse. But at midnight when no one speaks or gallops, and the thorn tree is perfectly still, it would be foolish to vex the moor with questions—what? and why?

The church clock, however, strikes twelve.

Twelve

THE WATER fell off a ledge like lead—like a chain with thick white links. The train ran out into a steep green meadow, and Jacob saw striped tulips growing and heard a bird singing, in Italy.

A motor car full of Italian officers ran along the flat road and kept up with the train, raising dust behind it. There were trees laced together with vines—as Virgil said. Here was a station; and a tremendous leave-taking going on, with women in high yellow boots and odd pale boys in ringed socks. Virgil's bees had gone about the plains of Lombardy. It was the custom of the ancients to train vines between elms. Then at Milan there were sharp-winged hawks, of a bright brown, cutting figures over the roofs.

These Italian carriages get damnably hot with the afternoon sun on them, and the chances are that before the engine has pulled to the top of the gorge the clanking chain will have broken. Up, up, up, it goes, like a train on a scenic railway. Every peak is covered with sharp trees, and amazing white villages are crowded on ledges. There is always a white tower on the very summit, flat red-frilled roofs, and a sheer drop beneath. It is not a country in which one walks after tea. For one thing there is no grass. A whole hillside will be ruled with olive trees. Already in

April the earth is clotted into dry dust between them. And there are neither stiles nor footpaths, nor lanes chequered with the shadows of leaves nor eighteenth-century inns with bow-windows, where one eats ham and eggs. Oh no, Italy is all fierce-ness, bareness, exposure, and black priests shuffling along the roads. It is strange, too, how you never get away from villas.

Still, to be travelling on one's own with a hundred pounds to spend is a fine affair. And if his money gave out, as it prob-ably would, he would go on foot. He could live on bread and wine — the wine in straw bottles — for after doing Greece he was going to knock off Rome. The Roman civilization was a very inferior affair, no doubt. But Bonamy talked a lot of rot, all the same. "You ought to have been in Athens," he would say to Bonamy when he got back. "Standing on the Parthenon," he would say, or "The ruins of the Coliseum suggest some fairly sublime reflections," which he would write out at length in let-ters. It might turn to an essay upon civilization. A comparison between the ancients and moderns, with some pretty sharp hits at Mr. Asquith — something in the style of Gibbon.

A stout gentleman laboriously hauled himself in, dusty, baggy, slung with gold chains, and Jacob, regretting that he did not come of the Latin race, looked out of the window.

It is a strange reflection that by travelling two days and nights you are in the heart of Italy. Accidental villas among olive trees appear; and men-servants watering the cactuses. Black victorias drive in between pompous pillars with plaster shields stuck to them. It is at once momentary and astonish-ingly intimate — to be displayed before the eyes of a foreigner. And there is a lonely hill-top where no one ever comes, and yet it is seen by me who was lately driving down Piccadilly on an omnibus. And what I should like would be to get out among the fields, sit down and hear the grasshoppers, and take up a handful of earth—Italian earth, as this is Italian dust upon my shoes.

Jacob heard them crying strange names at railway stations through the night. The train stopped and he heard frogs croaking close by, and he wrinkled back the blind cautiously and saw a vast strange marsh all white in the moonlight. The carriage was thick with cigar smoke, which floated round the globe with the green shade on it. The Italian gentleman lay snoring with his boots off and his waistcoat unbuttoned. . . . And all this business of going to Greece seemed to Jacob an intolerable weariness—sitting in hotels by oneself and looking at monuments—he'd have done better to go to Cornwall with Timmy Durrant. . . . "O—h," Jacob protested, as the darkness began breaking in front of him and the light showed through, but the man was reaching across him to get something—the fat Italian man in his dicky, unshaven, crumpled, obese, was opening the door and going off to have a wash.

So Jacob sat up, and saw a lean Italian sportsman with a gun walking down the road in the early morning light, and the whole idea of the Parthenon came upon him in a clap.

"By Jove!" he thought, "we must be nearly there!" and he stuck his head out of the window and got the air full in his face.

It is highly exasperating that twenty-five people of your acquaintance should be able to say straight off something very much to the point about being in Greece, while for yourself there is a stopper upon all emotions whatsoever. For after washing at the hotel at Patras, Jacob had followed the tram lines a mile or so out; and followed them a mile or so back; he had met several droves of turkeys; several strings of donkeys; had got lost in back streets; had read advertisements of corsets and of Maggi's consommé; children had trodden on his toes; the place smelt of bad cheese; and he was glad to find himself suddenly come out opposite his hotel. There was an old copy of the *Daily Mail* lying among coffee-cups; which he read. But what could he do after dinner?

No doubt we should be, on the whole, much worse off than we are without our astonishing gift for illusion. At the age of twelve or so, having given up dolls and broken our steam engines, France, but much more probably Italy, and India almost for a certainty, draws the superfluous imagination. One's aunts have been to Rome; and every one has an uncle who was last heard of—poor man—in Rangoon. He will never come back any more. But it is the governesses who start the Greek myth. Look at that for a head (they say)—nose, you see, straight as a dart, curls, eyebrows—everything appropriate to manly beauty; while his legs and arms have lines on them which indicate a perfect degree of development—the Greeks caring for the body as much as for the face. And the Greeks could paint fruit so that birds pecked at it. First you read Xenophon; then Euripides. One day—that was an occasion, by God—what people have said appears to have sense in it; "the Greek spirit"; the Greek this, that, and the other; though it is absurd, by the way, to say that any Greek comes near Shakespeare. The point is, however, that we have been brought up in an illusion.

Jacob, no doubt, thought something in this fashion, the *Daily Mail* crumpled in his hand; his legs extended; the very picture of boredom.

"But it's the way we're brought up," he went on.

And it all seemed to him very distasteful. Something ought to be done about it. And from being moderately depressed he became like a man about to be executed. Clara Durrant had left him at a party to talk to an American called Pilchard. And he had come all the way to Greece and left her. They wore evening-dresses, and talked nonsense—what damned non-sense—and he put out his hand for the *Globe Trotter,* an international magazine which is supplied free of charge to the proprietors of hotels.

In spite of its ramshackle condition modern Greece is highly advanced in the electric tramway system, so that while Jacob sat in the hotel sitting-room the trams clanked, chimed, rang, rang, rang imperiously to get the donkeys out of the way, and one old woman who refused to budge, beneath the windows. The whole of civilization was being condemned.

The waiter was quite indifferent to that too. Aristotle, a dirty man, carnivorously interested in the body of the only guest now occupying the only arm-chair, came into the room ostentatiously, put something down, put something straight, and saw that Jacob was still there.

"I shall want to be called early to-morrow," said Jacob, over his shoulder. "I am going to Olympia."

This gloom, this surrender to the dark waters which lap us about, is a modern invention. Perhaps, as Cruttendon said, we do not believe enough. Our fathers at any rate had something to demolish. So have we for the matter of that, thought Jacob, crumpling the *Daily Mail* in his hand. He would go into Parliament and make fine speeches—but what use are fine speeches and Parliament, once you surrender an inch to the black waters? Indeed there has never been any explanation of the ebb and flow in our veins—of happiness and unhappiness. That respectability and evening parties where one has to dress, and wretched slums at the back of Gray's Inn—something solid, immovable, and grotesque—is at the back of it, Jacob thought probable. But then there was the British Empire which was beginning to puzzle him; nor was he altogether in favour of giving Home Rule to Ireland. What did the *Daily Mail* say about that?

———

FOR HE HAD grown to be a man, and was about to be im-
mersed in things—as indeed the chambermaid, emptying his
basin upstairs, fingering keys, studs, pencils, and bottles of
tabloids strewn on the dressing-table, was aware.

That he had grown to be a man was a fact that Florinda
knew, as she knew everything, by instinct.

And Betty Flanders even now suspected it, as she read his
letter, posted at Milan, "Telling me," she complained to Mrs.
Jarvis, "really nothing that I want to know"; but she brooded
over it.

Fanny Elmer felt it to desperation. For he would take his
stick and his hat and would walk to the window, and look perfectly absent-minded and very stern too, she thought.

"I am going," he would say, "to cadge a meal of Bonamy."

"Anyhow, I can drown myself in the Thames," Fanny cried,
as she hurried past the Foundling Hospital.

"BUT THE *Daily Mail* isn't to be trusted," Jacob said to himself,
looking about for something else to read. And he sighed again,
being indeed so profoundly gloomy that gloom must have been
lodged in him to cloud him at any moment, which was odd in
a man who enjoyed things so, was not much given to analysis,
but was horribly romantic, of course, Bonamy thought, in his
rooms in Lincoln's Inn.

"He will fall in love," thought Bonamy. "Some Greek woman
with a straight nose."

It was to Bonamy that Jacob wrote from Patras—to Bonamy
who couldn't love a woman and never read a foolish book.

There are very few good books after all, for we can't count
profuse histories, travels in mule carts to discover the sources of
the Nile, or the volubility of fiction.

I like books whose virtue is all drawn together in a page or
two. I like sentences that don't budge though armies cross them.

I like words to be hard—such were Bonamy's views, and they won him the hostility of those whose taste is all for the fresh growths of the morning, who throw up the window, and find the poppies spread in the sun, and can't forbear a shout of jubilation at the astonishing fertility of English literature. That was not Bonamy's way at all. That his taste in literature affected his friendships, and made him silent, secretive, fastidious, and only quite at his ease with one or two young men of his own way of thinking, was the charge against him.

But then Jacob Flanders was not at all of his own way of thinking—far from it, Bonamy sighed, laying the thin sheets of notepaper on the table and falling into thought about Jacob's character, not for the first time.

The trouble was this romantic vein in him. "But mixed with the stupidity which leads him into these absurd predicaments," thought Bonamy, "there is something—something"—he sighed, for he was fonder of Jacob than of any one in the world.

JACOB WENT to the window and stood with his hands in his pockets. There he saw three Greeks in kilts; the masts of ships; idle or busy people of the lower classes strolling or stepping out briskly, or falling into groups and gesticulating with their hands. Their lack of concern for him was not the cause of his gloom; but some more profound conviction—it was not that he himself happened to be lonely, but that all people are.

Yet next day, as the train slowly rounded a hill on the way to Olympia, the Greek peasant women were out among the vines; the old Greek men were sitting at the stations, sipping sweet wine. And though Jacob remained gloomy he had never suspected how tremendously pleasant it is to be alone; out of England; on one's own; cut off from the whole thing. There are very sharp bare hills on the way to Olympia; and between them blue sea in triangular spaces. A little like the Cornish coast. Well now, to go walking by oneself all day—to get on to that track and follow it up between the bushes—or are they small trees?—to the top of that mountain from which one can see half the nations of antiquity——

"Yes," said Jacob, for his carriage was empty, "let's look at the map."

Blame it or praise it, there is no denying the wild horse in us. To gallop intemperately; fall on the sand tired out; to feel the earth spin; to have—positively—a rush of friendship for stones and grasses, as if humanity were over, and as for men and women, let them go hang—there is no getting over the fact that this desire seizes us pretty often.

THE EVENING air slightly moved the dirty curtains in the hotel window at Olympia.

"I am full of love for every one," thought Mrs. Wentworth Williams, "—for the poor most of all—for the peasants coming back in the evening with their burdens. And everything is soft and vague and very sad. It is sad, it is sad. But everything has meaning," thought Sandra Wentworth Williams, raising her head a little and looking very beautiful, tragic, and exalted. "One must love everything."

She held in her hand a little book convenient for travelling—stories by Tchekov—as she stood, veiled, in white, in the window of the hotel at Olympia. How beautiful the evening was! and her beauty was its beauty. The tragedy of Greece was the tragedy of all high souls. The inevitable compromise. She seemed to have grasped something. She would write it down. And moving to the table where her husband sat reading she leant her chin in her hands and thought of the peasants, of suffering, of her own beauty, of the inevitable compromise, and of how she would write it down. Nor did Evan Williams say anything brutal, banal, or foolish when he shut his book and put it away to make room for the plates of soup which were now being placed before them. Only his drooping bloodhound eyes and his heavy sallow cheeks expressed his melancholy tolerance, his conviction that though forced to live with circumspection and deliberation he could never possibly achieve any of those objects which, as he knew, are the only ones worth pursuing. His consideration was flawless; his silence unbroken.

"Everything seems to mean so much," said Sandra. But with the sound of her own voice the spell was broken. She forgot the peasants. Only there remained with her a sense of her own beauty, and in front, luckily, there was a looking-glass.

"I am very beautiful," she thought.

She shifted her hat slightly. Her husband saw her looking in the glass; and agreed that beauty is important; it is an inheritance; one cannot ignore it. But it is a barrier; it is in fact rather a bore. So he drank his soup; and kept his eyes fixed upon the window.

"Quails," said Mrs. Wentworth Williams languidly. "And then goat, I suppose; and then . . ."

"Caramel custard presumably," said her husband in the same cadence, with his toothpick out already.

She laid her spoon upon her plate, and her soup was taken away half finished. Never did she do anything without dignity; for hers was the English type which is so Greek, save that villagers have touched their hats to it, the vicarage reveres it; and upper-gardeners and under-gardeners respectfully straighten their backs as she comes down the broad terrace on Sunday morning, dallying at the stone urns with the Prime Minister to pick a rose—which, perhaps, she was trying to forget, as her eye wandered round the dining-room of the inn at Olympia, seeking the window where her book lay, where a few minutes ago she had discovered something—something very profound it had been, about love and sadness and the peasants.

But it was Evan who sighed; not in despair nor indeed in rebellion. But, being the most ambitious of men and temperamentally the most sluggish, he had accomplished nothing; had the political history of England at his finger-ends, and living much in company with Chatham, Pitt, Burke, and Charles James Fox could not help contrasting himself and his age with them and theirs. "Yet there never was a time when great men are more needed," he was in the habit of saying to himself, with a sigh. Here he was picking his teeth in an inn at Olympia. He had done. But Sandra's eyes wandered.

"Those pink melons are sure to be dangerous," he said gloomily. And as he spoke the door opened and in came a young man in a grey check suit.

"Beautiful but dangerous," said Sandra, immediately talking to her husband in the presence of a third person. ("Ah, an English boy on tour," she thought to herself.)

And Evan knew all that too.

Yes, he knew all that; and he admired her. Very pleasant, he thought, to have affairs. But for himself, what with his height (Napoleon was five feet four, he remembered), his bulk, his inability to impose his own personality (and yet great men are needed more than ever now, he sighed), it was useless. He threw away his cigar, went up to Jacob and asked him, with a simple sort of sincerity which Jacob liked, whether he had come straight out from England.

"How very English!" Sandra laughed when the waiter told them next morning that the young gentleman had left at five to climb the mountain. "I am sure he asked you for a bath?" at which the waiter shook his head, and said that he would ask the manager.

"You do not understand," laughed Sandra. "Never mind."

STRETCHED ON the top of the mountain, quite alone, Jacob enjoyed himself immensely. Probably he had never been so happy in the whole of his life.

But at dinner that night Mr. Williams asked him whether he would like to see the paper; then Mrs. Williams asked him (as they strolled on the terrace smoking—and how could he refuse that man's cigar?) whether he'd seen the theatre by moonlight; whether he knew Everard Sherborn; whether he read Greek and whether (Evan rose silently and went in) if he had to sacrifice one it would be the French literature or the Russian?

"And now," wrote Jacob in his letter to Bonamy, "I shall have to read her cursed book"—her Tchekov, he meant, for she had lent it him.

THOUGH THE opinion is unpopular it seems likely enough that bare places, fields too thick with stones to be ploughed, tossing sea-meadows half-way between England and America, suit us better than cities.

There is something absolute in us which despises qualification. It is this which is teased and twisted in society. People come together in a room. "So delighted," says somebody, "to meet you," and that is a lie. And then: "I enjoy the spring more than the autumn now. One does, I think, as one gets older." For women are always, always, always talking about what one feels, and if they say "as one gets older," they mean you to reply with something quite off the point.

Jacob sat himself down in the quarry where the Greeks had cut marble for the theatre. It is hot work walking up Greek hills at midday. The wild red cyclamen was out; he had seen the little tortoises hobbling from clump to clump; the air smelt strong and suddenly sweet, and the sun, striking on jagged splinters of marble, was very dazzling to the eyes. Composed, commanding, contemptuous, a little melancholy, and bored with an august kind of boredom, there he sat smoking his pipe.

Bonamy would have said that this was the sort of thing that made him uneasy—when Jacob got into the doldrums, looked like a Margate fisherman out of a job, or a British Admiral. You couldn't make him understand a thing when he was in a mood like that. One had better leave him alone. He was dull. He was apt to be grumpy.

He was up very early, looking at the statues with his Baedeker.

Sandra Wentworth Williams, ranging the world before breakfast in quest of adventure or a point of view, all in white, not so very tall perhaps, but uncommonly upright—Sandra Williams got Jacob's head exactly on a level with the head of the Hermes of Praxiteles. The comparison was all in his favour. But before she could say a single word he had gone out of the Museum and left her.

Still, a lady of fashion travels with more than one dress, and if white suits the morning hour, perhaps sandy yellow with purple spots on it, a black hat, and a volume of Balzac, suit the evening. Thus she was arranged on the terrace when Jacob came in. Very beautiful she looked. With her hands folded she mused, seemed to listen to her husband, seemed to watch the peasants coming down with brushwood on their backs, seemed to notice how the hill changed from blue to black, seemed to discriminate between truth and falsehood, Jacob thought, and crossed his legs suddenly, observing the extreme shabbiness of his trousers.

"But he is very distinguished looking," Sandra decided.

And Evan Williams, lying back in his chair with the paper on his knees, envied them. The best thing he could do would be to publish, with Macmillans, his monograph upon the foreign policy of Chatham. But confound this tumid, queasy feeling— this restlessness, swelling, and heat—it was jealousy! jealousy! jealousy! which he had sworn never to feel again.

"Come with us to Corinth, Flanders," he said with more than his usual energy, stopping by Jacob's chair. He was relieved by Jacob's reply, or rather by the solid, direct, if shy manner in which he said that he would like very much to come with them to Corinth.

"Here is a fellow," thought Evan Williams, "who might do very well in politics."

"I intend to come to Greece every year so long as I live," Jacob wrote to Bonamy. "It is the only chance I can see of protecting oneself from civilization."

"Goodness knows what he means by that," Bonamy sighed. For as he never said a clumsy thing himself, these dark sayings of Jacob's made him feel apprehensive, yet somehow impressed, his own turn being all for the definite, the concrete, and the rational.

NOTHING COULD be much simpler than what Sandra said as she descended the Acro-Corinth, keeping to the little path, while Jacob strode over rougher ground by her side. She had been left motherless at the age of four; and the Park was vast.

"One never seemed able to get out of it," she laughed. Of course there was the library, and dear Mr. Jones, and notions about things. "I used to stray into the kitchen and sit upon the butler's knees," she laughed, sadly though.

Jacob thought that if he had been there he would have saved her; for she had been exposed to great dangers, he felt, and, he thought to himself, "People wouldn't understand a woman talking as she talks."

She made little of the roughness of the hill; and wore breeches, he saw, under her short skirts.

"Women like Fanny Elmer don't," he thought. "What's-her-name Carslake didn't; yet they pretend . . ."

Mrs. Williams said things straight out. He was surprised by his own knowledge of the rules of behaviour; how much more can be said than one thought; how open one can be with a woman; and how little he had known himself before.

Evan joined them on the road; and as they drove along up hill and down hill (for Greece is in a state of effervescence, yet astonishingly clean-cut, a treeless land, where you see the ground between the blades, each hill cut and shaped and out-lined as often as not against sparkling deep blue waters, islands white as sand floating on the horizon, occasional groves of palm trees standing in the valleys, which are scattered with black goats, spotted with little olive trees and sometimes have white hollows, rayed and criss-crossed, in their flanks), as they drove up hill and down he scowled in the corner of the carriage, with his paw so tightly closed that the skin was stretched between the knuckles and the little hairs stood upright. Sandra rode oppo-site, dominant, like a Victory prepared to fling into the air.

"Heartless!" thought Evan (which was untrue).

"Brainless!" he suspected (and that was not true either). "Still . . . !" He envied her.

When bedtime came the difficulty was to write to Bonamy, Jacob found. Yet he had seen Salamis, and Marathon in the dis-tance. Poor old Bonamy! No; there was something queer about it. He could not write to Bonamy.

"I SHALL GO to Athens all the same," he resolved, looking very set, with this hook dragging in his side.

The Williamses had already been to Athens.

ATHENS IS STILL quite capable of striking a young man as the oddest combination, the most incongruous assortment. Now it is suburban; now immortal. Now cheap continental jewellery is laid upon plush trays. Now the stately woman stands naked, save for a wave of drapery above the knee. No form can he set on his sensations as he strolls, one blazing afternoon, along the Parisian boulevard and skips out of the way of the royal landau which, looking indescribably ramshackle, rattles along the pitted roadway, saluted by citizens of both sexes cheaply dressed in bowler hats and continental costumes; though a shepherd in kilt, cap, and gaiters very nearly drives his herd of goats between the royal wheels; and all the time the Acropolis surges into the air, raises itself above the town, like a large immobile wave with the yellow columns of the Parthenon firmly planted upon it.

The yellow columns of the Parthenon are to be seen at all hours of the day firmly planted upon the Acropolis; though at sunset, when the ships in the Piraeus fire their guns, a bell rings, a man in uniform (the waistcoat unbuttoned) appears; and the women roll up the black stockings which they are knitting in the shadow of the columns, call to the children, and troop off down the hill back to their houses.

There they are again, the pillars, the pediment, the Temple of Victory and the Erechtheum, set on a tawny rock cleft with shadows, directly you unlatch your shutters in the morning and, leaning out, hear the clatter, the clamour, the whip cracking in the street below. There they are.

The extreme definiteness with which they stand, now a brilliant white, again yellow, and in some lights red, imposes ideas of durability, of the emergence through the earth of some spiritual energy elsewhere dissipated in elegant trifles. But this durability exists quite independently of our admiration. Although the beauty is sufficiently humane to weaken us, to stir the deep deposit of mud—memories, abandonments, regrets, sentimental devotions—the Parthenon is separate from all that; and if you consider how it has stood out all night, for centuries, you begin to connect the blaze (at midday the glare is dazzling and the frieze almost invisible) with the idea that perhaps it is beauty alone that is immortal.

Added to this, compared with the blistered stucco, the new love songs rasped out to the strum of guitar and gramophone, and the mobile yet insignificant faces of the street, the

Parthenon is really astonishing in its silent composure; which is so vigorous that, far from being decayed, the Parthenon appears, on the contrary, likely to outlast the entire world.

"AND THE GREEKS, like sensible men, never bothered to finish the backs of their statues," said Jacob, shading his eyes and observing that the side of the figure which is turned away from view is left in the rough.

He noted the slight irregularity in the line of the steps which "the artistic sense of the Greeks preferred to mathematical accuracy," he read in his guide-book.

He stood on the exact spot where the great statue of Athena used to stand, and identified the more famous landmarks of the scene beneath.

In short he was accurate and diligent; but profoundly morose. Moreover he was pestered by guides. This was on Monday.

But on Wednesday he wrote a telegram to Bonamy, telling him to come at once. And then he crumpled it in his hand and threw it in the gutter.

"For one thing he wouldn't come," he thought. "And then I daresay this sort of thing wears off." "This sort of thing" being that uneasy, painful feeling, something like selfishness—one wishes almost that the thing would stop—it is getting more and more beyond what is possible—"If it goes on much longer I shan't be able to cope with it—but if some one else were seeing it at the same time—Bonamy is stuffed in his room in Lincoln's Inn—oh, I say, damn it all, I say,"—the sight of Hymettus, Pentelicus, Lycabettus on one side, and the sea on the other, as one stands in the Parthenon at sunset, the sky pink feathered, the plain all colours, the marble tawny in one's eyes, is thus oppressive. Luckily Jacob had little sense of personal association; he seldom thought of Plato or Socrates in the flesh; on the other hand his feeling for architecture was very strong;

he preferred statues to pictures; and he was beginning to think a great deal about the problems of civilization, which were solved, of course, so very remarkably by the ancient Greeks, though their solution is no help to us. Then the hook gave a great tug in his side as he lay in bed on Wednesday night; and he turned over with a desperate sort of tumble, remembering Sandra Wentworth Williams with whom he was in love.

Next day he climbed Pentelicus.

The day after he went up to the Acropolis. The hour was early; the place almost deserted; and possibly there was thunder in the air. But the sun struck full upon the Acropolis.

Jacob's intention was to sit down and read, and, finding a drum of marble conveniently placed, from which Marathon could be seen, and yet it was in the shade, while the Erechtheum blazed white in front of him, there he sat. And after reading a page he put his thumb in his book. Why not rule countries in the way they should be ruled? And he read again.

No doubt his position there overlooking Marathon somehow raised his spirits. Or it may have been that a slow capacious brain has these moments of flowering. Or he had, insensibly, while he was abroad, got into the way of thinking about politics.

And then looking up and seeing the sharp outline, his meditations were given an extraordinary edge; Greece was over; the Parthenon in ruins; yet there he was.

(Ladies with green and white umbrellas passed through the courtyard—French ladies on their way to join their husbands in Constantinople.)

Jacob read on again. And laying the book on the ground he began, as if inspired by what he had read, to write a note upon the importance of history—upon democracy—one of those scribbles upon which the work of a lifetime may be based; or again, it falls out of a book twenty years later, and one can't remember a word of it. It is a little painful. It had better be burnt.

Jacob wrote; began to draw a straight nose; when all the French ladies opening and shutting their umbrellas just beneath him exclaimed, looking at the sky, that one did not know what to expect—rain or fine weather?

Jacob got up and strolled across to the Erechtheum. There are still several women standing there holding the roof on their heads. Jacob straightened himself slightly; for stability and balance affect the body first. These statues annulled things so! He stared at them, then turned, and there was Madame Lucien Gravé perched on a block of marble with her kodak pointed at his head. Of course she jumped down, in spite of her age, her figure, and her tight boots—having, now that her daughter was married, lapsed with a luxurious abandonment, grand enough in its way, into the fleshy grotesque; she jumped down, but not before Jacob had seen her.

"Damn these women—damn these women!" he thought. And he went to fetch his book which he had left lying on the ground in the Parthenon.

"How they spoil things," he murmured, leaning against one of the pillars, pressing his book tight between his arm and his side. (As for the weather, no doubt the storm would break soon; Athens was under cloud.)

"It is those damned women," said Jacob, without any trace of bitterness, but rather with sadness and disappointment that what might have been should never be.

(This violent disillusionment is generally to be expected in young men in the prime of life, sound of wind and limb, who will soon become fathers of families and directors of banks.)

Then, making sure that the Frenchwomen had gone, and looking cautiously round him, Jacob strolled over to the Erechtheum and looked rather furtively at the goddess on the left-hand side holding the roof on her head. She reminded him of Sandra Wentworth Williams. He looked at her, then looked

away. He looked at her, then looked away. He was extraordinarily moved, and with the battered Greek nose in his head, with
Sandra in his head, with all sorts of things in his head, off he
started to walk right up to the top of Mount Hymettus, alone,
in the heat.

THAT VERY AFTERNOON Bonamy went expressly to talk about
Jacob to tea with Clara Durrant in the square behind Sloane
Street where, on hot spring days, there are striped blinds over
the front windows, single horses pawing the macadam outside
the doors, and elderly gentlemen in yellow waistcoats ringing
bells and stepping in very politely when the maid demurely
replies that Mrs. Durrant is at home.

Bonamy sat with Clara in the sunny front room with the
barrel organ piping sweetly outside; the water-cart going slowly
along spraying the pavement; the carriages jingling, and all the
silver and chintz, brown and blue rugs and vases filled with
green boughs, striped with trembling yellow bars.

The insipidity of what was said needs no illustration—
Bonamy kept on gently returning quiet answers and accumulating amazement at an existence squeezed and emasculated within
a white satin shoe (Mrs. Durrant meanwhile enunciating strident politics with Sir Somebody in the back room) until the
virginity of Clara's soul appeared to him candid; the depths unknown; and he would have brought out Jacob's name had he not
begun to feel positively certain that Clara loved him—and
could do nothing whatever.

"Nothing whatever!" he exclaimed, as the door shut, and, for
a man of his temperament, got a very queer feeling, as he walked
through the park, of carriages irresistibly driven; of flower beds
uncompromisingly geometrical; of force rushing round geometrical patterns in the most senseless way in the world. "Was Clara,"

he thought, pausing to watch the boys bathing in the Serpentine, "the silent woman?—would Jacob marry her?"

BUT IN ATHENS in the sunshine, in Athens, where it is almost impossible to get afternoon tea, and elderly gentlemen who talk politics talk them all the other way round, in Athens sat Sandra Wentworth Williams, veiled, in white, her legs stretched in front of her, one elbow on the arm of the bamboo chair, blue clouds wavering and drifting from her cigarette.

The orange trees which flourish in the Square of the Constitution, the band, the dragging of feet, the sky, the houses, lemon and rose coloured—all this became so significant to Mrs. Wentworth Williams after her second cup of coffee that she began dramatizing the story of the noble and impulsive Englishwoman who had offered a seat in her carriage to the old American lady at Mycenae (Mrs. Duggan)—not altogether a false story, though it said nothing of Evan, standing first on one foot, then on the other, waiting for the women to stop chattering.

"I am putting the life of Father Damien into verse," Mrs. Duggan had said, for she had lost everything—everything in the world, husband and child and everything, but faith remained.

Sandra, floating from the particular to the universal, lay back in a trance.

The flight of time which hurries us so tragically along; the eternal drudge and drone, now bursting into fiery flame like those brief balls of yellow among green leaves (she was looking at orange trees); kisses on lips that are to die; the world turning, turning in mazes of heat and sound—though to be sure there is the quiet evening with its lovely pallor, "For I am sensitive to every side of it," Sandra thought, "and Mrs. Duggan will write to me for ever, and I shall answer her letters." Now the royal band marching by with the national flag stirred wider rings of emotion, and life became something that the courageous mount and ride out to sea on—the hair blown back (so she envisaged it, and the breeze stirred slightly among the orange trees) and she herself was emerging from silver spray—when she saw Jacob. He was standing in the Square with a book under his arm looking vacantly about him. That he was heavily built and might become stout in time was a fact.

But she suspected him of being a mere bumpkin.

"There is that young man," she said, peevishly, throwing away her cigarette, "that Mr. Flanders."

"Where?" said Evan. "I don't see him."

"Oh, walking away—behind the trees now. No, you can't see him. But we are sure to run into him," which, of course, they did.

BUT HOW FAR was he a mere bumpkin? How far was Jacob Flanders at the age of twenty-six a stupid fellow? It is no use trying to sum people up. One must follow hints, not exactly what is said, nor yet entirely what is done. Some, it is true, take ineffaceable impressions of character at once. Others dally, loiter, and get blown this way and that. Kind old ladies assure us that cats are often the best judges of character. A cat will always go to a good man, they say; but then, Mrs. Whitehorn, Jacob's landlady, loathed cats.

There is also the highly respectable opinion that character-mongering is much overdone nowadays. After all, what does it matter—that Fanny Elmer was all sentiment and sensation, and Mrs. Durrant hard as iron? that Clara, owing (so the character-mongers said) largely to her mother's influence, never yet had the chance to do anything off her own bat, and only to very observant eyes displayed deeps of feeling which were positively alarming; and would certainly throw herself away upon some one unworthy of her one of these days unless, so the character-

mongers said, she had a spark of her mother's spirit in her—
was somehow heroic. But what a term to apply to Clara Durrant! Simple to a degree, others thought her. And that is the very
reason, so they said, why she attracts Dick Bonamy—the young
man with the Wellington nose. Now *he's* a dark horse if you like.
And there these gossips would suddenly pause. Obviously they
meant to hint at his peculiar disposition—long rumoured
among them.

"But sometimes it is precisely a woman like Clara that men
of that temperament need . . ." Miss Julia Eliot would hint.

"Well," Mr. Bowley would reply, "it may be so."

For however long these gossips sit, and however they stuff
out their victims' characters till they are swollen and tender as
the livers of geese exposed to a hot fire, they never come to a
decision.

"That young man, Jacob Flanders," they would say, "so distinguished looking—and yet so awkward." Then they would
apply themselves to Jacob and vacillate eternally between the two
extremes. He rode to hounds—after a fashion, for he hadn't a
penny.

"Did you ever hear who his father was?" asked Julia Eliot.

"His mother, they say, is somehow connected with the
Rocksbiers," replied Mr. Bowley.

"He doesn't overwork himself anyhow."

"His friends are very fond of him."

"Dick Bonamy, you mean?"

"No, I didn't mean that. It's evidently the other way with
Jacob. He is precisely the young man to fall headlong in love and
repent it for the rest of his life."

"Oh, Mr. Bowley," said Mrs. Durrant, sweeping down upon
them in her imperious manner, "you remember Mrs. Adams?
Well, that is her niece." And Mr. Bowley, getting up, bowed politely and fetched strawberries.

So we are driven back to see what the other side means — the men in clubs and Cabinets — when they say that character-drawing is a frivolous fireside art, a matter of pins and needles, exquisite outlines enclosing vacancy, flourishes, and mere scrawls.

The battleships ray out over the North Sea, keeping their stations accurately apart. At a given signal all the guns are trained on a target which (the master gunner counts the seconds, watch in hand — at the sixth he looks up) flames into splinters. With equal nonchalance a dozen young men in the prime of life descend with composed faces into the depths of the sea; and there impassively (though with perfect mastery of machinery) suffocate uncomplainingly together. Like blocks of tin soldiers the army covers the cornfield, moves up the hillside, stops, reels slightly this way and that, and falls flat, save that, through field-glasses, it can be seen that one or two pieces still agitate up and down like fragments of broken match-stick.

These actions, together with the incessant commerce of banks, laboratories, chancellories, and houses of business, are the strokes which oar the world forward, they say. And they are dealt by men as smoothly sculptured as the impassive policeman at Ludgate Circus. But you will observe that far from being padded to rotundity his face is stiff from force of will, and lean from the effort of keeping it so. When his right arm rises, all the force in his veins flows straight from shoulder to finger-tips; not an ounce is diverted into sudden impulses, sentimental regrets, wire-drawn distinctions. The buses punctually stop.

It is thus that we live, they say, driven by an unseizable force. They say that the novelists never catch it; that it goes hurtling through their nets and leaves them torn to ribbons. This, they say, is what we live by — this unseizable force.

"WHERE ARE the men?" said old General Gibbons, looking round the drawing-room, full as usual on Sunday afternoons of well-dressed people. "Where are the guns?"

Mrs. Durrant looked too.

Clara, thinking that her mother wanted her, came in; then went out again.

They were talking about Germany at the Durrants, and Jacob (driven by this unseizable force) walked rapidly down Hermes Street and ran straight into the Williamses.

"OH!" CRIED SANDRA, with a cordiality which she suddenly felt. And Evan added, "What luck!"

The dinner which they gave him in the hotel which looks on to the Square of the Constitution was excellent. Plated baskets contained fresh rolls. There was real butter. And the meat scarcely needed the disguise of innumerable little red and green vegetables glazed in sauce.

It was strange, though. There were the little tables set out at intervals on the scarlet floor with the Greek King's monogram wrought in yellow. Sandra dined in her hat, veiled as usual. Evan looked this way and that over his shoulder; imperturbable yet supple; and sometimes sighed. It was strange. For they were English people come together in Athens on a May evening. Jacob, helping himself to this and that, answered intelligently, yet with a ring in his voice.

The Williamses were going to Constantinople early next morning, they said.

"Before you are up," said Sandra.

They would leave Jacob alone, then. Turning very slightly, Evan ordered something—a bottle of wine—from which he helped Jacob, with a kind of solicitude, with a kind of paternal solicitude, if that were possible. To be left alone—that was good for a young fellow. Never was there a time when the country had more need of men. He sighed.

"And you have been to the Acropolis?" asked Sandra.

"Yes," said Jacob. And they moved off to the window together, while Evan spoke to the head waiter about calling them early.

"It is astonishing," said Jacob, in a gruff voice.

Sandra opened her eyes very slightly. Possibly her nostrils expanded a little too.

"At half-past six then," said Evan, coming towards them, looking as if he faced something in facing his wife and Jacob standing with their backs to the window.

Sandra smiled at him.

And, as he went to the window and had nothing to say she added, in broken half-sentences:

"Well, but how lovely—wouldn't it be? The Acropolis, Evan—or are you too tired?"

At that Evan looked at them, or, since Jacob was staring ahead of him, at his wife, surlily, sullenly, yet with a kind of distress—not that she would pity him. Nor would the implacable spirit of love, for anything he could do, cease its tortures.

They left him and he sat in the smoking-room, which looks out on to the Square of the Constitution.

"EVAN IS happier alone," said Sandra. "We have been separated from the newspapers. Well, it is better that people should have what they want. . . . You have seen all these wonderful things since we met. . . . What impression . . . I think that you are changed."

"You want to go to the Acropolis," said Jacob. "Up here then."

"One will remember it all one's life," said Sandra.

"Yes," said Jacob. "I wish you could have come in the day-time."

"This is more wonderful," said Sandra, waving her hand. Jacob looked vaguely.

"But you should see the Parthenon in the day-time," he said. "You couldn't come to-morrow—it would be too early?"

"You have sat there for hours and hours by yourself?"

"There were some awful women this morning," said Jacob.

"Awful women?" Sandra echoed.

"Frenchwomen."

"But something very wonderful has happened," said Sandra. Ten minutes, fifteen minutes, half an hour—that was all the time before her.

"Yes," he said.

"When one is your age—when one is young. What will you do? You will fall in love—oh yes! But don't be in too great a hurry. I am so much older."

She was brushed off the pavement by parading men.

"Shall we go on?" Jacob asked.

"Let us go on," she insisted.

For she could not stop until she had told him—or heard him say—or was it some action on his part that she required? Far away on the horizon she discerned it and could not rest.

"You'd never get English people to sit out like this," he said.

"Never—no. When you get back to England you won't forget this—or come with us to Constantinople!" she cried suddenly.

"But then . . ."

Sandra sighed.

"You must go to Delphi, of course," she said. "But," she asked herself, "what do I want from him? Perhaps it is something that I have missed. . . ."

"You will get there about six in the evening," she said. "You will see the eagles."

Jacob looked set and even desperate by the light at the street corner; and yet composed. He was suffering, perhaps. He was credulous. Yet there was something caustic about him. He had in him the seeds of extreme disillusionment, which would come to him from women in middle life. Perhaps if one strove hard enough to reach the top of the hill it need not come to him—this disillusionment from women in middle life.

"The hotel is awful," she said. "The last visitors had left their basins full of dirty water. There is always that," she laughed.

"The people one meets *are* beastly," Jacob said.

His excitement was clear enough.

"Write and tell me about it," she said. "And tell me what you feel and what you think. Tell me everything."

The night was dark. The Acropolis was a jagged mound.

"I should like to, awfully," he said.

"When we get back to London, we shall meet . . ."

"Yes."

"I suppose they leave the gates open?" he asked.

"We could climb them!" she answered wildly.

Obscuring the moon and altogether darkening the Acropolis the clouds passed from east to west. The clouds solidified; the vapours thickened; the trailing veils stayed and accumulated.

It was dark now over Athens, except for gauzy red streaks where the streets ran; and the front of the Palace was cadaverous from electric light. At sea the piers stood out, marked by separate dots; the waves being invisible, and promontories and islands were dark humps with a few lights.

"I'd love to bring my brother, if I may," Jacob murmured.

"And then when your mother comes to London——," said Sandra.

The mainland of Greece was dark; and somewhere off Euboea a cloud must have touched the waves and spattered them—the dolphins circling deeper and deeper into the sea. Violent was the wind now rushing down the Sea of Marmara between Greece and the plains of Troy.

In Greece and the uplands of Albania and Turkey, the wind scours the sand and the dust, and sows itself thick with dry particles. And then it pelts the smooth domes of the mosques, and makes the cypresses, standing stiff by the turbaned tombstones of Mohammedans, creak and bristle.

Sandra's veils were swirled about her.

"I will give you my copy," said Jacob. "Here. Will you keep it?"

(The book was the poems of Donne.)

Now the agitation of the air uncovered a racing star. Now it was dark. Now one after another lights were extinguished. Now great towns—Paris—Constantinople—London—were black as strewn rocks. Waterways might be distinguished. In England the trees were heavy in leaf. Here perhaps in some southern wood an old man lit dry ferns and the birds were startled. The sheep coughed; one flower bent slightly towards another. The English sky is softer, milkier than the Eastern. Something gentle has passed into it from the grass-rounded hills, something damp. The salt gale blew in at Betty Flanders's bedroom window, and the widow lady, raising herself slightly on her elbow, sighed like one who realizes, but would fain ward off a little longer—oh, a little longer!—the oppression of eternity.

But to return to Jacob and Sandra.

They had vanished. There was the Acropolis; but had they reached it? The columns and the Temple remain; the emotion of the living breaks fresh on them year after year; and of that what remains?

As for reaching the Acropolis who shall say that we ever do it, or that when Jacob woke next morning he found anything hard and durable to keep for ever? Still, he went with them to Constantinople.

Sandra Wentworth Williams certainly woke to find a copy of Donne's poems upon her dressing-table. And the book would be stood on the shelf in the English country house where Sally Duggan's *Life of Father Damien* in verse would join it one of these days. There were ten or twelve little volumes already. Strolling in at dusk, Sandra would open the books and her eyes would brighten (but not at the print), and subsiding into the arm-chair she would suck back again the soul of the moment; or, for sometimes she was restless, would pull out book after book and swing across the whole space of her life like an acrobat from bar to bar. She had had her moments. Meanwhile, the great clock on the landing ticked and Sandra would hear time accumulating, and ask herself, "What for? What for?"

"What for? What for?" Sandra would say, putting the book back, and strolling to the looking-glass and pressing her hair. And Miss Edwards would be startled at dinner, as she opened her mouth to admit roast mutton, by Sandra's sudden solicitude: "Are you happy, Miss Edwards?"—a thing Cissy Edwards hadn't thought of for years.

"What for? What for?" Jacob never asked himself any such questions, to judge by the way he laced his boots; shaved himself; to judge by the depth of his sleep that night, with the wind fidgeting at the shutters, and half-a-dozen mosquitoes singing in his ears. He was young—a man. And then Sandra was right when she judged him to be credulous as yet. At forty it might be a different matter. Already he had marked the things he liked in Donne, and they were savage enough. However, you might place beside them passages of the purest poetry in Shakespeare.

But the wind was rolling the darkness through the streets of Athens, rolling it, one might suppose, with a sort of trampling energy of mood which forbids too close an analysis of the feel-

ings of any single person, or inspection of features. All faces—
Greek, Levantine, Turkish, English—would have looked much
the same in that darkness. At length the columns and the
Temples whiten, yellow, turn rose; and the Pyramids and St.
Peter's arise, and at last sluggish St. Paul's looms up.

The Christians have the right to rouse most cities with their
interpretation of the day's meaning. Then, less melodiously, dissenters of different sects issue a cantankerous emendation. The
steamers, resounding like gigantic tuning-forks, state the old old
fact—how there is a sea coldly, greenly, swaying outside. But
nowadays it is the thin voice of duty, piping in a white thread
from the top of a funnel, that collects the largest multitudes,
and night is nothing but a long-drawn sigh between hammer-
strokes, a deep breath—you can hear it from an open window
even in the heart of London.

But who, save the nerve-worn and sleepless, or thinkers
standing with hands to the eyes on some crag above the multi-
tude, see things thus in skeleton outline, bare of flesh? In Surbiton the skeleton is wrapped in flesh.

"The kettle never boils so well on a sunny morning," says
Mrs. Grandage, glancing at the clock on the mantelpiece. Then
the grey Persian cat stretches itself on the window-seat, and buf-
fets a moth with soft round paws. And before breakfast is half
over (they were late to-day), a baby is deposited in her lap, and
she must guard the sugar basin while Tom Grandage reads the
golfing article in the *Times,* sips his coffee, wipes his mous-
taches, and is off to the office, where he is the greatest authority upon the foreign exchanges and marked for promotion.

The skeleton is well wrapped in flesh. Even this dark night
when the wind rolls the darkness through Lombard Street and
Fetter Lane and Bedford Square it stirs (since it is summer-time
and the height of the season), plane trees spangled with electric
light, and curtains still preserving the room from the dawn.

People still murmur over the last word said on the staircase, or strain, all through their dreams, for the voice of the alarum clock. So when the wind roams through a forest innumerable twigs stir; hives are brushed; insects sway on grass blades; the spider runs rapidly up a crease in the bark; and the whole air is tremulous with breathing; elastic with filaments.

Only here — in Lombard Street and Fetter Lane and Bedford Square — each insect carries a globe of the world in his head, and the webs of the forest are schemes evolved for the smooth conduct of business; and honey is treasure of one sort and another; and the stir in the air is the indescribable agitation of life.

But colour returns; runs up the stalks of the grass; blows out into tulips and crocuses; solidly stripes the tree trunks; and fills the gauze of the air and the grasses and pools.

The Bank of England emerges; and the Monument with its bristling head of golden hair; the dray horses crossing London Bridge show grey and strawberry and iron-coloured. There is a whir of wings as the suburban trains rush into the terminus. And the light mounts over the faces of all the tall blind houses, slides through a chink and paints the lustrous bellying crimson curtains; the green wine-glasses; the coffee-cups; and the chairs standing askew.

Sunlight strikes in upon shaving-glasses; and gleaming brass cans; upon all the jolly trappings of the day; the bright, inquisitive, armoured, resplendent, summer's day, which has long since vanquished chaos; which has dried the melancholy mediaeval mists; drained the swamp and stood glass and stone upon it; and equipped our brains and bodies with such an armoury of weapons that merely to see the flash and thrust of limbs engaged in the conduct of daily life is better than the old pageant of armies drawn out in battle array upon the plain.

THIRTEEN

"THE HEIGHT of the season," said Bonamy.

The sun had already blistered the paint on the backs of the green chairs in Hyde Park; peeled the bark off the plane trees; and turned the earth to powder and to smooth yellow pebbles. Hyde Park was circled, incessantly, by turning wheels.

"The height of the season," said Bonamy sarcastically.

He was sarcastic because of Clara Durrant; because Jacob had come back from Greece very brown and lean, with his pockets full of Greek notes, which he pulled out when the chair man came for pence; because Jacob was silent.

"He has not said a word to show that he is glad to see me," thought Bonamy bitterly.

The motor cars passed incessantly over the bridge of the Serpentine; the upper classes walked upright, or bent themselves gracefully over the palings; the lower classes lay with their knees cocked up, flat on their backs; the sheep grazed on pointed wooden legs; small children ran down the sloping grass, stretched their arms, and fell.

"Very urbane," Jacob brought out.

"Urbane" on the lips of Jacob had mysteriously all the shapeliness of a character which Bonamy thought daily more sublime, devastating, terrific than ever, though he was still, and perhaps would be for ever, barbaric, obscure.

What superlatives! What adjectives! How acquit Bonamy of sentimentality of the grossest sort; of being tossed like a cork on the waves; of having no steady insight into character; of being unsupported by reason, and of drawing no comfort whatever from the works of the classics?

"The height of civilization," said Jacob.

He was fond of using Latin words.

Magnanimity, virtue — such words when Jacob used them in talk with Bonamy meant that he took control of the situation; that Bonamy would play round him like an affectionate spaniel; and that (as likely as not) they would end by rolling on the floor.

"And Greece?" said Bonamy. "The Parthenon and all that?"

"There's none of this European mysticism," said Jacob.

"It's the atmosphere, I suppose," said Bonamy. "And you went to Constantinople?"

"Yes," said Jacob.

Bonamy paused, moved a pebble; then darted in with the rapidity and certainty of a lizard's tongue.

"You are in love!" he exclaimed.

Jacob blushed.

The sharpest of knives never cut so deep.

As for responding, or taking the least account of it, Jacob stared straight ahead of him, fixed, monolithic — oh, very beautiful! — like a British Admiral, exclaimed Bonamy in a rage, rising from his seat and walking off; waiting for some sound; none came; too proud to look back; walking quicker and quicker until he found himself gazing into motor cars and cursing women. Where was the pretty woman's face? Clara's — Fanny's — Florinda's? Who was the pretty little creature?

Not Clara Durrant.

THE ABERDEEN terrier must be exercised, and as Mr. Bowley was going that very moment — would like nothing better than

a walk—they went together, Clara and kind little Bowley—
Bowley who had rooms in the Albany, Bowley who wrote letters to the *Times* in a jocular vein about foreign hotels and the
Aurora Borealis—Bowley who liked young people and walked
down Piccadilly with his right arm resting on the boss of his
back.

"Little demon!" cried Clara, and attached Troy to his chain.

Bowley anticipated—hoped for—a confidence. Devoted
to her mother, Clara sometimes felt her a little, well, her mother
was so sure of herself that she could not understand other
people being—being—"as ludicrous as I am," Clara jerked out
(the dog tugging her forwards). And Bowley thought she looked
like a huntress and turned over in his mind which it should
be—some pale virgin with a slip of the moon in her hair, which
was a flight for Bowley.

The colour was in her cheeks. To have spoken outright
about her mother—still, it was only to Mr. Bowley, who loved
her, as everybody must; but to speak was unnatural to her, yet
it was awful to feel, as she had done all day, that she *must* tell
some one.

"Wait till we cross the road," she said to the dog, bending
down.

Happily she had recovered by that time.

"She thinks so much about England," she said. "She is so
anxious——"

Bowley was defrauded as usual. Clara never confided in
any one.

"Why don't the young people settle it, eh?" he wanted to
ask. "What's all this about England?"—a question poor Clara
could not have answered, since, as Mrs. Durrant discussed with
Sir Edgar the policy of Sir Edward Grey, Clara only wondered
why the cabinet looked dusty, and Jacob had never come. Oh,
here was Mrs. Cowley Johnson . . .

And Clara would hand the pretty china teacups, and smile at the compliment—that no one in London made tea so well as she did.

"We get it at Brocklebank's," she said, "in Cursitor Street."

Ought she not to be grateful? Ought she not to be happy? Especially since her mother looked so well and enjoyed so much talking to Sir Edgar about Morocco, Venezuela, or some such place.

"Jacob! Jacob!" thought Clara; and kind Mr. Bowley, who was ever so good with old ladies, looked; stopped; wondered whether Elizabeth wasn't too harsh with her daughter; wondered about Bonamy, Jacob—which young fellow was it?—and jumped up directly Clara said she must exercise Troy.

THEY HAD reached the site of the old Exhibition. They looked at the tulips. Stiff and curled, the little rods of waxy smoothness rose from the earth, nourished yet contained, suffused with scarlet and coral pink. Each had its shadow; each grew trimly in the diamond-shaped wedge as the gardener had planned it.

"Barnes never gets them to grow like that," Clara mused; she sighed.

"You are neglecting your friends," said Bowley, as some one, going the other way, lifted his hat. She started; acknowledged Mr. Lionel Parry's bow; wasted on him what had sprung for Jacob.

("Jacob! Jacob!" she thought.)

"But you'll get run over if I let you go," she said to the dog.

"England seems all right," said Mr. Bowley.

The loop of the railing beneath the statue of Achilles was full of parasols and waistcoats; chains and bangles; of ladies and gentlemen, lounging elegantly, lightly observant.

" 'This statue was erected by the women of England . . .' "

Clara read out with a foolish little laugh. "Oh, Mr. Bowley! Oh!" Gallop—gallop—gallop—a horse galloped past without a rider. The stirrups swung; the pebbles spurted.

"Oh, stop! Stop it, Mr. Bowley!" she cried, white, trembling, gripping his arm, utterly unconscious, the tears coming.

"TUT-TUT!" SAID Mr. Bowley in his dressing-room an hour later. "Tut-tut!"—a comment that was profound enough, though inarticulately expressed, since his valet was handing his shirt studs.

JULIA ELIOT, TOO, had seen the horse run away, and had risen from her seat to watch the end of the incident, which, since she came of a sporting family, seemed to her slightly ridiculous. Sure enough the little man came pounding behind with his breeches dusty; looked thoroughly annoyed; and was being helped to mount by a policeman when Julia Eliot, with a sardonic smile, turned towards the Marble Arch on her errand of mercy. It was only to visit a sick old lady who had known her mother and perhaps the Duke of Wellington; for Julia shared the love of her sex for the distressed; liked to visit death-beds; threw slippers at weddings; received confidences by the dozen; knew more pedigrees than a scholar knows dates, and was one of the kindliest, most generous, least continent of women.

Yet five minutes after she had passed the statue of Achilles she had the rapt look of one brushing through crowds on a summer's afternoon, when the trees are rustling, the wheels churning yellow, and the tumult of the present seems like an elegy for past youth and past summers, and there rose in her mind a curious sadness, as if time and eternity showed through skirts and waistcoats, and she saw people passing tragically to destruction. Yet, Heaven knows, Julia was no fool. A sharper woman at a bargain did not exist. She was always punctual. The

watch on her wrist gave her twelve minutes and a half in which
to reach Bruton Street. Lady Congreve expected her at five.

THE GILT CLOCK at Verrey's was striking five.

Florinda looked at it with a dull expression, like an animal.
She looked at the clock; looked at the door; looked at the long
glass opposite; disposed her cloak; drew closer to the table, for
she was pregnant—no doubt about it, Mother Stuart said, recommending remedies, consulting friends; sunk, caught by the
heel, as she tripped so lightly over the surface.

Her tumbler of pinkish sweet stuff was set down by the
waiter; and she sucked, through a straw, her eyes on the looking-
glass, on the door, now soothed by the sweet taste. When Nick
Bramham came in it was plain, even to the young Swiss waiter,
that there was a bargain between them. Nick hitched his clothes
together clumsily; ran his fingers through his hair; sat down, to
an ordeal, nervously. She looked at him; and set off laughing;
laughed—laughed—laughed. The young Swiss waiter, standing with crossed legs by the pillar, laughed too.

The door opened; in came the roar of Regent Street, the
roar of traffic, impersonal, unpitying; and sunshine grained with
dirt. The Swiss waiter must see to the newcomers. Bramham
lifted his glass.

"He's like Jacob," said Florinda, looking at the newcomer.
"The way he stares." She stopped laughing.

JACOB, LEANING FORWARD, drew a plan of the Parthenon in
the dust in Hyde Park, a network of strokes at least, which may
have been the Parthenon, or again a mathematical diagram. And
why was the pebble so emphatically ground in at the corner? It
was not to count his notes that he took out a wad of papers and
read a long flowing letter which Sandra had written two days
ago at Milton Dower House with his book before her and in her

mind the memory of something said or attempted, some moment in the dark on the road to the Acropolis which (such was her creed) mattered for ever.

"He is," she mused, "like that man in Molière."

She meant Alceste. She meant that he was severe. She meant that she could deceive him.

"Or could I not?" she thought, putting the poems of Donne back in the bookcase. "Jacob," she went on, going to the window and looking over the spotted flower-beds across the grass where the piebald cows grazed under beech trees, "Jacob would be shocked."

The perambulator was going through the little gate in the railing. She kissed her hand; directed by the nurse, Jimmy waved his.

"*He's* a small boy," she said, thinking of Jacob.

And yet—Alceste?

"WHAT A NUISANCE you are!" Jacob grumbled, stretching out first one leg and then the other and feeling in each trouser-pocket for his chair ticket.

"I expect the sheep have eaten it," he said. "Why do you keep sheep?"

"Sorry to disturb you, sir," said the ticket-collector, his hand deep in the enormous pouch of pence.

"Well, I hope they pay you for it," said Jacob. "There you are. No. You can stick to it. Go and get drunk."

He had parted with half-a-crown, tolerantly, compassionately, with considerable contempt for his species.

EVEN NOW poor Fanny Elmer was dealing, as she walked along the Strand, in her incompetent way with this very careless, indifferent, sublime manner he had of talking to railway guards or porters; or Mrs. Whitehorn, when she consulted him about her little boy who was beaten by the schoolmaster.

Sustained entirely upon picture post cards for the past two months, Fanny's idea of Jacob was more statuesque, noble, and eyeless than ever. To reinforce her vision she had taken to visiting the British Museum, where, keeping her eyes downcast until she was alongside of the battered Ulysses, she opened them and got a fresh shock of Jacob's presence, enough to last her half a day. But this was wearing thin. And she wrote now— poems, letters that were never posted, saw his face in advertisements on hoardings, and would cross the road to let the barrel-organ turn her musings to rhapsody. But at breakfast (she shared rooms with a teacher), when the butter was smeared about the plate, and the prongs of the forks were clotted with old egg yolk, she revised these visions violently; was, in truth, very cross; was losing her complexion, as Margery Jackson told her, bringing the whole thing down (as she laced her stout boots) to a level of mother-wit, vulgarity, and sentiment, for she had loved too; and been a fool.

"One's godmothers ought to have told one," said Fanny, looking in at the window of Bacon, the mapseller, in the Strand—told one that it is no use making a fuss; this is life, they should have said, as Fanny said it now, looking at the large yellow globe marked with steamship lines.

"This is life. This is life," said Fanny.

"A very hard face," thought Miss Barrett, on the other side of the glass, buying maps of the Syrian desert and waiting impatiently to be served. "Girls look old so soon nowadays."

The equator swam behind tears.

"Piccadilly?" Fanny asked the conductor of the omnibus, and climbed to the top. After all, he would, he must, come back to her.

But Jacob might have been thinking of Rome; of architecture; of jurisprudence; as he sat under the plane tree in Hyde Park.

———

THE OMNIBUS stopped outside Charing Cross; and behind it were clogged omnibuses, vans, motor-cars, for a procession with banners was passing down Whitehall, and elderly people were stiffly descending from between the paws of the slippery lions, where they had been testifying to their faith, singing lustily, raising their eyes from their music to look into the sky, and still their eyes were on the sky as they marched behind the gold letters of their creed.

The traffic stopped, and the sun, no longer sprayed out by the breeze, became almost too hot. But the procession passed; the banners glittered far away down Whitehall; the traffic was released; lurched on; spun to a smooth continuous uproar; swerving round the curve of Cockspur Street; and sweeping past Government offices and equestrian statues down Whitehall to the prickly spires, the tethered grey fleet of masonry, and the large white clock of Westminster.

Five strokes Big Ben intoned; Nelson received the salute. The wires of the Admiralty shivered with some far-away communication. A voice kept remarking that Prime Ministers and Viceroys spoke in the Reichstag; entered Lahore; said that the Emperor travelled; in Milan they rioted; said there were rumours in Vienna; said that the Ambassador at Constantinople had audience with the Sultan; the fleet was at Gibraltar. The voice continued, imprinting on the faces of the clerks in Whitehall (Timothy Durrant was one of them) something of its own inexorable gravity, as they listened, deciphered, wrote down. Papers accumulated, inscribed with the utterances of Kaisers, the statistics of ricefields, the growling of hundreds of work-people, plotting sedition in back streets, or gathering in the Calcutta bazaars, or mustering their forces in the uplands of Albania, where the hills are sand-coloured, and bones lie unburied.

The voice spoke plainly in the square quiet room with heavy tables, where one elderly man made notes on the margin of type-written sheets, his silver-topped umbrella leaning against the bookcase.

His head—bald, red-veined, hollow-looking—represented all the heads in the building. His head, with the amiable pale eyes, carried the burden of knowledge across the street; laid it before his colleagues, who came equally burdened; and then the sixteen gentlemen, lifting their pens or turning perhaps rather wearily in their chairs, decreed that the course of history should shape itself this way or that way, being manfully determined, as their faces showed, to impose some coherency upon Rajahs and Kaisers and the muttering in bazaars, the secret gatherings, plainly visible in Whitehall, of kilted peasants in Albanian uplands; to control the course of events.

Pitt and Chatham, Burke and Gladstone looked from side to side with fixed marble eyes and an air of immortal quiescence which perhaps the living may have envied, the air being full of whistling and concussions, as the procession with its banners passed down Whitehall. Moreover, some were troubled with dyspepsia; one had at that very moment cracked the glass of his spectacles; another spoke in Glasgow to-morrow; altogether they looked too red, fat, pale or lean, to be dealing, as the marble heads had dealt, with the course of history.

TIMMY DURRANT in his little room in the Admiralty, going to consult a Blue book, stopped for a moment by the window and observed the placard tied round the lamp-post.

Miss Thomas, one of the typists, said to her friend that if the Cabinet was going to sit much longer she should miss her boy outside the Gaiety.

Timmy Durrant, returning with his Blue book under his arm, noticed a little knot of people at the street corner; conglomerated as though one of them knew something; and the others, pressing round him, looked up, looked down, looked along the street. What was it that he knew?

Timothy, placing the Blue book before him, studied a paper sent round by the Treasury for information. Mr. Crawley, his fellow-clerk, impaled a letter on a skewer.

Jacob rose from his chair in Hyde Park, tore his ticket to pieces, and walked away.

"Such a sunset," wrote Mrs. Flanders in her letter to Archer at Singapore. "One couldn't make up one's mind to come indoors," she wrote. "It seemed wicked to waste even a moment."

The long windows of Kensington Palace flushed fiery rose as Jacob walked away; a flock of wild duck flew over the Serpentine; and the trees were stood against the sky, blackly, magnificently.

"Jacob," wrote Mrs. Flanders, with the red light on her page, "is hard at work after his delightful journey . . ."

"The Kaiser," the far-away voice remarked in Whitehall, "received me in audience."

"Now I know that face—" said the Reverend Andrew Floyd, coming out of Carter's shop in Piccadilly, "but who the dickens—?" and he watched Jacob, turned round to look at him, but could not be sure——

"Oh, Jacob Flanders!" he remembered in a flash.

But he was so tall; so unconscious; such a fine young fellow.

"I gave him Byron's works," Andrew Floyd mused, and started forward, as Jacob crossed the road; but hesitated, and let the moment pass, and lost the opportunity.

Another procession, without banners, was blocking Long Acre. Carriages, with dowagers in amethyst and gentlemen spotted with carnations, intercepted cabs and motor-cars turned in the opposite direction, in which jaded men in white waistcoats lolled, on their way home to shrubberies and billiard-rooms in Putney and Wimbledon.

Two barrel-organs played by the kerb, and horses coming out of Aldridge's with white labels on their buttocks straddled across the road and were smartly jerked back.

Mrs. Durrant, sitting with Mr. Wortley in a motor-car, was impatient lest they should miss the overture.

But Mr. Wortley, always urbane, always in time for the overture, buttoned his gloves, and admired Miss Clara.

"A shame to spend such a night in the theatre!" said Mrs. Durrant, seeing all the windows of the coachmakers in Long Acre ablaze.

"Think of your moors!" said Mr. Wortley to Clara.

"Ah! but Clara likes this better," Mrs. Durrant laughed.

"I don't know—really," said Clara, looking at the blazing windows. She started.

She saw Jacob.

"Who?" asked Mrs. Durrant sharply, leaning forward.

But she saw no one.

Under the arch of the Opera House large faces and lean ones, the powdered and the hairy, all alike were red in the sunset; and, quickened by the great hanging lamps with their repressed primrose lights, by the tramp, and the scarlet, and the pompous ceremony, some ladies looked for a moment into steaming bedrooms near by, where women with loose hair leaned out of windows, where girls—where children—(the long mirrors held the ladies suspended) but one must follow; one must not block the way.

CLARA'S MOORS were fine enough. The Phoenicians slept under their piled grey rocks; the chimneys of the old mines pointed starkly; early moths blurred the heather-bells; cartwheels could be heard grinding on the road far beneath; and the suck and sighing of the waves sounded gently, persistently, for ever.

Shading her eyes with her hand Mrs. Pascoe stood in her cabbage-garden looking out to sea. Two steamers and a sailing-ship crossed each other; passed each other; and in the bay the gulls kept alighting on a log, rising high, returning again to the log, while some rode in upon the waves and stood on the rim of the water until the moon blanched all to whiteness.

Mrs. Pascoe had gone indoors long ago.

But the red light was on the columns of the Parthenon, and the Greek women who were knitting their stockings and sometimes crying to a child to come and have the insects picked from its head were as jolly as sand-martins in the heat, quarrelling, scolding, suckling their babies, until the ships in the Piraeus fired their guns.

The sound spread itself flat, and then went tunnelling its way with fitful explosions among the channels of the islands.

Darkness drops like a knife over Greece.

"THE GUNS?" said Betty Flanders, half asleep, getting out of bed and going to the window, which was decorated with a fringe of dark leaves.

"Not at this distance," she thought. "It is the sea."

Again, far away, she heard the dull sound, as if nocturnal women were beating great carpets. There was Morty lost, and Seabrook dead; her sons fighting for their country. But were the chickens safe? Was that some one moving downstairs? Rebecca with the toothache? No. The nocturnal women were beating great carpets. Her hens shifted slightly on their perches.

FOURTEEN

"HE LEFT EVERYTHING just as it was," Bonamy marvelled. "Nothing arranged. All his letters strewn about for any one to read. What did he expect? Did he think he would come back?" he mused, standing in the middle of Jacob's room.

The eighteenth century has its distinction. These houses were built, say, a hundred and fifty years ago. The rooms are shapely, the ceilings high; over the doorways a rose or a ram's skull is carved in the wood. Even the panels, painted in raspberry-coloured paint, have their distinction.

Bonamy took up a bill for a hunting-crop.

"That seems to be paid," he said.

There were Sandra's letters.

Mrs. Durrant was taking a party to Greenwich.

Lady Rocksbier hoped for the pleasure. . . .

Listless is the air in an empty room, just swelling the curtain; the flowers in the jar shift. One fibre in the wicker armchair creaks, though no one sits there.

Bonamy crossed to the window. Pickford's van swung down the street. The omnibuses were locked together at Mudie's corner. Engines throbbed, and carters, jamming the brakes down, pulled their horses sharp up. A harsh and unhappy voice cried something unintelligible. And then suddenly all the leaves seemed to raise themselves.

"Jacob! Jacob!" cried Bonamy, standing by the window. The leaves sank down again.

"Such confusion everywhere!" exclaimed Betty Flanders, bursting open the bedroom door.

Bonamy turned away from the window.

"What am I to do with these, Mr. Bonamy?"

She held out a pair of Jacob's old shoes.

THE END

A Note on the Text

This edition follows the text of the first U.S. edition of *Jacob's Room*.

Notes to *Jacob's Room*

Unless otherwise indicated in these notes, "Roe" refers to Virginia Woolf, *Jacob's Room,* edited with an introduction and notes by Sue Roe (Harmondsworth: Penguin, 1992). "Bishop" refers to Virginia Woolf, *Jacob's Room,* edited with an introduction and notes by Edward L. Bishop (Oxford: Shakespeare Head Press, 2004). *OED* refers to the online *Oxford English Dictionary.* Where a work's full citation is not given in a note, details can be found either in the introduction's list of works cited or in the suggestions for further reading.

gold nib [3]   Betty Flanders is using an expensive fountain pen to write her letter.

full stop [3]   British usage for period.

lighthouse [3]   The Godrevy Lighthouse at St. Ives, Cornwall, which also appears in Woolf's *To the Lighthouse,* but there is fictionalized and relocated to the Hebrides, islands off the coast of Scotland.

perambulator [3]   British term for baby carriage.

Scarborough is seven hundred miles from Cornwall [4]   Betty is staying in Cornwall, probably St. Ives, where Virginia Stephen spent summers from 1882 to 1895. Woolf visited St. Ives in 1921 while she was writing *Jacob's Room.* The town is only about 430 miles from

Scarborough. Scarborough was attacked by German battleships on December 16, 1914 (see Usui 7; Bradshaw 13–17).

Captain Barfoot is in Scarborough [4]   David Bradshaw (7–9) suggests that John, Betty Flanders's third son, was fathered by Captain Barfoot.

glass house [4]   A greenhouse.

widows stray solitary in the open fields, picking up stones, gleaning a few golden straws, lonely, unprotected, poor creatures [4]   A reference to the book of Ruth (book eight of the Hebrew Bible and the Old Testament). Ruth, given the option of staying with her own people in Moab after both her husband and her father-in-law die, chooses instead to follow her mother-in-law, Naomi, back to Bethlehem, where the two women survive by gleaning the fields for grain after the harvest. The fields belong to Naomi's relative Boaz, who eventually marries Ruth and saves her and her mother-in-law from poverty (see Neverow, "Return" 221).

Panama hat [4]   A Panama hat, first introduced in the nineteenth century, is made of plaited straw and has a brim.

greys flowing into lavenders . . . too pale as usual [4]   Charles Steele, like Mr. Paunceforte in *To the Lighthouse,* is self-taught. At least in his own perception, his style of painting seems not to align with the popular techniques of the moment. He is very conscious of how his work will be judged and assumes that the judgment will be negative. St. Ives in Cornwall has been an artists' community since the early nineteenth century. Throughout the novel, Woolf uses painterly techniques for verbal representation of visual scenes. With regard to her description of Steele's painting, she is using ekphrasis, a verbal description of a visual artwork (see Wall).

Archer lagged past him, trailing his spade [5]   Archer, Jacob's older brother, has a child's shovel; Jacob has the bucket that goes with the set of beach toys.

raw sienna [5]   A caramel color.

Titian [5]   Charles Steele is comparing himself to one of the greatest European painters in history. Tiziano Vecellio (ca. 1488–1576)—known as Titian—was a renowned sixteenth-century Italian painter who started a new phase of his creativity in his fifties and died at ninety-one.

parasol [5]   An umbrella used typically by women for protection from the sun.

early-closing day [6]   In the United Kingdom, the weekday when the shops close early.

bandanna handkerchiefs [6]   Large patterned squares of fabric.

sea holly [7]   *Eryngium maritimum,* a tall, spiky plant with blue flowers native to European coastlines.

lodgings [7]   Rental of a furnished living space; Mrs. Flanders is worried about the landlady's reaction to Jacob's sheep's jaw.

bonnet-pin [7]   A hat pin; the pin was used to secure a woman's bonnet against the wind by passing through her hair, which would have been twisted up into a bun.

purple aster [8]   An autumn-blooming flower. Its symbolic meaning is "afterthought"—perhaps a punning reference to Mrs. Flanders's forgetfulness.

Strand *magazines* [8]   An American-style periodical launched in 1891 that ceased publication in 1950. It was named after a famous street in London. Each issue offered articles on topics including the sciences and history, humorous items, and short fiction. The readership was mainly middle class.

Think of the fairies [9]   A very similar passage occurs in *To the Light-house* as Mrs. Ramsay soothes her son James and her daughter Cam (*To the Lighthouse,* Orlando: Harcourt, 2005: 116–17).

cistern [9]   A large receptacle for holding water to flush the toilet.

I say, won't that steamer sink? [9]   The sound of water flowing is linked by association to Archer's question about a ship at sea in the storm. Archer will eventually serve in the King's Navy. The novel continually foreshadows World War I.

spirit-lamp [9]   A small lamp with a lighted wick burning a volatile fuel such as alcohol.

cot [9]   A crib. Rebecca is in the room with John, Betty Flanders's youngest child, who has just fallen asleep.

ma'm [10]   The narrator marks the class distinction between Mrs. Flanders and her servant, Rebecca.

Dods Hill [14]   A fictitious name. Castle Hill is the dominating ge-ological feature in Scarborough.

the Crimea [14]   The Crimean War (1853–1856) was a confronta-tion over control of the Crimean Peninsula on the Black Sea and the Azov Sea. In the war, Imperial Russia confronted an alliance of the United Kingdom, France, the Ottoman Empire, and the Kingdom of Sardinia.

Roman fortress [14]   An exaggerated reference to the remains of the Roman beacon built in A.D. 370.

the whole of Scarborough [14]   The view from Castle Hill shows the entire town below.

the red spot where the villas were building [15]   The expansion of the town of Scarborough into a suburban area where the construction of new residences had started. The villas would have been made of red brick.

allotments . . . diamond flash of little glass houses in the sun [15]   Allotments are parcels of land allocated for the vegetable and flower plots and small greenhouses of the residents.

shingle [15]   Pebbly beachfront area where small boats would be launched.

Little pleasure boats . . . goats suddenly cantered their carriages through crowds [15]   In 1626, a resident of Scarborough had discovered a spring of spa water and as a result the town became Britain's first seaside resort. With the coming of the railway in the 1840s, the accessibility and popularity of Scarborough increased.

Corporation [15]   From 1163, Scarborough had been a borough run by a Corporation responsible for all aspects of the city's functions.

Numbers of sponge-bag trousers were stretched in rows [15]   Describing rows of men wearing checked trousers lying on Bath chairs at the Scarborough Spa, Woolf creates a literary synecdoche (the part standing for the whole) in this painterly style using a Postimpressionist technique (see Roe, "Impact"). Bishop notes that the trousers are "so called because of the resemblance to the print commonly used on bags for carrying sponges and other bath supplies" (150 n12).

Purple bonnets fringed soft, pink, querulous faces on pillows in bath chairs [15]   This synecdoche evokes the image of petulant women wearing elaborate bonnets as they rest their heads on pillows while lying in wheeled Bath chairs. The chairs are named for another spa resort in the city of Bath, a site of ancient Roman baths.

Triangular hoardings were wheeled along by men in white coats [15]   Large advertisements and breaking news displayed on boards.

So that was a reason for going down into the Aquarium [15]   The monster shark is being exhibited. Eugenius Birch (1818–1884) designed the elaborate Scarborough Aquarium in an Indo-Moorish style. The building was demolished in the 1960s.

spirits of salt [15]   Hydrochloric acid is used to preserve specimens.

Gladstone bag [15]   Named after the Victorian-era British prime minister William Ewart Gladstone (1809–1898), the lightweight hand luggage has two hinged compartments. The hinged compartments are a reference to the jaws of the shark.

it was only by standing in a queue that one could be admitted to the pier [15]   Visitors had to wait in line to pay in order to pass through a turnstile and have access to the pleasure pier. A pier is a structure supported by piles that serves as a walkway over water. Many of the pleasure piers in the United Kingdom were built during the Victorian era when the railways made mass tourism at seaside resorts like Scarborough possible.

The pale girls . . . same blurred, drugged expression [16]   The pale girls may be visiting the spa to improve their health. The reference to three Jews may be a playful insider allusion to Leonard Woolf's short story "Three Jews" (1917) (see introduction page xxxix).

But there was a time when none of this had any existence [16]   The narrator reverses time (see also note to page 118, "But what century have we reached?"). Several piers were built in Scarborough over the centuries, including the Vincent's Pier begun in 1732 and finished in 1753, as well as the North Bay Promenade Pier, designed by Eugenius Birch, completed in 1869.

crinoline [16]   A rigid undergarment worn by women beneath their skirts to create a particular shape. The crinoline could be made of stiffened fabric or even of metal.

Cannon-balls . . . faded writing on it [16]   This archaeological description emphasizes the Victorian interest in history, highlights elements of warfare, and notes the ancient Roman presence in the region. Verdigris is the greenish corrosion of metal. Rev. Jaspar Floyd is probably the father of Rev. Andrew Floyd, a character who appears later in the novel.

breeches [16]   Short pants typically worn by young boys in the later Victorian period.

orchid leaf . . . little brown spots [17]   Johnny is Betty's youngest son (see note to page 9, "cot"). Betty identifies it as a common spotted orchid (*Dactylorhiza fuchsii*), which is typically found in the United Kingdom.

Mr. Floyd [17]   Mr. Floyd, like his father before him, visits cottages miles away on the moors, and, like old Rev. Floyd, is a scholar.

the elder boys were getting beyond her [17]   Mrs. Flanders seems to have homeschooled her boys when they were very young. They need to study Latin, but she cannot afford to pay for a tutor, so Mr. Floyd will have to suffice.

after tea [17]   A reference to the British tradition of afternoon tea, usually served around four P.M., with small cakes and sandwiches.

work-box [18]   Used to hold Mrs. Flanders's sewing paraphernalia.

blotting-paper [18]   Absorbent paper used to blot wet ink and prevent smearing.

paper-knife [19]   Used to open envelopes and cut the pages of books (at the time, the pages of most books were not trimmed but rather were published with the folds of the signatures uncut).

Byron [19]   George Gordon, Lord Byron (1788–1824), was a major second-generation Romantic poet (his predecessors were William Blake, Samuel Coleridge, and William Wordsworth; his contemporaries were John Keats and Percy Bysshe Shelley). Byron was known for his keen wit, his sexual adventures, and his advocacy for the independence of the Greeks from the Ottoman Empire. Prepared to fight in the conflict, Byron died of a fever just before the Greek War of Independence began.

King's Navy [19]   The reference to the King's Navy places the narrative after the death of Queen Victoria in 1901. Archer would not go to university.

Rugby [19]   Rugby School, one of the oldest public schools in England, was founded in 1567. Public schools in the United Kingdom are actually fee based and private, not public in the sense that American schools are. Jacob may have won a scholarship to Rugby, but it is more likely that Captain Barfoot was paying for his education. Rugby is particularly well known because of the Victorian-era novel *Tom Brown's Schooldays,* by Thomas Hughes (1822–1896).

silver salver [19]   A silver tray, presumably presented as a parting gift by Mr. Floyd's parish.

Sheffield [19]   A city in South Yorkshire about ninety miles inland from Scarborough.

Hackney [19]   A borough of London located a few miles north of the center of the city.

Maresfield House [19]   Possibly a school in Sussex (there was a Maresfield National School in that area at the time).

Ecclesiastical Biographies [19]   Lives of historical church leaders. Virginia Woolf's paternal grandfather, Sir James Stephen (1789–1859), was the author of *Essays in Ecclesiastical Biography* (1842).

Hampstead [19]   A suburb north of central London.

Leg of Mutton Pond [19]   A pond located on Hampstead Heath.

Piccadilly [20]   Piccadilly Circus, a major thoroughfare in London, located in the West End of the City of Westminster.

Late Victorian- or Edwardian-era photograph of Piccadilly Circus, featuring the 1893 Memorial Fountain to Lord Shaftesbury with the statue of Eros, designed by Alfred Gilbert, A.R.A. (1854–1934).

Scarborough and Harrogate Courier [20]   A fictitious local newspaper.

Topaz [20]   Probably so named because the color of his fur is similar to that of an orange-hued precious stone.

gelded [20]   Castrated or neutered.

stag-beetle [20]   The male stag beetle (*Lucanus cervus*) has pincerlike mandibles that it uses to protect itself or to attack other stag beetles. Albrecht Dürer's 1505 extremely detailed watercolor of a male stag beetle shows its unusual characteristics.

whiff of rotten eggs [20]   The smell of sulfur. The substance was probably used by Jacob to asphyxiate insects captured for the study of entomology. As a child, Virginia and her siblings collected butterflies and moths. She describes how the moths were captured in a diary entry: "A Red underwing was on the tree. By the faint glow we could see the huge moth—his wings open, as though in ecstasy, so that the splendid crimson of the underwing could be seen—his eyes burning red, his proboscis plunged into a flowing stream of treacle. We gazed one moment on his splendour, & then uncorked the [poison-pot]" (*A Passionate Apprentice* 145).

pale clouded yellows [20]   *Colias hyale* is a small yellow butterfly.

furze bush [20]   Furze (*Ulex europaeus*) is a prickly, dense shrub that grows on the moors and has small yellow flowers. It is also known as gorse.

fritillary [20]   Possibly the heath fritillary (*Melitaea athalia*), an orange and black spotted butterfly.

death's-head moth [21]   A large hawk moth (*Acherontia atropos*) found mainly in the Mediterranean and Middle East. The distinctive feature of the moth is a skull-like pattern on its back. The death's-head moth is relatively rare in Britain, arriving in late summer and early fall. The adult moth steals honey from beehives; the caterpillars feed on potatoes. The species name of the moth derives from Atropos, the eldest of the Moerae, the mythic Greek Fates (see introduction page lii–liii). The genus name, as Bishop notes, is from "Acheron, the river of pain in the Greek underworld" (151 n16). Vincent van Gogh's 1889 painting of a death's-head moth emphasizes the skull-like formation on the back of the insect.

camphor [21]   A whitish crystalline substance with a strong unpleasant smell used to deter moths (mothballs were made of camphor) from destroying woolen clothing. The substance would have been used to preserve the insect specimens.

butterfly boxes [21]   The boxes in which the insect specimens were stored.

fulvous [21]   Reddish yellow, dull yellowish brown, or tawny (*OED*).

a volley of pistol-shots [21]   The tree falling sounds like pistol shots. The phrase is a memento mori and recurs, referring to the sound of the falling tree, in chapter 3 (see page 31). Woolf also refers to the fallen tree in her essay "Reading," written ca. 1919 (*Essays* 3: 152).

Morris [21]   A reference to Francis Orpen Morris (1810–1893), author of *A History of British Butterflies* (1853) and of *British Moths* among other works. Morris, according to his obituary in the *Entomologist*, "belonged to a well-known Yorkshire family" and was the vicar of Nafferton, near Driffield in East Yorkshire. In 1854 he moved to the rectory of Nunburnholme. Roe notes that the Stephen siblings had a copy of one of Morris's books (160 n20).

red underwing [21]   *Catocala nupta* is a large moth with red markings under its wings. The moth comes to both light and sugar used to trap it.

straw-bordered underwing [21]   Probably a straw underwing (*Thalpophila matura*) typically found in the north of England and in Scotland rather than a scarce bordered straw (*Helicoverpa armigera*), more common in the south. The straw underwing is nocturnal and has dark forewings. Its lighter hindwings are straw colored, marked with a darker border. It, too, comes to both light and sugar.

mowing-machine [21]   A lawn mower.

blues [22]   May be *Plemyria rubiginata,* blue-bordered carpet butterflies. Bishop suggests that they are common blue (*Lycaena icarus*) (152 n17).

painted ladies [22]   An orange butterfly (*Vanessa cardui*) with brown wing tips and white markings.

peacocks [22]   The peacock butterfly (*Inachis io*) has a distinctive eyespot on each wing used to deter predators.

teasles [22]   *Dipsacus fullonum* are tall bristly plants with spiky purple flowers.

commas [22]   The butterfly may be a shoulder-striped wainscot (*Mythimna comma*) or a *Polygonia c-album* (see Bishop 152 n17).

white admiral [22]   May be a *Limenitis camilla* or *Basilarchia arthemis*, a variety of butterfly. Bishop suggests that it is a *Limenitis sibylla* (152 n17).

Easter holidays [22]   Jacob is home from school but will be going back very soon. The butterflies and moths are summer insects, so the reference to the Easter holidays (which occur in March or April, depending on the phase of the moon) is an indication that the chronology has shifted forward to the next year.

serge [22]   A twilled woolen fabric.

rubber-shod stick [22]   A walking stick with a rubber tip or ferrule.

esplanade [22]   A boardwalk.

watering-carts [23]   Horse-drawn vehicles used to sprinkle the streets.

the Pierrots, or the brothers Zeno, or Daisy Budd and her troupe of performing seals [23]   Fictitious entertainers.

drapery stores [23]   Fabric stores.

swimming-bath [23]   The Scarborough Aquarium featured a swimming pool, added in 1893.

Mount Pleasant [23]   An actual street near North Cliff and Castle Hill in Scalby Mills, Scarborough.

mews [24]   A narrow passage or alley where stables are located. Mr. Dickens and his family live above a stable.

tram [24]   A trolley car, almost certainly horse drawn rather than electrified.

Rectory [24]   Home of an Anglican rector.

Nero [24]   Nero Claudius Caesar Drusus Germanicus (37–68) was a Roman emperor.

ferrule [26]   A cap at the end of a stick.

Bridge [26]   Location of command on a ship.

pea-jacket [26]   A double-breasted heavy woolen coat with large buttons worn by sailors and naval officers.

bandanna handkerchief [26]   See note to page 6.

hearth-brush [26]   A brush used to clean the fireplace.

after twenty years [26]   The time frame suggests that Mrs. Flanders's relationship with Captain Barfoot may have preceded her marriage to Seabrook.

I have a very nice report from Captain Maxwell [27]   Archer is now serving in the King's Navy.

Cricket [27]   A British and Commonwealth game played with a bat and ball. As a child, Virginia herself was known by her siblings as a "demon bowler" in cricket (George Rylands, *Portrait of Virginia Woolf*, BBC Home Service, 29 August 1956, quoted in Quentin Bell, *Virginia Woolf: A Biography*, vol. I [New York: Harcourt Brace Jovanovich, 1972]: 33).

went up to Cambridge in October, 1906 [27]   The date establishes that Jacob is around nineteen when he starts his university studies; he goes up to Cambridge the same year as Virginia Woolf's friend Rupert Brooke did. It was in 1906 that Woolf's brother Thoby Stephen died at age twenty-six from typhoid.

smoking-carriage [28]   Jacob enters the compartment of a train car that does not permit the smoking of tobacco.

jumped in [28]   Jacob entered the compartment from the station platform. At the time British train cars did not have corridors but were divided into separate compartments, each with their own door on either side and no access to other compartments or to lavatories; because of the isolation, women traveling alone could be quite anxious about their safety. Woolf's holograph draft indicates that Jacob is "about eighteen or a twenty" and that the compartment is third class (Bishop, *Holograph* 25).

spring of her dressing-case [28]   The latch of the small piece of luggage containing toiletries.

scent-bottle [28]   A perfume or cologne bottle.

Mudie's [28]   Mudie's Select Library, for subscribers who paid for the service and for the assurance that the selection process had eliminated any likelihood of indecency (see Guinevere L. Griest, *Mudie's Circulating Library and the Victorian Novel*, Bloomington: Indiana University Press, 1970). A one-year subscription to Mudie's Select Library cost at least a guinea (twenty-one shillings).

communication cord [28]   An emergency chain or cord in a train.

Morning Post [28]   A conservative daily newspaper published in London from 1772 to 1937 and then purchased by the owners of the *Daily Telegraph*.

Daily Telegraph [28]   A conservative British broadsheet newspaper, founded in 1855.

Mr. Norris's novels [29]   William Edward Norris (1847–1925), a prolific late Victorian British writer whose work would have met
the standards of Mudie's Select Library.

Out at sea a great city will cast a brightness into the night [30]   The phrase
resonates with Thomas Hardy's description, in *Jude the Obscure*
(1895), of Cambridge (renamed Christminster in the novel) and
its lights and spires seen from a great distance. Jude never
attains his dream of being educated at Cambridge. Like Jude,
Virginia Stephen was excluded from the halls of learning at
Cambridge. In her case, she was barred based on gender rather
than class since neither her father nor her mother wanted her to
be educated at a public school or university. Her short fictional
piece "A Woman's College from the Outside" was originally included in the manuscript of *Jacob's Room* as chapter 9 but later
excised (see introduction page lviii).

gowns [30]   The gowns worn by the boy choristers and other participants in the religious service. All members of the university
community wore gowns appropriate to their standing and role
in the institution.

subservient eagle . . . white book [30]   The large Bible is open on the
lectern, which is made of metal cast in the shape of an eagle.
However, Roe indicates that there was no such lectern at King's
College Chapel (161 n8).

illumines the tree-trunks [30]   This passage and the similar one below
both refer back to chapter 2. The passage recalls Virginia and
Thoby Stephen's childhood collecting of moths using sugaring
and lanterns (see *A Passionate Apprentice* 144–45). In her essay
"Reading" (ca. 1919), Woolf revises the "bug-hunting" passage

from her early diary entry: "The lantern had not stood upon the ground for ten seconds before we heard . . . little crackling sounds which seemed connected with a slight waving and bending in the surrounding grass. Then there emerged here a grasshopper, there a beetle, and here again a daddy longlegs. . . . They went straight . . . to the lantern" (*Essays* 3: 150).

approaching a pillar . . . So do these women [31]   Jacob thinks that women should not be permitted to attend services at the chapel and envisions them as dogs defiling a sacred place. This negative comparison of women to dogs in a religious setting is reiterated in *A Room of One's Own* when the narrator alludes to Samuel Johnson's infamous bon mot: "A woman's preaching is like a dog's walking on his hind legs. It is not done well; but you are surprised to find it done at all" (*A Room of One's Own,* Orlando: Harcourt, 2005: 54).

Waverley [31]   A series of early nineteenth-century historical novels by Sir Walter Scott that begin with the one titled *Waverley* in 1814.

Girton [31]   The first residential women's college in England, founded in 1869. For many decades women were not permitted to earn degrees at either Cambridge or Oxford. Woolf angrily criticizes this exclusionary practice in chapter 1 of *Three Guineas* (1938).

Scott [31]   Sir Walter Scott (1771–1832), a Scottish historical novelist and poet, and author of the Waverley novels. Virginia Woolf's father was very fond of Scott and read aloud to the family from his work.

touched the bell [32]   Rang the bell for the servant to begin serving lunch.

went down [32]   Graduated from university.

suburbs of Manchester [33]   Manchester is one of the largest cities in

England but would, from Woolf's perspective, have been considered exceedingly provincial. In the Victorian period, Manchester was an industrial city with numerous textile factories, but it was also the site of a number of workers' uprisings including the Peterloo Massacre in St. Peter's Fields in 1819. Friedrich Engels (1820–1895), the collaborator of Karl Marx (1818–1883), wrote his 1844 study *The Condition of the Working Class in England* based on Manchester. Mrs. Plumer, however, is seeking to climb the social ladder.

Persia [33]   Now known as Iran, Persia was an ancient empire with a long and complex history including the Greco-Persian Wars (499–448 B.C.). Persia was peripherally involved in World War I.

Trade winds [33]   Equatorial winds.

Reform Bill [33]   The 1832 Reform Act significantly increased the number of men eligible to vote (no women had the vote at that time).

Wells [33]   Herbert George Wells (1866–1946), a novelist and a member of the Fabian Society, a group that advocated socialism. Wells was one of several Edwardian writers whose literary approach Woolf challenged in her 1923 essay "Mr. Bennett and Mrs. Brown."

Shaw [33]   George Bernard Shaw (1856–1950) was a prolific Anglo-Irish playwright, polemical writer, and member of the Fabian Society, a group that advocated socialism.

sixpenny weeklies [33]   Weeklies, costing sixpence, included the *New Age,* edited by A. R. Orage and Holbrook Jackson. This particular publication emphasized such topics as Fabian socialism and women's suffrage.

Bloody beastly [34]   "Bloody" is "foul language, a vague epithet expressing anger, resentment, detestation; but often a mere intensive" (*OED*); Richard A. Spears's *Slang and Euphemism* (3rd rev. and abridged ed., New York: Signet, 2001) traces the word back to a blurred pronunciation of "by your lady." "Beastly" is a British word that means offensive or vulgar.

Homer [34]   The ancient Greek epic poems *The Iliad* and *The Odyssey* are attributed to Homer.

Elizabethans [34]   Contemporaries of William Shakespeare (1564–1616) such as Christopher Marlowe (1564–1593), Ben Jonson (1572–1637), Edmund Spenser (1552–1599), Sir Thomas Wyatt (1503–1542), Sir Philip Sidney (1554–1586), and Sir Walter Raleigh (1554–1618).

poor devils [34]   British usage for unfortunate people.

against a red and yellow flame [34]   The narrator indicates that the world created by Jacob's elders has metaphorically been set on fire by the next generation. A similar image is invoked in *Three Guineas* in the context of feminist resistance to patriarchy: "Shall I ask them to rebuild the college on the old lines? Or shall I ask them to rebuild it, but differently? Or shall I ask them to buy rags and petrol and Bryant & May's matches and burn the college to the ground?" (*Three Guineas*, Orlando: Harcourt, 2006: 42).

young man of substance [34]   A man of substance is "well-to-do, wealthy" (*OED*); however, it is unlikely that Jacob qualifies as a man of substance.

Byron [34]   Another mention of Lord Byron (see note to page 19). Byron's work includes *Don Juan,* a satirical account of a young man's sexual adventures, reversing the Don Giovanni legend by making Don Juan the victim of female predation, as Jacob seems to be. As Roe notes, canto xxi of Byron's *Childe Harold's Pilgrimage* focuses on the Napoleonic Wars and the Duke of Wellington (162 n18).

thin green water of the graveyard grass [35]   The scanty grass in the graveyard where Seabrook Flanders is buried is being compared to water.

white dresses [36]   A synecdoche referring to women wearing white.

Falmouth [36]   A port city in Cornwall.

Harrogate [36]   A spa town in North Yorkshire.

Mohammedan [36]   Now an archaic term for a Muslim.

beastly [37]   See note to page 34.

chestnut blossoms [37]   The flowers of the chestnut trees.

cow-parsley [37]   *Anthriscus sylvestris,* a common wild plant in Britain, blooms in May. It is sometimes also known as *Daucus carota,* the wild carrot, which is called Queen Anne's Lace in the United States (http://www.carrotmuseum.co.uk/queen.html).

Trinity [37]   Trinity College, Cambridge University, where Leslie Stephen, Thoby Stephen, Leonard Woolf, and Lytton Strachey all were educated. All of these men were also members of the Cambridge Conversazione Society, a secret society known informally as the Apostles. The organization, founded in 1820, was devoted to intellectual debate; however, there is no direct reference to the Apostles in *Jacob's Room.*

Great Court [37]   The open quadrangle of the college.

Neville's Court [37]   Correctly spelled Nevile's Court, it is named after one of the college masters at Trinity College, Thomas Nevile. Bishop notes that Lytton Strachey and Leonard Woolf both had rooms on Nevile's Court (154 n30).

at the top [37]   Before the invention of elevators, residents who had limited resources typically lived in rooms on higher floors because they could not afford the more accessible and thus more desirable living spaces.

yellow flags [37]   Water iris (*Iris pseudacorusis*).

Does History consist of the Biographies of Great Men? [37]   In part, this query is a reference to Thomas Carlyle's claim that "the history of the world is but the biography of great men." However, there is also an element of humor since Virginia Woolf's father, Leslie Stephen, was the editor of the *Dictionary of National Biography* (which, of course, mostly featured the biographies of great men, as one would expect in the Victorian period).

Lives [37]   Biographies.

Duke of Wellington [37]   Arthur Wellesley (1769–1852), the 1st Duke of Wellington, known as the Iron Duke, fought and defeated Napoleon at the Battle of Waterloo in 1815. There are multiple references to the Duke of Wellington and the Napoleonic Wars in the novel (see Smith; Bradshaw 25–28).

Spinoza [38]   Born Baruch de Spinoza (1632–1677), later Benedictus de Spinoza, he was a Dutch philosopher. He was born into a Jewish family but later banished from that faith because of his views on the nature of God.

Dickens [38]   Charles Dickens (1812–1870), a prolific Victorian novelist.

Faery Queen [38]   *The Faerie Queen,* by Edmund Spenser (ca. 1552–1599), first published in 1590, is an allegorical epic poem written in honor of Queen Elizabeth I.

Greek dictionary with the petals of poppies [38]   The poppy petals are dried between the pages of the dictionary. See introduction (lxxxv) regarding the significance of the poppy in war poetry.

Elizabethans [38] Jacob's books include the poets and play-
wrights mentioned above (see note to page 34). Rupert Brooke
(see introduction lxxi) was very interested in Elizabethan
drama.

photographs from the Greeks [38] These may be photographs of the
Elgin Marbles, which consist of some statuary as well as elements of the Parthenon Frieze that were removed from Athens
in the early 1800s after Thomas Bruce, 7th Earl of Elgin (who
was at the time the ambassador to the Ottoman Empire), negotiated the removal of the artifacts at his own expense from
Greece to England. In 1816 the artifacts were purchased by the
British Museum. Another possibility is that Jacob has photographs of Greece itself taken by such British photographers as
George Wilson Bridges and James Robertson (some of these
photographs are included in the Getty Research Library, Special
Collections and Visual Resources, Early Photography in Greece
and the Mediterranean, an extensive archive of nineteenth-
century photography of Greece).

mezzotint [38] A reproduction of an image using the intaglio
process, in which an image is cut into a surface, usually a metal
plate, and then covered with ink. When the ink is wiped away,
the image, cut into the plate and saturated with the ink in every
crevice, is ready to print.

Sir Joshua [38] Sir Joshua Reynolds (1723–1792), who specialized
in portraits, was one of the most important and influential of
eighteenth-century English painters.

all very English [38] Jacob's collection of reading material and
images is typical of an English culture that featured an obses-
sive passion for ancient Greece. Woolf, in her short story "A
Dialogue upon Mount Pentelicus," asserts humorously that

"Germans are tourists and Frenchmen are tourists but Englishmen are Greeks" (*The Complete Shorter Fiction* 63). The attribu-
tion is apt since, as Rowena Fowler notes, the story is based on
the behavior of Thoby and Adrian Stephen, whose philhellenic
obsession made them feel as if they had "borrowed ancestors"
from ancient Greece (237).

works of Jane Austen . . . to some one else's standard [38]   Jane Austen
seems to be the only female author in Jacob's entire library. The
reference to "some one else's standard" indicates that Austen is
not to his taste.

Carlyle was a prize [38]   Thomas Carlyle (1795–1881) was a Victorian essayist, known for *Sartor Resartus,* the autobiographical
fragments of the life of a fictional character, Diogenes Teufels-
dröckh, who discovers the importance of work as a means of
overcoming material desires. Throughout the novel, Jacob actively seeks the gratification of his material desires and avoids
work. Jacob did not choose the book for himself; rather, he received it as an honor.

Italian painters of the Renaissance [38]   Painters of the period include Leonardo da Vinci (1452–1519) and Sandro Botticelli
(1444/45–1510), both of whom are discussed in *The Renaissance*
(1873; 1878; 1901) by Walter Pater (1839–1894). Woolf was familiar with Pater's work and had been tutored in Greek by his sister, Clara Pater. The Renaissance (rebirth) was a cultural shift in
Europe that began in the late medieval period.

old man, with his hands locked behind him, his gown floating black [38]
Woolf is describing a Cambridge don (professor) wearing the
traditional academic attire that dates back to the medieval period. Undergraduates at the university also wore gowns (see
note to page 30).

Then another . . . another [38]   A reference to two other professors and their quirks. The professors are fictitious but represent Woolf's satiric view of male educational traditions.

Greek burns here . . . philosophy on the ground floor [38]   A metaphor of the professors' disciplines or areas of study—Greek, science, and philosophy.

Rossetti's [38]   Paintings by Dante Gabriel Rossetti (1828–1882), a member of the Pre-Raphaelite Brotherhood, a poet, and the brother of Christina Rossetti (1830–1894). As Marshik notes, Rossetti was attacked by Robert Buchanan for the indecency of two of his poems, "Jenny," depicting a prostitute, and "Nuptial Sleep," depicting the postcoital pleasure of a married couple (34–37). Rossetti's sister was the author of "Goblin Market" among other poems. Virginia Woolf's mother, Julia Prinsep Jackson, served as a model for several pre-Raphaelite painters, posing for the depiction of Mary in *The Annunciation* by Edward Burne-Jones (1833–1898) and for drawings by her cousin Valentine Cameron Prinsep (1838–1904).

Van Goch [38]   His name spelled unconventionally in the novel, Vincent van Gogh (1853–1890) was a Dutch Postimpressionist artist known for his experimental work and his psychological problems (in a bout of severe depression, he cut off his left ear, and eventually committed suicide). His work was included in Roger Fry's provocative first Postimpressionist exhibition at Grafton Galleries in 1910. The subject of the reproduction Jacob has is unidentified, but Roe reminds the reader of Van Gogh's painting *A Pair of Shoes* (164 n30), since Jacob's shoes are an important motif, particularly at the end of the novel.

rusty pipes [38]   Used tobacco pipes.

We are the sole purveyors of this cake [38]   The narrator is referring to the mystique of university education by comparing Cambridge University to a merchant who boasts about having exclusive rights to a particular product.

change of dress [39]   Old Professor Huxtable has removed his academic gown and changed into more comfortable clothing.

chose his paper [39]   He subscribes to more than one newspaper. There were at the time numerous newspapers written for different readerships.

underground railway carriage [39]   A reference to the London Underground, which most North Americans would call a subway or a metro.

Huxtable's head will hold them all [39]   He knows more than the collective knowledge of all the passengers on the subway seat.

runnels [39]   Small streams.

whole hall, dome, whatever one calls it [39]   Another reference to Professor Huxtable's mind — the image is of his skull and brain, like a dome over a hall. The image of the dome will recur in chapter 9 in a description of the British Museum Reading Room.

gout [39]   A painful inflammation of the joints caused by the buildup of uric acid.

Strange paralysis and constriction — marvellous illumination [39]   A description of the professor's complex and peculiar personality traits.

on a pillow of stone he lay triumphant [39]   A description of a burial tomb with an effigy of the dead person carved into the stone.

nobody got up when they went or when they came [39]   It was common courtesy at the time for a man to stand up when someone entered a room. However, the undergraduates are not observing this tradition.

port [40]   Sweet red fortified wine from Portugal.

Virgil [40]   (also spelled Vergil) Publius Vergilius Maro (70–19 B.C.), a Roman poet of the classical period and author of the epic poem *The Aeneid* as well as the *Georgics* (a poem about agricultural life) and the *Eclogues* (also known as the *Bucolics*), mythologizing Roman politics. *The Aeneid* recounts the founding of Rome by Aeneas, a Trojan hero who survives the triumphant Greek victory over Troy.

Catullus [40]   Gaius Valerius Catullus (ca. 84–ca. 54 B.C.) was a celebrated poet who wrote vividly of heterosexual desire thwarted and fulfilled. Woolf's elegiac dedication to her brother Thoby is taken from "Catullus 101" (see introduction lxvi).

arms, bees, or even the plough [40]   "Arms" is probably a reference to the first line of *The Aeneid* ("Of arms and the man I sing"). In Book I of *The Aeneid,* there is a simile of bees likened to the building of Carthage: "As bees in early summer / In sunlight in the flowering fields / Hum at their work, and bring along the young / Full-grown to beehood" (I: 587–89). In the *Georgics,* the plough is a key motif but so are the bees. *Georgics* IV begins: "Of air-borne honey, gift of heaven, I now / Take up the tale" (1–2); in lines IV: 149–78, Virgil describes the nature of the bees and their habits (see Bradshaw 17–26). C. G. Perkell argues in "A Reading of Virgil's Fourth Georgic" (*Phoenix* 32.3 [Autumn 1978]: 211–21) that Virgil emphasizes the "bees' mores." While "many critics, noting such apiary virtues as loyalty and selflessness, have seen in the bees Virgil's model for the moral and political renewal of Rome," Perkell does not believe that "Virgil intends the bees to serve here as a positive social model for Romans." Rather, the bees are flawed creatures:

They fall into two categories, physical and spiritual. . . . The beekeeper plunders their wealth at will (228–29); in self-defense they lose their lives (238); finally, the entire hive, as Virgil represents it, can be lost through disease (281). Here Virgil intends to dramatize the bees' vulnerability, for he exaggerates the incidence of fatal disease among them. . . . The moral flaws of the bees are, perhaps, even more suggestive. Their mindless and passive loyalty to their king is contrary to Roman republican tradition. . . . Furthermore, the bees' labor is mindless. . . . Virgil's bees are passionate for war, especially civil. Although they do not weaken their bodies with sexual activity (198–99), they do expend them carelessly in battle (217 f.). Yet even their lauded continence (198–99) is more apparent than real. Bees are not truly continent for they have merely replaced sexual amor with another sort. (212–13)

Backs [41]   Several of the colleges at Cambridge University have their backs to the River Cam.

Clare Bridge [41]   A very beautiful bridge of Clare College that spans the River Cam.

Newnham [41]   A women's college at Cambridge University. Miss Umphelby probably has rooms at Newnham. Her character may be modeled on Janet Case, who tutored Virginia Stephen in Latin.

hanging lists above doors [41]   Professor Cowan seems also to be engaged in academic administrative activities, perhaps reporting scores on examinations.

foaming window-box [41]   Probably a window box filled with blooming flowers.

hive full of bees, the bees home thick with gold [41–42]   The undergraduates in their quarters are described as bees in a hive; the phrase "thick with gold" evokes the image of bees covered with the yellow pollen gathered during the day's work. The reference to the bees is probably also another allusion to Virgil's poetry (see Bradshaw 17–26).

Moonlight Sonata [42]   The Piano Sonata no. 14 in C-sharp minor, "Quasi una fantasia," op. 27, no. 2, was written in 1801 by German composer Ludwig van Beethoven (1770–1827).

waltz [42]   A piece of music in triple meter, usually in three-quarter time with a 1–2–3 count. Typically, a waltz is dance music.

shilling shockers [42]   Inexpensive British periodical publications with illustrations and serial stories. The genre of shilling shockers is related to halfpenny marvels, dime novels, and penny dreadfuls.

no need to think of them grown old [42]   Often referred to as the Lost Generation, university-educated men from the United Kingdom and the British Empire died in disproportionate numbers in the First World War (see introduction l).

Jo—seph! Jo—seph! [42]   This cry marks the absence of someone and thus is a deliberate variant on the earlier cry "Ja—cob! Ja—cob!" when, in the beginning of the novel, Jacob's brother Archer is looking for him.

elderly man . . . pile of tin covers [42]   A waiter or other college servant is carrying plates and plate covers.

clergymen's sons [42]   Because of the British laws of patrilineal primogeniture, generally requiring that the estate of the father pass to his eldest living son, younger male siblings often had no option for income except to join the armed forces or become clergymen. The sons of clergymen would have been the poor cousins of their more privileged uncles who had inherited the estate.

Keats [42]   John Keats (1795–1821), one of the great second-generation Romantic British poets. He died very young—at the age of twenty-five—of tuberculosis in Italy. The reference can be read as another reminder of the premature death of young men.

Holy Roman Empire [42]   The Holy Roman Empire was primarily Germanic in culture and was founded with the coronation of Charlemagne by Pope Leo III as the first Holy Roman Emperor in the year 800. Mention of the Holy Roman Empire is relevant to the historical grounding of the narrative of *Jacob's Room* since the Central Powers—the Austro-Hungarian, German, Ottoman, and Bulgarian remnants of the empire—were the forces that fought against the Entente Powers of France, Imperial Russia, and Britain (and eventually Italy and the United States) in the First World War.

making long pink spills from an old newspaper [43]   A spill is "a thin slip of wood, a folded or twisted piece of paper, used for lighting a candle, pipe, etc." (*OED*).

brutality . . . division between right and wrong [43]   The hints of this debate evoke the intellectual activities of the Cambridge Apostles as well as the "Thursday Evenings" that Thoby Stephen initiated in 1905, founding the Bloomsbury Group (see preface xiii).

fender [43]   A metal screen placed in front of a fireplace to prevent coals from falling out onto the floor (it is unlikely that, given the time of year and the reference to a hot spring night, there is a fire lit, but the fender is a permanent component of the fireplace).

date-stones [43]   The pits of the dried dates that Jacob has eaten.

swaddlings [44]   Wrappings or bandages used for babies and corpses.

Simeon [44]   Simeon may be a surrogate of Leonard Woolf. The name *Simeon* is from the Hebrew and means "harkening, listening." Simeon was the second son of the biblical Jacob. The tribe of Simeon is one of the ten lost tribes of Israel.

Julian the Apostate [44]   Flavius Claudius Julianus (A.D. 331–363) was the last pagan Roman emperor and ruled briefly from 361–363. Known as Julian the Apostate because he not only rejected Christianity but actively tried to suppress it, he ended special taxes imposed on Jews and also sought to rebuild Jerusalem. However, he failed in his ambitions and held his position for only the briefest period of time, dying from a wound sustained in battle. Julian was Thoby Stephen's first given name. Like his sister Adeline Virginia, Thoby was known by his middle name instead.

Scilly Isles [46]   The Isles of Scilly are off the coast of Cornwall.

tin of beef [46]   Canned beef.

glass [47]   A spyglass or small handheld telescope.

line [47]   The shipping company that owned the vessel.

Primus stove [47]   The brainchild of Frans Wilhelm Lindqvist, a Swedish inventor who in 1892 developed a small, portable appliance that burned paraffin and thus allowed travelers to heat their food in almost any setting. However, Jacob, by clumsily breaking the small pin or handle that turned the stove on, has made it impossible to heat anything.

calling pilchards [48]   A street vendor is selling a small fresh-caught fish similar to a sardine that was a mainstay of the fishing industry in Cornwall until the 1950s. As a child summering in St. Ives,

Cornwall, Virginia Stephen was intrigued by the pilchard fishery but did not actually see the pilchard catch until 1905, when she and her siblings returned to St. Ives after her father had died (*Moments of Being* 130–31).

mourning emblem [48]   A reference to traditional mourning symbols. The Victorians were particularly interested in the paraphernalia of death and mourning.

spats [49]   Cloth or leather coverings of the shoe uppers and ankles, generally with buttons down the side of the ankle and a strap fastened under the shoe. Spats were considered stylish.

Domesday Book [50]   William the Conqueror's 1086 census of England, conducted mainly for the purposes of taxation. *Domesday* or *doomsday* refers to the day of reckoning when the ruler accounts for his subjects' debts. In Christian eschatological belief, Christ judges all the people who have ever lived on the day of reckoning, which is known as the Last Judgment. The event follows the resurrection of the dead and the Second Coming of Christ.

Lord Chancellor [50]   The lord chancellor is one of the great officers of the state in the government of Great Britain.

Duke of Wellington [50]   See note to page 37.

Keats [50]   John Keats was born to a working-class family and his father worked in a stable in London caring for horses. See note to page 42.

Lord Salisbury [50]   Robert Arthur Talbot Gascoyne-Cecil, 3rd Marquess of Salisbury (1830–1903), participated in the Congress of Berlin (1878) in the aftermath of the Russo-Turkish War (1877–1878), negotiating for "peace with honour" and protecting British interests in the contested area. The intent of the gathering was to redistribute control of the Balkans after the Russian attempt to take the Balkan Peninsula from the Ottoman Empire.

tombs of crusaders [50]   Burial places of the Christian combatants who fought in the four successive religious wars known as the Crusades (1095–1291), intended to take the Holy Land from the Muslims.

Abide with me [51]   A Christian hymn written in 1847 by Henry Francis Lyte while he was close to death from tuberculosis. The hymn is used in military services on Remembrance Day each year (the event was formerly known in the United Kingdom as Armistice Day and is observed as Veterans Day in the United States). As Bishop notes, Edith Cavell (a World War I nurse who helped combatants of the Entente Powers escape from Belgium to the Netherlands, was court-martialed by the Germans, and was executed by firing squad), "repeated the words of the song with a clergyman" just before her death (156 n41). Her final words were, "I am glad to die for my country." Her execution was a key element of British war propaganda. A statue in her honor stands in St. Martin's Place near Trafalgar Square.

Great God, what do I see and hear? [51]   The hymn, originally in German, was probably written around 1556. It refers to the Last Judgment.

cormorant [51]   A coastal seabird.

Rock of Ages [51]   A popular Christian hymn that may reflect a conflict between Anglican and Methodist views of faith and salvation.

an icefield [51]   Winds blow toward Great Britain from the ice fields in the Arctic Ocean.

gold-beater's skin [52]   The treated membrane of the large intestine of oxen. For centuries, goldbeater's skin was used to repair torn vellum and parchment. Here, the image suggests an opaque crumpling of the water surface.

red lacquer box [52]   Lacquer is a very shiny finish; Timmy has been out in the sun all day and his skin is very sunburned and very sweaty.

scullery [52]   A kitchen area where dishes are washed.

Wesleyan [52]   Methodist.

Cardiff [52]   The capital of Wales, located on the south coast.

foxglove [52]   The common foxglove (*Digitalis purpurea*) is a tall flowering plant with fuzzy leaves and bell-shaped purple, pink, and white blossoms. The plant grows wild throughout Cornwall. It is also the source of digitalis, a medicine used to treat heart conditions.

gorse [52]   See note to page 20, "furze bush."

the victim's blood [52]   The narrator is referring to ancient sacrificial rituals practiced by the Celtic peoples. The passage is a memento mori.

Gurnard's Head [52]   A large coastal headland in Cornwall.

Look . . . [53]   A tourist's perspective on the life of Mrs. Pascoe.

glasses [53]   Binoculars.

tramp steamer [53]   A steam-driven ship that does not have a regular schedule for ports of call.

luggers [53]   A small boat used for fishing or sailing and equipped with two or three masts for lugsails, quadrilateral sails without a boom.

teasle [53]   See note to page 22.

peacock butterfly [53]   See note to page 22, "peacocks."

cream pan [53]   A shallow, open dish or vessel, typically made of metal, and used to set and skim cream.

signifying in a room full of sophisticated people the flesh and blood of life [53] From the perspective of upper-class people, Mrs. Pascoe is a stereotypical symbol of the wholesomeness and strength of her class. In Woolf's holograph draft, Mrs. Pascoe is sketched in a very earthy fashion, including references to her menstrual cycle and copulation with her husband (Bishop, *Holograph* 58).

dried skate [53]   An oddly shaped cartilaginous fish.

picture papers [54]   Weekly newspapers featuring photographs and illustrations.

Lady Cynthia's wedding at the Abbey [54]   Lady Cynthia Mary Evelyn Charteris, a descendant of William the Conqueror, married Herbert Asquith, the second son of Prime Minister H. H. Asquith, on July 28, 1910, at Westminster Abbey in London. The narrator's reference to a specific year indicates that Jacob has completed four years of university study. (See also introduction page lviii.)

carriage with springs [54]   A horse-drawn carriage with suspension. The rural horse-drawn wheeled vehicles would not have had any springs to break the impact of bumps and ruts in the dirt roadways.

soft, swift syllables [54]   Another comparison—in reverse—between the wealthy and the laboring classes. In British culture, the class divisions are often strongly marked by pronunciation.

hansom cabs [54]   Hansom cabs were small vehicles drawn by a single horse. The vehicle held two passengers comfortably and the driver sat on a sprung seat behind the vehicle. The word *cab* is a shortening of *cabriolet.*

wise old woman [54]   A reference back to the "pure gold" of her cherished thoughts and the class divisions that make her seem wholesome and worthy to the talkative class.

a Highland race, famous for its chieftains [54]   Mrs. Durrant is descended from Scottish clan leaders.

St. John's wort [54]   Saint-John's-wort (*Hypericum*) is a plant with small yellow flowers.

Falmouth [54]   See note to page 36.

blight was on her potatoes [55]   The potato blight caused the Great Irish Famine in Ireland in the 1840s.

pampas grass [56]   Tall, plumed grasses that grow near water.

convolvulus moth [56]   *Agrius convolvuli* is a member of the *Sphingidae* family and is known as a hawk moth. The convolvulus moth gathers nectar from flowers. The narrator compares herself (and all others who are fascinated by Jacob) to the convolvulus moth that, with its extremely long proboscis and swing-hovering behavior, attempts to drink the nectar of his mysterious being (see page 74).

nasturtium [56]   A brightly colored edible flower.

tobacco plant [56]   Flowering tobacco (*Nicotiana*).

passion flower [56]   *Passiflora* generally grows as a vine and produces stunning flowers.

scared sleepy wings into the air again [56]   The sound of the dinner bell at the Durrants' house frightened the rooks (rooks are members of the crow family and may be a harbinger of the crows in Flanders). The image of rooks settling and rising is repeated frequently in Woolf's works.

hazy, semi-transparent shapes of yellow and blue [57]   A synecdoche for young women in evening dress.

escallonia [57]   A fast-growing plant in the *Escalloniaceae* family, typically with crimson flowers and a honeylike scent.

old man with the beard went on eating plum tart [58]   This character is crafted from Woolf's childhood memories: "Mr Wolstenholme was a very old gentleman who came every summer to stay with us [at St. Ives]. . . . He fitted into a brown wicker beehive chair as if it had been his nest. . . . He had only one characteristic— that when he ate plum tart he spurted the juice through his nose so that it made a purple stain on his grey moustache. . . . By way of shading him a little I remember that we had to be kind to him because he was not happy at home; that he was very poor, . . . that he had a son who was drowned in Australia" ("A Sketch of the Past" 73). Possibly Jacob's uncle Morty is based on Mr. Wolstenholme's son. In Woolf's holograph draft, it is Mr. Clutterbuck who "was seized with an attack of sneezing" while eating plum tart (63).

a sovereign [58]   A gold coin worth one pound. Great Britain used the gold standard until World War I.

"Charlotte won't pay you" . . . "How dare you . . ." said Charlotte [58]   It was unseemly for genteel women to wager, so Charlotte is a very daring young woman.

Andromeda, Bootes, Sidonia, Cassiopeia [59]   Constellations of stars. Bishop notes that Sidonia is an asteroid (157 n47).

Andromeda [59]   Andromeda's mother, Cassiopeia, the wife of

Cepheus, king of Ethiopia, defied the gods and claimed that she and her daughter were more beautiful than the daughters of the sea god Nereus. Her reckless boasting provoked the wrath of Poseidon, and Cassiopeia had to offer her daughter as a sacrifice to a sea monster to protect Ethiopia from destruction. However, Andromeda was unexpectedly rescued from her dreadful fate by a hero, Perseus, who subsequently married her. Clara is specifically compared to Andromeda later in the novel (see note to page 129).

verbena leaf [59]   Probably *Verbena officinalis,* which is also known as common vervain.

silver-spangled stuff [61]   Costume material.

private theatricals [61]   Generally, respectable women would not have performed in public settings. Private theatricals, however, were common forms of amusement in the homes of the wealthy.

Lord Lansdowne's speech [61]   Henry Charles Keith Petty-Fitzmaurice, 5th Marquess of Lansdowne (1845–1927). He was probably speaking in relation to the 1909 vote in the Conservative-dominated House of Lords to block the so-called People's Budget, an effort on the part of the Liberal government to redistribute wealth. The Parliament Act of 1911 confirmed the dominance of the House of Commons in all legislative matters.

skein [62]   A ball of yarn.

make you act in their play [62]   This is one of several instances in which Jacob is a willing victim in a performance or game of some sort (see note to page 130, "And suppose one wreathed Jacob in a turban . . .").

"You're too good—too good" . . . No, no, no [63]   Clara hopes that Jacob will propose to her. In her holograph draft, Woolf struck out the lines "can't say it. Clara! Clara! Clara!" indicating Jacob's attraction to her (Bishop, *Holograph* 70).

"Not to sit for me" . . . planting her tripod upon the lawn [63]   Like Virginia Woolf's maternal great-aunt Julia Margaret Cameron (1815–1879), Miss Eliot is a photographer and is setting up her equipment. Woolf's mother, Julia Prinsep Jackson, frequently posed for Cameron.

Virgil [64]   See note to page 40.

Lamb's Conduit Street [64]   Lamb's Conduit Street is in Bloomsbury, where the Stephen siblings lived after the death of their father in 1904. Jacob's rooms are in a house located on or very near Lamb's Conduit Street, which runs from Guilford Place to Theobald's Road. The streets intersecting Lamb's Conduit are Long Yard, Great Ormond Street, Rugby Street, Emerald Street, Dombey Street, and Richbell Place.

pillar box [64]   A British mailbox. A pillar box is typically a tall red column with a mail slot near the top (which is why the little girl has to stand on her tiptoes to mail her letter).

kerb [64]   Curb.

Long ago great people lived here . . . and let them in [64]   In the seventeenth and eighteenth centuries, the area now known as Bloomsbury was developed by wealthy families. Southampton Square (later renamed Bloomsbury Square) was designed by Thomas Wriothesley, 4th Earl of Southampton, in 1660. However, by the nineteenth century the area was no longer fashionable. The bitter eighteenth-century rain rushing down the "kennel" might suggest that the area's high-class desirability is being washed into the gutter.

Southampton Row . . . a tailor [64]   The once fashionable area has become a commercial zone where the dominant business is tailoring. Jacob has left his rooms near Lamb's Conduit Street and has walked, perhaps via Great Ormond Street, to Southampton Row, then has probably turned left onto Old Gloucester Street and right onto Bloomsbury Street to New Oxford Street, where Mudie's Select Library was located.

Mudie's corner [65]   Mudie's Select Library (see note to page 28) was located at this intersection.

red and blue beads . . . on the string [65]   That is, omnibuses owned by different public transportation companies.

motor omnibuses were locked [65]   The reference to motor omnibuses indicates that there are still horse-drawn omnibuses as well. The motor omnibus is a two-decker. The buses are caught in a traffic jam. Jacob is on one of the buses traveling toward the City of London.

city [65]   The boundaries of the City of London date back to the medieval period. The City is located within Greater London.

Shepherd's Bush [65]   A district in West London.

proximity of the omnibuses . . . each other's faces [65]   The seating on the upper deck of the omnibus was open to the elements, allowing the passengers going in opposite directions to look directly at one another.

a young man in grey smoking a pipe [65]   This could be a rare glimpse of Jacob (Jacob does enjoy smoking his pipe and thus would want to sit on top of the omnibus).

swing down the staircase [65]   The spiral staircase leading to the upper deck of the omnibus.

steak and kidney pudding [65]   A popular British dish made of beef and animal organs in a pastry case.

Holborn [65]   Jacob's omnibus is passing through an area in central London en route to the City.

volute [65]   A spiral-shaped element (in this case, one similar to the shape of a snail shell). The narrator is describing a feature of St. Paul's Cathedral's architecture—probably the dome designed by Christopher Wren to replace the earlier structure destroyed in the Great Fire of London in 1666. The new cathedral was completed in 1708.

Late Victorian- or Edwardian-era photograph of St. Paul's Cathedral.

ghosts of white marble [66]   Carved effigies of the dead on the slabs that cover their tombs.

chaunts [66]   An archaic variant of the word *chants*.

verger with his rod [66]   A church official; the rod is called a "verge" and represents his authority.

marble shoulders . . . the folded fingers [66]   Another reference to the effigies on the tombs.

requiem — repose [66] A funeral or memorial service that concludes with prayers for the repose of a departed soul.

Prudential Society's [66] An insurance company, also known as the Prudential Assurance Company, located at the time at 142 Holborn Bars, High Holborn, London.

great Duke's tomb [66] The tomb of the Duke of Wellington was not unveiled until 1912; thus, the year should be 1912, but the chronology in *Jacob's Room* is sometimes blurry (regarding the Duke of Wellington, see note to page 37).

she never fails . . . on her own tomb [66] Mrs. Lidgett, like Mrs. Pascoe, has fantasies of grandeur regarding the privileges of the wealthy and famous — in this case, fantasies of an elaborate funeral and burial (see Clewell 200–1).

leathern curtain [66] Leather curtains were hung in the entryways of nineteenth-century churches.

Old Spicer, jute merchant [66] Spicer probably sells products made from jute such as cheap rope and coarse fabrics like burlap for sacks.

churchyard [66] The graveyard of the cathedral.

Where's Nelson's tomb? [66] Vice Admiral Horatio Nelson, 1st Viscount Nelson (1758–1805), was killed in the Battle of Trafalgar during the Napoleonic Wars. Nelson is buried in St. Paul's Cathedral and was commemorated most famously by the column in Trafalgar Square, which displays his statue.

Finlay's Byzantine Empire [66] George Finlay (1799–1875) was a British historian whose works focused primarily on Greece and the Byzantine Empire. His works included *History of the Byzantine Empire, 716–1057*. He, like Byron, was an advocate of Greek independence from the Ottoman Empire. Finlay actually fought in the war (Byron died before seeing action).

Ludgate Hill [66]   The ancient site of a Roman temple to the goddess Diana on which the original St. Paul's Cathedral was later constructed.

three elderly men . . . parlour [67]   The men, who are spaced so that they will not compete with one another, are selling mechanical toys to passersby, probably windup penny toys manufactured in Germany.

a woman stares . . . to buy [67]   Another street vendor.

The posters . . . a race won [67]   Newspaper companies used posters to display the most current headlines.

beneath the sky . . . horse dung shredded to dust [67]   The particulate pollution in London air was the cause of the famous London fogs; the steel filings are a by-product of industrial production; the horse dung dust results from the numerous horse-drawn vehicles that were still a main mode of transportation in the 1910s. Additional contributing factors included coal-burning fireplaces.

green shade [67]   Possibly a glass shade on an office worker's desk lamp. Alternatively it could be a transparent green celluloid eyeshade, a visor worn by office workers.

provender [67]   Food provisions.

industrious pen [67]   Various prototypewriters were developed in the 1800s, but it was not until the 1920s that the machine became an essential fixture of the office.

Innumerable overcoats . . . along the pavement [67]   The workers are depicted as mechanical figures. Probably, the figures "split apart into trousers" are men and the ones that are "a single thickness" are women.

dropped into darkness [67]   Entered the Underground or the Tube (the London transport system).

Beneath the pavement . . . circuses of the upper [67]   The narrator is describing the lighting in the Underground stations. "Circuses" refer to the proper names of streets such as Oxford Circus and Piccadilly Circus (*circus* is derived from the Greek word *kirkos,* meaning circle; in Roman culture, the circus came to be a site of competition, whether horse racing or gladiatorial combat or other spectator events). The underworld is another term for Hades, which, in classical Greek mythology and literature, is the final destination for the shades of the dead.

Marble Arch . . . a blue ground [67]   The Marble Arch is located at the northeast corner of Hyde Park where Edgeware Road, Oxford Street, and Park Lane intersect. Shepherd's Bush is several stops farther west from Marble Arch on the Central Line. Signs in the Underground (the Tube) are in white lettering on blue enamel plaques.

Only at one point . . . a bedroom [67]   Aside from the area near their own station, most commuters never see what is above ground on their route.

Acton, Holloway, Kensal Rise, Caledonian Road [67]   Various areas outside of central London accessed by different Tube lines— Acton is on the central Line, Holloway and Caledonian Road are on the Piccadilly Line, and Kensal Rise is on the Bakerloo Line.

Union of London and Smith's Bank [67]   A major Victorian-era bank.

clasping a brown mongrel . . . against her breast [67–68]   In a diary entry, Woolf notes: "An old beggar woman, blind, sat against a stone wall in Kingsway holding a brown mongrel in her arms & sang aloud. There was a recklessness about her; much in the spirit of London. Defiant—almost gay, clasping her dog as if for warmth. How many Junes has she sat there, in the heart of London? How she came to be there, what scenes she can go through, I can't imagine. O damn it all, I say, why cant [*sic*] I know all that too?" (*Diary* 2: 47).

Bank [68]   A stop on the Central Line of the Underground, Bank is in the City of London and named for the Bank of England. As Ward, Lock and Company's *Pictorial and Descriptive Guide to London and Its Environs* (London, 1914) indicates, "It is the busiest spot in restless London. Here converge no fewer than seven of the most important thoroughfares . . . Of omnibuses alone, a recent official count gave an average at the Bank of 690 per hour, . . . while underground 600 trains a day bring people to or from this busy centre. Here may be seen, . . . that glorious spectacle of the policeman with uplifted arm which nearly always moves the wonder and admiration of visitors from abroad" (199). Facing the Bank of England is the Royal Exchange, and close by is the Mansion House, the official residence of the lord mayor. Woolf refers to this same "spectacle of the policeman" as an icon of patriarchal machinery in chapter 13 (see 164).

eternally the pilgrims trudge [68]   The pilgrims in this case are probably the city dwellers and workers. Pilgrims generally travel to visit a distant religious site, often on foot.

Of all the carriages . . . condemn [68]   The operagoers are traveling by horse-drawn vehicles, the men wearing formal black and white and the women pastel-colored evening attire. Wealthy neighborhoods such as Mayfair and Kensington are located in the West End of London. The Royal Opera House is near Covent Garden, which at the time was a fruit, vegetable, and flower market located close to a slum area known as Seven Dials; the "little thief" probably lives in the immediate vicinity.

Thomas à Kempis [68]   (1380–1471), author of *The Imitation of Christ,* was a Roman Catholic monk. Lady Charles is trying to find spiritual solace even though she does no good works (a passage from *The Imitation of Christ* reads: "At the Day of Judgement we shall not be asked what we have read but what we have done" [Book I, chapter 3]).

autumn season [68]   According to *The Musical Times,* vol. 52, no. 822 (August 1911), 533–34, "The season of German opera at Covent Garden in October and November will be under the musical direction of Dr. Hans Richter. The works to be given will [include] 'the Ring' [and] 'Tristan und Isolde.'"

Tristan [68]   A performance of Richard Wagner's *Tristan and Isolde,* a tragic love story based on misunderstandings and betrayals that ends with the death of both lovers. (See note to page 71 for more information about Wagner.)

pink faces and glittering breasts [68]   The operagoers' faces are reduced to mere pink ovals and their bodies to the shimmer of their jewelry and evening clothes.

When a Royal hand attached . . . a name worth dying for [68]   The reference is to Queen Mary, the wife of King George V, who ascended to the throne upon the death of his father Edward VII in 1910.

Walpole [69]   Horace Walpole, 4th Earl of Orford (1717–1797), a politician and writer, was known for his keen and stinging wit.

As one scholar puts it, "Seldom free of malice, Walpole's wit has bequeathed a chaplet of gems that shine the brighter for those who know their eighteenth century. How can one forbear to smile at the thought of stuffy Bute voiding a 'quarry of gall-stones,' one so large as to deserve a place in the British Museum? . . . Or at the listing, among other art objects, of 'one bedpan having the queen's arms enamelled at the end?'" (W. S. Lewis and A. Dayle Wallace, *Horace Walpole's Correspondence with the Countess of Upper Ossory,* reviewed by Charles F. Mullett in *The American Historical Review* 71.2 [January 1966]: 562–64).

Victoria . . . her ministers [69]   On June 20, 1837, King William IV, the uncle of Princess Victoria, died. The new monarch was awakened in the early hours of the morning and, according to a report by Miss Frances Williams Wynn, she appeared before her ministers in her nightgown and with her hair down (Frances Williams Wynn, *Diaries of a Lady of Quality from 1797 to 1844,* edited by A. Hayward, 2nd ed. [London: Longman, Green, Roberts & Green, 1864]).

opera glass [69]   A special kind of binoculars used to see the stage and the performers in more detail.

bald-headed men . . . wand [69]   Men in leadership roles who are seated next to the queen during the performance are mingling with other members of the audience during the intermission; they do not take their seats until the conductor raises his baton.

Clara Durrant said farewell . . . sweetness of death in effigy [69]   Saying good night to Jacob, Clara envisions herself as Isolde. In the last act of the opera, Tristan dies of his wounds in Isolde's arms and, in a moment of transfigured grief, Isolde dies of love itself.

Brangaena [69]   More typically spelled Brangäne, she is Isolde's attendant.

suspended in the gallery . . . his miniature score [69]   Edward Whittaker is high up in the gallery, where the seats are very cheap; he has to use a flashlight (a torch) to follow the performance (he probably has a vocal score that would include English translations from the German).

Only to prevent . . . stalls, boxes, amphitheatre, gallery [69]   The opera theater is divided into categories based on rank; the most privileged operagoers have the stalls and boxes and the best view of the stage; those who are the next level down in society are seated in the amphitheater relatively close to the stage, while the least privileged who can still afford the opera are seated high in the gallery, very far from the stage.

Wellington nose [70]   The man has a large hooked nose like that of the Duke of Wellington (see note to page 37).

seven-and-sixpenny seat [70]   Probably a moderately priced single ticket (rather than season ticket) for a reserved seat.

By Jove! [70]   The exclamation is a mild oath and expresses surprise. It circumvents the objectionable phrase "by God!" by invoking Jove (also known as Jupiter), the supreme deity of the ancient Roman gods, rather than the Christian deity, Jehovah.

Virgil [70]   See note to page 40.

Lucretius [70]   Titus Lucretius Carus (ca. 99–ca. 55 B.C.), a Roman poet and philosopher, known for his philosophical and scientific epic poem *De rerum natura* (*On the Nature of Things*).

Damned swine! [70]   A rather extreme insult.

Professor Bulteel, of Leeds [70]   A fictitious professor at the University of Leeds, only granted a royal charter as a university at the beginning of the twentieth century. Leeds is a city in West Yorkshire. Jacob, as a Cantabrigian, regards the University of Leeds as an inferior institution.

Wycherley [70]   William Wycherley (ca. 1640–1716) was a Restoration-era playwright whose sexually fraught comedies included *Love in a Wood, The Country Wife,* and *The Plain Dealer.*

Aristophanes [70]   A dramatist (ca. 450–388 B.C.) who wrote satirical and political plays, including *Lysistrata,* in which women attempt to end the Peloponnesian War (431–404 B.C.) by withholding sex from their husbands to force them to lay down their weapons.

copied his pages [70]   Wrote a clean copy of the essay by hand.

the Fortnightly . . . Nineteenth Century [70]   The *Fortnightly Review,* published biweekly, was founded by Anthony Trollope and others in 1865 and was one of the major periodicals of the era. Its focus was secular and, for a time, liberal. The *Contemporary Review,* founded in 1866 by Alexander Strahan, was a religiously oriented response to the *Fortnightly.* It was in the *Contemporary Review* that Robert Buchanan published his scathing attack on Dante Gabriel Rossetti in his essay "The Fleshly School of Poetry: Mr. D. G. Rossetti" (see note to page 38). In 1882, Percy Bunting took over the editorial responsibilities at the *Contemporary Review* and transformed it into a liberal political publication. Founded in 1877 by James Knowles, one of the editors of the *Contemporary Review, Nineteenth Century* (which added *and After* to its title in 1901) was a literary periodical. Leslie Stephen, Woolf's father, contributed to the *Fortnightly Review.*

old flannel trousers [70–71]   Soft, woven woolen pants.

with the Cornish postmark [71]   Letters from Cornwall, probably from Clara Durrant.

black wooden box . . . in white paint [71]   This coffinlike box was probably the trunk in which Jacob shipped his belongings to London from Cambridge.

furniture . . . came from Cambridge [71]   The furniture was in Jacob's rooms at the university. A gate-legged table has legs that swing out to support the hinged leaves.

These houses . . . have their distinction [71]   Jacob rents rooms on one floor of a row house in the Bloomsbury area. The landlady, Mrs. Whitehorn, is the daughter of Mrs. Garfit, a neighbor in Scarborough. The house would have been built in the mid-1700s. The sitting room (living room) faces the street; the bedroom probably faces into a garden space in the back of the house. The narrator does not say that Jacob's room actually has the ram's skull motif over his doorways—it might be the carved rose instead.

Wagner [71]   Wilhelm Richard Wagner (1813–1883) was a German composer. His operas (also known as "music dramas") include *Tristan and Isolde* (see note to page 68) and *The Ring of the Nibelung* (*Der Ring des Nibelungen*), an epic cycle of four individual operas based on Norse mythology.

which seat in the opera house was his [71]   Jacob's social standing is difficult to categorize in terms of class. Using the metaphor of opera seating to analyze social rank, Woolf blurs Jacob's status to make him an everyman of the educated classes (see note to page 69, "Only to prevent . . .").

Mr. Letts . . . shilling diaries [72]   In 1812, John Letts, a stationer, combined the format of the calendar with that of a journal to create the daily diary, providing a single small page for each day of the year.

She wished . . . that July morning [72]   As she stands in the green-house where she had cut the grapes for Jacob in July 1910, Clara is recalling Jacob's visit to Cornwall.

I'm twenty-two [73]   Since Jacob went up to Cambridge in 1906 when he was about nineteen, he was born in 1887 or thereabout (Woolf's holograph draft indicates that he is between eighteen and twenty when he goes to university [Bishop, *Holograph* 25]). If he is twenty-two, the year is 1909—but there are a number of other indications that at least four years have passed since he began his studies at Cambridge University, in which case the year is 1911 or 1912. Thus the chronology of the novel is not entirely reliable—and Jacob should be twenty-four in this chapter.

wearing a tail coat [73]   Tailcoats were required for men at formal events.

Beethoven [73]   Ludwig van Beethoven (1770–1827), a German composer.

all those Frenchmen [73]   Bonamy's personality is very similar to that of Lytton Strachey, whose first book-length work was *Landmarks in French Literature* (1912). The book covers French literary history from the Middle Ages through the nineteenth century.

talking rot [73]   Talking nonsense.

Tennyson [73]   Alfred Tennyson, 1st Baron Tennyson (1809–1892), was the poet laureate from 1850 until his death. His poetry includes *In Memoriam,* a long elegiac poem written in honor of Arthur Hallam, a dear friend from Trinity College, Cambridge, who died prematurely. Both were members of the Apostles. In addition, Tennyson wrote *Idylls of the King,* an epic based on

Arthurian legends, as well as "The Charge of the Light Brigade," a poem celebrating the bravery of the British combatants who fought in a botched attack on the Russian forces during the Crimean War.

market carts [73]   Large, heavy wheelbarrows filled with produce and used for selling fruits and vegetables.

pocket-book [73]   A pocket-sized case or folder for money and papers.

hawk moth [74]   The hawk moth (see also note to page 21, "death's-head moth") has an unusual flying pattern and is able to move rapidly from side to side while hovering (a trait called "swing-hovering"). Since the hawk moth feeds on flower nectar, it has an unusually long proboscis.

Parliament [74]   The seat of British government.

Late Victorian- or Edwardian-era photograph of the Houses of Parliament, Westminster Hall, and the Clock Tower.

hob [74]   A flat raised area in a fireplace used to warm food and heat water.

burning Guy Fawkes on Parliament Hill [74]   It is November 5, 1909, and celebrations of Bonfire Night or Guy Fawkes Night are under way. Guy Fawkes (1570–1606) was born in Yorkshire, as was Jacob Flanders. Fawkes, a Roman Catholic, joined in the

Gunpowder Plot of 1605 to enable the succession of a Catholic monarch. The intent was to blow up the House of Lords on November 5 during the state opening of Parliament, thereby killing the Protestant king James I, his eldest sons, and many members of Parliament. The attempt was thwarted. Guy Fawkes and his co-conspirators were executed on January 31, 1606, in the courtyard of St. Paul's Cathedral. The annual event, November 5, celebrates the failure of the plot by burning straw effigies of Guy Fawkes. Parliament Hill is near Hampstead Heath in northwest London. The hill was formerly called Traitor's Hill because the conspirators gathered there to plot. It was renamed Parliament Hill during the English Civil War when the troops loyal to the Parliamentarians held the hill.

flames had fairly caught [75]   The bonfire for burning the straw effigies of Guy Fawkes on Parliament Hill is lit.

city of London [75]   The City of London.

A hand descending . . . white hat of a pierrot [75]   "Chequered" means *checkered,* creating sharp bright and dark contrasts. Pierrot is the French name for a sad clown who always wears a distinctive pointed hat. The Bonfire Night festivities always include costumes.

billycock hats [75]   Low-crowned and wide-brimmed bowler hats made of felt.

polished tortoiseshell [75]   The water is colored brown and red by the light from the fire.

Guy Fawkes [76]   See note to page 74.

"Auld Lang Syne" [76]   A song written by Robert Burns, a Scottish poet. Singing "Auld Lang Syne" on Bonfire Night is a tradition. In Lewes, Sussex, near Rodmell, where Leonard and Virginia

Woolf bought Monks House in 1919, Bonfire Night festivities are also a remembrance of the seventeen Protestant martyrs who were burned alive in Lewes High Street from 1555 to 1557, under the Catholic reign of Mary Tudor.

barrel organ [76]   A barrel organ is typically a mechanical musical instrument with bellows, pipes, and a crank.

So they wreathed his head . . . figure-head of a wrecked ship [76]   Jacob is sitting on a white and gold chair that resembles a throne. See introduction li.

Then Florinda . . . in his waistcoat [76]   Only a promiscuous woman or a prostitute would sit on a strange man's knee in public and rest her head against his vest.

Haverstock Hill [77]   The most direct road leading back to Jacob's rooms in Bloomsbury from the Parliament Hill area.

Aeschylus [77]   Aeschylus (525/524–456 B.C.) was a Greek dramatist who is considered the founder of tragedy. His play *The Persians* was based on the Battle of Salamis (480 B.C.), in which the Persians were defeated by the Greeks. Aeschylus himself had fought in this battle.

Sophocles [77]   (ca. 496–406 B.C.) was, like Aeschylus, a great Greek tragedian. His surviving works include *Oedipus Rex* and *Antigone*.

It is true that no Greek . . . Never mind [77]   Woolf is drawing on her experiences traveling in Greece with her brothers (see 1906 in *A Passionate Apprentice;* "A Dialogue on Mount Pentelicus" in *Complete Shorter Fiction;* Fowler).

boy at Gibraltar [77]   The man's son is probably serving in the Royal Navy, which has a base on the Rock of Gibraltar, a territory on the Iberian Peninsula of Spain that has been held by the British since 1713 under the provisions of the Treaty of Utrecht.

Duke of Wellington [77]   See note to page 37.

surfeit of print [77]   Too much time spent reading books and newspapers.

specific [78]   A remedy that is especially effective in treating a particular ailment.

Acropolis [78]   A very high rock formation overlooking the city of Athens. The archaeological remains of ancient Athenian culture include the ruins of the Parthenon and the Erechtheum (known in Greek as the Erechtheion).

called him Jacob without asking his leave [78]   Florinda has violated social conventions, which excites Jacob.

wavering, quavering, doleful lamentation [78]   Probably the sound of a factory siren.

doors in back streets . . . stumped forth [78]   The workday has begun.

Inferno [78]   The Italian poet Dante Alighieri (1265–1321) wrote the epic poem *The Divine Comedy* in three parts. The first section is *Inferno,* a depiction of the nine circles of hell. The second is *Purgatorio,* and the third is *Paradiso.*

bedroom seemed fit for these catastrophes . . . rosaries pendent from the gas brackets [78]   Florinda has decorated her space in a bohemian fashion with various odds and ends, including the tall stovepipe-shaped hats worn by Welsh women, and religious objects displayed as decor. A gas bracket is a lighting fixture.

name had been . . . maidenhood was still unplucked [78]   Her name supposedly indicates that she is still a virgin.

was without a surname [79]   She does not have a last name. Sue Roe sees this absence as evidence of Florinda's illegitimate birth.

Mother Stuart [79]   *Mother* is a common term for a madam, a woman who runs a brothel.

transmigration of souls [79]   A belief that the soul survives after death and can be transferred from the body of the dead to another living body.

read the future in tea leaves [79]   Tell fortunes.

powdered her cheeks in omnibuses [79]   Women were just beginning to use cosmetics in the 1910s, defying the Victorian standards that branded any woman who used makeup as a prostitute. In her article, "The Make-up of Jean Rhys's Fiction," Rishona Zimring comments on a passage in *Mrs. Dalloway* (1925), noting that

> the audaciousness of the girl's public performance signals a new femininity that Woolf broadcasts as part of a post-war transition from Victorian to modern. Five years have blurred, if not erased, the line between private and public space, and also that between art and life; for a young woman, powdering in public means asserting one's freedom from domesticity and Victorian conventions of femininity that assign women to the natural, not the artificial. (*NOVEL: A Forum on Fiction* 33.2 [Spring 2000]: 212–34; 219).

A.B.C. shop [79]   The Aerated Bread Company Ltd was a chain of tearooms that offered inexpensive meals and, as Bishop notes, allowed "unchaperoned women" to eat alone or meet with friends. He notes that "the young Woolf patronized them regularly" (160 n63).

detected glass in the sugar bowl [79]   By claiming that there was broken glass in the sugar, Florinda is attempting to avoid paying for her tea.

dirty Jews [79]   In the holograph draft, Florinda asks Jacob if he is a Jew: "She told him how a Jew had played her a dirty trick, leaving all his dirty clothes scattered over the room, & she having to pawn her mothers watch to pay for the rent" (Bishop, *Holograph* 85, 86).

drew off her gloves [79]   A respectable woman would have had to have a chaperone to go out in the streets or to visit a man in his rooms; she would definitely not have removed her gloves.

tea-cosy [79]   Made of cloth or knitted wool, it covers a teapot to keep the tea hot.

took her word for it that she was chaste [79]   Jacob's naïveté is evidence that Florinda is not a virgin.

left with one of Shelley's poems beneath her arm [80]   Percy Bysshe Shelley (1792–1822), one of the second-generation Romantic poets, died young, as did his contemporaries, Keats and Byron.

Marvellous are the innocent [80]   In the book of Matthew in the New Testament, Jesus tells the crowds who the blessed are (for example, he says: "Blessed are the poor in spirit, for theirs is the kingdom of heaven" [5:3]). Here, "innocent" refers to Jacob's naïveté, not to his virtue.

unanchored life [80]   The bohemian life.

his own seeming petted and even cloistered in comparison [80]   Jacob is thinking of his sheltered upbringing and relatively comfortable lifestyle. "Cloistered" refers to the life of monks in a sequestered religious community with limited contact with the outside world and thus, by association, to the all-male environment of Cambridge University.

sovereign specifics . . . Shakespeare [80]   "Sovereign" means supreme, and "specifics" (as on page 78) is a reference to healing agents.

Thus Jacob believes that both Percy Bysshe Shelley's elegiac poem *Adonais* and the plays of Shakespeare are the ultimate remedy for the spiritual suffering of an educated man.

washed her head [80]   Florinda would not have had running water in her lodgings; most likely she washed herself with water from a basin and pitcher.

opened Shelley [80]   Opened the volume of Shelley's poems—or possibly a single volume of *Adonais*—lent to her by Jacob; the poem is elaborately constructed and involves extensive references to sources that would be obscure or even incomprehensible to an uneducated reader like Florinda. *Adonais* refers to many other poetic elegies, such as Milton's "Lycidas." The poem is in the ancient tradition of grieving for the gifted loved one's premature death.

formidable sights in the streets [80]   Possibly a reference to accidents. During one week in May 1897, Virginia Stephen witnessed several serious street accidents (*A Passionate Apprentice* 82–86).

beck and call of life [80]   Again, a description of the bohemian life.

All night men and women seethed up and down the well-known beats [80]   The "well-known beats" would refer to the nightlife in London—and the areas where prostitutes worked the streets.

shadows against the blinds even in the most respectable suburbs [80]   Illicit sexual encounters silhouetted against the drawn window blinds.

a square [80]   A square is typically a garden space surrounded on all four sides by streets and buildings. The amorous couple would be taking advantage of the darkness in the garden area.

Mozart [81]   Wolfgang Amadeus Mozart (1756–1791) was a prolific Austrian composer.

Bishop Berkeley [81]   George Berkeley (1685–1753), known as Bishop Berkeley, was an Irish philosopher who argued that one could only know sensations and ideas directly.

British Museum [81]   Located in Bloomsbury, the British Museum is a treasure trove of artifacts. The Elgin Marbles are among the collections (see note to page 38). Florinda is the first woman in the novel to see a strong resemblance between Jacob and statuary. Sandra Wentworth Williams (see note to page 165, "Jacob . . ."), Clara Durrant (see note to page 176, "This statue . . ."), and Fanny Elmer (see note to page 180, "battered Ulysses") see his qualities in relation to specific statues.

lamps of Soho . . . Jacob and Florinda approached [82]   Soho was one of the main thoroughfares for prostitution. Prostitutes often stood under streetlamps to attract customers. Both women and men prostituted themselves in the area at the time. In *Three Guineas,* Woolf mocks the idea that women, lacking the vote, could still have a political role by influencing powerful men with their sexual wiles: "If such is the real nature of our influence, . . . many of us would prefer to call ourselves prostitutes simply and to take our stand openly under the lamps of Piccadilly Circus rather than use it" (*Three Guineas,* Orlando: Harcourt, 2006, 19).

dropped her glove [82]   A prostitute entices Jacob by dropping her glove. As Bishop notes (161 n66), Woolf recorded an incident in which a woman dropped her glove (*Diary* 2: 21).

Further on . . . soundness of London [83]   Jacob and Florinda are walking through various neighborhoods as they return to his rooms. They have left Soho and now are probably in Holborn, walking west.

There they sit, plainly illuminated . . . the crochet basket has to be moved [83]   The residents of this particular boardinghouse (a lodging that provides both rooms and meals) are at the dinner table dressed *like* ladies and gentlemen. In the narrator's class analysis, she uses the word *like* to indicate that they are actually imposters and not of the class that they claim to be.

And so on again into the dark . . . the women with veiled hair [83]   Jacob and Florinda have entered another area where prostitution is common—"a girl here for sale" refers to a brothel. The Tube station may be Russell Square, near Lamb's Conduit Street where Jacob lives.

In spite of defending indecency, Jacob doubted whether he liked it in the raw [83]   A reference to Jacob's essay on indecency, regarding the omission of indecent language in an edition of plays by Wycherley (see note to page 70).

He had . . . the classics [83]   Jacob was educated in an all-male environment at Cambridge. The all-male ambience resembles the lives of monks—earlier he has thought of himself as "cloistered" in an isolated way; now he yearns for the safety of a masculine community where ideas are shared.

He told her his head ached [84]   Jacob invokes the classic excuse women supposedly use to deflect sexual advances—but eventually succumbs.

little paper flowers [85]   A pellet of paper, dropped into a vessel of water, would rehydrate into tiny paper flowers, floating in finger bowls, small shallow bowls used to rinse the fingertips after eating.

little cards [86]   Calling cards, left by visitors who arrive at a time when the person they wish to see is not at home (i.e., not receiving visitors).

battle of Waterloo [86]   A passing mention of the final conflict of the Napoleonic Wars; it is also, by association, a reference to the Duke of Wellington (see note to page 37).

Six yards of silk will cover one body [86]   In the early part of the twentieth century, dresses for the wealthy would not have been sold off the rack but handmade by personal dressmakers. The measuring, fitting, and design of the garment took substantial time (see Woolf's short story "Moments of Being: 'Slater's Pins Have no Points,'" *Complete Shorter Fiction* 215–20). With regard to the expense of such attire, Woolf recalls in "A Sketch of the Past" how "on an allowance of fifty pounds [a year] it was difficult, . . . to be well dressed for an evening. A home dress . . . could be had for a pound or two; but a party dress . . . cost fifteen guineas." When Virginia Stephen, in the interest of frugality, had a dress made from upholstery material, her half brother George Duckworth was enraged and told her harshly, "Go tear it up" (*Moments of Being* 150–51).

pudding with tufts of green cream and battlements of almond paste [86]   An elaborate dessert in the form of a castle with defensive ramparts. In the United Kingdom, any cooked dessert is called pudding.

flamingo hours fluttered softly through the sky [86]   The image is of the brightly colored pink and red plumage of the flamingo, a bird that would be considered extremely rare in England. Starting around 1910, inhabitants of Flanders in Belgium were known as Flamingos (*A Dictionary of Slang and Unconventional English,* edited by Eric Partridge, 8th ed. [New York: Macmillan, 1984]).

Notting Hill [86]   A primarily middle- and upper-middle-class community with some poorer areas, located near Kensington, north and west of Hyde Park, relatively close to where Virginia Stephen grew up.

purlieus of Clerkenwell [86]   Clerkenwell is to the east of the Bloomsbury area where Virginia Woolf lived most of her adult life. A purlieu is an old and poor district. The area was a hotbed of political activism for centuries. Activist groups in the area include the Lollards in the sixteenth century, the Chartists in the nineteenth century, and the Communists in the early twentieth century.

No wonder . . . the same sonata [86]   Young women of the privileged classes do not have time to master these accomplishments because of their social responsibilities.

elastic stockings [86]   Therapeutic treatment for vein disease.

Mrs. Page, widow, aged sixty-three [86]   The narrative style changes in the description of Mrs. Page, mimicking the case studies of the working class such as Charles Booth's *Inquiry into the life and labour of the people in London,* a project he conducted between 1886 and 1903. Woolf's half brother George was Booth's private secretary from 1892–1902.

five shillings out-door relief [86]   The British welfare system of the period, based on the 1601 Poor Laws, provided assistance to those not in an institution (a workhouse or hospital provided "indoor relief"). In this case, the recipient is given five shillings (a pound was twenty shillings) a week.

Messrs. Mackie's dye-works [86]   A company that dyes fabrics.

Edwin Mallett . . . her sobs [87]   Clara is pressured by both society and family members to marry. The marriage proposal Clara rejects from the "ridiculous young man" resembles the offer Virginia Stephen declined from Edward Hilton Young (1879–1960), who eventually became a British politician and writer. She also later received a marriage offer from Lytton Strachey, who has a strong resemblance to the character Richard Bonamy in personal appearance (the Wellington nose), literary interests (French literature), and sexual orientation (homosexuality) (see introduction lxxvi).

Which is the result of enjoying yourself [87]   Clara has been inappropriately dancing with the same man at balls and gatherings.

Three young men stood at the doorway looking about for their hostess [88]   Eligible young men—but not Jacob—seem to be vying for Clara's attention as Miss Eliot and Mr. Salvin speculate about Clara's marriage prospects.

You don't remember Elizabeth as I do [88]   Mrs. Durrant, Clara's mother, who was raised in Scotland.

Highland reels [88]   One of the vigorously athletic dances derived from ancient Scots traditions of sword and shield dancing to celebrate a victorious battle.

Banchorie [88]   The burgh of Banchory is located in Aberdeenshire.

Are you going away for Christmas? [89]   The query marks the approach of a new year—probably 1911, but the chronology of the novel is not always reliable.

What regiment is he in? [89]   Miss Edwards's brother is in the Twentieth Hussars, a cavalry regiment that was sent to Belgium on August 17, 1914, where they fought on horseback at Mons and during the retreat from Mons. Leonard Woolf's brothers Cecil and Philip were in this regiment. Philip was wounded and Cecil killed by the same shell at the Battle of Cambrai in 1917.

Charles James Fox [89]   Fox (1749–1806), a Whig politician, was known for his antislavery stance as well as his support for both

American independence and the French Revolution, and was a close friend of Edmund Burke. Fox was also known for his fashion statement—bringing the foppish continental couture of the macaronis to London.

Going about as girls do nowadays [89]   Typical of the new woman, this new generation of young women rejects the rigidly controlled and narrow lives of respectable young women like Clara.

There's not much to be said . . . Women like it. [90]   Timothy and Jacob are excruciatingly bored, but Jacob thinks that women enjoy this sort of event. For women, it is the high-stakes marriage market that matters.

"Like what?" . . . "I don't see why not," said Charlotte [90]   A flirtation between Timothy and Charlotte continues from an earlier chapter. Her behavior illustrates what "girls . . . nowadays" do.

"People must go downstairs," said Clara, passing. "Take Charlotte, Timothy. How d'you do, Mr. Flanders." [90]   Etiquette of the period required that a woman be accompanied. Similarly, Clara must greet Jacob formally by his surname even though she has known him for some time.

Who is Silvia? what is she? / That all our swains commend her? [90]   The lines are from Shakespeare's *Two Gentlemen of Verona* (IV.ii. 40–41), a comedy driven by complications in the marriage plot. Silvia, wooed both by Thurio and Proteus (who is already engaged to Julia), is in love with another character, Valentine. Proteus not only betrays his fiancée, Julia, who witnesses his seductive behavior, but also betrays his friend, Thurio, by pretending that he will woo Silvia on his behalf. Roe indicates that a song lauding female chastity and combining the Shakespearean words with a melody by Franz Schubert (1797–1828) was popular in the mid-1820s.

"Ah!" ... his bare ones [90–91]   Respectable women of the period were expected to wear gloves at gatherings and in public spaces. The same standards did not apply to men.

There is Mr. Clutterbuck [91]   See note to page 58.

Harrogate [91]   See note to page 36.

"Will you come and have something to eat?" he said to Clara Durrant [91] An indication that Jacob is interested in Clara and might even propose to her.

But half-way down they met Mr. and Mrs. Gresham [92]   Because Clara is the hostess, she must attend to the needs of the guests — even the uninvited one that the guests "dared to bring," a violation of courtesy that they attempt to justify. As a result of this encounter, Clara must leave Jacob and return to her duties. The chapter ends with the sentence, "So Clara left him," and the brief window of opportunity has closed.

About half-past nine ... as other people do [93]   The narrator describes Jacob's routine when leaving for work. For white-collar employees, the day began later than for blue-collar workers.

telephone [93]   A unified telephone system only became available in Britain in 1912.

books bound in green leather [93]   An indication that Jacob works at a law firm.

electric light [93]   Electric light in the workplace was a relatively new development. In 1860, a year before Thomas Edison, Sir Joseph Wilson Swan in the United Kingdom received a British patent for the lightbulb. However, while electricity rapidly replaced other sources of lighting in the United States, its introduction into the United Kingdom was slower. The first major generator, the Deptford Power Station, designed by Sebastian Ziani de

Ferranti, was completed by 1889 and supplied electricity to parts of London. However, the "battle of the systems" (alternating current, or AC, vs. direct current, or DC) slowed the process of electrification. Resistance from the competing gas companies was fierce. Furthermore, there was no regulation of competing companies, and some areas had no electrical supply at all. Not until 1926 was there a standardized national electrical grid.

Fresh coals, sir? . . . Your tea, sir. . . . [93]   Jacob's office does not have central heating. A servant attends to his needs.

football [93]   Known in the United States as soccer.

Hotspurs [93]   Tottenham Hotspurs is a soccer club that takes its name from Harry Hotspur, Sir Henry Percy (1364–1403), who led a rebellion against King Henry IV and was killed in battle. Henry IV had Hotspur's body dismembered and his head displayed on a spike outside the gates to the city of York in Yorkshire (Jacob grew up in Scarborough, Yorkshire).

Harlequins [93]   A rugby union team, founded in 1866 under the name Hampstead Football Club and renamed in 1870. In 1906, the Harlequins began to play at the Twickenham Stadium, a site located in the London borough of Richmond upon Thames, near Hogarth House, where Leonard and Virginia Woolf moved in March 1913 and started the Hogarth Press in 1917.

Star [93]   An evening newspaper intended for a popular rather than educated readership.

Gray's Inn [93]   One of the four Inns of Court, located in Holborn, a seedy area (see note to page 146). The Inns of Court derive their name from where masters of the law would gather in the thirteenth century to teach their apprentices. To this day they are legal societies that control admission to the English bar.

Verdict . . . winner [93]   Newspaper boys shouting "verdict" and "winner" as they hawk their papers to passersby. In *A Room of One's Own,* the narrator, casually scanning the headlines of a "lunch edition of the evening paper," discovers a similar theme: "Somebody had made a big score in South Africa. . . . A meat axe with human hair on it had been found in a cellar. Mr Justice —— commented in the Divorce Courts upon the Shamelessness of Women. . . . The most transient visitor to this planet, I thought, who picked up this paper could not fail to be aware, even from this scattered testimony, that England is under the rule of a patriarchy" (Orlando: Harcourt, 2005: 33).

pictures in Bond Street [93]   Sue Roe suggests that Jacob is visiting the galleries to view paintings in this fashionable street (172 n4).

Nelson on his column surveying the horizon [93]   See note to page 66.

second post [93]   The British postal system provided two mail deliveries a day.

mothers down at Scarborough . . . tea's cleared away [93–94]   Scarborough is actually north of London, not south, but it was conventional to say one was traveling "up" to London from wherever in the United Kingdom one was coming. Betty Flanders is warming her feet at the coal fire while writing her letter to Jacob. The tea would have been served and cleared away by a servant.

bad women [94]   Florinda is a "bad woman" by contemporary standards.

whooping-cough [94]   The bacterium *B. pertussis* causes severe symptoms ranging from gasping and apnea (not breathing) to choking and convulsions. The disease can be fatal. A vaccine for the disease was not developed until the 1940s.

Old Mouse gets very stiff . . . the smallest hill [94]   Betty Flanders's cart horse. He is too elderly to pull the cart up the steep hills of Scarborough.

sucking her thread [94]   Preparing the thread to put it through the eye of a sewing needle.

peat [94]   The remains of plant material that grows in a very wet environment.

Parrot's great white sale [94]   A reference to the January department-store sales in the United Kingdom. Parrot's seems to be a fictitious store.

unpublished works of women . . . the nib cleft and clotted [94]   Woolf was very interested in the marginalized writings of women (see *A Room of One's Own*). Nib pens used liquid ink and the nib, a sharp metal point, eventually split after long use. Whether the writer used a fountain pen or dipped the pen in an ink bottle, blotting paper was needed to absorb excess wet ink and prevent smearing.

sciatica [94]   Pain in the leg and buttock caused by damaged lumbar vertebrae.

Captain says things look bad . . . Ireland or India [94]   During the period prior to the Great War there was much anxiety in Britain that Ireland would collapse into civil war. At the same time, there was significant unrest in India related to the partitioning of Bengal in 1905 and the rise of the Muslim League in 1906. King George V and his wife, Queen Mary, visited India in December 1911. Also, Roe notes that the Indian Councils Act became effective in 1909, a marker of progress toward self-rule in India (173 n9).

had the natives got him . . . would the Admiralty tell her? [94–95]   Betty Flanders's brother, Morty, was an explorer or adventurer who traveled by sea to dangerous areas where "natives" (indigenous people) were often in confrontation with colonists who sought to advance imperial expansion. Possibly he traveled clandestinely under the auspices of the Royal Navy.

Leghorns, Cochin Chinas, Orpingtons [95]   Various breeds of chickens.

letter lay upon the hall table [95]   The letter from Betty Flanders came in the second post and was left in the entryway. Florinda, coming up to see Jacob, brings the mail with her. He kisses Florinda with his eyes open, glancing down at the letter on the table, and recognizes his mother's handwriting.

the obscene thing [95]   *Obscene* is from the Greek term *ob skene* meaning "offstage," but in Latin the word evolved toward its current meanings, such as indecent, offensive, lewd, or repulsive. The use of the term also refers to Woolf's immediate concerns as a writer and publisher. The Hogarth Press would have been at risk for legal action under the obscenity laws if Woolf had described the sex act (see Marshik, *British Modernism* 23–24).

Let us consider letters . . . sweet beneath the leaf [96–97]   This long passage reveals Virginia Woolf's deep interest in letter writing. The narrator mentions Byron (see notes to pages 19 and 34) and William Cowper (1731–1800), an eighteenth-century poet who suffered from severe depression. In *To the Lighthouse,* Mr. Ramsay recites the last lines from Cowper's "The Castaway" (Orlando: Harcourt, 2005: 151).

Russian dancers [96]   Roe notes that Diaghilev's Russian dancers first performed in London in 1909. Bishop indicates that Virginia Stephen went to one of the performances and also observes that the dancer Lydia Lopokova was living with John Maynard Keynes in Bloomsbury in 1921 when Woolf was writing *Jacob's Room* (162). Sergei Pavlovich Diaghilev (1872–1929), founder of the Ballets Russes, was also known as an art critic. His innovative and often shocking modernist experiments in dance were tremendously influential. He collaborated with the composer Igor Stravinsky and commissioned *The Firebird* (1910), *Petrushka* (1911), and *The Rite of Spring* (1913). The first performance of *The Rite of Spring* in Paris was so controversial that it actually triggered a riot.

these little prostitutes . . . an inviolable fidelity [97–98]   The image of Florinda holding a mirrored compact of face powder invokes the ancient motif of a woman regarding herself in a looking glass.

Greek Street upon another man's arm [98]   The reference to Greek Street harks back to its nineteenth-century notoriety as a den of prostitution. And, of course, there is the irony that Jacob has compared Florinda to women of ancient Greece (see page 78).

The light from the arc lamp . . . This was in his face [98]   Jacob is standing under an electric arc streetlamp that forms the intensely bright "arch" of light by igniting a current between two rods.

obliterated [98]   Derived from the Latin *oblittero,* the root meaning of *obliterate* is "to strike out (a letter)," an ironic resonance with the narrator's commentary on letter writing.

whetstone [98]   Used to sharpen blades.

switchback railway [98]   A roller coaster.

Prince of Wales's secretary [99]   The secretary serves the eldest son of the ruling monarch. Prince Edward's investiture as Prince of Wales was in 1911.

Azores [99]   An archipelago controlled by Portugal in the North Atlantic Ocean.

couchant [100]   Crouching or lying down with the head raised, a motif from heraldry and coats of arms.

now Jimmy feeds crows in Flanders and Helen visits hospitals [100]   As the narrator knows, Jimmy will die in Flanders, in Belgium, in a battle fought during the trench war. Those who were wounded or killed in the no-man's-land between the trenches could not be recovered. The wounded died in agony and the corpses decomposed within view of their comrades. The remains that could be retrieved were buried in Flanders rather than shipped back to the United Kingdom. There is little certainty that the body of a given individual actually lies beneath the grave marker bearing his name in the cemeteries in Belgium. Jacob's last name is an obvious reference to this bloody battlefield. Helen, unwed, has no other solace than to care for those who survived.

The lamps of London uphold the dark as upon the points of burning bayonets . . . oh, here is Jacob's room [100–1]   A bayonet, a sharp knife attached to the muzzle of a rifle, was used by military personnel in close combat during World War I. Street lighting was first introduced in London in the mid-eighteenth century to address rising crime rates. The narrator turns time back to the eighteenth and then on to the nineteenth century in the description of Soho seen by gaslight. The women of the period would have worn large scarves rather than coats or jackets. The narrator returns to the present moment when she and the reader arrive at Jacob's room.

Globe [101]   A conservative newspaper intended for the educated classes. Some British newspapers were printed on colored paper. Roe indicates that the *Globe* was printed on pink paper (165 n38).

in his new voice the ancient words [102]   A similar passage occurs in *Three Guineas* with regard to radio broadcasts during the build-up to World War II: "And if, Sir, pausing in England now, we turn on the wireless of the daily press we shall hear what answer

the fathers who are infected with infantile fixation now are making to those questions now. . . . As we listen to the voices we
seem to hear an infant crying in the night, the black' night that
now covers Europe, and with no language but a cry, Ay, ay, ay,
ay. . . . But it is not a new cry, it is a very old cry" (Orlando: Harcourt, 2006: 166–67).

Prime Minister's speech [102]   The prime minister is Herbert Henry
Asquith (1852–1928), whose term ran from 1908 to 1916. His
speech regards the hotly debated Third Irish Home Rule Bill.
The year is probably 1911. The debate over Irish Home Rule, a
form of self-government, began in the 1870s. The first Irish
Home Rule Bill, introduced by Prime Minister William Gladstone, was defeated in the House of Commons in 1886. The
Second Irish Home Rule Bill was passed in 1893 by the House
of Commons and defeated in the House of Lords. In 1914, the
Third Irish Home Rule Bill was passed by Royal Assent but
because of the onset of World War I in 1914 and the Easter Uprising in 1916 was not implemented. As Bishop notes, Protestant Ulster rejected the bill when it passed in April 1912,
initiating a decade of conflict. As he remarks: "Woolf's cousin,
H. A. L. Fisher (1865–1940) was a member of the Coalition
Cabinet's Committee on Ireland, the body that sent the Black
and Tans (so called because of their combination of black con-
stabulary and khaki military uniforms) into Ireland to fight the
nationalists in 1920" (162 n81).

The snow . . . He went to bed [102–3]   The snowfall echoes the last
paragraph of James Joyce's short story "The Dead" (published
in *Dubliners* in 1914). The protagonist, Gabriel, realizes that his
wife still has an emotional attachment to a young man who had
died of love for her. A culvert is a drain that runs underground
beneath a road or through an embankment. The end of the

chapter also echoes the first two stanzas of Thomas Hardy's "The Darkling Thrush," a poem that he wrote as a death knell for the nineteenth century (*The Complete Poems,* edited with an introduction by James Gibson [New York: Palgrave, 2001]: 150):

> I leant upon a coppice gate
> When Frost was spectre-gray,
> And Winter's dregs made desolate
> The weakening eye of day.
> The tangled bine-stems scored the sky
> Like strings of broken lyres,
> And all mankind that haunted nigh
> Had sought their household fires.
>
> The land's sharp features seemed to be
> The Century's corpse outleant,
> His crypt the cloudy canopy,
> The wind his death-lament.
> The ancient pulse of germ and birth
> Was shrunken hard and dry,
> And every spirit upon earth
> Seemed fervourless as I.

The grim description of the winter night presciently evokes the no-man's-land of the trenches in World War I. The chiming of the clocks suggests the inevitable progress toward the outbreak of the war.

Grosvenor Square [104]   Pronounced "Grove-nuh," an extremely exclusive residential square in the Mayfair neighborhood of London.

Walworth [104]   Located in the southeast London borough of Southwark, a poorer area.

Putney [104]   A middle-class district in southwest London where Leonard Woolf and the novelist E. M. Forster grew up.

Joseph Chamberlain [105]   A British politician (1836–1914) who was a supporter of the Boer War and an opponent of Irish Home Rule.

moments before a horse jumps [105]   The description of horseback riding has a cinematic quality that suggests Woolf may have seen the sequential photographs taken in the 1870s and 1880s by photographers like Eadweard Muybridge (1830–1904) documenting bodies in motion, including galloping horses.

galloped over the fields [105]   The fox-hunting season begins in October.

Essex [105]   A county in the east of England, northeast of London.

clipped, curt [105]   The speech patterns of the upper classes.

wattles [105]   Fleshy red appendage like that of a turkey's neck, hanging from the throat or chin.

using free speech [105]   Language inappropriate in the presence of women.

Mrs. Papworth [106]   The charwoman (housekeeper) for Richard Bonamy.

Endell Street, Covent Garden [106]   A lower-class area southwest of Lincoln's Inn.

New Square, Lincoln's Inn [106]   A residence for barristers (lawyers) located at the oldest of the four Inns of Court.

Mr. Sanders [106]   Jacob Flanders.

"good," he said, and "absolute" and "justice" and "punishment," and "the will of the majority" [106]   The debate between Bonamy and

Jacob is modeled on the traditions of the Cambridge Apostles and Thursday Evenings at 46 Gordon Square (see preface xiii).

her gentleman [106]   Richard Bonamy.

Objective something [106]   A philosophical debate similar to those of the Cambridge Apostles.

having at each other [106]   Roughhousing. A similar scene is mentioned in *Mrs. Dalloway* (Orlando: Harcourt, 2005: 84). There is also a hint of D. H. Lawrence's *Women in Love* (1920), in which the protagonist, Rupert Birkin, and his friend Gerald Crich wrestle naked in front of a fireplace. (See introduction page lxxxviii.)

bulls of Bashan [107]   Powerful and dangerous animals mentioned in Psalm 22: "Many bulls have compassed me: strong [bulls] of Bashan have beset me round" (22:12).

Mudie's library [107]   See note to page 28.

Spectator [107]   Founded in 1711 by Joseph Addison (1672–1719) and Richard Steele (1672–1729), major writers of the Enlightenment period, the publication was revived in 1828 after its demise in 1714 and still exists. In 1861, R. H. Hutton became the editor and served in that capacity until 1897. During his tenure, he "exercise[d] both political influence in support of the Liberal Party and religious influence in what was to become support of High Anglicanism" (78) (Malcolm Woodfield, "Victorian weekly reviews and reviewing after 1860: R. H. Hutton and the 'Spectator,'" *The Yearbook of English Studies* 16 [1986]: 74–91). Bishop notes that "from 1898 to 1925 [it was] owned by Lytton Strachey's cousin, John St. Loe Strachey, who disapproved of Strachey's pacifism, and denounced *Eminent Victorians* when it appeared in 1918" (163 n85). Today the publication is political in focus and tends to be very conservative.

fire screen [107]   A handheld guard against heat from the fireplace.

Jacob 25 [108]   The year is probably 1912.

kettle-holder [108]   A pot holder.

Saturday Westminster [108]   The *Saturday Westminster Gazette,* a weekly
periodical that was a spin-off of the parent publication, the *Westminster Gazette,* a liberal evening paper. The Saturday weekly published poems by Rupert Brooke as well as by Katherine Mansfield
and D. H. Lawrence, and included a Problems and Prizes page.
Mr. Benson's and Miss Rosseter's winnings refer to the Saturday
edition competitions, which consisted of witty prose passages,
poems, and epigrams.

style of Whistler [108]   James Abbott McNeill Whistler (1834–1903)
was an American-born painter who lived in the United Kingdom. Whistler, though heterosexual, was associated with the
flamboyant style of Oscar Wilde and had an ongoing competition of witticisms with him. The reference is probably to the ornate design of the Peacock Room.

a contemptible ass [108]   An insulting comparison to a donkey.

moving towards the bell [108]   Ringing for the servant to show Jacob
out.

Britannia leaning on her spear [108–9]   The female warrior with
helmet and spear personifying Britain. Britannia resembles
Boudica (Boadicea), the first-century warrior queen who led a
revolt against the Romans in 60 A.D.

ground glass [109]   Sandblasted translucent glass for privacy. This
episode is based on a conversation Woolf had with her young
friend Ralph Partridge: "He described a brothel the other
night—how, after the event, he & the girl sat over the fire, dis-

cussing the coal strike. Girls paraded before him—that was what pleased him—the sense of power" (*Diary* 2: 75).

Laurette's skirts were short [109]   An indication that she is a fallen woman.

Only Madame herself... the whole bag of ordure [109]   The madam who runs the brothel reveals the sleazy side of prostitution. The narrator compares the practice to fecal matter spilling from a bag.

Not so very long ago the workmen had gilt the final "y" [109]   A reference to Thomas Babington Macaulay, 1st Baron Macaulay (1800–1859), a historian as well as a poet and a politician. Jacob is visiting the circular, domed British Museum Reading Room, with long tables divided into individual spaces for researchers arranged as spokes radiating from a central desk, where requests for materials were submitted. The materials were brought to the researchers by the staff. The gilded *y* in Macaulay concluded a six-month closure of the Reading Room in 1907. Nineteen names of great British writers were inscribed along the base of the dome. In *A Room of One's Own,* Woolf refers to the Reading Room as a "huge bald forehead which is so splendidly encircled by a band of famous names" (Orlando: Harcourt, 2005: 26). Benjamin Harvey lists the "nineteen 'great names'" in "The Twentieth Part: Virginia Woolf in the British Museum Reading Room," *Literature Compass* 4 (1): 218–34: Geoffrey Chaucer (ca. 1342–1400), a poet who wrote *The Canterbury Tales;* William Caxton (ca. 1422–1491), who introduced the printing press to England; William Tyndale (also spelled Tindal, Tindall, or Tindale) (ca. 1494–1536), who translated the Bible into English and was later burned at the stake for heresy; Edmund Spenser (ca. 1552–1599), author of *The Faerie Queen;* the playwright and poet William Shakespeare (1564–1616); Francis Bacon (1561–1626), a philosopher and essayist; John Milton (1608–1674), author of *Paradise Lost;* John Locke (1632–1704), a philosopher; Joseph Addison (1672–1719), an essayist and poet, cofounder of the *Spectator;* Jonathan Swift (1667–1745), an Irish satirist and essayist; Alexander Pope (1688–1744), a poet known for his satire; Edward Gibbon (1737–1794), author of *The History of the Decline and Fall of the Roman Empire;* William Wordsworth (1770–1850), a first-generation Romantic poet; Sir Walter Scott (1771–1832), a Scottish novelist and poet; George Gordon, Lord Byron (1788–1824), a second-generation Romantic poet; Thomas Carlyle (1795–1881), a Scottish satirist and essayist; Thomas Babington Macaulay (see above); Alfred, Lord Tennyson (1809–1892), a Victorian poet who wrote *In Memoriam* and *Idylls of the King;* and poet and playwright Robert Browning (1812–1889). Regarding Woolf's view of the British Museum Reading Room, see also Anne E. Fernald, "The Memory Palace of Virginia Woolf," in *Virginia Woolf: Reading the Renaissance,* edited by Sally Greene (Athens, OH: Ohio University Press, 1999): 88–114. Bishop notes that the Reading Room "could accommodate 458 readers" at a time, but access was restricted to "persons over 21 years of age, with letters of recommendation" (161 n65).

claret [110]   A dark, wine-red color.

chilblains [110]   A painful and disfiguring swelling of the skin caused by exposure to cold.

Hyde Park [110]   Possibly a reference to Speakers' Corner on the northeast side of Hyde Park, where Marble Arch is located and where anyone can express ideas to passersby as long as the speech is not offensive. Also, possibly, Miss Marchmont has rented a chair and is inflicting her ideas on whoever is seated near her.

Queen Alexandra [110]   Wife of Edward VII (1841–1910), Queen Alexandra (1844–1925) was born in Denmark. Edward VII ascended the throne upon the death of his mother, Queen Victoria. He ruled from 1901–1910. Alexandra survived him, becoming Queen Mother during the rule of George V, her son.

Marlowe [111]   Christopher Marlowe (1564–1593), a playwright and contemporary of Shakespeare, who may have been a spy and was stabbed to death at the age of twenty-nine in a brawl.

Eliot [111]   George Eliot, the pen name of Mary Ann Evans (1819–1880), a prolific Victorian novelist and essayist who transgressed social constraints by living with a married man.

Brontë [111]   Charlotte (1816–1855), Emily (1818–1848), and Anne (1820–1849) Brontë were early Victorian novelists who, like George Eliot, wrote under pseudonyms (Currer, Ellis, and Acton Bell respectively) because of social restrictions on women writers.

Mr. Masefield [111]   John Masefield (1878–1967), a well-known novelist and poet. He served with the Red Cross in France and on a hospital ship at the Battle of Gallipoli and solicited the British government to let him write *Gallipoli* (1916), an autobiographical account of the events intended for an American audience and designed to justify the British military losses.

Mr. Bennett [111]   Arnold Bennett (1867–1931), a novelist and writer whom Woolf viewed as both a misogynist and as a literary adversary. Bennett's *Our Women* (1920) resulted in a scathing response from Woolf. His remarks about *Jacob's Room* provoked Woolf to retort with her first version of "Mr. Bennett and Mrs. Brown" (see introduction page lxxxvii; see also Daugherty 269–93).

Stuff them into the flame of Marlowe and burn them to cinders [111]   Compare to note to page 000 on burning down the past. Woolf and her contemporaries had similar feelings about the previous generation of writers. Woolf may have playfully chosen the word *savage* (a synonym is *heathen*) to evoke Rupert Brooke's involvement with the "neo-pagans" such as Marjorie Strachey and Brooke's sometime lover Ka Cox.

Detest your own age. Build a better one [111]   Woolf may be mocking the anti-Bloomsbury writer Wyndham Lewis (1882–1957) for his Vorticist publication, *BLAST*. Lewis was assisted by Ezra Pound, and contributors included Rebecca West and T. S. Eliot. The first of the two volumes begins with a list of the "Blessed" and the "Blasted," and includes assertions such as, "We are primitive Mercenaries in the Modern World."

Useless to trust to the Victorians, who disembowel [111]   Bishop notes the pun on Dr. Thomas Bowdler (1754–1825), who expurgated unsavory passages from his *Family Shakespeare* (1807) (164 n88). While 1807 precedes the Victorian era (1837–1901), there is no doubt that censorship continued to be widely practiced. The eponym *bowdlerize* derives from his censorship.

six young men [112]   Roe speculates that Woolf is making an insider reference to her brother Thoby Stephen and his friends Clive Bell, Lytton Strachey, Saxon Sydney-Turner, Desmond McCarthy, and John Maynard Keynes (176 n18).

Elgin Marbles [112]   See note to page 38.

Hobbes [113]   Thomas Hobbes (1588–1679) was a political philosopher; he is known for his argument in *Leviathan* that society needs a social contract to prevent a "war of all against all." Without such a contract, life is "solitary, poor, nasty, brutish, and short."

Gibbon [113]   See note to page 109.

octavos [113]   Refers to sheets of paper folded three times to create

signatures of eight pages or a book smaller than six inches by
ten inches.

quartos [113]   Sheets of paper folded twice to create signatures of
four pages measuring about nine inches by twelve inches.

folios [113]   Sheets of paper folded once to create signatures of two
pages; books of folio size are at least fifteen inches tall.

ivory pages [113]   The paper has faded to a vanilla color over the
years.

morocco bindings [113]   Made from specially treated goatskin, they
are decorative and very expensive.

pigeon-holes [113]   Cubbyholes.

Plato [113]   Best known for his Socratic dialogues, Plato
(428/427–348/347 B.C.) was one of the greatest ancient Greek
philosophers.

Aristotle [113]   A prolific Greek philosopher (384–322 B.C.) whose
work included treatises on poetics, rhetoric, logic, metaphysics,
and natural history.

Huxtable [113]   See notes to page 39.

Bentley [113]   Richard Bentley (1662–1742), a renowned scholar of
Greek who was named master of Trinity College, Cambridge,
in 1700.

Great Russell Street [113]   The street facing the entrance of the
British Museum and linking Southampton Row to Tottenham
Court Road.

chemist's [113]   A pharmacy.

carriages [113]   Horse-drawn vehicles.

Kentish Town [114]   North of the Bloomsbury area where the British Museum is located.

Highgate [114]   Located north of Kentish Town in Islington, Highgate Cemetary is one of seven burial sites created in the Victorian period outside of the center of London. Among the dead buried there are Karl Marx and George Eliot.

Great Ormond Street [114]   Intersects with Lamb's Conduit Street, where Jacob lives.

Hamlet [114]   The protagonist in Shakespeare's play of the same name.

Elgin Marbles [114]   See note to page 38.

Ulysses [114]   A fragment of a sculpture possibly representing Odysseus, one of the heroes of Homer's *Iliad* and *Odyssey* (see Bishop xxxviii for a photograph of the sculpture from *A. H. Smith's catalogue of sculpture in the Department of Greek and Roman Antiquities, British Museum,* London, 1892).

Phaedrus [114]   Plato's dialogue, in which Socrates and Phaedrus discuss homosexual pederastic desire and the madness of love as well as the rhetoric of speechmaking.

vociferating [114]   Shouting.

Gibson [115]   A fictitious painter. Possibly Woolf is drawing on a glittering and diverse party held by Ottoline Morrell at her Bedford Square home. Invited to bring a guest of her own choice, Virginia Stephen chose Rupert Brooke (see "Old Bloomsbury," *Moments of Being* 199).

Magdalen [115]   A fictitious actress. The description of Magdalen may be a parody of gossip about Virginia and her sister, Vanessa. For example, at the ball that celebrated the closing of the Second Post-Impressionist Exhibition in 1912, the sisters "dressed [them]selves up as Gauguin pictures" and shocked the onlookers with their near nakedness. According to Woolf, many old friends of the Stephen family viewed the sisters as "abandoned women" ("Old Bloomsbury" 200–1). Mary Magdalen was a devotee of Jesus and the first to witness the empty tomb where he had been laid after his crucifixion. She has at times been regarded as a fallen woman or prostitute.

jodelling [116]   Yodeling.

Magdalen had got upon his knees; now his pipe was in her mouth [116] Outrageous behavior for a respectable woman of the period.

Dick Graves, being a little drunk . . . more beautiful than women's friendships [116]   Dick's surname is a memento mori. His adoration of Jacob verges on the homoerotic. Helen's impression of both men as "heroes" is a foreshadowing of the coming war. Woolf would not concur with Helen's view of women's friendships.

drums and trumpets [117]   Musical instruments associated with the military. In a review titled "The 'Pageant' of History" in the *Nation & Athenaeum,* 19 January 1924, Leonard Woolf commented on the contemporary turn toward social history represented by the work of writers such as Eileen Power, and away from the history of "drums and trumpets" (148), thus the phrase must have been in use at the time Virginia Woolf was writing *Jacob's Room.*

Waterloo Bridge [117]   The original bridge, built to celebrate the 1815 victory at the Battle of Waterloo, opened to traffic in 1817. "They cross the Bridge incessantly" resonates with T. S. Eliot's reference to London Bridge in "The Burial of the Dead," (section I of *The Waste Land*): "A crowd flowed over London Bridge, so many, / I had not thought death had undone so many" (62–63). The Waterloo station still runs nonstop trains to

Surbiton, a suburb about twelve miles southwest of London, where some of the Pre-Raphaelite Brotherhood painters lived during the Victorian period.

lorry [117]   A truck.

a mason's van with newly lettered tombstones [117]   Another memento mori. A mason is a stonecutter.

Surrey [118]   A county southwest of London.

Strand [118]   A busy London thoroughfare.

They are hatless. They triumph. [118]   All decent women were expected to cover their hair and avoid unruly behavior. These triumph over social conventions.

tiller [118]   A lever that lets the helmsman control the rudder and steer the vessel.

But what century have we reached? [118]   As in several earlier passages, the narrator travels back in time—here, to the early 1300s (see note to page 16, "But there was a time . . ."). At the time, a different St. Paul's Cathedral stood on the site. Consecrated in 1300, it was destroyed in the Great Fire of London in 1666. The current St. Paul's was designed by Christopher Wren and completed in 1708. The derelict old man whom the narrator describes as a pilgrim is a reminder of an age of faith.

Somerset House [118]   New Somerset House (construction began in 1775) is located in the Strand near the Waterloo Bridge on the same site as the Old Somerset House, which had been built in the 1550s and was demolished to make space for the new construction. The new structure housed the War Office (which oversaw the Army) and the Navy Office (which included the Sick and Hurt Office for sailors).

Lothair [119]   A very popular novel by Benjamin Disraeli (1804–1881), published in 1870, that focuses on religious tensions between Anglicanism, Catholicism, and Judaism, and on Giuseppe Garibaldi's confrontation with the papacy in the 1860s.

Temple Bar [119]   Named after the Knights Templar (Poor Fellow-Soldiers of Christ and of the Temple of Solomon); the order was founded in the twelfth century after the First Crusade.

disused graveyard in the parish of St. Pancras [120]   Fanny has walked about three miles northwest from the City of London to St. Pancras Old Church. St. Pancras New Church was consecrated in 1822 and St. Pancras Old Church became a Chapel of Ease. Its graveyard was no longer used as a place of burial but was disturbed by the Midland Railway in 1865 when it cut through the burial site to access St. Pancras Station. Thomas Hardy, the Victorian novelist and poet, then an apprentice architect, oversaw the exhumation of the coffins and the reburial of the remains during the project. Hardy's wrenching poem "Channel Firing" was written in 1914 when the naval force had begun to prepare for the war by testing its artillery. In the poem, the dead are disturbed in their coffins; God reassures them that it is not Judgment Day but "All nations striving strong to make / Red war yet redder" (13–14).

crossing the grass to read a name [120]   Among the tombstones is the memorial to Mary Wollstonecraft (1759–1797), an early feminist and author of *A Vindication of the Rights of Woman;* and William Godwin (1756–1836), a novelist and philosopher. Wollstonecraft died in childbirth. Her daughter, Mary Wollstonecraft Shelley (née Godwin), was the author of *Frankenstein* and the wife of the poet Percy Bysshe Shelley.

silk stockings, and silver-buckled shoes [120]   Fanny can afford silk stockings (very expensive at the time) and stylish shoes.

Madame Tussaud's [120]   Madame Tussauds (no apostrophe) is a wax museum and tourist attraction in London, located first on Baker Street (1835) and then later on Marylebone Road (1884).

ankles of a stag [120]   Her ankles are very slim and elegant.

She sat in a flowered Spanish shawl . . . that's right [121]   Fanny is posing nude with a shawl around her shoulders. Nick Bramham wants her to lower the shawl to expose her breasts more.

yellow novel [121]   Probably a "yellow-back novel," a cheap paperback reprint sold for sixpence and generally intended for a female readership (see Anthony Rota, *Apart from the Text* [New Castle, DE: Oak Knoll Press, 1998]: 221–26).

His head might have been the work of a sculptor . . . stiff with sitting [121–22]   The narrator aligns the ugly personal appearance of Nick Bramham with the fleeting beauty of all women. The description of woman's inconstant beauty is an echo of Virgil, in *The Aeneid:* "Varium, et mutabile semper femina"—"A woman is ever a fickle and changeable thing" (IV.569).

pink sticks of sweetstuff [122]   Probably rock candy, which was, until later in the century, invariably pink.

Pickford's van [122]   Pickfords Removals, a company first founded in 1670s. Bishop indicates that the company had its offices at 205 High Holborn at that time (165 n96).

Leicester Square [123]   In the West End of London, it became a center for entertainment during the Victorian period. In the 1910s, the theaters and entertainment halls at Leicester Square included the Alhambra, the Empire, Daly's, and the Hippodrome.

the King [123]   George V.

promenade at the Empire [123]   The Empire was a variety theater (known as vaudeville in the United States) offering a series of short performances including song-and-dance numbers as well as magic performances and the like. According to Ward, Lock and Company's *Pictorial and Descriptive Guide to London and Its Environs* (London: 1914), it offered "entertainments of high class" (123). However, until 1916, the Empire was also notorious for its promenade. The promenade, partially concealed by a barrier located behind the royal circle, was a clublike gathering place for men about town enjoying themselves and prostitutes seeking customers. The barrier was a compromise to placate those who had tried to stop the practice, which was tolerated by the police (see Joseph Donoghue, *Fantasies of Empire: The Empire Theatre of Varieties, Leicester Square, and the Licensing Controversy of 1894* [Iowa City: University of Iowa Press, 2005]).

Bloody rot [123]   Nonsense. Jacob thinks Nick was deliberately ignoring him.

"Miss Elmer," said Nick [123]   Conforming to polite conventions, Nick formally introduces Fanny to Jacob. Fanny's social status is best described as bohemian. She is clearly not a respectable woman but neither is she a prostitute.

sat upon a plush sofa and let the smoke go up between them [123]   Jacob, Nick, and Fanny are all sitting comfortably on upholstered furniture in the promenade, smoking cigarettes. Decent women were expected not to smoke cigarettes at this time.

for ever the beauty of young men . . . she thought [123]   Echoes the earlier passage regarding the beauty of women. Fanny's fantasies painfully foreshadow the Great War. For example, the image of young men "set in smoke" alludes both to the smoke of battle and to the terrible evanescence of their lives. The mention of games echoes the cheerful propaganda representing battle as a playing field (see introduction li). Young men losing their beauty suggests the disfiguration of the wounded and disabled. The motif of "the eyes of faraway heroes" at "their station among us" suggests the great divide between the military personnel who experienced the front lines of the war and the civilians who knew nothing of the war firsthand.

each word falling like a disc new cut, not a hubble-bubble of small smooth coins such as girls use [123]   This passage recalls chapter 3 and the conversation of young men in the Cambridge rooms of Professor Sopwith. The comparison significantly devalues women's words as used pocket change in relation to men's newly minted linguistic wealth.

isn't it pleasant . . . in a purse? [124]   Just as men seem to have more weighty words and thoughts, so, too — from Fanny's perspective — they naturally and legitimately have more money than women.

Her screwed-up black glove dropped to the floor . . . fall in love [124]   This passage, reiterating the motif of a woman's glove as her sexuality, echoes the narrator's fear of Jacob after Florinda betrays him. Roe suggests that Fanny has made a prostitute's offer to Jacob (179 n4).

Hampstead Garden Suburb [124]   Hampstead Garden Suburb, built in 1907, is in northwest London. The planned community was created by a dedicated social reformer, Dame Henrietta Barnett.

bench in Judges Walk looking at Hampstead Garden Suburb [124]   Judges Walk is on the other side of Hampstead Heath and about two miles southwest of Hampstead Garden Suburb. Bishop notes that it was so named because, in 1665 during the Great

Plague, which killed as many as 100,000 Londoners, the law courts relocated to a safer place. In the following year, 1666, the Great Fire of London destroyed much of the city, killing many of the disease-bearing animals such as rats that caused the contagion.

to launch little boats [125]   The boating pond is near Parliament Hill at the southern end of Hampstead Heath.

She spent tenpence on lunch . . . Express Dairy Company's shop [125] Fanny Elmer has bought her lunch at the Express Dairy Company's shop for less than a shilling (a shilling was twelve pence). Most restaurants in London would have charged at least 1/6d (one shilling and sixpence) according to Ward, Lock and Company's *Pictorial and Descriptive Guide to London and Its Environs* (London: 1914). The Express Dairy Company was founded in 1864 by George Barham because he thought that the milk from cows in London was unhygienic. The company opened its first tea shops and cafés in the 1890s. Regarding cows in London, see E. H. Whetham, "The London Milk Trade, 1860–1900," *Economic History Review, New Series,* 17.2 (1964): 369–80.

plaits [125]   Braids.

Pie and greens [126]   Probably shepherd's pie (lamb and vegetables under a crust of mashed potatoes) with a green vegetable.

crumpets [126]   Crumpets resemble English muffins but are flatter.

Foundling Hospital [127]   Located near Lamb's Conduit Street, the hospital was originally supposed to be a refuge for orphaned and abandoned children from the countryside. When Virginia took a house in Brunswick Square with her brother Adrian and several male friends, including Leonard Woolf, more socially prim friends were horrified. Vanessa, however, pointed out that the site was close to the Foundling Hospital ("Old Blooms-bury," *Moments of Being* 201).

How exquisite it was . . . of the next comer [127] Fanny is a true flâneuse and a dedicated window-shopper, wandering through London and its environs, free to meander while other young women of her age are working in offices or as seamstresses. Re-garding the flâneuse, see Rachel Bowlby, "Walking, Women and Writing: Virginia Woolf as flâneuse," *New Feminist Discourses: Critical Essays on Theories and Texts,* edited by Isobel Armstrong (London: Routledge, 1992): 26–47.

Swan and Edgars [127] In 1911, the department store was the tar-get of suffragette window-smashing protests. In 1917, it was struck by a zeppelin bomb attack.

parts of a woman were shown separate . . . slashed with scarlet [128] The contents of the shop window are described in delectable detail but with grim hints of mutilation. The women's hats are explic-itly compared to decapitation—specifically the eighteenth-century practice of displaying the severed heads of traitors on pikes on top of the Temple Bar arch designed by Christopher Wren.

Feasted upon by the eyes of women . . . in a baker's window [128] An image of decay—a "fly-blow" is "the egg deposited by a fly in the flesh of an animal, or the maggot proceeding there from" (*OED*) and thus "flyblown" means "filled with fly-blows; tainted, putrid, impure" (*OED*).

Gerrard Street [128] Runs parallel to Shaftesbury Avenue and inter-sects with Greek Street, Dean Street, and Wardour Street.

Virgil [128] See note to page 40.

Scott [128] See note to page 31.

Dumas [128]   Alexandre Dumas, père (1802–1870), was best known for his novels of adventure such as *The Count of Monte Cristo* and *The Three Musketeers*. His son, Alexandre Dumas (1824–1895), was known for the novel *La dame aux camélias (The Lady of the Camellias)*, the account of a privileged young man's affair with a courtesan who ultimately dies tragically of tuberculosis. The novel was later produced as the play *Camille* and adapted by Verdi as the opera *La Traviata*.

Slade [128]   The Slade School of Fine Art, on Gower Street in London, was founded in 1871. Woolf's sister, Vanessa, was a student there.

Tonks and Steer [128]   Henry Tonks and Philip Wilson Steer were protégés of Frederick Brown, a devotee of drawing in the eighteenth-century style of Jean Auguste Dominique Ingres, the French neoclassical artist. Brown advocated the use of charcoal (Nick Bramham's preferred medium for drawing). Brown, according to Randolph Schwabe ("Three Teachers: Brown, Tonks and Steer," *The Burlington Magazine for Connoisseurs* 82.483 [June 1943]: 141–46), routinely treated models in an insulting fashion: "Communication was restricted to short words of command" (142). Tonks was sarcastic in general and particularly harsh with female students (145). Richard Shone notes that "in 1904 Vanessa Stephen . . . briefly attended the Slade and . . . was 'crushed by Tonks'" ("The Friday Club," *Burlington Magazine*, 117.866, [May 1975]: 278–84; 280. Woolf also seems to have integrated elements of the painter Dora Carrington, who studied at the Slade School of Fine Art with Tonks, into the chapter.

Fielding [128]   Henry Fielding (1707–1754) was one of the earliest English novelists and author of the picaresque *Tom Jones* (1749) as well as satirical work such as *Shamela*, a spoof on Samuel Richardson's *Pamela*.

Charing Cross Road [128]   The street, which runs north from Trafalgar Square and intersects with Shaftesbury Avenue, was the site of numerous bookshops until the early twenty-first century when rents were raised to market value, forcing out many of the booksellers.

Tom Jones [128]   The novel, a comic bildungsroman, traces the life of a foundling infant, Tom Jones, who is raised by a rich landowner, but despised and ridiculed as a bastard. Leading a rambunctious life with many sexual adventures, Tom is rescued from the gallows at the last possible moment, comes into an inheritance, and eventually marries the woman who loves him.

shared with a school teacher [128]   Neither Fanny nor her roommate can afford her own lodgings. The narrator is subtly pointing out the economic limitations on the lives of women.

mystic book [128]   Fanny, bored and confused by *Tom Jones,* forces herself to read some of the book to please Jacob but has a reaction similar to Florinda's encounter with Shelley's *Adonais.* For Fanny, "mystic" means incomprehensible.

fancy-dress dance [129]   A costume ball; Woolf may have been thinking of Dora Carrington's 1913 pencil-and-watercolor sketch (probably a self-portrait), *Slade Student in Fancy Dress.*

three and sixpence [129]   Three shillings and sixpence (3s. 6d.) was close to a fifth of a pound (a pound was twenty shillings), a rather significant amount of money. Fanny has spent more than four times as much for a copy of *Tom Jones* than she did for her tenpence lunch in Hampstead.

virgin chained to a rock . . . playing Bach [129]   A reference to Andromeda (see note to page 59). Lowndes Square is in the wealthy neighborhood south of Knightsbridge Road, near Hyde Park and Grosvenor Square, where Lady Rocksbier resides. The young Virginia Stephen and her sister, Vanessa, who lived about a mile and half west of Clara at 22 Hyde Park Gate, were expected to entertain family friends and other guests, serving afternoon tea to elderly men and making small talk ("A Sketch of the Past" 142–43).

fetched her head-dress; her trousers; her shoes with red tassels. What should she wear? [130]   The garments are strongly reminiscent of Virginia Stephen's daring 1910 experiment in cross-dressing as one of the pranksters who perpetrated what is known as the Dreadnought Hoax. While Horace Cole, the organizer of the prank, and Adrian Stephen, Virginia's brother, were only slightly disguised for the adventure, the other participants blackened their faces (Virginia sported a false beard as well) and donned robes and turbans to disguise themselves as the emperor of Abyssinia and his entourage. The group was given full military honors and a tour of a secret warship, the HMS *Dreadnought.* When it was discovered, the hoax caused great consternation in the British Admiralty. See Peter Stansky, "The *Dreadnought* Hoax," in *On or About December 1910: Early Bloomsbury and Its Intimate World* (Cambridge: Harvard University Press, 1996): 17–46; and Adrian Stephen, *The "Dreadnought" Hoax* (London: Hogarth Press, 1936).

Purple Emperor [130]   A very beautiful butterfly (*Apatura iris*) that is attracted to foul smells and feeds on dead carcasses and feces.

glow-worms [130]   *Lampyris noctiluca,* a European firefly; the females are wingless but emit light to attract the winged males. The larvae develop over a two- to three-year period feeding on slugs and snails. As adults, they live from May to July, devoting their entire energy to reproduction and then dying.

the New Forest [130]   In 1079, William the Conqueror designated the forest for hunting. As Bishop notes, "By Jacob's time it was famous for fox-hunting, but in 1914 all the horses would be called up for the war" (167 n102). Most of the deciduous trees of the New Forest were cut down during the war.

And suppose one wreathed Jacob in a turban? . . . (and he let her blacken his lips and clenched his teeth and scowled in the glass) [130]   Another possible allusion to the Dreadnought Hoax; Jacob has agreed to go to the event in blackface.

Gibraltar [131]   See note to page 77. Archer is in the navy.

Here was Jacob Flanders gone abroad [131]   Woolf accompanied her sister, Vanessa, to Paris in 1904 to visit artists' studios and cafés (see Richard Shone, "The Friday Club," *The Burlington Magazine,* 117.866 [May 1975]: 278–84, n2); Jacob cannot tell his mother what he is doing.

left him a hundred pounds [131]   Jacob can travel to France and Greece only because of the money he inherited. One hundred pounds is a substantial amount—significantly more than $10,000 today—but Jacob is spending the principal itself, unlike the narrator in *A Room of One's Own* who inherited a legacy of £500 a year from her maiden aunt but is spending only the interest. Virginia Stephen, too, had an inheritance that altered her financial situation—she inherited £2,500 from Caroline Emelia Stephen, her paternal great-aunt, in 1909.

Velasquez [132]   The Spanish painter Diego Velázquez (1599–1660), known for his portraiture. His style and technique were an inspiration for impressionist and postimpressionist painters, including Édouard Manet. Bishop notes that one of Velasquez's "most famous early works is *Los Borrachos* (The Drunkards)" (167 n104), which is very appropriate to the occasion, Jacob and his acquaintances being quite drunk.

Hang there like fruit my soul. [132]   A line from *Cymbeline,* one of Shakespeare's problem plays, in which the character Imogen, daughter of King Cymbeline, secretly marries Posthumus, a man of low birth. Later she must feign her own death to shield herself from lies about her virtue as a wife. The line marks Posthumus's realization that his wife is alive (V.v.263–64).

frogs [132]   An ethnic slur describing a French person. The term is derived from a French culinary delicacy, frogs' legs.

The devil damn you black, you cream-faced loon! [132]   From Shakespeare's *Macbeth* (V.iii.13). On the verge of the battle in which he will be slain, Macbeth abuses and insults his servant.

grilled bone [132]   Broiled steak with the bone in.

juggins [133]   Jacob is drunk, doesn't speak French well, and is hungry. He is mildly rude when he calls the waiter, Adolphe, a fool.

Hey diddle diddle, the cat and the fiddle [133]   A line from a nursery rhyme.

Boulevard Raspaille [133]   A misspelling of boulevard Raspail in Montparnasse, the notorious Left Bank haven for artists and their models, as well as for lesbians, bohemians in general, and prostitutes.

Chardin [133]   Probably the painter Jean-Baptiste-Siméon Chardin (1699–1779).

swell [133]   Someone who does something very well (Partridge); thus Cruttendon is paying Mallinson homage. Although it is hard to tell from the narrative, Mallinson—who Cruttendon says sells his paintings to pay for his dinner—may also be spending his pittance on the lifestyle of a man about town.

Pierre Louÿs [133]   Pseudonym of Pierre Louis (1870–1925) who was known for his novels about lesbians and for his friendships with famous male homosexuals such as André Gide (1869–1951) and Oscar Wilde (1854–1900). Bishop notes that Louÿs was particularly famous for "erotica set in Hellenistic Greece such as *Aphrodite* (1896) and *Les Chansons de Bilitis* (1894)" (168 n105).

a daughter of the church [134]   Probably Jinny's father is (or was) a clergyman (as opposed to her having taken religious vows).

painter men [134]   The phrase suggests that there are also painter women, like Vanessa Bell and Dora Carrington.

Teddy [134]   Cruttendon's given name is Edward.

Half a jiff [134]   Half a second.

Versailles [135]   Jacob, Jinny, and Cruttendon have traveled about fourteen miles southwest of Paris to the Château de Versailles, the palace of Louis XIV, and center of political power for the Ancien Régime that was eventually toppled by the French Revolution in 1789. Bishop observes that Versailles gave its name to the punitive treaty that formally ended the war in 1919 (168 n106).

military music [135]   A reminder of the impending war.

air-ball [135]   A balloon.

summer-house [135]   Le petit hameau de la Reine, where Marie Antoinette and her attendants also dressed up as shepherdesses and milkmaids and played at farming, or Le Petit Trianon.

sitting on the handle of his walking-stick [135]   Also known as a shooting stick, the curved handle folds out into two halves creating a seating support. The tip of the stick, pressed against the ground, would stabilize the seat.

Hang it all [136]   An expression of vexation or anger.

will King George give way about the peers? [136]   In 1910, when George V ascended the throne, he agreed to address a constitutional crisis by threatening to create a sufficient number of peers to oppose the Conservative resistance in the House of Lords. Ultimately, the Parliament Act of 1911, asserting the legislative authority of the House of Commons, made it unnecessary to create the new peers. The chronology of the novel is problematic here. Chapters 11 and 12 are almost certainly set in the year 1913, not 1910.

Gare des Invalides [136]   Trains from Gare des Invalides run to Versailles.

being of course unable to foresee how it fell out in the course of time [137]   A hint that Jacob will predecease Cruttendon and Jinny Carslake — the narrator knows how their lives will evolve.

Lefanu [137]   Possibly alluding to the well-known supernatural tale, "Strange Event in the Life of Schalken the Painter" (1839) by Sheridan Le Fanu (1814–1873).

rampart [138]   A defensive fortification.

garnet brooch [138]   A brooch is a pin. A garnet is a semiprecious gem that resembles the dark, wine-colored seeds of the pomegranate (see Neverow, "Return" 227), a reminder of the six seeds of a pomegranate that the mythic Greek goddess Persephone ate while captive in the underworld. Abducted by Hades, the god of the dead, Persephone was required to spend six months of the year in the underworld, away from her mother, Demeter, the goddess of the harvest.

furze [139]   See note to page 20.

Bertha Ruck [139]   The name Woolf chose for the tombstone, perhaps at random, created a fuss by offending a living writer, Amy

Roberta Ruck, who found the similarity disturbing. Her husband, Oliver Onions, threatened legal action, but all was resolved peaceably. See Diane F. Gillespie, "Virginia Woolf and the Curious Case of Berta Ruck," *Woolf Studies Annual* 10 (2004): 109–38, for a detailed discussion of the events and contexts.

Did the bones stir, or the rusty swords? . . . The Roman skeletons are in safe keeping [139–41]   Reminders of death, battle, and the Anglican burial traditions. "Ghosts flocked thick" echoes the underworld of Virgil's *Aeneid* and Dante Alighieri's *Inferno* as well as T. S. Eliot's *The Waste Land*.

Virgil's bees . . . vines between elms [142]   Regarding the bees, see note to page 40. The vines are mentioned both in the *Georgics* and the *Eclogues*. Roe cites the *Georgics* II: 221: "Illa tibi laetas intexet vitibus ulmos" (One kind of land will twine your vines with elms) (181 n1).

flat red-frilled roofs [142]   The roofs are made of curved terra-cotta tiles.

ruled with olive trees [142]   Olive trees planted in straight rows.

neither stiles nor footpaths . . . ham and eggs [143]   The narrator contrasts England with Italy. Stiles are steps or rungs that allow one to cross a barrier, such as a fence, without letting farm animals pass through. Footpaths in Great Britain give ramblers and hikers the right to cross private property.

black priests [143]   Priests in black gowns or black clothing.

Parthenon [143]   The Parthenon is the Athenian temple built after the Persians sacked the temples in 480 B.C. The building was begun in 447 B.C. and completed in 432 B.C. The metopes, which are carved elements of the frieze, a horizontal architectural band, depict mythical battles against the Amazons (Amazonomachy), the Centaurs (Centauromachy), the Giants (Gigantomachy), and the Trojans. During the sixth century A.D., the Parthenon served as a Christian church dedicated to the Virgin. In the early 1460s, following the Ottoman conquest, the Parthenon was converted into a mosque. Then, in 1687, an explosion of Ottoman ammunition caused severe damage to the building and the sculptures. In the first decade of the nineteenth century Thomas Bruce, 7th Earl of Elgin, removed at his personal expense some of the surviving sculptures with Ottoman permission. The Elgin Marbles were sold in 1816 to the British Museum in London.

Coliseum [143]   The ancient amphitheater in Rome.

Asquith [143]   See note to page 102 ("Prime Minister's speech").

Gibbon [143]   See note to page 109 ("Not so very long ago . . .").

Latin race [143]   Italians, the descendants of Roman culture.

victorias [143]   A horse-drawn carriage that seats two passengers.

pompous pillars with plaster shields stuck to them [143]   Probably the columns of a villa.

waistcoat [144]   A vest.

dicky [144]   A partial shirtfront.

we must be nearly there! [144]   Jacob is arriving at the city of Bari in the Apulia region of Italy. From there, he will take the ferry to Patras in Greece, one of the main ports linking western Greece to Italy. Virginia Stephen and her sister, Vanessa, followed a similar route when they visited Greece in 1906.

corsets [144]   A woman's close-fitting undergarment.

Maggi's consommé [144]   A Swiss product developed by Julius Michaël Johannes Maggi (1846–1912) based on a formula he came up with in 1863; advertising claimed that instant soup liberated women from housework.

Daily Mail [145]   The *Daily Mail,* first published in Britain in 1896, was a warmongering publication that represented Germany as a massive threat to England in the buildup to the war and also advocated conscription when the war began. A few paragraphs later the reader finds out that Jacob does not trust the reporting in the *Daily Mail.*

Rangoon [145]   Rangoon (now called Yangon) was the capital of Burma, then a British colony, from 1885 to 1948 (now called Myanmar by the military junta). The reference is to Jacob's uncle Morty.

governesses [145]   Genteel single women of limited means of the Victorian and Edwardian periods often earned their living by educating the young of the middle and upper classes.

Look at that for a head . . . the Greeks caring for the body as much as for the face [145]   The governesses seemingly were entranced by the beautiful Greek sculpture (and somewhat smitten by "manly beauty," especially given their status as unwed and unlikely to wed. Jacob is compared to statuary by all four of the women who are attracted to him (Florinda [81], Clara Durrant [176], Fanny Elmer [180], and Sandra Wentworth Williams [153]).

And the Greeks could paint fruit so that birds pecked at it [145]   An allusion to Zeuxis, fifth-century B.C. Greek painter whose work was so realistic that birds were said to peck at the grapes in his pictures; the governesses would also teach painting to their young charges, which would further explain their interest in Greek painting.

First you read Xenophon; then Euripides . . . we have been brought up in an illusion [145]   Having been intellectually seduced by their governesses, the adolescents begin to study Greek and eventually to read Greek literature. The first and most accessible texts a student of Greek would read (as Virginia Stephen herself almost certainly did) would be those of Xenophon (ca. 431–352 B.C.), a contemporary of Socrates. The playwright Euripides (ca. 484–406 B.C.) was the author of many tragedies, among them *Alcestis, Medea, Electra,* and *The Bacchae.*

Pilchard [145]   The man's name was Pilcher. A pilchard is a small oily fish similar to a sardine.

Globe Trotter [146]   A fictitious publication.

Olympia [146]   The original site of the Olympic Games and of the ruins of a major temple to Zeus.

This gloom, this surrender to the dark waters which lap us about, is a modern invention [146]   Jacob slumps into depression. Woolf may be referring to psychoanalysis (her brother Adrian Stephen was one of the first British psychoanalysts).

wretched slums at the back of Gray's Inn [146]   Gray's Inn is one of the four Inns of Court (the others are Lincoln's Inn, the Middle Temple, and the Inner Temple). Both Gray's Inn and Lincoln's Inn are in Holborn, a seedy and poverty-ridden area from the Victorian period well into the twentieth century.

British Empire [146]   By 1909, the British possessions constituted 20 percent of the global landmass.

Home Rule to Ireland [146]   See note to page 102 ("Prime Minister's speech").

cadge [147]   To beg or wheedle.

Foundling Hospital [147]   See note to page 127.

I like books . . . the charge against him [147–48] Bonamy's taste in the books he reads is very similar to those Lytton Strachey wrote. By the time *Jacob's Room* was published in 1922, Strachey had written *Landmarks in French Literature* (1912), *Eminent Victorians* (1918), and *Queen Victoria* (1921). Bonamy's aversion to literary fecundity hints at the kind of poetry that Rupert Brooke wrote.

three Greeks in kilts [148] The men Jacob sees are in the military. Like the men Virginia Stephen saw while in Greece, they are wearing traditional military garb called Fustanella (see *A Passionate Apprentice* 328).

like the Cornish coast [148] Like Virginia Stephen in her diary entries regarding Greece (*A Passionate Apprentice* 338), Jacob notices that Greece, with its hills and glimpses of the sea, is similar to Cornwall.

Tchekov [149] Anton Pavlovich Chekhov (1860–1904) is known for his poignant short stories and modernist plays. *The Black Monk and Other Stories,* the first translation of Chekhov's short stories into English—translated by R. E. C. Long—was published by Duckworth and Co. in 1903, the company founded by Woolf's half brother. Long's second collection of Chekhov stories, *The Kiss and Other Stories,* was published in 1908. In 1921 the Hogarth Press published Maxim Gorky's *The Note-Books of Tchekov Together with Reminiscences of Tchekov* as part of their series of Russian translations.

moving to the table where her husband sat reading . . . there was a looking-glass [149–50] Possibly the relationship between Sandra Wentworth Williams and Evan Williams parallels that of Mrs. Jarvis and her husband, Herbert. Sandra's admiring herself in the mirror invokes the mythic and cultural tradition of the goddess of love, Aphrodite (Venus), looking at herself in a mirror. The motif of the woman looking at herself also occurs earlier in the novel (see note to pages 97–98).

Quails . . . goat . . . Caramel custard [150]   Local food staples; crème caramel is also a standard Greek dessert. Quails migrate to Greece from North Africa in the spring (in the autumn migration, quails can be poisonous).

villagers have touched their hats . . . the Prime Minister [150]   Sandra Wentworth Williams is upper class and very well-to-do. Thus she receives the servile deference of villagers near her estate as well as from her numerous servants. Walking in her garden with the prime minister, who must have been a house guest, further marks her status.

Chatham [151]   William Pitt, 1st Earl of Chatham, Privy Counsellor (1708–1778), was a British Whig statesman and served as prime minister from 1766–1768.

Pitt [151]   William Pitt the Younger (1759–1806) was a British politician. He served as prime minister twice. He is known as William Pitt the Younger to distinguish him from his father, William Pitt the Elder, who was also prime minister.

Burke [151]   Edmund Burke (1729–1797) was a Whig. An Irish statesman for many years, he was also known as a political theorist and a philosopher.

Charles James Fox [151]   See note to page 89.

pink melons are sure to be dangerous [151]   A sexually suggestive phrase since Jacob enters the dining room at the exact moment that Sandra replies "beautiful but dangerous."

Napoleon was five feet four [151]   Born Napoleone di Buonaparte, Napoléon I (1769–1821) eventually crowned himself Emperor of the French in 1804 and was the instigator of the Napoleonic Wars. Popular belief, as indicated here by Evan, is that Napoléon was quite short—an attribute that did not prevent him from exercising immense power.

threw away his cigar . . . straight out from England [151]   Evan's gesture may suggest that he has voided his sexual claim on his wife. He initiates the possibility of an affair much as Pandarus brokered a relationship between Troilus and Cressida (see, for example, Geoffrey Chaucer's *Troilus and Criseyde* and Shakespeare's *Troilus and Cressida*).

wild red cyclamen [152]   A small wild flower (*Cyclamen graecum*) native to Greece, typically an autumn-blooming plant.

Margate [153]   A seaside town in Kent.

Baedeker [153]   A tourist guide from Verlag Karl Baedeker, a German publisher.

Hermes of Praxiteles [153]   A nude statue of Hermes, the messenger of the Greek gods, holding the infant Dionysus. The statue of Hermes is missing the right arm (see *A Passionate Apprentice* 319).

Balzac [153]   Honoré de Balzac (1799–1850), a prolific French writer.

Macmillans [153]   A prestigious publishing house, correctly known as Macmillan.

Corinth [153]   A city in Greece on the Isthmus of Corinth.

Acro-Corinth [154]   The heavily fortified citadel overlooking Corinth.

Park was vast [154]   A reference to the estate Sandra Wentworth Williams inherited.

wore breeches, he saw, under her short skirts [154]   Sandra wears short
pants under daringly short skirts.

like a Victory prepared to fling into the air [155]   Nike, the Goddess of
Victory, is always depicted with wings. There is an ancient statue
of Nike in the museum at Olympia, and Virginia Stephen mentions a statue of Nike at Eleusis in *A Passionate Apprentice* (324).
Bishop points out that she is the "daughter of Pallas and Styx,
who presided over all contests," and that her attire is always "di-
aphanous" (171 n122), clinging to her body.

Salamis, and Marathon [155]   Ancient sites of the Persian Wars
(499–449 B.C.). The Battle of Marathon, fought in 490 B.C., was
the site of a major Greek victory over the Persians. In the Battle
of Salamis in 480 B.C., the first major naval battle in history, the
Greeks defeated the Persians resoundingly.

Athens [155]   The capital of modern Greece and the site of one of
the greatest ancient Hellenic city-states. The description of
Athens is related to Virginia Stephen's diary entries from 1906
in *A Passionate Apprentice*.

royal landau [155]   A horse-drawn open carriage, with front and
back passenger seats, probably carrying one or more members
of the royal family of Constantine I of Greece, who ascended
the throne in March 1913 after the assassination of his father,
George I.

ships in the Piraeus [156]   Piraeus is a port city to the south of
Athens; the firing of the guns is a reminder of impending war.

pediment [156]   The wide, low triangular gable of a Grecian-style
building.

Temple of Victory [156]   A very small temple on the Acropolis erected around 420 B.C. and dedicated to Athena Nike, the Athenian goddess of victory.

Erechtheum [156]   Also known as the Erechtheion, an ancient Greek temple located on the north side of the Acropolis. The Porch of the Maidens is famous for its caryatides—six architectural support elements in the form of draped female figures. One was removed and replaced with a reproduction. The original is included among the Elgin Marbles. Virginia Stephen describes the caryatides as "the fat Maidens" who "stand smiling tranquil ease" (*A Passionate Apprentice* 323).

stucco [156]   A type of plaster typically used for exterior walls.

great statue of Athena [157]   The goddess after whom the city of Athens was named. The forty-foot-high statue was the centerpiece of the structure and was made of chryselephantine (gold and ivory). (See *A Passionate Apprentice* 323.)

he was pestered by guides [157]   Guides are offering to give Jacob a tour of the site for a price.

the sight of Hymettus, Pentelicus, Lycabettus on one side [157]   The three mountains of Athens, visible from the Acropolis.

Plato [157]   See note to page 113.

Socrates [157]   The ancient Greek philosopher (ca. 470–399 B.C.) whose ideas are recounted, perhaps accurately, in the dialogues of Plato.

Constantinople [158]   The city of Istanbul in Turkey, also known historically as Byzantium.

women standing there holding the roof on their heads [159]   The draped female figures of the caryatides.

Madame Lucien Gravé [159]   The surname of the woman who takes his picture reiterates a memento mori—*gravé* derives from the Latin *gravis,* meaning "heavy" or "serious" (as in "a grave wound"); for an English reader the word also subliminally suggests a site of burial. Furthermore, the word *grave* resonates with *engraving,* such as the etching on a tombstone.

kodak pointed at his head [159]   The pocket camera was first introduced by Kodak in 1895. Madame Lucien Gravé is probably using the very inexpensive Brownie camera, made available by Kodak in 1900.

looked rather furtively at the goddess on the left-hand side holding the roof on her head [159]   Jacob compares Sandra to one of the caryatides just as Sandra aligned Jacob's profile with that of the statue of Hermes in Olympia.

Sloane Street [160]   Sloane Street runs parallel to Lowndes Square in a fashionable area of London. See note to page 129 ("virgin chained to a rock . . .")

single horses pawing the macadam outside the doors [160]   Either a reference to the mounts of riders who circle the ring at Hyde Park on horseback or to a carriage drawn by a single horse.

at home [160]   To be receiving guests.

barrel organ [160]   See note to page 76.

water-cart [160]   See note to page 23.

chintz [160]   A brightly colored fabric.

existence squeezed and emasculated within a white satin shoe [160]   The kind of sheltered life that Virginia Stephen and her sister, Vanessa, endured, resisted, and finally ended with their migration to the Bloomsbury area in 1905 (see "22 Hyde Park Gate" and "Sketch of the Past" in *Moments of Being*).

man of his temperament . . . would Jacob marry her? [160–61]   As a man and a homosexual, Bonamy is not keenly aware of the narrow lives of women; but, momentarily, he senses the maze in which women of a certain class were trapped. The narrator's mention of Bonamy watching boys bathing marks his sexual leanings.

Serpentine [161]   An artificial lake in Hyde Park.

silent woman [161]   Possibly a reference to Ben Jonson's Renaissance play *Epicoene: Or the Silent Woman,* a comedy in which the so-called silent woman is neither silent nor female. *Epicene* (as it is now usually spelled) means having both male and female attributes or being unmanly, effeminate.

almost impossible to get afternoon tea [161]   In Britain, afternoon tea is a ritual, but the tradition is not observed in Greece.

Sandra Wentworth Williams . . . her cigarette [161]   She is smoking a cigarette and extending her legs, both very daring things for a woman to do during the 1910s.

Square of the Constitution [161]   Syntagma (Constitution) Square celebrates the establishment of a constitution after an uprising in 1843 and is linked historically to the Greek War of Independence.

Mycenae [161]   An ancient archaeological location in Greece where a site, now known as Shaft Grave Circle A, was excavated in 1876 by Heinrich Schliemann. In *A Passionate Apprentice,* Virginia Stephen refers to Schliemann's discovery of artifacts at the site (333).

Father Damien [161]   The Belgian Catholic priest who devoted himself to caring for Hawaiians suffering from leprosy (now called Hansen's disease).

kisses on lips that are to die [161]   A possible reference to a line in Wilfred Owen's war poem "Greater Love": "Red lips are not so red / As the stained stones kissed by the English dead" (1–2)

(*The War Poets: An Anthology of the War Poetry of the 20th Century,* edited with an introduction by Oscar Williams, New York: The John Day Company, 1945: 35).

royal band marching by with the national flag [161]   A reference to the king of Greece and to nationalist pride.

mere bumpkin [162]   An unsophisticated provincial.

But we are sure to run into him [162]   The English community in Greece is so small that such a meeting would be inevitable.

age of twenty-six [162]   The age at which Thoby Stephen died of typhoid upon returning from Greece. Since Jacob was probably nineteen in 1906 when he went up to Cambridge, the year is now 1913 (or, possibly, 1914, depending on his birth date).

character-mongering [162]   Gossiping. Roe also notes Woolf's subhead "The Character-Mongers and Comedians" in her essay "Phases of Fiction" (183 n12).

Simple to a degree [163]   Clara is free of guile, very naive, and lacking mental acuity.

Now he's *a dark horse . . . long rumoured among them* [163]   The gossips know that Bonamy is a homosexual but they avoid saying so. Bonamy is the type of person who chooses not to reveal much about himself.

Did you ever hear who his father was? [163]   A suggestion that Seabrook Flanders is Jacob's legal but not biological father.

It's evidently the other way with Jacob [163]   Jacob is entirely heterosexual as far as the gossips are concerned—and perhaps has too many casual sexual relationships.

the men in clubs and Cabinets . . . mere scrawls [164]   The narrator is referring to such male bastions of patriarchy, including government positions. Such men view gossip as either feminine or effeminate and as a pointless pastime.

The battleships ray out over the North Sea . . . like fragments of broken match-stick [164]   Possibly a reference to the First Battle of Heligoland Bight, the initial naval battle of the First World War, fought on August 28, 1914. Later in the same year on December 16, 1914, German battleships in the North Sea attacked Scarborough, Hartlepool, and Whitby. All told, the attack resulted in 137 British fatalities and 592 casualties, many of them civilians. The Royal Navy failed to prevent the raid despite prior intelligence reports and the deployment of naval forces. The German invasion into Belgium triggered the Battle of Liège, the first land battle of the war. The siege of the city lasted from August 5–16, when the fort finally surrendered to the Germans. The narrator's descriptions do not distinguish between enemies and allies. The young men cut down in the cornfields is a reminder of the grim reaper with his scythe, suggesting that it is August, the harvest month in the United Kingdom. The word *corn* in British usage refers to any cereal grain such as wheat or barley. By using the term *tin soldiers,* the narrator caustically points out that those in charge of the war are playing with the lives of young men like toys. However, as in several other instances, the chronology is either unreliable or indicates a leap forward or backward.

chancellories [164]   Or chancery, the residence of a chancellor (such as the chancellor of the exchequer, the office that oversees the finances of the nation) or the offices of an embassy or consulate.

Jacob . . . ran straight into the Williamses [165]   The narrator leaps from London to Athens. In this case, the force is sexual attraction. The meeting on Hermes Street is a reminder of the statue of Hermes in Olympia, to which Sandra compared Jacob.

The dinner which they gave him . . . glazed in sauce [165]   Jacob would not have been able to afford such a meal. The narrator's observation that the meat in the main course "scarcely needed" a vegetable disguise may be a sly dig at Sandra's age.

Greek King's monogram [165]   Probably the monogram of Constantine I.

Delphi [167]   Located at the foot of Mount Parnassus, the site of the ancient Delphic oracle who predicted the future cryptically.

light at the street corner [168]   See notes to pages 98 ("The light from the arc lamp...") and 100 ("The lamps of London...").

"I suppose they leave the gates open?" ... she answered wildly [168]   Possibly a reference to lines from Andrew Marvell's "To His Coy Mistress": "Let us roll all our strength and all / Our sweetness up into one ball, / And tear our pleasures with rough strife / Thorough the iron gates of life" (41–44) (*The Complete Poems,* edited by Susan Story Donno; introduction by Jonathan Bate [New York: Penguin Classics, 2005]: 50–51).

Euboea [169]   Also known as Negropont, Euboea is one of the Greek Aegean islands. The city of Eretria on Euboea was sacked by the Persians in 490 B.C.

Violent was the wind now rushing down the Sea of Marmara between Greece and the plains of Troy [169]   See introduction page lxxix.

Albania [169]   Bordered by Greece to the south, Albania is located in the Balkans.

Turkey [169]   A nation bordering on Greece to the west, Turkey was the center of the six centuries of the Ottoman Empire's rule in the region. By the 1900s, the empire was in remnants. Turkey lost most of its Balkan territories in the Balkan Wars (1912–1913).

cypresses [169]   Cypresses in Greek mythology are associated with Hades, the underworld.

Mohammedans [169]   See note to page 36.

"I will give you my copy," said Jacob. "Here. Will you keep it?" (The book was the poems of Donne.) [169]   Jacob gives something to Sandra to "keep"—later the reader finds out that Sandra has given birth to a baby boy named Jimmy. Thus Jacob may have given her a "copy" of himself as well as a volume of poems. John Donne (1572–1631) was a metaphysical poet who in the early part of his life was especially known for his erotic poetry.

Now one after another lights were extinguished [169]   Night is falling—in more than one sense. Symbolically the darkness of war is spreading from the Balkans, where in Serbia the Archduke Franz Ferdinand of Austria will be—or has been—killed by an assassin on June 28, 1914, triggering the First World War. The imagery prefigures the words of British foreign secretary Lord Grey of Fallodon at twilight on August 3, 1914: "The lamps are going out all over Europe; we shall not see them lit again in our lifetime" (see note to page 175).

fain ward off a little longer … the oppression of eternity [169]   "Fain ward off" means to wish to avoid; "the oppression of eternity" suggests death.

They had vanished [169]   The narrator, distracted by Betty Flanders, has lost track of Jacob and Sandra. Similarly, when Jacob went to bed with Florinda in chapter 8 and Betty's letter lay on the table during the encounter, "the obscene thing" occurred off-stage. Such indecent details would have provoked punitive legal action against the publisher and the author in 1922.

Miss Edwards [170]   A companion, personal assistant, or poor relative of Sandra Wentworth Williams.

half-a-dozen mosquitoes singing in his ears [170]   Although the narrative had moved forward to describe Sandra at her estate in England, perhaps more than a year later, it now loops back to the night that Jacob and Sandra spent climbing the Acropolis. The mosquitoes may allude to Virginia Stephen's encounter with an army of bedbugs at one of the hotels in Olympia or Corinth (*A Passionate Apprentice* 320).

Already he had marked the things he liked in Donne, and they were savage enough [170]   Much of Donne's poetry is quite sexually explicit, such as "To His Mistress Going to Bed," or misogynist, such as "Love's Alchemy."

Levantine [171]   The designation applies to a range of peoples in the Sinai Peninsula.

Pyramids [171]   The morning breaks over the Egyptian pyramids at Giza.

St. Peter's [171]   The morning light strikes St. Peter's Basilica in Rome.

sluggish St. Paul's looms up [171]   The morning light has reached London.

The Christians have the right to rouse most cities with their interpretation of the day's meaning [171]   Bells chiming the time or marking a service.

Then, less melodiously, dissenters of different sects issue a cantankerous emendation [171]   For example, the *adhan* (or *adan*), the Muslim call to worship, occurs five times a day at every mosque.

hammer-strokes . . . an open window even in the heart of London [171]   Either gunnery practice or the sound of the artillery on the western front in August 1914 when the weather was warm enough for windows to be open.

Surbiton [171]   A suburb of London (see note to page 117, "Waterloo Bridge").

Lombard Street [171]   A street in the City of London and the location of the headquarters of most UK banks, including the Bank of England. The war caused tremendous disruption in the financial system.

Fetter Lane [171]   The Fetter Lane Society marked the founding of Methodism and the great eighteenth-century religious revival in England. Among the major figures in the society were John Wesley, Charles Wesley, and George Whitefield. Wesley was a vehement pacifist and condemned all war.

Bedford Square [171]   44 Bedford Square was the home of Lady Ottoline Morrell and her husband, Philip Morrell. The Morrells were pacifists and offered conscientious objectors from the Bloomsbury Group the opportunity to live at their country house, Garsington Manor, and work on the farm to fulfill their military service.

Bank of England [172]   The central bank of the United Kingdom, responsible for monetary policy.

Monument with its bristling head of golden hair [172]   The monument was designed by Christopher Wren (or an associate) to commemorate the Great Fire that began on September 2, 1666, and

Late Victorian- or Edwardian-era photograph of the Monument.

burned for four days, destroying more than 80 percent of London's buildings including churches, public buildings, and homes. The "bristling head of golden hair" refers to the gilded urn of fire that tops the 202-foot-tall Roman Doric column. The Monument stands near London Bridge and close to Pudding Lane, the street where the fire began.

dray horses . . . show grey and strawberry and iron-coloured [172]   A dray horse is a workhorse, able to pull heavy loads; strawberry is the color roan, a mixture of white and darker hair.

London Bridge [172]   Opened in 1831, the bridge connected the City of London to Southwark.

a whir of wings as the suburban trains rush into the terminus [172]   Pigeons are disturbed by the arriving trains. The London Bridge Railway Station is the oldest in London (1836). Trains from London Bridge go to southern and southeastern suburbs, East Surrey and Kent.

Sunlight strikes . . . battle array upon the plain [172]   The narrator mentions multiple accoutrements, insignia, and paraphernalia that are markers of authority and power. Victorian descriptions of warfare are evident in the passage. A pageant is a spectacle, so the idea of a performance rather than a conflict is suggested. Matthew Arnold repeatedly used variations of the "old pageant of armies drawn out in battle array upon the plain." In his poem "Cromwell," he uses the phrase: "The surging battle and the mail'd array!"; in *Sohrab and Rustum,* he refers to "the battle in the plain," and in "Dover Beach," he writes: "And we are here as on a darkling plain / Swept with confused alarms of struggle and flight, / Where ignorant armies clash by night."

The height of the season [173]   The summer London Season, during which members of high society enjoyed such events as the

Epsom Derby (pronounced "darby"), the horse races held just outside of London at Epsom Downs Racecourse; the Royal Academy Summer Exhibition of new art, which began the year after the founding of the Royal Academy in 1768; and the Chelsea Flower Show, formerly known as the Royal Horticultural Society's Great Spring Show, renamed in 1913 when it was held for the first time at the Royal Hospital Chelsea. The Season also included Trooping the Colour, a military display, as well as charity events, numerous balls, and extravagant dinners. As chapter 7 suggests, the height of the Season was also the height of courtship rituals for young women like Clara Durrant, Helen Aitken, and Elsbeth Siddons. It seems to be the month of June.

green chairs in Hyde Park [173]   See a 1912 article in the *Los Angeles Times* entitled "London's Famous Season: When the Green Chairs Are Set Out in Hyde Park the Curtain Rises on the Annual Show" (August 13, 1912: 13). Chairs are still available to rent by the hour.

plane trees [173]   Probably the London plane tree (*Platanus x acerifolia*), a hybrid of the American and Oriental sycamore.

Hyde Park was circled . . . turning wheels [173]   Horse-drawn vehicles are following a circuit through the park consisting of the remaining parts of the Ring (created by King Charles II but partially destroyed by the addition of the Serpentine, a lake) and the carriage drive along the south side of the park.

Greek notes [173]   Foreign currency.

the chair man came for pence [173]   Payment for use of the chairs; Jacob is, as always, short of cash.

motor cars . . . bridge of the Serpentine [173]   The cars are on the West Carriage Drive of the Ring, where it divides the Serpentine from the Long Water.

the upper classes walked upright . . . flat on their backs [173]   The narrator marks a class distinction that indicates the social constraints of the privileged and the freedoms of the lower classes.

the sheep grazed [173]   Sheep were allowed to graze in Hyde Park until 1935.

civilization [174]   An ironic foreshadowing of the collapse of civilized culture in Europe during the coming war. Woolf may also be alluding to a bitter commentary on the Great War in Ezra Pound's 1920 poem *Hugh Selwyn Mauberley:* "There died a myriad, / And of the best, among them, / For an old bitch gone in the teeth, / For a botched civilization" (I:v.1–4). The word *civilization* is not directly derived from classical Latin.

Magnanimity [174]   Great generosity, nobility of spirit; the word is of postclassical Latin derivation (*OED*); it evokes the debates of the Apostles and the Bloomsbury Group members.

virtue [174]   Manliness, valor, worth; the word originates from the Latin *vir,* man (*OED*). As above, a topic of interest to the Apostles.

like an affectionate spaniel . . . rolling on the floor [174]   See note to page 106 ("having at each other").

European mysticism [174]   Possibly a reference to Theosophy, the religious philosophy of Helena Petrovna Blavatsky (Madame Blavatsky). Another widely known mystic of the era was George Ivanovitch Gurdjieff, an Armenian Greek. Regarding Woolf's interest in mysticism, see Madeline Moore, *The Short Season Between Two Silences: The Mystical and the Political in the Novels of Virginia Woolf* (Boston: Allen & Unwin, 1984); Gough; Hussey, *Singing;* Julie Kane, "Varieties of Mystical Experience in the Writings of Virginia Woolf," *Twentieth Century Literature* 41.4 (Winter 1995): 328–50; Stephanie Paulsell, "Writing and

Mystical Experience in Marguerite d'Oingt and Virginia Woolf," *Comparative Literature* 44 (1992): 249–67. Roe thinks that Jacob may be recoiling from Christianity in favor of paganism (184 n1).

Constantinople [174]   Woolf makes recurrent references to Constantinople as a site of illicit passion or failed intimacy (see David Roessel, "The Significance of Constantinople in *Orlando*," *Papers on Language and Literature* 28 [1992]: 398–416).

fixed, monolithic—oh, very beautiful!—like a British Admiral [174] The description suggests Jacob's statuesque beauty and compares him to a monument or effigy like those of Lord Nelson, a British admiral.

the Albany [175]   An elite residence for bachelors located in Piccadilly.

Troy [175]   The dog's name recalls the mythic Trojan War as well as the nickname of the breed, Little Diehard—so designated in the nineteenth century by the 4th Earl of Dumbarton, who dubbed his regiment, the Royal Scots, the Diehards. The regiment lost 40,000 men in the Great War.

she looked like a huntress . . . a slip of the moon in her hair [175] Artemis, the Greek goddess of the hunt (known as Diana in Roman mythology). Mr. Bowley serves as Clara's chaperone.

Why don't the young people settle it, eh? [175]   Possibly an ironic reference to the war, initiated by the old and fought by the young.

Sir Edward Grey [175]   Grey (1862–1933), the foreign secretary, failed to communicate to Germany that Britain would declare war if the neutrality of Belgium were to be breached until the Germans had already mobilized for the attack on Belgium. It was he who commented that "the lamps are going out all over Europe" (see note to page 169).

hand the pretty china teacups, and smile at the compliment [176]   The tea table as a site of torment (see "A Sketch of the Past" 116–17).

Cursitor Street [176]   A street in the City of London near Lincoln's Inn.

Morocco [176]   Possibly a reference to the Entente cordiale between France and Britain, which resolved some disputes over colonial 'issues in Egypt and Morocco but also provoked Germany. The 1904 Franco-British declaration led to the First Moroccan (or Tangier) Crisis between Germany and France. The Entente cordiale was one of the factors that led to World War I.

Venezuela [176]   The South American nation was not involved in World War I. Clara may have misunderstood her mother's remarks.

old Exhibition [176]   Also known as the Great Exhibition, the international exhibition was a showcase of industry and culture and was held in Hyde Park, London, at the Crystal Palace, from May 1 to October 15, 1851.

This statue was erected by the women of England [176]   The monument is a memorial for the Duke of Wellington (see note to page 37). The inscription reads: "To Arthur, Duke of Wellington, and his brave companions in arms / this statue of Achilles / cast from cannons won at the victories / of Salamanca, Vittoria, Toulouse and Waterloo is inscribed by their countrymen." According to legend, when Achilles was an infant, his mother, Thetis, dipped him into the waters of the river Styx in Hades to protect him from death. The place where she had held the child—his heel—was vulnerable. He was killed in the Trojan War when Paris shot a poisoned arrow into his heel.

a horse galloped past without a rider. The stirrups swung [177]   A riderless horse is often used in funerals of military leaders above the rank of colonel (see Smith); however, the actual event in Hyde Park on this summer day is droll, an embarrassing accident in which no one is even injured. Jacob is specifically linked to the motif of the horse because of his interest in horseback riding and fox hunting. Horses were involved in the war's first military conflict involving Great Britain—the cavalry attack of the Twentieth Hussars (see note to page 89, "What regiment is he in?") near Mons in August 1914. Eight million horses were killed in the war.

shirt studs [177]   Typically, small metal fasteners, sometimes inlaid with mother-of-pearl or other decorative materials, used instead of buttons for pleated or stiff-front dress shirts.

Marble Arch [177]   A marble monument near Speakers' Corner in Hyde Park. Passage through the arch is restricted to members of the royal family and to the King's Troop, Royal Horse Artillery.

a sick old lady who had known . . . the Duke of Wellington [177]   The old lady is a living link to the Napoleonic Wars almost one hundred years earlier (the Battle of Waterloo was won in 1815 and the Great War began in 1914).

slippers at weddings [177]   The tradition marks the completion of the marriage transaction, but Jacob will never marry.

The watch on her wrist . . . twelve minutes and a half [178]   Synchronization of watches was used by the Germans to launch effective attacks at the front (see William Balck, *Development of Tactics,* trans. Harry Bell, Fort Leavenworth, KS: General Service Schools Press, 1922: 84).

Bruton Street [178]   Located in the Mayfair area, close to Grosvenor Square (where Lady Rocksbier lives), one of the most prestigious residential districts in London.

Lady Congreve [178]   A possible reference to the Restoration play-wright William Congreve (1670–1729), whose work was as inde-cent as that of his contemporary, the dramatist Wycherley (see note to page 70). Famous for such comic works as *Love for Love* and *The Way of the World*, Congreve is also known for his single tragedy, *The Mourning Bride*—a work that by its title alone is deeply relevant to the ominous theme of the novel.

Verrey's [178]   A high-end restaurant on Regent's Street near Pic-cadilly Circus.

long glass [178]   A mirror.

recommending remedies, consulting friends [178]   Various suggestions for abortifacients or other methods to bring on a miscarriage.

caught by the heel [178]   Pregnancy depicted as a woman's version of Achilles' heel.

that man in Molière . . . Alceste [179]   French playwright known as Molière (1622–1673) but born Jean-Baptiste Poquelin. The pro-tagonist of *The Misanthrope* despises social conventions and val-ues sincerity. However, he is also an extremist in his views and thus is a laughingstock.

Jacob would be shocked. . . . Jimmy waved [179]   Sandra has given birth to a baby boy. The implication is that Jacob is his father. How-ever, the chronology of this pregnancy and birth is difficult to follow.

battered Ulysses [180]   A carved head, tentatively identified as Ulysses, one of the Greek warriors who fought in the Trojan War and survived, unlike Achilles. Earlier, Jacob glances repeatedly at the "battered Greek nose" of a caryatid at the Erechtheum to as-suage his desire for Sandra Wentworth Williams.

Bacon, the mapseller [180]   There were a number of map sellers located in the Strand; Bacon's Maps and Publications was founded by George Washington Bacon, an American map-maker. Roe notes that there was much demand for maps at the onset of the Great War (185 n11).

Syrian desert [180]   Beginning in 1914, Syria was used as a military base by the Ottoman Empire and an Ottoman force under German command attacked the British at the Suez Canal in 1915.

Charing Cross [181]   See note to page 128.

a *procession with banners was passing* [181]   Possibly a specific march such as a National Union of Women's Suffrage Societies (NUWSS) march. Fifty thousand women reached Hyde Park on July 26, 1913, in the culmination of a series of meetings all over England. The women's suffrage societies did not respond to the war in the same way. One group, the Women's Social and Political Union, led by Christabel Pankhurst and her mother, Emmeline, gave their allegiance to the war effort instead of to suffrage, while Christabel's sister, Sylvia, organized the East London Federation of Suffragettes, a rival suffrage group that advocated pacifism and the vote. The voting rights granted to women age thirty and older in 1918 were a quid pro quo for the WSPU's loyal support of the war. Roe speculates that it is a prowar demonstration (185 n13).

Whitehall [181]   A main thoroughfare in Westminster and the concentrated center of government ministries. The government offices in the area include 10 Downing Street, the residence of the prime minister; the Cabinet War Rooms; the Home and Foreign Office; the Horse Guards; the Admiralty Building (now the Old Admiralty Building); and the War Office (constructed in 1906), now the Old War Office.

paws of the slippery lions [181]   Roe suggests that this is a reference to the "four bronze lions at the foot of Nelson's Column" in Trafalgar Square (185 n13).

Cockspur Street [181]   A street joining Trafalgar Square to Pall Mall and the Haymarket.

equestrian statues down Whitehall [181]   One of the statues is of Charles I on horseback; known as Charles the Martyr, he was defeated in the Second English Civil War, tried as a traitor, and executed in front of the Banqueting House on Whitehall on January 30, 1649. After his death, the monarchy was abolished and the Commonwealth of England was established with Oliver Cromwell as its leader.

prickly spires, the tethered grey fleet of masonry [181]   The Houses of Parliament.

the large white clock of Westminster [181]   The Clock Tower and the Great Clock of Westminster.

Big Ben [181]   The bell of the Clock Tower.

Nelson received the salute [181]   The statue of Nelson at Trafalgar Square.

Reichstag [181]   The building where the German parliament met.

entered Lahore [181]   Possibly a reference to the mobilization of the Third Lahore Division of the Indian Army as they moved from their base in Ferozepore, India, to set out for France, where in 1914 they would fight in Flanders (also see Knowles regarding these quasihistorical references). Bishop notes that Lahore was, at the time, an independent state (174 n143).

said that the Emperor travelled [181]   Probably Franz Joseph (1830–1916) whose nephew, Archduke Franz Ferdinand, was assassinated along with his wife, Sophie, by Gavrilo Princip while riding in a motorcade through the city of Sarajevo on June 28, 1914. His death triggered the Austro-Serbian crisis that resulted in World War I. Franz Joseph signed the declaration of war against Serbia on July 26, 1914.

in Milan they rioted [181]   In August 1913, a general strike supporting an increase in wages for metal workers became violent, and at least forty police were injured in the rioting (*New York Times* August 8, 1913).

the Ambassador at Constantinople had audience with the Sultan [181]   In summer 1914, the sultan sent felicitations to the new American Ambassador, Henry Morgenthau (*New York Times* July 5, 1914); the Russian ambassador was in communication with the sultan during the buildup to the Battle of Gallipoli regarding the renaming of two German battleships (*New York Times* August 15, 1914).

the fleet was at Gibraltar [181]   The Royal Navy is positioned at a key military site controlled by the British, guarding access to the Mediterranean Sea.

utterances of Kaisers [181]   Possibly a blurring of Kaiser Wilhelm II and Czar Nicholas II of Imperial Russia.

gathering in the Calcutta bazaars [181]   Possibly a reference to the All-India Muslim League (AIML, later the Muslim League). The league was founded in 1906 by Aga Khan III to protect the political interests of Muslims in India. The league initially advocated the rule of Britain and did not support the *swadeshi* (self-sufficiency) movement, urged by such activists as Mohandas (later Mahatma) Gandhi. While the Indian National Congress had originally supported the Great War in hopes of winning greater autonomy from Britain, the Muslim League had been concerned about the impending threat the war posed to the

Ottoman Empire, the last great Islamic power. In 1916, the Muslim League joined with the Indian National Congress in the Lucknow Pact calling for independence from Britain. Bishop notes that the decision to replace Calcutta with Delhi as the capital on December 12, 1911, would have caused disruptions (174 n143).

mustering. . . Albania [181]   Albania was one of the areas involved in the Balkan Wars of 1912–1913. Bishop notes that Albania's independence had been negotiated in 1912 by Britain, was no longer controlled by the Ottoman Empire, and declared neutrality during the Great War (174 n143).

carried the burden of knowledge . . . to control the course of events [182]   The narrator sardonically notes that these sixteen men think that they can control the world. The reference to sixteen men may be an indication that two members of the cabinet, Viscount Lord Morley (the president of the council) and John Burns (president of the local government board), had resigned in opposition to the war. Lord Kitchener replaced the prime minister as secretary of state for war.

Pitt and Chatham, Burke and Gladstone [182]   Statues in the New Palace of Westminster (the Houses of Parliament) located in St. Stephen's Hall of the House of Commons with eight other figures of English statesmen.

Blue book [182]   A government document on policy or intelligence.

the placard tied round the lamp-post [182]   Probably a recruitment notice urging British men to join the army. Lord Kitchener, the war secretary, announced his recruiting effort for a "second army" of 100,000 men on August 7, 1914.

her boy [182]   Her boyfriend.

the Gaiety [182]   A theater in the West End of London featuring musical comedies.

impaled a letter on a skewer [183]   A way of organizing papers using a metal spike to secure them; also a grim image suggesting a bayonet wound.

Such a sunset [183]   The sunset suggests the end of the Belle Epoque; at the time the phrase "the sun never sets on the British Empire" was geographically accurate since Britain's colonial possessions literally circled the globe. Rudyard Kipling, in his 1897 poem "Recessional," foresaw the diminishing power of the empire. For the significance of sunrise and sunset for the troops on the western battlefront see Fussell 51–63.

Singapore [183]   One of the ports for the Royal Navy. Singapore was the site of a military mutiny in 1915 when Muslims among the troops from India killed their officers and a number of British civilians.

Kensington Palace [183]   A royal residence in Kensington Gardens.

Another procession . . . intercepted cabs [183]   Possibly a description of wealthy theater- and operagoers wearing evening dress, their horse-drawn carriages lined up along Long Acre, known for its coach makers and later for car dealerships. Roe suggests that the procession is "an anti-war Suffragette meeting at Kingsway Hall, addressed by Mrs. Fawcett on behalf of the National Union of Women's Suffrage Societies" (186 n2).

motor-cars . . . billiard-rooms [183–84]   Government officials and other civil servants on their way to their homes in the suburbs or to their clubs.

Putney [184]   See note to page 104.

Wimbledon [184]   A privileged suburb southwest of London.

barrel-organs [184]   See note to page 76.

Aldridge's with white labels on their buttocks straddled across the road and were smartly jerked back [184]   Located in St. Martin's Lane, near Long Acre, Aldridge's auctioned horses. The white labels may indicate the names of the purchasers.

steaming bedrooms . . . where children [184]   A suggestion either of poverty or of a brothel with child prostitutes.

Phoenicians [184]   From ancient Carthage, the Phoenicians were world traders in tin; Britain was known as Cassiterides, the Tin Islands.

the chimneys of the old mines [184]   The mines in Cornwall were vertical shafts that continually pumped water out of the depths.

heather-bells [184]   *Calluna vulgaris,* a low-growing shrub with small bell-shaped purple and lavender flowers commonly found on the moors and heaths.

the red light was on the columns of the Parthenon [185]   This later sunset marks the end of a subsequent day.

sand-martins [185]   *Riparia riparia,* a small insect-eating bird that summers in Europe and the Mediterranean.

the ships in the Piraeus fired their guns [185]   See note to page 156.

Darkness drops like a knife over Greece [185]   Possibly another reference to the words of Sir Edward Grey (see note to page 169).

"The guns?" . . . as if nocturnal women were beating great carpets [185]   Betty Flanders thinks she may have heard the guns firing at the front, but decides that Scarborough is too far away for the

sound to travel. However, Scarborough itself was attacked during the war (see Usui; Bradshaw 13–17).

her sons fighting for their country [185]   All three of her boys have been deployed. In *Three Guineas,* Woolf asserts that "as a woman, I have no country," despite the propaganda that fosters loyalty (Orlando: Harcourt, 2006: 129).

hunting-crop [186]   A small whip for horseback riding with a handle that can also open to be used to open gates.

Greenwich [186]   Located southeast of London, Greenwich is the site of the Royal Observatory (built in the 1670s). Bishop notes that Greenwich was "a former burial site after the Black Death in 1353" (175 n147).

Pickford's van [186]   See note to page 122.

Mudie's corner [186]   See note to page 28.

SUGGESTIONS FOR FURTHER READING:
Virginia Woolf

Editions

The Complete Shorter Fiction. Edited by Susan Dick. 2nd ed. San Diego: Harcourt, 1989.

The Diary of Virginia Woolf. Edited by Anne Olivier Bell. 5 vols. New York: Harcourt, 1977–84.

The Essays of Virginia Woolf. Edited by Andrew McNeillie. 6 vols. [in progress]. San Diego: Harcourt Brace Jovanovich, 1986–.

The Letters of Virginia Woolf. Edited by Nigel Nicolson and Joanne Trautmann. 6 vols. New York: Harcourt Brace Jovanovich, 1975–80.

Moments of Being. Edited by Jeanne Schulkind. San Diego: Harcourt, 1985.

A Passionate Apprentice: The Early Journals, 1897–1909. Edited by Mitchell A. Leaska. San Diego: Harcourt, 1990.

Biographies and Reference Works

Briggs, Julia. *Virginia Woolf: An Inner Life.* San Diego: Harcourt, 2005.

Hussey, Mark. *Virginia Woolf A to Z: A Comprehensive Reference for Students, Teachers, and Common Readers to Her Life, Works, and Critical Reception.* New York: Facts on File, 1995.

Kirkpatrick, B. J., and Stuart N. Clarke. *A Bibliography of Virginia Woolf.* 4th ed. Oxford: Clarendon, 1997.

Lee, Hermione. *Virginia Woolf.* New York: Knopf, 1996.

Marder, Herbert. *The Measure of Life: Virginia Woolf's Last Years.*
Ithaca, NY: Cornell University Press, 2000.

Poole, Roger. *The Unknown Virginia Woolf.* 4th ed. Cambridge:
Cambridge University Press, 1995.

Reid, Panthea. *Art and Affection: A Life of Virginia Woolf.* New York:
Oxford University Press, 1996.

General Criticism

Abel, Elizabeth. *Virginia Woolf and the Fictions of Psychoanalysis.*
Chicago: University of Chicago Press, 1989.

Bazin, Nancy Topping. *Virginia Woolf and the Androgynous Vision.*
New Brunswick, NJ: Rutgers University Press, 1973.

Beer, Gillian. *Virginia Woolf: The Common Ground.* Ann Arbor: University of Michigan Press, 1996.

Cuddy-Keane, Melba. *Virginia Woolf, the Intellectual, and the Public
Sphere.* Cambridge: Cambridge University Press, 2003.

DiBattista, Maria. *Virginia Woolf's Major Novels: The Fables of Anon.*
New Haven, CT: Yale University Press, 1980.

Fleishman, Avrom. *Virginia Woolf: A Critical Reading.* Baltimore:
Johns Hopkins University Press, 1975.

Froula, Christine. *Virginia Woolf and the Bloomsbury Avant-Garde:
War, Civilization, Modernity.* New York: Columbia University Press,
2005.

Guiguet, Jean. *Virginia Woolf and Her Works.* 1965. Reprint, New
York: Harcourt Brace Jovanovich, 1976.

Harper, Howard. *Between Language and Silence: The Novels of Virginia
Woolf.* Baton Rouge: Louisiana State University Press, 1982.

Hussey, Mark. *The Singing of the Real World: The Philosophy of Virginia
Woolf's Fiction.* Columbus: Ohio State University Press, 1986.

———, ed. *Virginia Woolf and War: Fiction, Reality and Myth.* Syracuse, NY: Syracuse University Press, 1991.

Majumdar, Robin, and Allen McLaurin, eds. *Virginia Woolf: The Critical Heritage*. Boston: Routledge, 1975.

Marcus, Jane. *Art and Anger: Reading Like a Woman*. Columbus: Ohio State University Press, 1988.

———, ed. *New Feminist Essays on Virginia Woolf*. Lincoln: University of Nebraska Press, 1981.

———, ed. *Virginia Woolf: A Feminist Slant*. Lincoln: University of Nebraska Press, 1983.

———, ed. *Virginia Woolf and Bloomsbury: A Centenary Celebration*. Bloomington: Indiana University Press, 1987.

———. *Virginia Woolf and the Languages of Patriarchy*. Bloomington: Indiana University Press, 1987.

McLaurin, Allen. *Virginia Woolf: The Echoes Enslaved*. Cambridge: Cambridge University Press, 1973.

McNees, Eleanor, ed. *Virginia Woolf: Critical Assessments*. 4 vols. New York: Routledge, 1994.

Minow-Pinkney, Makiko. *Virginia Woolf and the Problem of the Subject: Feminine Writing in the Major Novels*. New Brunswick, NJ: Rutgers University Press, 1987.

Phillips, Kathy J. *Virginia Woolf Against Empire*. Knoxville: University of Tennessee Press, 1994.

Roe, Sue, and Susan Sellers, eds. *The Cambridge Companion to Virginia Woolf*. Cambridge: Cambridge University Press, 2000.

Ruotolo, Lucio. *The Interrupted Moment: A View of Virginia Woolf's Novels*. Stanford, CA: Stanford University Press, 1986.

Silver, Brenda R. *Virginia Woolf Icon*. Chicago: University of Chicago Press, 1999.

Zwerdling, Alex. *Virginia Woolf and the Real World*. Berkeley: University of California Press, 1986.

SUGGESTIONS FOR FURTHER READING:
Jacob's Room
(in addition to the works cited in the introduction)

Andres, Isabel M. "Is It in His Feet? The Role of Cripple and Dismemberment in *Jacob's Room*." *Virginia Woolf Miscellany* 70 (2006): 26–27.

Archer, Jane. "The Characterization of Gender-Malaise: Gazing up at the Windows of *Jacob's Room*." In *Gender Studies: New Directions in Feminist Criticism*. Edited by Judith Spector, 30–42. Bowling Green, OH: Popular, 1986.

Banfield, Anne. "Time Passes: Virginia Woolf, Post-Impressionism, and Cambridge Time." *Poetics Today* 24.3 (2003): 471–516.

Barber, Keri. "Virginia Woolf's Changing Vision of the Soldier from Jacob Flanders to North Pargiter." *Virginia Woolf Bulletin* 14 (September 2003): 26–34.

Bell, Kevin. "Something Savage, Something Pedantic: Imaginary Portraits of Certitude in *Jacob's Room*." In *Ashes Taken for Fire: Aesthetic Modernism and the Critique of Identity*, 71–108. Minneapolis: University of Minnesota Press, 2007.

Bishop, Edward L. "The Subject in *Jacob's Room*." *Modern Fiction Studies* 38 (1992): 147–75.

Blain, Virginia. "Narrative Voice and the Female Perspective in Virginia Woolf's Early Novels." In *Virginia Woolf: New Critical Essays*. Edited by Patricia Clements and Isobel Grundy, 115–36. Totowa, NJ: Barnes and Noble, 1983.

Blodgett, Harriet. "From *Jacob's Room* to *A Passage to India:* A Note." *ANQ: A Quarterly Journal of Short Articles, Notes, and Reviews* 12.4 (1999): 23–24.

Bodenheim, Maxwell. "Underneath the Paint in *Jacob's Room.*" *Nation* (March 28, 1923): 368–69.

Bowlby, Rachel. "Jacob's Type." In *Feminist Destinations and Further Essays on Virginia Woolf,* 85–99. Edinburgh: Edinburgh University Press, 1997.

Carpentier, Martha C. "Why an Old Shoe?: Teaching *Jacob's Room* as l'écriture féminine." In *Re: Reading, Re: Writing, Re: Teaching Virginia Woolf: Selected Papers from the Fourth Annual Conference on Virginia Woolf.* Edited by Eileen Barrett and Patricia Cramer, 142–48. New York: Pace University Press, 1995.

Church, Margaret. "Joycean Structure in *Jacob's Room* and *Mrs. Dalloway.*" *International Fiction Review* 4.2 (1977): 101–9.

Daugherty, Beth Rigel. "The Whole Contention Between Mr. Bennett and Mrs. Woolf, Revisited." In *Virginia Woolf: Centennial Essays.* Edited by Elaine K. Ginsberg and Laura Moss Gottlieb, 269–94. Troy, NY: Whitson, 1983.

De Gay, Jane. "Literature and Survival: *Jacob's Room* and *Mrs. Dalloway.*" In *Virginia Woolf's Novels and the Literary Past,* 67–95. Edinburgh: Edinburgh University Press, 2006.

Dobie, Kathleen. "This is the Room that Class Built: The Structure of Sex and Class in *Jacob's Room.*" In *Virginia Woolf and Bloomsbury: A Centenary Celebration.* Edited by Jane Marcus, 195–207. Bloomington: Indiana University Press, 1987.

Dowling, David. "Virginia Woolf's Own *Jacob's Room.*" *Southern Review: Literary and Interdisciplinary Essays* 15.1 (March 1982): 60–72.

Doyle, Laura. "Transnationalism at Our Backs: A Long View of Larsen, Woolf, and Queer Racial Subjectivity in Atlantic Modernism." *Modernism/modernity* 13.3 (September 2006): 531–59.

Fernald, Anne E. "A Very Sincere Performance: Woolf, Byron and

Fame." In *Virginia Woolf: Feminism and the Reader,* 117–60. New York: Palgrave, 2006.

Fisher, Jane. *"Jacob's Room* and the Canon." In *Re: Reading, Re: Writing, Re: Teaching Virginia Woolf: Selected Papers from the Fourth Annual Conference on Virginia Woolf.* Edited by Eileen Barrett and Patricia Cramer, 203–9. New York: Pace University Press, 1995.

Freedman, Ralph. "The Form of Fact and Fiction in *Jacob's Room."* In *Virginia Woolf: Revaluation and Continuity.* Edited by Ralph Freedman, 123–40. Berkeley: University of California Press, 1980.

Froula, Christine. "War, Civilization, and the Conscience of Modernity: Views from *Jacob's Room."* In *Virginia Woolf: Texts and Contexts: Selected Papers from the Fifth Annual Conference on Virginia Woolf.* Edited by Beth Rigel Daugherty and Eileen Barrett, 280–95. New York: Pace University Press, 1996.

Gough, Val. "With Some Irony in Her Interrogation: Woolf's Ironic Mysticism." In *Virginia Woolf and the Arts: Selected Papers from the Sixth Annual Conference on Virginia Woolf.* Edited by Diane F. Gillespie and Leslie K. Hankins, 85–90. New York: Pace University Press, 1997.

Hancock, Kami A. "Deviant Snapshots: Re-visiting *Jacob's Room." Virginia Woolf Miscellany* 70 (2006): 10–11.

Hattaway, Judith. "Virginia Woolf's *Jacob's Room:* History and Memory." In *Women and World War I: The Written Response.* Edited by Dorothy Goldman, 14–30. New York: St. Martin's, 1993.

Hollander, Rachel. "Novel Ethics: Alterity and Form in *Jacob's Room." Twentieth Century Literature* 53.1 (Spring 2007): 40–66.

Hynes, Samuel. "The Whole Contention between Mr. Bennett and Mrs. Woolf." *NOVEL: A Forum on Fiction* 1.1 (Autumn 1967): 34–44.

Ippolito, Maria F., and Ryan D. Tweney. "The Journey to *Jacob's Room:* The Network of Enterprise in Virginia Woolf's First

Experimental Novel." *Creativity Research Journal* 15.1 (January 2003): 25–43.

Kiely, Robert. "*Jacob's Room* and *Roger Fry:* Two Studies in Still Life." In *Modernism Reconsidered.* Edited by Robert Kiely and John Hildebidle, 147–66. Cambridge: Harvard University Press, 1983.

Koutsoudaki, Mary. "The 'Greek' Jacob: Greece in Virginia Woolf's *Jacob's Room.*" *Papers in Romance* 2.1 (1980): 67–75.

Lilienfeld, Jane. "Accident, Incident, and Meaning: Traces of Trauma in Virginia Woolf's Narrativity." In *Virginia Woolf: Turning the Centuries: Selected Papers from the Ninth Annual Conference on Virginia Woolf.* Edited by Ann Ardis and Bonnie Kime Scott, 153–58. New York: Pace University Press, 2000.

Little, Judy. "Feminizing the Subject: Dialogic Narration in *Jacob's Room.*" *LIT: Literature Interpretation Theory* 3.4 (October 1992): 241–51.

Mackay, Marina. "The Lunacy of Men, the Idiocy of Women: Woolf, West, and War." *NWSA Journal* 15.3 (Fall 2003): 124–44.

Marshik, Celia. "Publication and 'public women': Prostitution and censorship in three novels by Virginia Woolf." *Modern Fiction Studies* 45.4 (Winter 1999): 853–86.

McNeillie, Andrew. "Bloomsbury." In *The Cambridge Companion to Virginia Woolf.* Edited by Sue Roe and Susan Sellers, 1–28. Cambridge: Cambridge University Press, 2000.

Mepham, John. "Mourning and Modernism." *Virginia Woolf: New Critical Essays.* Edited by Patricia Clements and Isobel Grundy, 137–56. Totowa, NJ: Barnes and Noble, 1983.

Moore, Madeline. "Virginia Woolf and the Good Brother." In *Virginia Woolf: Texts and Contexts: Selected Papers from the Fifth Annual Conference on Virginia Woolf.* Edited by Beth Rigel Daugherty and Eileen Barrett, 157–76. New York: Pace University Press, 1996.

Novak, Jane. "Freedom and Form: *Jacob's Room.*" In *The Razor Edge of Balance: A Study of Virginia Woolf,* 86–105. Coral Gables, FL: University of Miami Press, 1975.

Olin-Hitt, Michael R. "Power, Discipline, and Individuality: Subversive Characterization in *Jacob's Room*." In *Virginia Woolf: Texts and Contexts: Selected Papers from the Fifth Annual Conference on Virginia Woolf*. Edited by Beth Rigel Daugherty and Eileen Barrett, 128–34. New York: Pace University Press, 1996.

Putnam, Ron. "Summer Study Day: *Jacob's Room*." *Virginia Woolf Bulletin* 17 (September 2004): 79–80.

Raitt, Suzanne. "Finding a Voice: Woolf's Early Novels." In *The Cambridge Companion to Virginia Woolf*. Edited by Sue Roe and Susan Sellers, 29–49. Cambridge: Cambridge University Press, 2000.

Reginio, Robert. "Virginia Woolf and the Technologies of Exploration: *Jacob's Room* as Counter-Monument." In *Woolf and the Art of Exploration: Selected Papers from the Fifteenth International Conference on Virginia Woolf*. Edited by Helen Southworth and Elisa Kay Sparks, 86–95. Clemson, SC: Clemson University Digital Press, 2006.

Roe, Sue. "The Impact of Post-Impressionism." In *The Cambridge Companion to Virginia Woolf*. Edited by Sue Roe and Susan Sellers, 164–90. Cambridge: Cambridge University Press, 2000.

Ronchetti, Ann. "*Jacob's Room*." In *The Artist, Society & Sexuality in Virginia Woolf's Novels*, 41–48. New York: Routledge, 2004.

Ruddick, Sara. "Private Brother, Public World." In *New Feminist Essays*. Edited by Jane Marcus, 185–215. Lincoln: University of Nebraska Press, 1981.

Ruotolo, Lucio P. "On the Margins of Consciousness: *Jacob's Room*." In *The Interrupted Moment: A View of Virginia Woolf's Novels*, 69–94. Stanford, CA: Stanford University Press, 1986.

Sakamoto, Tadanobu. "A New Relation Between the Narrator and the Reader in *Jacob's Room*." *Virginia Woolf Bulletin* 19 (May 2005): 41–47.

Salomon, Alyza Lee. "Naming Defoe's Influence in *Jacob's Room*." *Virginia Woolf Miscellany* 55 (Spring 2000): 3–4.

Schaefer, Josephine O'Brien. "Sterne's *A Sentimental Journey* and *Jacob's Room.*" *Modern Fiction Studies* 23 (1977): 189–97.

Stewart, Jack. "Impressionism in the Early Novels of Virginia Woolf." *Journal of Modern Literature* 9.2 (May 1982): 237–66.

Sutherland, Cori. "Substantial Men and Transparent Women: Issues of Solidity in *Jacob's Room.*" In *Virginia Woolf: Emerging Perspectives: Selected Papers from the Third Annual Conference on Virginia Woolf.* Edited by Mark Hussey and Vara Neverow, 65–70. New York: Pace University Press, 1994.

Swanson, Diana L. "With Clear-Eyed Scrutiny: The Narrator as Sister in *Jacob's Room.*" In *Virginia Woolf Out of Bounds: Selected Papers from the Tenth Annual Conference on Virginia Woolf.* Edited by Jessica Berman and Jane Goldman, 46–52. New York: Pace University Press, 2001.

Takai, Hiroko. "On Not Speaking Out: *Jacob's Room* as a Conflation of Modernism and Feminism." *Virginia Woolf Bulletin* 4 (May 2000): 7–12.

Usui, Masami. "The German Raid on Scarborough in *Jacob's Room.*" *Virginia Woolf Miscellany* 35 (Fall 1990): 7.

Walkowitz, Judith R. "Going Public: Shopping, Street Harassment, and Streetwalking in Late Victorian London." *Representations* 62 (Spring 1998): 1–30.

Zappa, Stephanie. "Woolf, Women, and War: From Statement in *Three Guineas* to Impression in *Jacob's Room.*" In *Virginia Woolf: Texts and Contexts: Selected Papers from the Fifth Annual Conference on Virginia Woolf.* Edited by Beth Rigel Daugherty and Eileen Barrett, 274–79. New York: Pace University Press, 1996.

ILLUSTRATION CREDITS

Virginia Woolf Annotated Editions

Top Woolf scholars provide valuable introductions, notes, suggestions for further reading, and critical analysis in this paperback series. Students reading these books will have the resources at hand to help them understand the text as well as the reasons and methods behind Woolf's writing.

Between the Acts
Annotated and with an introduction by Melba Cuddy-Keane
978-0-15-603473-9 • 0-15-603473-5

Jacob's Room
Annotated and with an introduction by Vara Neverow
978-0-15-603479-1 • 0-15-603479-4

Mrs. Dalloway
Annotated and with an introduction by Bonnie Kime Scott
978-0-15-603035-9 • 0-15-603035-7

Orlando: A Biography
Annotated and with an introduction by Maria DiBattista
978-0-15-603151-6 • 0-15-603151-5

A Room of One's Own
Annotated and with an introduction by Susan Gubar
978-0-15-603041-0 • 0-15-603041-1

Three Guineas
Annotated and with an introduction by Jane Marcus
978-0-15-603163-9 • 0-15-603163-9

To the Lighthouse
Annotated and with an introduction by Mark Hussey
978-0-15-603047-2 • 0-15-603047-0

The Waves
Annotated and with an introduction by Molly Hite
978-0-15-603157-8 • 0-15-603157-4

The Years
Annotated and with an introduction by Eleanor McNees
978-0-15-603485-2 • 0-15-603485-9

Each volume includes a preface by Mark Hussey, professor of English and women's and gender studies at Pace University, and editor of *Woolf Studies Annual*.

Harcourt | HARVEST BOOKS
www.HarcourtBooks.com